Lethal Suggestions

Lethal Suggestions

Steven Laine

iUniverse, Inc.
New York Lincoln Shanghai

Lethal Suggestions

Copyright © 2005 by Steven Lewis Laine

All rights reserved. No part of this book may be used or reproduced by any means, graphic, electronic, or mechanical, including photocopying, recording, taping or by any information storage retrieval system without the written permission of the publisher except in the case of brief quotations embodied in critical articles and reviews.

iUniverse books may be ordered through booksellers or by contacting:

iUniverse
2021 Pine Lake Road, Suite 100
Lincoln, NE 68512
www.iuniverse.com
1-800-Authors (1-800-288-4677)

ISBN-13: 978-0-595-37529-5 (pbk)
ISBN-13: 978-0-595-67520-3 (cloth)
ISBN-13: 978-0-595-81921-8 (ebk)
ISBN-10: 0-595-37529-4 (pbk)
ISBN-10: 0-595-67520-4 (cloth)
ISBN-10: 0-595-81921-4 (ebk)

Printed in the United States of America

PROLOGUE

▼

Jim Wells had never woken up like this before.

The smell of antiseptic assaulted his nostrils. He opened his eyes groggily. They seemed glued shut. He didn't know how much time had passed, but he felt it had not been too long since he had crawled onto the cold park bench and gone to sleep. He looked around at his new surroundings hoping to make sense of his predicament. He was strapped down in a chair. He had a vague notion that he was in a dentist's chair, or something close to it.

He was in a small, windowless, yet brightly lit room filled with what appeared to be hospital equipment. A large mirror and a door took up most of the wall to his left. Cupboards lined the upper portion of two of the walls. Their glass doors permitted Jim to see their contents. They were filled with vials, test tubes, syringes, and other hospital-like apparatus. The numerous hi-tech machines surrounding his chair were completely alien to him.

It was not until he surveyed the entire room that he noticed there was a man standing with his back to him in front of one of the counters which lined the institutionally colored walls. They were a pale green that no self-respecting couple would paint their living room. The man seemed to be too involved with whatever he was doing to notice that Jim had woken up. Jim strained against the numerous straps holding him down in an attempt to see what the room's only other occupant was doing but found he could not even flex his muscles. He was completely immobilized. At that moment, the stranger turned around and seemed surprised that Jim was awake.

"Back to the land of the living are we?" The man, dressed in a doctor's smock, approached Jim from the side with a loaded syringe in his hand. Jim tried to open his mouth to speak but found that he could not operate the muscles in his jaw.

"Cat got your tongue?" the doctor smirked. "The anesthesia has that effect sometimes, you can think clearly, but the rest of you is pretty much paralyzed. It'll wear off within a few minutes though. Did you know that it's not entirely uncommon for patients undergoing surgery to feel everything during an operation despite being completely anaesthetized? It doesn't happen too often, but could you imagine? Being able to feel every incision made, every suture, everything going on while you're being operated on and not being able to cry out, while your doctor continues to poke, probe, and cut your insides." Jim began to sweat as the doctor approached. The doctor held out the large syringe at arm's length and gave it a few taps with his finger to get the air bubbles out.

"Now, you're probably wondering what you're doing here and what I'm doing with this nasty looking syringe aren't you?" Jim tried once more in vain to answer but to no avail. The fear in his eyes was answer enough.

"Don't worry, in time all of your questions will be answered. But first, I have some questions for you." The doctor, as Jim now thought of him despite the fact that Hippocrates would be rolling in his grave had he known this man had taken his oath, took Jim's left arm and prepared to inject him. Jim watched as the doctor professionally punctured the largest vein in his left forearm and the needle's contents flowed into his bloodstream when the doctor depressed the plunger.

"In case you're wondering, which I'm sure you are," the doctor paused for emphasis and smiled caustically, "what I have just injected into your arm is sodium amytal, or more commonly known to the layperson, such as yourself, as truth serum. It's a bit of a cocktail really with some other drugs mixed in, but I won't bore you with the details. Once the drug has taken effect, I will ask you a series of questions and you will answer me truthfully. Actually, given the properties of this particular drug, you will have no choice in the matter. So just sit back and relax and we'll get started."

The doctor pulled up one of the many rolling units in the room and proceeded to hook up a dazzling array of wires to Jim's head, chest, and limbs. Jim guessed that one of the machines was probably a lie detector to determine whether he was lying or not just in case the drug was not entirely effective. Another machine appeared to be measuring the beating of his heart. Jim watched the pulsing green light bounce across the screen. Its path seemed a little erratic to him.

Jim Wells tried to remain calm. His heart was racing, as were his thoughts as he tried to figure out just what in hell was going on and what this crazy doctor had planned for him. Just as he had no friends to speak of, Jim also had no enemies that he could think of. He had never knowingly hurt, deceived, or harmed anyone in his entire life and he could not possibly imagine what it was that this doctor, if that was what he really was, could want from him. A sadistic doctor, forcible restraints, truth serum, none of it made any sense. Jim felt as if he had plunged headfirst down the rabbit hole of Lewis Carroll lore. Only, he did not think he was going to be invited to tea.

The doctor, having finished hooking Jim up to several impressive looking machines, dimmed the lights and took a seat opposite. Half an hour had passed since his patient had regained consciousness. He looked in the direction of the mirror, nodded his head once and began speaking in a soft, gentle voice.

He's hypnotizing me, Jim thought as he struggled to block out what the doctor was saying. Despite his best efforts, Jim felt himself losing control of his own thoughts, as the doctor spoke in a smooth, almost seductive manner, his voice devoid of emotion and intonation.

"Let's begin," the doctor said matter-of-factly. "The drugs which prevented you from speaking earlier should have worn off by now, so I don't think you should have any problem answering my questions." Jim wanted to scream but another part of him wanted to answer all of the doctor's questions.

"First of all, what is your full legal name and your birth date?" the doctor asked lifting a clipboard up to his knee, preparing to take notes.

"Jim Barnaby Wells, March twentieth, nineteen-fifty-eight," Jim heard himself answer, though he felt oddly detached from the process of speaking.

"And what is your current address?" the doctor continued.

"I don't have one."

"I am assuming you had some sort of occupation before you left it to live the high life?" the doctor asked sardonically.

"I was a janitor at a publishing house but lost my job when it went bankrupt last year." Jim felt no emotion as he rhymed off the name of his former employer, the job he had held for so many years.

"Have you ever had any alcohol related illnesses? Ever been addicted to drugs, prescription or otherwise?"

"No."

"Are you taking drugs now, prescription or otherwise? Do you drink on a regular basis? Do you drink at all?" the doctor continued his questioning.

"No, I don't take drugs, and I don't drink."

"Have you ever needed medical treatment, had any operations, any diseases?"

"I've had my wisdom teeth removed."

"Have you ever suffered a mental illness, in the past or currently? Is there any history of mental illness in your family?" The doctor's questions seemed to have shifted gear and become focused on something that Jim couldn't quite grasp in his hypnotically and chemically induced state.

"No."

"You've been very cooperative Jim. I appreciate that. Now do you have any living relatives, any next of kin, any close friends who might miss you?" The doctor leaned closer to Jim awaiting his response.

"No, my wife died two years ago. Cancer. Parents are dead. No children. No friends." Again, Jim felt no emotion as he recalled his past, including the drawn out death of his wife. Painful hours filled with grief and torment spent in a room with a similar feel to the one he was in now. He watched passively as the doctor jotted down some more notes on his clipboard. The doctor looked up pensively and regarded Jim with a curious satisfaction.

"I've talked a bit to Jim, but I think that perhaps there might be another part of Jim that I haven't talked to. I would like very much to talk to that other part. Are you with me?"

Jim frowned and looked quizzically at the doctor. *Other part, what the hell was he talking about?* "I don't understand. What other part?"

"Don't worry," the doctor replied, "just answer the question. Let that other part talk to me. We'll take good care of you. We'll take good care of all of you."

CHAPTER 1

▼

Monday
7:53 a.m.
Meadowvale Clinic

It did not look like a madhouse.

The grounds surrounding the Meadowvale Clinic for the Treatment of Dissociative Disorders were well tended and detracted from its stark architecture and purpose. An impeccably manicured California Native hedge, wrapped around the entire building, formed a natural five-foot barrier which served to hide the modern building's bare foundation. The Clinic was a large gray institutional structure made entirely of concrete and mirrored glass fashioned in the Brutalism tradition of architecture; it seemed diametrically opposed to anything Mother Nature had ever intended.

Situated on a plot of land which had previously been occupied by a farmhouse, the six storey structure overlooked lush rolling lawns on five of its sides and asphalt parking lots on the remaining two. Some claimed that from a bird's eye view, the building was shaped like a piano, although in reality it looked more like a mangled stop sign. Protected within the walls of the building, yet exposed to the elements, a square courtyard in the center of the Clinic gave it the appearance of a misshapen donut.

Despite the weather forecaster's call for a sunny, cloudless day, the day was indeed sunny and cloudless. A perfect day for the Clinic's opening ceremony.

On the sixth floor, nestled in a sparsely, yet expensively furnished corner office, Dr. Walter Flemming, Chief of Psychiatry and co-director of the newly established Meadowvale Clinic had chosen to skip the ribbon-cutting ceremony taking place below. He had to finish writing his speech for the assembly that would take place immediately after the ribbon-cutting. Hunched over his massive mahogany desk reviewing his speech for the umpteenth time, he paused to take a drink from a tall glass of liquid resting on the corner of his ink-blotter. He couldn't quite get used to the taste of prune juice.

He plodded on with his speech. Scribbling occasionally in the margins as he thought of another point he wanted to make or something upon which he wanted to elaborate, he couldn't help but smile. He was thinking back twenty-five years. His undergraduate days. He had decided then that he would one day be the greatest psychiatrist in his field.

Today, after a quarter of a century, his dreams, no, not his dreams, but rather his goals, had finally come to fruition. Today was the pinnacle of his career. Everything he had worked so hard for was finally being realized. Self-Actualization was not just a psychological term dreamed up by the likes of Rogers and Maslow, it was indeed attainable. It was that point in one's life where everything comes together and the individual's full potential is realized.

His new office, with its extravagantly expensive decor, was a reflection of his own diligence and perseverance. Not only the new office however. The entire institution which he himself had created out of scratch with Grant Foley, which was being officially opened at that moment, was largely his doing.

The Meadowvale Clinic served as testimony to his greatness, his superiority in a field where so many others had tried and failed or simply achieved mediocrity. Reflecting upon all he had accomplished, Flemming glanced up to the clock hanging on the same wall which proudly displayed his numerous degrees and citations from the most prestigious institutions in the country, in the world in fact, and realized that he had an audience to address in less than ten minutes. He looked out his office window and saw that the crowd had already made its way inside.

Gathering up his notes, Flemming stood up, adjusted his silk tie and admired himself in the full length mirror affixed to the back of his office door. At six feet, with a trim figure and a thick, silver mane of hair, Flemming was an impressive man. Cool, calculated, and with a practiced icy gaze, he would have no difficulty in seducing any woman he chose. However, most of the time he chose not to.

With a final glance in the mirror, Flemming ran his fingers through his hair, opened a heavy oak door and stepped out of his plush office. He was greeted by the clicking of keys on a keyboard.

"Good morning, Marjorie, and how are we today?" Flemming asked his secretary as he eased his office door shut behind him.

"Just fine, doctor, knock 'em dead with your presentation," Marjorie Newman, a plump and matronly woman in her late forties, replied jovially without missing a beat in her typing.

Her lightweight, aluminum wheelchair groaned under her weight as she shifted about. Flemming himself had interviewed her at the behest of Grant Foley, Marjorie's brother-in-law. She was well aware that her physical condition and her nepotistic position would bode her well in the interview. That was why she told Flemming straight away that she wanted no special treatment. She believed that respect was something a person earned. It was not a given, and she said as much in her interview. Flemming hired her on the spot.

"Thank you, Marjorie, I intend to do just that," Flemming called back. He had taken only a few steps when his secretary called out to him.

"Oh, Doctor Flemming, I almost forgot to tell you, a new patient came in over the weekend. The file is right here when you want it," she pointed to a folder on her desk with her bright red polished nails.

"Yes, I know, Marjorie, I know." Flemming continued on towards the auditorium where he would be speaking momentarily.

Flemming took the elevator downstairs and headed for the main doors of the Arthur Montgomery auditorium, named after a missing colleague and friend, partially responsible for the development of the Meadowvale Clinic. Flemming preferred using the main doors rather than the small door leading to the side of the stage. He thoroughly enjoyed entering a crowded room and reveled in the hush that fell over the crowd as he did so this morning.

Heading purposefully towards the stage, Flemming could hear the whispers and see the hushed awe in the faces of the auditorium's occupants. He could easily imagine himself as a famous celebrity or a well-known politician. Being a prominent psychiatrist, a leader in his field, however, earned him the same amount of respect among those who knew anything about dissociative disorders.

Flemming took the steps leading up to the stage one at a time, always measuring his movements and being careful of the image he conveyed to those around him. Five chairs were set up in the middle of the stage.

Sitting at the chair on the left end was Dr. Ruth Tanner. A graduate of Brown University, Dr. Tanner had little else going for her. Though exceptionally brilliant in the field of clinical psychiatry, especially in the more concise field of dissociative disorders, Dr. Tanner was less than attractive, and possessed minimal people skills. She had short black hair, pale white skin, a sharp angular nose, and a long neck which gave the impression that she was always trying to peer over some invisible wall. Lacking people skills, Dr. Tanner's main function at the

Clinic was research, although she too had to see patients. Surprisingly, her patients enjoyed the time spent with her. This was more than her colleagues could say of her.

Sitting next to Dr. Tanner was Dr. Clyde Henderson, a short, balding, scholarly looking African. Henderson had a heavy Ghanaian accent which sometimes made it difficult to understand what he was saying but he was very patient. Specializing in the treatment of amnesiacs, Henderson was a valuable member of the Clinic's elite staff.

The middle seat was vacant. It was reserved for Flemming. To the right of it sat Dr. Carl Sanford. Along with Flemming, Sanford had worked at the San Francisco Psychiatric Hospital. Flemming had been there for just over nine years while Sanford had been there for eight. Sanford's hands were continuously fidgeting. The only time they remained steady was when he was hypnotizing his patients. Sanford was renowned for his abilities and techniques in hypnosis. Dozens of papers in numerous professional publications attested to his qualifications.

The institution's co-director and chief administrator, Dr. Grant Foley, who had been sitting in the last of the five chairs in the middle of the stage, stood up, approached Flemming and pumped his hand energetically. Foley was a wiry man bursting with energy. His graying hair belied his youthful enthusiasm that his bright eyes and ready smile could not hide. He too had been employed at the San Francisco Psychiatric Hospital, though only for half as many years as Carl Sanford.

"Good morning, Walt. It looks like we have a full house today. Good turn out by the local press as well. You'll be happy to know the ribbon-cutting went off without a hitch. I'll start off with a few introductory remarks and hand the stage over to you. Why don't you have a seat right here. Oh, by the way, if you could stop by my office before noon I'd appreciate it. I've got something important to discuss with you." Foley motioned toward the chair in the middle, waited for the doctor to sit down and sauntered over to the podium in the middle of the stage. Adjusting the microphone to make it level with his mouth, Foley addressed the crowd.

"Good morning, and welcome all. I want to thank you all for attending so early in the morning. As you know, today is the official opening of Meadowvale. Having worked with most of the outdated equipment and facilities we have had to put up with at the psychiatric hospital, I can barely convey the significance of this event." Foley paused for laughter and was not disappointed.

"Not only will the new Clinic provide for us the proper equipment and environment we need to adequately treat our patients, but it will also enable us to join the ranks of the most prominent dissociative disorder treatment facilities in the world." Foley had to pause again, this time for a full minute as he waited for the clapping to subside.

"For those of you who are old hands from the psychiatric hospital, and for those new employees, I hope that you come to think of Meadowvale as your home away from home, or as my wife often refers to it, as the only building in the city which allows in ten times as many people as fire regulations permit." Laughter rippled through the crowd of just over two hundred individuals made up of the Clinic's staff, numerous patients, San Francisco city officials, and the press, personally invited by Flemming. Foley was sure some of them didn't understand the subtle reference to multiple personality disorder and were laughing out of politeness more than anything.

"But, in all seriousness folks, there is only one reason that we have been blessed with this new state of the art clinic, one driving force behind its inception, and one man to thank personally for all his crowning achievements and the recognition he has drawn to our field and institution. For most of you, this man needs no introduction. It is with great pleasure that I hand over the floor to Doctor Walter Flemming." The crowd burst into applause as Flemming rose and approached the podium, shaking Foley's hand on the way.

"Good morning and thank you." Flemming set his notes down on the podium and surveyed the audience. "I see several new faces out there, bright, young, and ready to take on the challenges that our field has to offer. It is with humble grace that I present to you this new clinic, it, and not the world, is your oyster. In these tumultuous times we live in, it is not surprising that our expertise is called upon at an ever increasing rate. It is our duty, and our privilege to answer that call. Here at the Meadowvale Clinic, we hope to further expand upon our groundbreaking discoveries and completely revamp society's attitudes towards dissociative disorders. Furthermore…"

Chapter 2

▼

Rachel Miller raced through an alleyway, craning her neck to catch a glimpse of her unknown pursuer. A shadowy figure was chasing after her through the dark city streets for no apparent reason. Rachel had just left the movie theatre alone planning on going home and getting some shuteye.

Having walked two blocks, she developed the oddest sensation that someone, or something, was following her. Stopping periodically to tie her shoe and for late night traffic, she attempted to clandestinely sneak a peek behind her. Indeed, there was someone following her. What his agenda was, Rachel could hardly surmise. He was about a block behind her and was matching her pace without showing any signs of slowing down. At this distance, Rachel could not discern who it was that was tailing her but decided not to wait to find out. That was when she had ducked into the alleyway in which she was now running.

Garbage dumpsters and their overflowing refuse lined both sides of the darkened alley yet offered no secure place to hide. Looking back once more, Rachel could just make out a fleeting figure making its way down the alley in obvious pursuit. Rachel stumbled briefly over a stray bag of garbage but managed to maintain her balance.

Running as fast as possible, perspiration poured down Rachel's face, her blouse clung to her sweat soaked body, her heart beat strenuously and threatened to burst through her ribcage if she did not calm down. The combination of the exertion from running and the fear she was experiencing at being chased through the night prevented calmness.

Up ahead in the alley, a brick wall loomed. Rachel caught sight of it for the first time; darkness and a light fog had prevented her from seeing it earlier.

Rachel slowed down as she neared the wall, debating what to do next. She could not possibly scale the wall which was at least ten feet high, therefore her only chance would be to turn around and face her pursuer.

Conceding to herself that she would have to defend herself against a total, and perhaps even armed, stranger, Rachel almost failed to notice that, despite the presence of the impenetrable wall at the end of the alley, the alley itself did not end. It continued to the right.

Energized by this new discovery, Rachel pumped her burning legs even harder and sprinted for the corner. Footsteps echoed loudly behind her and she risked one more look back. Her pursuer was directly behind her and lunged just as she turned the corner. A hand brushed her calf and briefly attempted to latch onto her ankle but with a violent kick, Rachel managed to shake it free.

Now in another alley, Rachel looked for the end but could not see that far ahead. Instead, she saw two blinking red lights approaching her at a rapid clip. She heard what sounded like a hydraulic press being operated and it dawned on her that a city garbage truck was bearing down on her.

It was too late to move out of the lumbering vehicle's path and, looking back, she saw that her pursuer was coming after her again. Before she could decide on a course of action, the steel lip of the rear end of the garbage truck slammed into her midsection as the truck emanated an incredibly piercing beeping sound as it backed up over her.

Rachel Miller woke up drenched in sweat, springing forward as if her lower back were operated on a spring mechanism. In doing so, she launched her cat Spooky across the bed. The cat had decided to pounce on her stomach as it heaved up and down while she lay sleeping.

Slamming the snooze button on her alarm clock in order to halt its incessant beeping Rachel opened her eyes and was greeted by a pair of very green, very perturbed feline eyes. Spooky was apparently not impressed with this method of waking up. Anything that involved being flung involuntarily through the air was not high on the cat's fun activities list. Especially at six-thirty in the morning.

"Sorry, Spooky," Rachel called back to her three year old cat as she threw back the sheets, got out of bed and made for the bathroom. The pressure of the shower washed away the sweat and the last remnants of her dream, but it couldn't get rid of the chill Rachel experienced when she first woke up.

This was not the first time she had woken up in a cold sweat wanting to scream. The mysterious figure who had pursued her in this most recent of dreams had made several cameo appearances in other dreams. They were more like nightmares as opposed to dreams. Dreams were supposed to be comforting and rejuvenating, not terrifying and draining. Despite her training in psychiatry, she had no idea what this particular dream signified.

Her contacts popped in easily, making her eyes seem even brighter and bluer than they were naturally. Stepping out of the bathroom while toweling off her short brown hair, Rachel turned on her stereo to catch the morning news. The DJ announced that it was to be a clear and sunny day with no chance of rain. She ignored the following sports results of last night's numerous games and matches and headed for the kitchen to make breakfast.

Spooky rubbed up against her smoothly shaven legs as she put the coffee on and depressed a pair of waffles into the toaster. Sunlight streamed into the kitchen glaring brightly off the chrome of the sink and the numerous layers of high gloss varnish that covered the wooden wraparound cupboards.

Rachel grabbed her waffles when they popped up and centered them on a plate she had placed on the kitchen island which dominated the middle of the room. She looked down at Spooky when he clawed at her bathrobe. Bending down, she lifted the cat up onto the island and set him down beside her breakfast. She enjoyed the company.

"I hope you slept better than I did," Rachel said to her furry companion as she poured herself a cup of coffee. The aroma of the coffee alone was enough to perk her up.

Spooky found a patch of sunlight on the ceramic countertop and lay down in it, sprawling as only cats can. Rachel was terribly envious.

Finishing her breakfast, Rachel went back to her bedroom to dress. Today was a big day for the Clinic where she worked. She had started work two weeks ago when it first opened, but today was its official opening. Most of the staff had had a chance to move in and orient themselves and the majority of the rooms available were filled by patients who had been placed on waiting lists at the first mention of the proposed opening of the Clinic over two years ago.

She tried to listen to the radio as she pulled on a blouse to go with her pantsuit. There was still no mention of the opening of the Clinic. She knew it would be announced soon however. For the past two months, it had dominated a small portion of the local news.

Spooky was still stretched out on the kitchen island and had apparently fallen asleep while Rachel was changing. She briefly considered getting revenge on him by waking him up with a jolt but decided not to, it wasn't in her nature, and she knew he had not woken her intentionally. Looking at the digital clock on her microwave, Rachel saw that she still had plenty of time to get to work. It was only seven-thirty. She still had thirty minutes.

Rachel turned off the coffee pot and radio and grabbed her keys and purse from atop a small crescent shaped table near the door to her apartment. She unlocked her door and stepped out into the hallway.

The apartment door next to hers was open, and a large black man was leaning over the threshold reaching for a newspaper on the floor.

"Oh, good morning, Rachel," her next door neighbor said as he quickly straightened himself up clutching at his housecoat to ensure it didn't fall open. Rachel caught a glimpse of his muscular chest. His ebony complexion made if difficult for Rachel to tell if he was blushing. To Rachel, he looked like what she envisioned James Patterson's fictional detective/psychologist, Alex Cross, would look like.

"Good morning, Ted," Rachel replied locking her door.

"Heading off for another exciting day at work I see." Ted had regained his composure and held his paper on his thigh.

Rachel laughed. "Oh yeah, fun and games all day long. At least you only have to deal with people who don't know what they want. I, on the other hand, have to work with people who don't even know who they are." Ted Harpingham, an ex-cop, smiled at Rachel's comparison of their respective lines of work. Ted worked at a number of local high schools as a guidance counselor. He helped kids with their applications to colleges and universities, set them up in a variety of co-op programs, and with all his contacts in the city, managed to get quite a few of them part and full-time jobs.

Rachel was right to a large extent about his having to deal with people who did not know what they wanted. A lot of students came to him as a last resort. They would tell him they didn't know what they wanted out of life or what they wanted to be when they grew up.

"True enough, and on top of that, you have to be at work an hour earlier than I do." Ted gave Rachel a broad grin, pointed his paper at her and stepped back into his apartment.

"Thanks, as if it isn't hard enough waking up at six-thirty, I don't need you rubbing it in," Rachel said over her shoulder as she headed for the stairs.

Her car was parked in a lower level parking lot behind the apartment building. A recent rash of vandalism had plagued the neighborhood resulting in thousands of dollars worth of damage to storefront windows and unattended vehicles. Most likely the work of some of the students Ted Harpingham couldn't help no matter how hard he tried. Rachel scanned the other tenant's cars as she approached her own looking for signs of destruction. She failed to notice any; that is until she reached her nineteen eighty-four Volkswagen Rabbit. The front tires had been slashed.

Rachel looked up at the sky and mouthed, "Why me?" Of all the days for this to happen, today was probably the worst.

Realizing there was no sense in standing around waiting for the tires to magically re-inflate themselves, Rachel stormed back into her apartment building.

When she got back into her apartment she called a taxi first, she didn't have time to bike to work but she could bike home. She then called Triple A to come and replace the tires. She told them she would leave her keys with her neighbor, Ted. As she described her car to the woman on the other end of the line, she looked again enviously at Spooky who had not budged even when she had burst into her apartment. Spooky seemed to smile in his sleep; presumably chasing dogs up trees in his dream. *Must be nice*, Rachel thought.

After leaving her apartment for the second time that morning and leaving her car keys and Triple A card with Ted, Rachel made her way downstairs carrying her bicycle to the front of the building to meet the cab. She was going to be late for the beginning of the opening ceremony.

The cab arrived ten minutes later. Rachel took her front tire off, put her bike in the trunk and hopped in without preamble.

"The Meadowvale Clinic please," she told the cabby as he pulled away from the curb.

"That's that new hospital, isn't it? The one outside town?" the cabby asked.

"That's right. If you could hurry I'd appreciate it. I'm running late this morning." The cab driver depressed the accelerator at the mere mention of hurry.

"So are you a doctor or something?" the cabby asked Rachel, making conversation.

"Psychiatrist actually, I treat the mind as opposed to the body."

"Huh, I know a few people who could use your services." Rachel just smiled politely. She doubted that anyone the cab driver knew suffered to the same extent as the people she was trained to deal with.

Rachel looked out the side window of the taxi as it left the city and headed for the Clinic. The taxi driver had thankfully stopped talking. Rachel didn't like loquacious drivers. Driving was one of the few times Rachel felt she could truly relax. The steady thrum of the wheels on the pavement below and the pleasant smell of the pine scented car-deodorizer hanging from the rearview mirror provided an atmosphere conducive to relaxing.

The taxi slowed as it approached the turnoff to the Clinic. It passed through a set of tall wrought-iron gates with a wave from a security guard sitting in an enclosed booth.

The driver sped halfway around the front circle immediately outside the entrance of the Clinic and came to a surprisingly gentle stop.

"That'll be seventeen-fifty, lady."

Rachel passed a twenty to the cabby, thanking him as she hopped out. She was glad she brought her bike; she wouldn't have to shell out another twenty dollars to get home. She locked her bike up outside the building. Smoothing the creases in her trousers, she power-walked through the front lobby smiling at the girls behind the reception desk. She paused to take a look at herself in the clear reflective glass covering a fire hose. Satisfied with her appearance, and taking a breath to relax, she made her way to the Arthur Montgomery Auditorium, located on the first floor. She took one last look at her watch; she was twenty minutes late.

Chapter 3

▼

Walter Flemming was just concluding his speech when the rear doors of the auditorium opened. A number of heads turned to look at the late arrival.

Flemming recognized her immediately. It was the young doctor who Grant Foley had taken a shining to: Rachel Miller. Pausing only for the briefest of moments so as to be almost imperceptible, Flemming made his closing remarks as Dr. Miller found a seat to occupy. He would have a word with her later about the virtue of punctuality.

"Now are there any questions?" Flemming asked the crowd. A number of hands shot up among the members of the press. Flemming pointed to a sharply dressed reporter he recognized from the *San Francisco Globe*. "How about you, sir?"

"Yes, thank you, Doctor Flemming," the *Globe* said. "There has been a lot of talk about the technique you use to treat dissociative disorders in your patients, and as I'm sure you're aware, a lot of controversy as well."

"Yes, I'm well aware of the critics' opinions. Do you have a question?" Flemming had expected the press to take such an approach so he had decided to take a mildly defensive stance in return. Flemming despised having to justify his every action to a sensation mongering media.

"My question for you, Doctor Flemming, is," the *Globe* continued, "in the case of the treatment offered here at the Clinic, do the ends justify the means?" The reporter held up his mini-cassette recorder awaiting the doctor's reply.

"Do the ends justify the means?" Flemming repeated the question mulling it over. He paused to let an expectant hush fall over the crowd. "What we do here at the Meadowvale Clinic is treat people who suffer from some of the most mentally debilitating disorders known to science. Our methods demonstrate no long-term negative effects, nor do they violate any ethical principles or standards set by the A.P.A., that is, the American Psychiatric Association. To answer your question of whether the ends justify the means, I challenge you to explore the lives of some of the patients we look after and once you have done so, if you can honestly tell me they are better off in their current state prior to our treatment, then I invite you to come up with something better. In the meantime, our methods, as demonstrated by several published papers on the subject, have proven to be more reliable, more valid, and more beneficial to patients with dissociative disorders than any other." A good portion of the Clinic's staff began clapping. A very cowed reporter mumbled a thank you and sat down.

"Now, are there any questions about the Clinic itself?" Flemming beamed, proud of his retort. He pointed to another reporter, a middle-aged woman sitting near the back of the auditorium. She represented *The Oakland Times*.

"Doctor Flemming, given the fact that it's only been just over six months since the disappearance of Doctor Arthur Montgomery, don't you think it's a little premature to name an auditorium in his memory?" Flemming had to wait a moment before answering to measure his response.

"No, I don't think so at all," Flemming spoke directly to the *Times* woman. "First of all, the auditorium is not dedicated to Doctor Montgomery's memory, it is dedicated to his integrity, perseverance, and his tireless efforts in the field of dissociative disorders. And secondly, I have been keeping in close touch with the San Francisco Police Department and the Federal Bureau of Investigation in terms of Doctor Montgomery's disappearance. There is no evidence to support the media's belief that he is no longer alive, and until we discover otherwise, I, the doctor's family, and the rest of the staff at this Clinic, will not give up hoping for his safe return. Now, if you'll excuse me, Doctor Foley will give you a tour of the facilities. I have patients to see." Flemming quickly gathered his notes and marched to the back of the stage. "Damn muckrakers," he muttered under his breath.

"Walter, hold on a second," it was Foley, "I'm sorry, I was hoping they wouldn't bring up the business about Arthur."

"It's not your fault Grant, they're vultures, they can't seem to let well enough alone." Flemming was fuming but didn't hold Foley responsible. "I just need to get back to my office to cool down for a few minutes. I'll drop by before noon to see you about whatever it was you wanted to discuss." With that, Flemming left the auditorium through a rear door and headed back to his office.

If only everyone would just forget Arthur Montgomery ever existed.

Chapter 4

▼

Rachel left her seat as soon as Flemming left the podium. She didn't blame him. She would have left too. Reporters could be so thoughtless. Today's ceremony had been intended to celebrate the official opening of a clinic designed to help others. Instead, the media had used it as an opportunity to sensationalize old stories.

Rachel wasn't wild about Flemming, but she sympathized with him this morning. The two had been introduced shortly after Dr. Foley had hired her. They didn't hit it off quite as well as she and Foley had. Rachel thought he was arrogant and imagined he thought she was green. And perhaps a bit insecure.

The auditorium emptied quickly, reminding Rachel that she too had patients to see. She took the elevator up to the sixth floor where her office was situated toward the rear of the building.

Draping her coat over the back of her chair, she scrutinized her schedule for the day. She had four patients to see before noon and two after lunch. With any luck, no new patients had come in over the weekend. She was up for the next patient.

There were six doctors on staff at the Clinic, she the youngest by at least ten years. The others were Walter Flemming, Grant Foley, Carl Sanford, Ruth Tanner, and Clyde Henderson. Originally, Arthur Montgomery was to be the sixth, but since he vanished half a year ago, a replacement had been necessary. It was just by serendipity that Rachel met Grant Foley when she did.

The Meadowvale Clinic could provide full treatment and residence for up to forty-eight patients on an in-patient basis and hundreds of others on an out-patient basis. The system that Foley and Flemming had established for assigning patients was based on a rotation schedule. Rachel was up next in the rotation. Once the Clinic became fully operational and filled all its vacancies, Rachel could have as many as thirty-five patients. Today she only had the six to see.

Her current position was a far cry from her previous job at UCLA making minimum wage as a research assistant for a social psychologist. She had actually been more of a gopher; go for this, go for that. She saw very little in the way of actual research. Having worked two years for the same demanding woman, Rachel had vowed that she would never work directly under someone else again. She wanted to be autonomous in her work. She wanted her own patients and her own office.

Once she successfully defended her Master's thesis and began her MD program, she realized that such a goal was a long way off. That was until she met Grant Foley.

Six months ago, Rachel had attended a lecture at Berkeley with her boyfriend who attended the University. He was in social psychology. He was a behavioralist whereas she leaned toward psychoanalysis, or Freudian psychiatry.

The lecture they attended was sponsored by the Meadowvale Clinic which was still under construction at the time. Grant Foley was the speaker. He spoke at length about Rachel's main interest: dissociative disorders.

His argument focused on the value of hypnotherapy used in conjunction with dynamically oriented psychotherapy in terms of re-integrating patients' personalities. Coincidentally, Rachel's MA was based on physiological evidence of multiple personality disorder, thus making Dr. Foley's presentation all the more interesting.

Rachel had been so impressed with Foley's unique view of dissociative disorder treatment that she waited for him after the lecture. He was a very amiable fellow and he and Rachel hit it off immediately. Foley had expressed an interest in Rachel's work and asked to see her the next day. Rachel agreed, although she was a bit leery. She thought maybe he was interested in something else.

During her residency at the Langley-Porter Psychiatric Hospital, she got used to the men in her profession constantly asking her out. It seemed they all had the same opening line. As a result, she came up with her own line in return. One which was pretty effective. Whenever someone asked, "What's a pretty girl like you doing in a place like this?" Rachel would always reply, "I'm a patient here," and start twitching. Most of the would-be-Casanovas beat a hasty retreat.

Fortunately, in the case of Grant Foley, he was happily married and was genuinely interested in Rachel's studies.

Over the course of a week, Foley and Rachel came to know each other quite well. Rachel was extremely curious about the new Clinic he was involved with. When asked if she would like a tour of the new facility she couldn't refuse. The Clinic itself was still being built when she saw it for the first time, but Rachel could imagine what it would look like once it was completed.

The two of them had lunch at the university after the tour and that was when Foley proposed to Rachel.

"Rachel, I have a confession to make."

"What's that?" Rachel asked.

"I gave you the tour and buying your lunch because I want to propose to you."

Rachel was taken aback. "I'm sorry?"

"I want to offer you a position at the Clinic. You would have your own office, your own patients and the freedom to carry out your own research." He then told her the starting salary which was better than Rachel could have hoped for at twenty-nine years of age and the job itself could not have been better tailored to her desires if she had made it up herself.

"I accept," she heard herself say. "But when would I start?"

"As soon as the Clinic is completed and you've finished your residency."

"Don't I have to have an interview or something?"

"Think of the past week as an informal interview. Besides, you'll be on the market soon and I don't want to risk someone else discovering you."

The first week at work had been extremely hectic. There was an overlap between contractors finishing up and moving out and doctors and Clinic staff moving in. The building resembled Grand Central Station on a busy day. As promised, Rachel was provided with her own furnished office. Although not large, it suited her perfectly.

The second week wasn't too much better. The only reminder of the contractors' presence was the lingering smell of paint in the hallways and it was the week that a large number of patients were being transferred from the San Francisco Psychiatric Hospital and several other local facilities to the Meadowvale Clinic.

Now, on the day that the Clinic was officially opened, things were in relative order. Rachel knew most of the staff at the Clinic by this time but had still not made any close friends. There was a cliquiness among the staff at Meadowvale. Many of them had been employed at the San Francisco Psychiatric Hospital prior to their being lured away by Dr. Foley. Rachel felt a bit like an outsider. Not to be discouraged however, she had made an effort to be as friendly as possible towards everyone.

Her main concern was for her patients. How well she fit in wouldn't affect her job as much as how her patients felt about her.

Grabbing her clipboard and a pen from the top of her desk, Rachel decided to waste no time and headed for the long-term patient ward on the third floor to see her first patient of the day.

Stepping off the elevator onto the third floor was like stepping out of an aquarium without glass; the difference was instantaneous and complete. The floor had an intensity about it that the other floors lacked. The air was electric and conveyed an atmosphere of perpetual expectancy.

Patients filled the halls and common areas. Many were smoking and some seemed to have forgotten the cigarettes dangling from their mouths or charred fingertips. Several patients suffering from akathisia paced restlessly rushing from room to room without destination, a side effect of drugs such as Haldol used to treat schizophrenia. On the other end of the psychiatric spectrum, other patients remained perfectly still in the oddest positions for hours on end in catatonic poses. Patients', nurses', and doctors' voices ensured that the ward was never silent. Getting used to the sensory overload took getting used to. Despite the chaotic atmosphere of the floor, Rachel always felt revitalized when she saw her patients, knowing she was making a difference.

The floor consisted of forty-eight rooms designed to hold one patient each. The spacious rooms were located on the outer perimeter of the building and each had a window facing the sprawling lawn. Two well appointed common areas, one for eating and one for entertainment, were located roughly in the middle of the wing. Both overlooked the courtyard.

Rachel looked at her clipboard; the first patient she had to see was Donna King. She was one of the patients who had been transferred from the San Francisco Psychiatric Hospital. According to the records sent over with her and Rachel's own observations, Donna suffered from dissociative fugue.

Rachel found Donna in her room brushing her long blond hair. She was counting the strokes out loud.

"Good morning, Donna," Rachel said as she stepped into the patient's room.

"Good morning," Donna said without looking away from the mirror she was staring into. Rachel held up her clipboard and prepared to ask Donna whether her memories were coming back at all when one of the floor nurses, Kevin Cheung, rushed up behind her.

"Doctor Miller, thank God you're here. I'm sorry to interrupt," he glanced at Donna apologetically, "but we have an emergency of sorts and you're the only doctor on the floor at the moment."

"Okay, hold on one second," Rachel rolled her eyes towards Donna indicating to Kevin that she couldn't just leave her.

"Donna? I have to go help Kevin with something important. I'll be back soon, Okay?" Rachel said. Donna nodded her head up and down telling Rachel that it was okay. Her right arm moved in sync with her head so that she could continue brushing her hair. She was past one hundred strokes.

"Let's go," Rachel turned to Kevin ushering him out of the room, "now what's going on?" She noticed Kevin's usual cool demeanor was missing.

"Dean and I were giving out the patients' medication when we noticed one of them wasn't on the floor." Dean Campbell was a floor nurse as well.

Rachel had a good idea of what Kevin meant but asked anyway, "What do you mean, 'Wasn't on the floor?'"

"Exactly that. We assumed she was watching TV or in the dining area the first time we saw that her room was empty. But when we finished distributing the patients' meds and went back to give her her medicine, she still wasn't there. Dean is checking the other rooms right now."

"Who is it?"

"Amanda."

"Amanda Rutherford? Doctor Sanford's patient?" Rachel asked.

"Yep."

"Has he been told?"

"I paged him right before I started looking for you, but he hasn't shown up yet."

"Page him again. I know he's here. I just saw him at the opening ceremony."

"Okay, what are you going to do?"

"I'm going to see how far Dean has gotten and start asking the other patients if they know where Amanda went. Meet me by your station."

"I'll join you as soon as I can." Kevin turned to leave when Rachel called out to him.

"Notify security and the guard at the front gate as well, Amanda can be quite resourceful." Kevin gave her a dubious look but didn't question her. He sprinted down the hall for the phone.

Rachel headed in the opposite direction in search of Dean Campbell. Dean was the other nurse on shift and often worked with Kevin. Whereas Dean was tall and lanky with a shock of red hair, Kevin was short and built like a tank. The two of them both shared a friendly demeanor and Rachel got along with both of them. Rachel peered into each room as she passed by and almost collided with Dean when he stepped out of one of the rooms.

"Oh God, Doctor Miller I'm sorry, I wasn't looking where I was going."

"Never mind that, I'm fine. Kevin just told me what's going on. Any luck in finding her?"

"Not yet, but I've only checked half of the rooms."

"Good, I'm going to start on the other side of the floor. Kevin's just gone to page Doctor Sanford again, then he's going to help me."

"Good luck," Dean said as he stepped into the next room. Rachel found Kevin waiting for her near the elevators.

"He's on his way," Kevin said when he saw Rachel.

"Good. I found Dean," she said, "He's checked half of the rooms so far but hasn't found her. Let's start asking the other patients if they've seen her. You take the even numbered rooms, I'll take the odds. Let's just hope we find her before something happens to her," Rachel neglected to say *again* out loud. It wouldn't be the first time Amanda had disappeared.

Chapter 5

▼

Flemming paced his office, threatening to wear a path right through to the fifth floor below him. His fists clenched, he swore under his breath. How dare those insolent reporters turn his shining moment into a farce.

His turbulent thoughts were interrupted by the buzz of his intercom. Striding across to his desk, Flemming punched a button.

"What is it?"

"I'm so sorry to bother you Doctor Flemming but there's a young woman who desperately wants to see you," Marjorie said quickly, sensing the mood her boss was in.

"Who is it?" he asked, his curiosity aroused at Marjorie's mention of a 'young woman.'

"She says she's a student at Berkeley who works on the school paper and wants to ask you a few questions."

"All right, send her in. Her name?"

"Tanya Perkins."

Flemming had just enough time to sit down behind his desk when Tanya Perkins bounced into the room. Flemming fought not to gasp.

Tanya Perkins was stunning to say the least. With long, curly fire-red hair, a pixie face, and a body that would have sent Venus running to Jenny-Craig, Tanya had a presence all her own.

"Doctor Flemming," she gushed, "thank you so much for seeing me. I'm such a big fan of yours." Tanya offered a dainty hand and leaned far over the mahogany desk giving Flemming a breathtaking view of her ample cleavage. Flemming managed to keep eye contact which he found was not too difficult given the woman's deep green eyes.

"Thank you, Miss Perkins. Please sit down."

"Thank you." Tanya sat down and crossed her legs. Images of Sharon Stone leapt to Flemming's mind.

"What can I do for you?"

"Like you're secretary said, I'm a student at Berkeley. I'm in my fourth year of psychology and I also work on the school paper. I was hoping I could do an interview with you. Something a little more personal than a press conference."

"Of course, I would be delighted. Unfortunately, I'm tied up all morning but perhaps we can arrange a time to meet over dinner perhaps?"

"That would be great," Tanya said excitedly.

Flemming stood up and Tanya took his lead letting him lead her to the door.

"Speak with my secretary and she can set something up this week." Flemming reached for the door and pulled it open. Tanya was standing directly behind him and made no effort to move. Flemming's arm brushed her breasts and still she held her ground.

"Thank you so much, Doctor Flemming. I'm really looking forward to it," she said with a broad smile.

"Me too. I'll see you soon. Thanks for stopping by."

"It was my pleasure," she said with a wink and she was out the door.

Flemming closed the door and smiled wickedly. It was all too easy. Within seconds of Tanya Perkins departure, Flemming switched his mind back to the events of the morning and the smile fell from his face. It wasn't long before he worked himself up again.

He knew he probably shouldn't meet with Foley in his condition but he couldn't possibly get any work done until the turgid veins in his forehead abated. Besides, he wanted to have a word with Foley regarding his tardy protégé. He looked at his watch and noticed an hour had passed since his speech had finished. Foley should have finished his tour by now.

Grant Foley's office was three doors down from his own. He needn't bother calling as he had been invited. He nodded curtly to Foley's secretary and let himself in without introduction. Foley's office was similar in design to Flemming's but what Flemming's lacked in personal mementos, Foley's all but made up for.

Pictures of his family lined the edges of his desk, and although he couldn't see them when he entered, Flemming knew the back of the office door was covered with children's bright Crayola drawings and chaotic finger and potato-print paintings.

Foley, who was talking on the phone, motioned towards one of two chairs opposite his desk when he saw who his unannounced visitor was.

"Thanks, Hal. I'll have one of the doctors on staff give him a tour and explain to him what it is we do here. In the meantime, that fax will be on your desk within the hour. I'll talk to you soon." Grant hung up the phone and smiled. "Well, at least things are going well for me this morning. I hope that reporter didn't upset you too much."

"Never mind that damn reporter, who does this Rachel Miller think she is coming to work twenty minutes late. Of all the people at this Clinic, she should have been here first. It's hardly a way to start a career," Walter barked. He realized his anger was somewhat misplaced, but he felt the urgent need to vent his frustrations. Displacement could be so relieving.

"I'll have a word with her myself," Foley responded calmly, "although I hardly see why you're so worked up over her coming in late."

"It's not her specifically, it's just that from here on in, everything has to go perfectly. We can't afford to have some young upstart put the entire project in jeopardy." The two men rarely discussed the project in their offices, especially with their secretaries sitting right outside.

"I think you're behaving a little irrationally. Rachel Miller is a fine psychiatrist, a little green, yes, but with time I think we can even consider her to join us."

"Let's not jump the gun, Grant. She may be bright, but I don't think we're ready to assume any more risks."

"Risks!" Grant sputtered. He could scarcely believe what he had just heard. "Who are you to lecture me on taking risks! If it wasn't for you, we wouldn't be in this mess with Arthur."

"Arthur was opposed to what we're doing and would have taken the whole project to the A.P.A. And need I remind you that we are both in this together. Besides, what's done is done. Arthur Montgomery won't come back to haunt us."

"I hope you're right," Foley said, tapping an unlit pipe on his desk and stroking his chin. The two men had a way of getting under each other's skin although they were both professional enough not to let their emotions cloud their judgment. Having known each other so long, they knew how to annoy each other.

They had met under quite morbid circumstances. Both had attended Columbia in pursuit of their medical degree, and due to the proximity of their surnames on the class roster, they had been assigned as dissection partners. They shared a cadaver. Their shared interest in psychiatry and black humor resulted in a camaraderie of sorts.

Once they graduated, they went their separate ways, keeping in contact only sporadically. It was Flemming who had re-initiated their friendship five years ago by making Foley an offer he couldn't refuse.

"Let's shift this conversation to a more pleasant topic, shall we?" Flemming felt better having aired his discontent. "I gather you wanted to see me this morning regarding our new patient."

"Yes. He was brought in over the weekend. His name is Jim Wells. He hasn't been officially assessed yet however. I thought I would let Doctor Miller do the honors. She is next on the rotation," Grant informed his colleague.

"How appropriate. How very appropriate." Flemming chuckled, his tensions relieved. He left the office in much higher spirits.

Chapter 6

"Good morning, Steinbeck & Wainfleet insurance. Ed Morgan speaking, how may I help you?"

"Yes, good morning, I need home insurance," the caller replied.

"Certainly, are you a customer with us right now, sir?" Ed asked.

"No, I'm not. Is that a problem?"

"No, of course not. I just need some basic information from you that's all."

"How long will this take?" the man on the line asked.

"Not long at all, sir, I will need you to come in and sit down so I can go over some things with you and of course we have to evaluate the house and…"

"That won't be good for me."

"I'm sorry, sir?"

"I said that won't be good for me."

"How do you mean?"

"I'm afraid I can't come in to see you and I don't want anyone seeing the house."

"We can't give you insurance without seeing the house."

"There's not that much left to see."

"When you say 'not that much left,' what do you mean exactly?" Ed asked slowly.

"The fire has gutted most of it."

"Your house was on fire?" Ed asked, not sure he had heard correctly.

"Was on fire, yeah, the firefighters left about an hour ago."

"Let me get this straight. You want to insure your house that just burned down?"

"Yeah."

"That kind of defeats the purpose of having insurance, don't you think?"

"Well I didn't need it before," the caller answered sincerely.

"I'm sorry you lost your home, sir, but I don't think I can help you."

"Oh, alright, thanks for your time."

"Bye." Ed hung up, removed his thin telephone headset and placed it on top of his cluttered desk almost knocking over a full can of Dr. Pepper in the process. He massaged his temples in an effort to soothe his boggled mind.

The door to his small, sparsely decorated office opened, unpreceded by a knock. Only one person would enter without knocking.

"Good morning, Hal," Ed said without looking away from his computer, tucking a well-gnawed pencil behind his ear.

"A very good morning indeed, Ed," Hal shot back jovially. Ed spun around in his ergonomically and posturepedically correct chair and faced his boss of seven years. Hands planted firmly on the desk between them, Hal Rosenberg towered over Ed and smiled a Cheshire cat smile revealing perfect white teeth. A perfectly tailored brown Armani suit hid his growing paunch and expanding love-handles. His thinning hair could not be as well disguised.

Hal had insurance in his blood. His great-great-grandfather had been one of the first agents with Hancock Insurance and passed down his love of the business to his son, who passed it onto his son, who passed it onto Hal's father, who passed it on to him. By the time he was sixteen Hal could quote insurance rates on pretty much anything. He met Ed seven years ago when Ed was twenty-one and delivering pizza's to supplement his non-existent income as an undergraduate.

Ed had delivered over twenty pizzas to the top floor of the Steinbeck and Wainfleet building for a staff party. He wheeled them in on a dolly and placed them on a large banquet table in stacks of four.

As a joke, Hal asked out loud, "Hey, kid, I'll give you an extra fifty bucks if you can tell me what's on each pizza." To everyone's amazement, especially Hal's, Ed went through each stack and rhymed off what each pizza was covered in. He got every single topping right. Despite his shock and embarrassment, Hal coughed up the fifty bucks, and asked Ed to come to his office the next day for an interview. He recognized Ed's uncanny memory and his ability to recall insignificant trivia as a useful tool in the insurance business. He wanted to be the one who discovered Ed. Now, seven years after Ed received his degree, Hal still spun that yarn every chance he could get. He never once regretted hiring Ed. He thought of him as his protégé.

"What's got you in such a good mood this morning?" Ed smiled back, "Let me guess, they've discovered a cure for old age? All speed limits have been reduced by half? The discovery of fireproof homes?"

"No, no, and no." Hal beamed, enjoying the curiosity he had aroused in his best agent.

"Well, what could be so exciting that you would come all the way to my office when you could have simply called and invited me to yours?" Ed tapped the headset on his desk.

"I'm sure you're aware of the new clinic that opened just outside town?" Hal asked innocently.

"I heard a word or two around town," Ed replied equally innocently. He had spent the majority of the past month thinking about nothing else. "Do they want to cancel their coverage after I spent the last three weeks getting their portfolio in order?"

"Not exactly." Hal's walnut brown eyes were sparkling with excitement and seemed ready to burst forth blinding rays of light.

"What do you mean, 'Not exactly'?" Ed was no longer sharing the contagious energy Hal had brought in with him, as it became replaced by suspicion and a sense of unease. The insurance business was one of the most unpredictable and frustrating businesses in existence. Policy holders constantly canceled their policies not realizing the amount of work they were undoing. And similar to the credit card industry, insurance companies suffered huge losses every year due to fraud which was becoming more and more widespread despite industry assurances that it was under control. People constantly complained about the exorbitant prices they had to pay for insurance. If they knew how much of it was due to covering losses from fraud, they would probably try it themselves to get their money's worth.

"I don't want to talk about it in here, let's go up to my office and I'll fill you in over a cup of coffee, or perhaps a real drink, and not that sweetened-acid you pour down your gullet first thing every morning." He pointed to the brown can on Ed's desk. "I feel in the mood to celebrate." With that, Hal straightened up, spun sharply on his heel and reached the door in two steps. He looked back when he realized Ed had not made a move to get up.

"Coming?" Hal asked. Ed stood, grabbed his jacket which hung loosely on the back of his seat, and made for the door. He wasn't quite sure what to think, and even less sure of what to expect. Hal stepped into the hallway first and turned right towards the elevators.

Ed slipped into his navy-blue blazer, reached up for his pencil, and without looking, threw it straight up where it stuck firmly in the ceiling tile. Closing his office door, he trotted down the hall to catch up to his boss who was already stepping into the elevator.

The two men rode up three floors in silence, stopping only once to let off a bereaved woman who Ed knew had just recently lost her husband but had reaped a substantial amount of money from two insurance policies she had been unaware her husband had taken out on his own life. Ed had sold one of them to him. Tears dragged down her face as she stepped out of the elevator, but it was unclear whether they were a sign of grief or joy. She was now a very rich widow.

Hal pushed the 'door open' button repeatedly when the elevator car reached the ninth floor, which housed all of the executive offices. Ed hoped to be making the same trip to this floor every morning within a few years to his own office.

Stepping into the hallway of the top floor of the Steinbeck & Wainfleet insurance building was nothing like entering the fast-paced, hectic floor where Ed worked. He often wondered if the architects and interior decorators had used up all of their inspiration and talent on the top floor and the lobby and made do with the leftover materials to construct and furnish the rest of the building. Ed ran his hand along the smooth pine paneling which lined the walls.

Hal Rosenberg's office was at the end of a long hall. He maintained his vigil of silence leaving Ed's curiosity to simmer as they walked. Ed opened the door for his superior and followed him in catching a whiff of Aramis cologne as he did. Closing the heavy oak door behind him, Ed marveled at the luxuriously appointed office he had just entered. At least four times as big as his own, Hal's office was thickly carpeted in burgundy broadloom, commanding an entire corner of the top floor, and offering a panoramic view of the city. The Oakland Bay Bridge was just barely visible, but the rest of the city could be seen clearly. The building itself was located in the heart of San Francisco's financial district. In front of one of four bay windows stood a huge desk, adorned only by an ink blotter, computer, telephone, and a silver-framed picture of Hal and his family. Hal stepped behind it and eased himself down in a well-worn black leather chair. Two glasses, an ice bucket, and a bottle of Scotch sat innocuously on the corner of the desk.

"Have a seat, Ed," Hal said, motioning to the two chairs in front of the desk. Ed chose the one on the right so that he could take advantage of the view outside. Hal poured himself three fingers. Ed declined when he was offered.

Hal opened one of the drawers in the desk and reached in. He lifted out a file and placed it squarely in the middle of the desk. It faced Ed in such a way that if he craned his neck he could read the cover without twisting his neck in an attempt to read upside down.

"What is it?" Ed asked, dying to know, yet not wanting to reveal how anxious he truly was. Ed looked at Hal and reached for the file between them.

"Go ahead," Hal said, taking a sip of his drink, relishing the moment as if Ed were his son and the file a deceptively wrapped bicycle on Christmas morning. Hal had done such a good job of piquing his curiosity that Ed had to restrain himself from lunging at the file. He casually slid it towards himself, off the desk, and into the palm of his left hand. Opening the file, he noticed that it was a collection of faxes, correspondence between two parties spanning a period of three weeks, the most recent of which was dated today. The letterhead of the faxes were both familiar to him. One was of the very company he worked for, Steinbeck & Wainfleet, and the other was one which he had had the opportunity to get to know quite well. It was from a Dr. Grant Foley at the Meadowvale Clinic.

"What are they about?" Ed asked looking up across the desk at Hal.

Hal smiled. "Read them and find out. It's something I've been working on for the past three weeks."

"Something that *you've* been working on?"

"That's right. Go on, read them." Ed crossed his legs and began to read the contents of the file. He had just recently completed providing insurance coverage for the property and equipment at the Meadowvale Clinic, so although he could have guessed what the faxes suggested, he was nonetheless flabbergasted. He looked up at Hal.

"They want us to provide them with malpractice insurance as well?"

"That's right!" Hal snapped his fingers on both hands and pantomimed a pair of six-shooters which he pointed at Ed, "And better yet, they want you to be in charge."

"That's great. But what the heck do we know about malpractice insurance for a psychiatric clinic?"

"Very little, as far as I know."

"So what are we doing with this?" Ed waved the file in the air, the contents threatening to spill out.

"Ed. Let me ask you something. Remember that obstetrician who came in here two years ago looking for malpractice coverage and we told him we couldn't help him because we didn't handle that type of insurance?"

"Yeah?"

"Do have any idea how much he has to pay each year just to deliver babies?"

"I'm a property, vehicle and life kind of guy, but I would guess around ten thousand?"

"Would you believe that that doctor is paying over eighty-thousand dollars a year, to another insurance company?"

"Eighty-thousand dollars? Are you serious?"

"Dead serious."

Ed was shocked.

"Now do you see why we're hoping to cover the Meadowvale people?"

"I'm starting to."

"Ed, they have six doctors over there messing with people's heads. Just think of the commissions alone."

"But psychiatry is nowhere near the same as delivering babies. How do we know how much to charge them?"

"I've been working on that. I've been in contact with a large number of insurance companies gathering information on what they charge psychiatrists for malpractice insurance."

"But the Meadowvale Clinic is unique. It's one of the few places in the world which deals exclusively with dissociative disorders. Their psychiatrists are extremely specialized."

"I know that, that's why our work isn't done yet."

"You mean 'our' in the royal sense, right?" Ed asked apprehensively.

"No, I mean me and you."

"So what do I have to do?"

"Well, we need someone to go over there and check out what it is they do, how long it takes, and most importantly, how much it costs."

"Alright, I'll have Bernard go down there today and by the end of the week he'll know the place inside and out."

"That's not what I had in mind."

"You don't expect me to go down there do you?"

"Doctor Grant Foley requested you himself just this morning."

"Come on, Hal, that's a flunky's job, we can send somebody from accounting over and they can do it. Someone like Bernard."

"I don't have to tell you how big a contract this would be and how it would make you look in the eyes of Steinbeck and Wainfleet. This is the first step for this firm into the realm of malpractice insurance. Think of yourself as a pioneer. Besides, Doctor Foley specifically requested that you take care of it. When I told him that it was you who were responsible for all the work done thus far he insisted I send you over."

"But I haven't even met the man."

"Your reputation precedes you. Also, we need someone who can fill the rest of us in. We can't provide them with insurance if nobody here knows what they do, you're young, you'll pick it up quickly. You're my top agent, Ed, and you should see this as a measure of my faith in you and not an attempt to get you out of my hair for a couple of weeks. By the way, we only have two weeks. That's when their coverage under the psychiatric hospital expires."

"Two weeks!? You owe me big time for this, Hal. This is worse than when you sent in that crazy old dame to insure her pets. Who dries their poodle in the microwave after giving it a bath?"

"You'll thank me for this."

"I'm going to spend the next two weeks surrounded by stuffy old doctors, psychiatric patients, and mountains of paperwork, and you think I'm going to thank you? Unlikely."

"If anything, it'll be an interesting experience. Where else can you go where you can meet one new person yet make ten new friends?" Hal laughed at his own joke. Ed simply rolled his eyes.

Ed left Hal's office not knowing whether to be as excited as his boss or annoyed at the fact that he would have to spend another two full weeks working on the Meadowvale Clinic portfolio. He felt he already knew the Clinic inside and out even though he had never set foot in the place. He had spent days and nights pouring over blueprints and property deeds to assess the true value of the land and the structure built upon it. Now he was being asked to go to the Clinic in person and dive into a world as alien to him as Mars.

When he opened the door to his office, Ed looked up at the ceiling; his pencil was no longer there. It had fallen to the ground. That was not a good sign. He bent over and picked it up. Whenever he left his office, Ed liked to throw his pencil up into the ceiling tiles where it stuck easily. If it fell in his absence he believed it meant bad luck. If it was still in place when he returned that meant good luck. Ed didn't consider himself to be exceedingly superstitious, but he enjoyed playing little games to keep his mind occupied and guessing. Since the pencil had fallen while he was talking to Hal about the new Meadowvale contract, Ed assumed that his suspicions would prove correct; the job would be tedious and devoid of any mental stimulation.

Chapter 7

▼

Never a dull moment in a psychiatric clinic, Rachel thought.

Rachel bought a small cup of strawberry-banana yogurt and a poppy-seed bagel with cream cheese for lunch from the Clinic cafeteria, and ate in her office while she poured over the notes she had made on her patients that morning. Once they had found Amanda, the rest of the morning flew by. It was Dean who had discovered her. Rachel, Kevin, and Dean had checked all the rooms in a fruitless search and not one of the patients could tell them where Amanda could be found. Rachel wasn't surprised that none of the other patients could help them find one of their floormates. Most of them didn't know who Amanda was. For that matter, most of them didn't know who they were.

Amanda had crawled into the small freight elevator located in the serving area behind the patient dining room. The elevator was used to send meals up to the patients and to bring the dirty dishes down. It saved the Clinic from having to build two kitchens. Fortunately, it could not be operated from within as normal elevators could be. This is what had prevented Amanda from escaping the floor and the Clinic altogether. If she'd had an accomplice she may have been successful.

Dr. Sanford arrived on the floor just when Dean found Amanda curled up in the elevator. A short, balding, cherubic-faced man, he knew better than anybody Amanda's penchant for freedom. Just over a week ago, during the transfer of patients from the San Francisco Psychiatric Hospital to the Clinic, Amanda had escaped. All of the patients who were to be transferred, thirteen in total, were gathered in the lobby of the psychiatric hospital without incident. Rachel hadn't been there herself but Foley told her all about it afterwards. Everything went smoothly until Flemming pulled up to the front of the hospital in a fifteen passenger van. Amanda took one look at the van and decided she wasn't going.

Before anyone could stop her, she bolted back the way she had come and disappeared. No one had seen where she ran off to. The entire hospital was closed and searched floor by floor, room by room. Once it became apparent that she was no longer within the confines of the hospital, the SFPD was called in to help search the immediate vicinity. The local radio station was notified and they broadcast a special bulletin regarding the missing patient.

Amanda suffered from dissociative identity disorder, also known as multiple personality disorder, as well as borderline personality disorder and mild depression. Amanda didn't pose a serious threat to anyone, but as a patient with a severe dissociative disorder, she was not in any condition to be running around the streets of San Francisco. The rest of the patients were transferred safely while the search for Amanda continued. Hundreds of shop clerks and pedestrians were questioned but no one had seen her. Only in a large city such as San Francisco could a woman run around in a hospital patient's outfit and a plastic identification bracelet without being noticed.

It wasn't until the next morning that she was found by a very surprised homeowner seven blocks away from the hospital. Amanda had simply walked into someone's house and helped herself to breakfast. Needless to say, the gentleman who found this strange woman eating at his breakfast table mumbling something about the breakfast of champions was somewhat taken aback. He had heard the broadcast on the radio the previous day however and quickly deduced that the woman sitting in his kitchen was the same who had escaped from the psychiatric hospital. Realizing she wasn't dangerous, he soon regained his composure, called the police, and sat down and ate breakfast with her. When the police arrived, they found Amanda drinking orange juice on the porch with her new-found friend. She was returned unharmed to the Clinic and up until today, had not shown any inclination to take flight again.

Rachel hadn't told Dean this because Foley had asked her not to tell anyone. Now thinking back to the morning's events, she was glad Amanda wasn't her patient. She already had her hands full with her own. A knock on her office door interrupted the bagel's journey to her mouth and Foley walked in.

"Rachel, good morning, I heard about your game of hide and seek this morning, everything all right?" he said.

"Yes, we found Amanda in the kitchen lift. Aside from a cramp in her leg she appeared to be fine."

"Good, I'm glad someone was here to take care of her," his voice soured a bit and Rachel took it to mean that he wasn't happy about Sanford's absence. Not knowing what to say, Rachel didn't respond.

"The reason I came to see you," Foley continued, "was that a new patient was admitted over the weekend and as you know your next up on the rotation."

"Has he or she been diagnosed yet?"

"He. And no he hasn't. I thought we would wait until you had a chance to do so. If you don't mind, I would like to sit in and observe your diagnosis. You remember how I told you about the pro-bono work each doctor at the Clinic will be doing?"

"The two patients a month?"

"That's right. This will be your first pro-bono case." Each doctor at the Clinic was to *volunteer* several hours a week on a pro-bono basis, to see patients who couldn't afford proper treatment. Rachel had yet to do any pro-bono work. But now the rotation called her up to do her part.

"Sure, just give me a minute to finish lunch and I'll join you downstairs." Rachel said.

"Actually, just swing by my office and get me, I have a couple of phone calls to make."

"Okay, I'll see you in a few minutes." Rachel hastily finished her lunch, stuffed a fresh set of sheets onto her clipboard and went to Foley's office.

The patient was already downstairs on the fourth floor waiting for the two doctors and seemed to be disoriented. His shaggy brown hair hung over the back of the wide, cushioned chair he was sitting in. His eyes scanned the room nervously and he couldn't stop touching his face. He seemed to perk up a little when he saw Rachel enter the room. Foley sat down on one of two chairs opposite the patient's and invited Rachel to do the same.

"Jim, I'd like you to meet Doctor Miller, she's here to ask you some questions," Foley said.

"Hi, Jim," Rachel said. "My name is Rachel and I'm a doctor here at the Clinic."

"Hello."

"Do you know where you are, Jim?" Rachel asked. Jim slowly looked around the room as if he was seeing it for the first time.

"No," he said finally.

"This is the Meadowvale Clinic. You were brought in this weekend. Do you remember that?" Again, Jim paused before he answered.

"No."

"Can you remember anything from your past?"

"Not really."

"When you say not really, do you mean not at all, or do you mean that you do remember some things but not everything?"

Jim remained silent. He was looking at Rachel but not seeing her.

"Jim, do you understand what I'm asking you?"

"What? Sorry, I didn't hear you there." He shook his head as if gathering his thoughts.

"I asked what you could remember from your past."

"I can remember some stuff," Jim said pointing to the file Foley held in his hands. Rachel glanced at the file on Foley's lap and thought she understood.

"You mean you remember personal information about yourself? Is that what you mean Jim?"

"Yes."

"Has he been given a physical examination yet, Grant?" Rachel asked Foley.

"Not that I'm aware of, why?"

"It looks like he has a bruise on the side of his head," Rachel leaned towards Jim and pointed to a large welt on the right side of his head.

"How did you get this bump on your head?" she asked Jim. He reached up to touch the side of his head, he winced as he touched the bruise. A look of perplexion crossed his face. "I don't know," he answered. He continued to explore the bruise with the tips of his fingers. Rachel held up three fingers and asked Jim how many she was holding up.

"Three," he said. Rachel then held up her index finger and asked Jim to follow it with his eyes only as she moved it side to side and up and down. He did so without difficulty. Rachel then withdrew a blank sheet of paper from her clipboard, drew a circle on it and passed it to Jim along with a pencil.

"Jim," she said, "this circle represents a clock. Could you draw ten minutes to two on it for me?" Jim took the pencil and paper and quickly drew two hands on the clock. They correlated with the time Rachel had asked him to draw.

"Well there doesn't appear to be any brain damage or signs of dementia," Rachel said, "Jim, think hard, try to remember how you got that bruise on your head." Jim's face was a mask of concentration, he struggled to think of the origins of the contusion but could not. He shook his head and said he still could not remember.

"Do you remember my name, Jim?" Rachel asked as she covered up her nametag.

"Doctor Miller," he said.

"Good, and his?" she pointed to Foley who covered his own nametag.

"Doctor Foley."

"Good," Rachel stood up "Grant, could I speak with you outside for a moment?" she asked Foley.

"Sure, Doctor Miller." Foley stood up as well.

"Jim? Doctor Foley and I are going to step out for a minute to talk but we'll be right back, okay?"

Jim nodded his head.

"From what I can determine thus far, I would say he has post-traumatic amnesia but not dissociative," Rachel told Grant once they had left the room.

"Why do you say that?" Foley asked. Rachel thought he looked puzzled or annoyed and wondered if she had missed something.

"Well, he remembers personal information, ruling out retrograde amnesia, he's able to learn new things which he demonstrated by remembering our names, so he doesn't have anterograde amnesia. He knows who he is and doesn't seem to be confused about his identity which rules out fugue. He passed the clock test which would suggest he doesn't suffer from any form of dementia, and finally, the bump on his head indicates that he suffered some kind of blow to the head which would explain his memory loss."

"I think you're right, Rachel. What do you propose we do now?" Foley asked, although Rachel thought he seemed a little pained to admit she was right, almost as if he wanted her to be wrong.

"Well, I think we should tell Jim what we think happened, and if he consents, I'd like to run a CT scan and an EEG over at San Francisco General just to be sure there is no internal damage. Otherwise, I think with a little time and encouragement, he'll remember what happened to him and we can let him go."

"Good work, doctor," Foley smiled, "arrange the tests as soon as you can and check him into one of the short-term rooms on the fourth floor, I imagine he won't be here long."

"Sure thing," Rachel said as Foley walked down the hall.

"Oh, Rachel, by the way," Foley said as he stopped and turned around, "I'm meeting a gentleman from Steinbeck and Wainfleet Insurance tomorrow morning and I was hoping that you could show him around the Clinic. You know, give him a tour and show him what we do around here. I'm assuming he doesn't have much of a background in psychiatry so I'll need you to explain to him the nature of our work and as much as you can about dissociative disorders without completely overwhelming him.

"He'll be here for the next two weeks working on the Clinic's insurance needs. I've already arranged it so that tomorrow your patients will be taken care of, the other doctors and I will split them up between us. If you could take him under your wing so to speak and just make yourself available if he has any questions it would be greatly appreciated. Thanks, Rachel." The elevator doors closed before Rachel could slip a word in edgewise.

Babysitting some insurance agent was the last thing Rachel needed. Her hands were going to be full now that she had another patient. She would have to come in to work an hour or two earlier tomorrow morning. Sighing in resignation, Rachel went back into the room where Jim was waiting to tell him the news.

Chapter 8

"Walter, we have a problem," Grant Foley said marching into Flemming's office.

"Oh? What is it?" Flemming asked with a bit of concern in his voice. He was used to Carl Sanford rushing into his office with his 'problems', but to have Grant rushing in saying they had a problem was a bit disconcerting.

"Rachel Miller and I just diagnosed the new patient, Jim Wells, well actually she diagnosed while I observed, and she came up with post-traumatic amnesia, non-dissociative."

"Post-traumatic amnesia?" Flemming frowned.

"Yes, that was my reaction as well."

"How did she come up with that?" Foley recounted the diagnosis to Flemming and concluded with Rachel's observation of the bruise on the side of Jim's head.

"How did he get a bruise on his head?" Flemming asked.

"I'm not sure, but I intend to find out."

"Well do so soon. In the meantime, I think we should have another round with Jim Wells."

"Isn't that a little premature?"

"Is it? I don't think so. You said it yourself, he was diagnosed by one of our own doctors as suffering from post-traumatic amnesia. Surely you don't think we should diagnose the man ourselves?"

"No, of course not, I was just thinking perhaps we should wait awhile and observe what happens."

"We've already waited too long. If not for the incessant whining of Montgomery and Sanford, we would have done this a long time ago."

"Well, when should we see Jim again?"

"Bring him down later this afternoon and Sanford and I will take care of it. This time we'll go even further."

"More hypnosis?"

"Yes. That and more."

"What should I tell Doctor Miller?"

"Don't tell her anything, you're the chief administrator of this Clinic, you don't have to answer to anybody. Once she's done her rounds tomorrow have her take another look at her new patient. With a little luck, she'll change her diagnosis."

"She's not doing rounds tomorrow."

"What?"

"The agent from Steinbeck and Wainfleet is coming tomorrow, remember?"

"Yes, so what of it?"

"Well, I've asked Doctor Miller to give him a tour of the Clinic and show him the ropes."

"Oh, for crying out loud."

"Don't worry, she'll be free on Wednesday. This way you and I will have more time to take care of Jim. Besides, he's not going anywhere."

"I suppose you're right," Flemming conceded, "alright, have her examine him again on Wednesday and let's see to it that she sees things our way."

Chapter 9

▼

Once she had sent Jim Wells over to the San Francisco General Hospital to be tested, and seen the rest of her patients, Rachel left the Clinic an hour later than she had intended. The sun shone brightly and a warm September breeze chased billowy cumulus clouds across a pale blue sky. It was perfect bike riding weather.

As she crossed over the Oakland Bay Bridge, Rachel noticed the hand railings on the bridge were only four feet high. She hoped that one day soon, the city's bridge authorities would get around to installing suicide barriers as they were now doing on the Golden Gate Bridge. Since it was first opened in nineteen thirty-seven, over twelve hundred people had committed suicide by jumping off the Golden Gate Bridge. Forty more had already jumped to their deaths in the last year. Although not as popular, the Oakland Bay Bridge was no stranger to suicides either. Both the Eiffel Tower in Paris and the Empire State Building in New York had suicide barriers and the numbers of jumpers had been dramatically reduced as a result. It didn't take much yet it could make all the difference in the world.

Few people would even notice the barrier once it was installed as it was designed with the notion that it should not hamper the view the bridge currently afforded. To mental health activists, whom Rachel actively supported, and the people they represented the barrier represented a small, but important, victory. It meant that at least a few lives would be spared the tragic fate that so many others had chosen.

After a harrowing bike ride through rush-hour traffic, Rachel reached her downtown apartment building. The building itself had been built shortly after WWII and was showing its age. Ownership of the Brownstone had changed hands so frequently over the past half century that management never bothered to maintain it.

Now weeds grew unchecked in what used to be flower gardens on either side of the steps; peeling lead-based paint framed every window and covered the soffits ten stories overhead; the mortar, struggling to hold the bricks together, was crumbling. Rachel could not help but look upwards every time she climbed the front steps anticipating a brick to come loose and jar her skull, killing her instantly.

Striding up those steps now with her ten-speed's cross-bar digging into her shoulder, Rachel fumbled for her keys. Once in a blue moon, the lock caught on the first attempt. This was not one of those times. Rachel jiggled the keys for what seemed an eternity before the door finally opened, all the while, her Schwinn dug deeper and deeper into her shoulder, grinding her clavicle.

Not that she really needed keys however; one good yank on the handle and the door would most likely come off of its hinges. Some security she thought. For the price she was paying for her one bedroom apartment one would expect a doorman, twenty-four hour security and free coffee and donuts in the lobby. No such luck.

The interior was in no better shape than the exterior of the building. The front entrance's carpet was threadbare due to uncountable tenants moving in and out over the years. Decades of cigarette smoke stained the walls and ceiling a putrid yellow, and the overhead lamp, a lightbulb hanging by a very worn wire, served as a piniata for drunken college students.

Lugging her bicycle up five flights of stairs (the elevator was forever being repaired), Rachel reached her apartment out of breath. Upon entering her apartment, she quickly scanned the room for anything missing or out of place. It was not a rare occurrence that the maintenance people would pilfer a tenant's belongings. Assuring herself that everything was in order, Rachel put her bike away in the hall closet and made a beeline for the kitchen to prepare dinner. She picked up the phone and ordered Chinese for one.

Rachel took a quick shower while she waited for her food to arrive. The hot water sluiced off the sweat and city air that seemed to get thicker every day. Stepping out of the shower, Rachel made for the telephone and checked her messages as she toweled off her short brown hair. There were three messages.

"Rachel, it's Mom. I just wanted to see if you were still alive, you never call. How is work? I know it's only your third week, but I worry about you surrounded by all those crazies, sorry hon, I mean, 'psychologically challenged individuals.' I hope you're still seeing that Marty fellow, he seems like such a nice boy, he really has his head on straight. You know I don't want to be the last one in my bridge club to be a grandmother. Anyway, call me when you get the chance or have the time. Bye dear." Rachel sighed in exasperation. Her overprotective mother called her at least twice a week. Rachel truly thought the woman was living vicariously through her, all her mother had was her bridge club to keep her busy, that and gloating about her daughter the doctor.

A woman's monotone voice interrupted Rachel's thoughts notifying her of the next message.

"Hi Rachel, it's Marty," he sounded nervous. "Look, I realize this isn't the best way to do this, but I don't think things are working out between us. I mean, all you ever do is study and work and I feel like I'm playing second fiddle in your life. Call me if you want, don't take this personally, it's not you, it's me, bye." *Yeah right*, Rachel thought, *it was never the other person*. She had heard the same line all through high school, her undergraduate years, grad school, and now, keeping with consistency, the same disclaimer would no doubt haunt her throughout her professional life as well. At least it wasn't a surprise. "Message erased, next message."

"Hi Rachel, it's Chris Landry from Imperial Bank and Trust. I was just calling to remind you of your outstanding college loan. If you have a minute, give me a call, or drop by and see me, it won't take long. I just want to go over a payment plan with you. Talk to you soon." The last thing she needed was another reminder of her loan. The bank seemed to hold it over her head just to vex her. They sent her a notice every week and called every two. Rachel pushed the erase button. "Message erased, you have no more new messages," the recorded voice stated matter-of-factly.

Rachel finished drying off and began to get dressed. Just as she finished putting on a pair of jeans and a T-shirt, the front door buzzer sounded, signaling the arrival of her dinner. She buzzed the delivery man in. Every time she ordered Chinese he would deliver to her and they would have the same conversation each time. Rachel opened the door before the delivery boy had a chance to finish knocking.

"Hi, Bryan, how's it going today?" Rachel asked leaning against the doorframe.

"Tired. When are they going to fix that stupid elevator? It's a good thing you don't order every night," Bryan said smiling. Rachel pinned him at about seventeen years old. He was a tall gangly fellow with dark hair. His face was pocked with acne, and he was always smiling despite his braces.

"I couldn't afford to order out every night, and as for the elevator, we might as well be waiting for Godot." Rachel laughed at the perplexed look on Bryan's face. "Never mind," she told him.

"Okay, well here's your gourmet meal, madam." Bryan extended two brown paper bags. "That'll be twelve-sixty-three."

"What about delivery charges?" Rachel asked knowing the answer in advance.

"For you Rachel, never. You just have to promise me a date someday." Bryan smiled again, this time his cheeks flushed as he did so.

"Sure Bryan, we'll do that sometime, a real night on the town, and who knows where it will all lead to," Rachel said as she handed him a ten and a five. Bryan's face turned a scarlet red. He mumbled something unintelligible as he rummaged in his pockets for Rachel's change.

"Well, here's your change," Bryan handed her a bill and a handful of coins. Rachel gave him a dollar tip.

"Thanks Rachel, see you later," Bryan turned and walked down the hall with a new bounce in his step. Rachel felt guilty about not being able to give him a bigger tip but she was barely getting by herself and had just started her first full-paying job. She could barely afford to buy new tires for her car.

Rachel closed the door with her hip and made for the living room. The room itself was cramped even by a student's standards. Measuring ten by twelve, the room barely afforded room for a sofa, a makeshift entertainment unit, and a coffee table. The decorations were sparse. Two Van Gogh prints and a Monet adorned the walls. The Monet was covering a hole the last tenant had put in the plaster. Despite numerous assurances by the landlord that he would get it fixed soon, Rachel had decided to cover it on her own.

A single waist high plant commanded the attention of an entire corner of the living room as it leaned precariously towards the window struggling for what little light the grime covered glass would let in during the daytime.

Branching off from the living room was a bathroom no bigger than a closet, a surprisingly well equipped kitchen given the amenities, or lack thereof provided in the rest of the apartment, and her bedroom. A twin bed took up half of the floorspace while the other half was dominated by a six foot banquet table which served as her desk. Piles of notes and case studies, and two bookshelves overflowing with books written by such authors as, Jung, Adler, Freud, Erikson, Horney, Fromm, and Rogers.

Rachel sat down on her twenty dollar sofa courtesy of the local thrift store and spread her feast before her. Digging into her shrimp fried rice she channel-surfed, looking for something to entertain yet educate at the same time. She settled on an X-Files re-run.

She enjoyed the widely divergent points of view the two FBI agents had. In a world where there seems to be no absolutes, despite Mulder's claim that *the truth is out there*, perspective is everything. That was partially why Rachel decided to become a psychiatrist. She found it fascinating that people see the world in such radically different ways. She wanted to understand how and why people interpreted events the way they did and whether or not there was an objective reality independent of what humans thought as philosophers such as Plato and Ayn Rand postulated. For the time being she believed that humans interpreted the world in their own way based on their experiences and perspective.

With her meal finished and the X-Files over, Rachel turned off the lights to her apartment, double checked the lock on her door, and turned in early to read an Oliver Sacks book. She hoped her nocturnal stalker would give it a rest this evening.

Chapter 10

▼

Tuesday
8:46 a.m.

Ed Morgan's cherry red, four-year-old, F-150 pickup streaked down the highway towards the Meadowvale Clinic. The five-liter V8 truck was leased, so Ed didn't mind pushing it once in awhile to get his money's worth. Singing along to one of his *Hits of the Eighties* tapes, he paid little attention to the scenery as it whizzed by. Despite the fact that he was singing, his mind was going over what he had to do in a short two week period. He was being asked to learn everything he could about dissociative disorders, from how they developed to how they were treated. It was not going to be an easy task especially given the minimal time frame in which to accomplish it.

The Clinic emerged into view and Ed took his foot off the gas. He turned right onto an off-ramp and was stopped at a set of tall iron gates by a man in a security booth. Ed told the guard who he was and why he was there and was let through without incident. He followed a long, winding driveway lined with towering oak trees. The trees' branches formed a loose canopy in a feeble attempt to block out the sun.

Arriving at the front circle of the Clinic, Ed turned right into the parking lot and searched for the visitor's parking spaces. Several cameras mounted on the Clinic itself followed his every move. Not surprisingly, the visitor parking spaces were located at the far back right corner of the lot. Ed sighed as he drove to the furthest parking spot from the Clinic. Killing the ignition, he cut off the *Naked Eyes* in the middle of a song, grabbed his attaché case and laptop and proceeded to the front entrance.

Two sets of glass doors and one revolving door set in between offered passageway into the Clinic. Ed pushed himself through the revolving door and stepped into the most modern institution he had ever set foot in. Dark wooden wainscotting lined the walls separating the pale green of the lower half from the off white of the top half. The black marble floor appeared to have been buffed just moments ago. Rows of fluorescent lights high overhead made the lobby seem even brighter than it really was and gave life to the numerous plants which seemed to occupy every corner.

Two young women stood behind a large crescent-shaped reception desk busily answering phones and sorting and organizing files. Ed stepped up to the front desk in awe of his surroundings and of the two pretty women behind the desk. He set his belongings down on the floor beside him.

"Good morning, can I help you, sir?" one of the two receptionists greeted Ed before he had a chance to open his mouth. Her long brown hair matched her big brown eyes and complemented her full figure. A plastic tag pinned over her right breast indicated that her name was Daniela.

"Yes, good morning..., Daniela," Ed placed his right elbow on the counter top taking some of the weight off his feet. "My name is Ed Morgan, I have a nine o'clock with the Chief Administrator, Doctor Grant Foley."

"Okay, Mister Morgan. If you take the elevator located to your right up to the sixth floor, his office is the sixth door on the left. That door leads to his outer office so just walk right in and his secretary will let him know you're here. Her name is Barbara." Daniela pointed to the elevators and gave Ed a big smile.

"Thank you very much, Daniela, I'll see you later." Ed leaned down to collect his case and PC and headed towards the elevators with a smile on his face. *Maybe this wouldn't be such a bad job after all*, he thought to himself.

He was halfway to the elevator when Daniela called out to him, "Mister Morgan, I almost forgot," she was waving a small rectangular piece of plastic in her hand, "you need a visitor's pass." Ed doubled back, took the pass and affixed it to his coat.

"Thank you, I wouldn't want to be gunned down by one of the guards," Ed joked. Daniela smiled again.

Ed made his way to the elevator and pushed the button for the sixth floor. The elevator's walls were a rich walnut paneling and reminded Ed of a five-star hotel he had stayed at during a conference in London. Upon reaching the sixth floor, the doors opened to reveal a long hallway broken up by several doors on each side. Off-whites and greens predominated on the sixth floor as well. Ed made his way down the hall glancing at the names and titles on each door as he passed. All of them had about ten extra letters after their names. The sixth door on his left, plain and unassuming, bore a nameplate: Dr. Grant Foley Chief Administrator & Co-Director.

Ed knocked lightly and walked in. A secretary looked up from the document she was reading and greeted him.

"Hi, I'm here to see Doctor Foley. I'm Ed Morgan from Steinbeck and Wainfleet Insurance. I have a nine o'clock." Ed closed the door gently behind him.

"Certainly, Mister Morgan. Doctor Foley is on the phone right now but if you'll have a seat I'll let him know you're here as soon as he's done." Barb continued reading her document. The document was actually a Harlequin Romance novel. Several years ago, she had discovered a small company which published Harlequin-type books cleverly disguised as official looking documents so that people in her position could read on the job. Barb and the other secretaries in the Clinic took turns buying the disguised books and they passed them around. They cost roughly twice the actual cost of the book itself but they were well worth it. None of the doctors had caught on thus far.

Barb undressed the lean, dark-haired young insurance agent sitting across from her with her eyes. She longed for some sort of adventure in her life. An affair would do the trick, unfortunately, she knew it would never happen and she would be forever destined to work for other people and spend the rest of her days with the same man. Such was the problem with living vicariously through fictional characters. Barb sighed longingly, and continued reading.

Chapter 11

Ed glanced at his watch: eight fifty-five. He was early as usual. Although most wouldn't consider it an annoying habit, Ed had come to rue his punctuality. He was always early, he could not comprehend how anyone could be late for anything. If you knew you had to be somewhere, all you had to do was plan your time and get organized. It wasn't that hard. Ed learned over a number of years however that most people were unable to do this. He also discovered that most people didn't like it when you were constantly early, it made them look bad. Now sitting in an Indian red leather chair that made an ominous noise every time he shifted his weight, Ed regretted being early once again. Just then, Barb set down the 'file' she was reading and told Ed that Dr. Foley could see him now and that he should just walk right in. Ed was relieved, the secretary couldn't seem to take her eyes off him.

Ed stood up, rolled his shoulders to compose himself and let himself into Grant Foley's office. The office itself was fairly standard with numerous degrees and citations framed on the left wall. A faint hint of tobacco smoke lingered in the air. Ed spied the source of the smell; a black wooden pipe rested upon the doctor's desk. Several picture frames stood on the expansive wooden desk which dominated the room. Ed couldn't see what the pictures were of but assumed they were pictures of the doctor's family. A short wiry man of about fifty stood up from behind the desk and came over to greet Ed.

"Hi, I'm Doctor Grant Foley, Co-Director and Chief Administrator of Meadowvale, although you probably already know that." Ed smiled at the easygoing manner of this energetic man as they shook hands.

"It's a pleasure to meet you, Doctor Foley. I'm Edwin Morgan from Steinbeck and Wainfleet. That's a lot of paper you have up on your wall," Ed nodded his head towards the degrees, "I'm afraid I wouldn't have the patience to spend so much time in school."

"Well, the ivory tower isn't for everybody. Frankly, I prefer the clinical side of my profession, hence my position here and not at some university." Grant Foley winked at Ed and waved his hand toward a seat inviting him to sit down. The doctor made his way back around his desk, cleared a pile of folders, and sat down, smoothing his tweed jacket as he did so.

"So, you're the young man Hal sent to learn in two weeks everything I learned over a period of thirty-five years?" It was a statement more than it was a question. Hal Rosenberg and Dr. Foley had established quite a rapport over the past month having talked on the phone so often and even meeting for lunch on occasion.

"That seems to be about the size of it," Ed said, only now realizing the enormity of his task. "I'm afraid I don't know the first thing about dissociative disorders. I've seen *The Three Faces of Eve* with Joanne Woodward, but I don't think that will earn me an honorary degree anywhere."

"No, I think you may be right my boy. Although that case may not be the best example to use given recent developments. Unfortunately, as with most Hollywood productions, its glaring inaccuracies by far outweigh any value the film had in creating awareness of multiple personality disorder, which as you may or may not know was renamed in nineteen ninety-four by the American Psychiatric Association and is now known as dissociative identity disorder."

"I did not know that," Ed said politely.

"Just so you know, dissociative identity disorder is the Clinic's pet disorder. It's by far the most interesting and most complex of the numerous types of dissociative disorders."

"From what little I know, I would have to agree. I'm looking forward to finding out more."

"Excellent," Foley said, then added, "So if you didn't take psychology at college what did you take, if you don't mind my asking?" Foley leaned forward with interest.

"I'm a history major, or was, I studied resistance throughout history." Ed said, his cheeks flushed a bit as he did so thinking back to his undergraduate years. He never had a strong enough math background to go into commerce or engineering and he had no inclination to follow in his father's footsteps and go into medicine. History had seemed like the most interesting alternative at the time. He wasn't embarrassed that he was a history major despite all of his friend's assurances that he would surely be unemployed or flipping burgers somewhere, but he always felt as if others would look down upon him. Grant Foley was not one of these people.

"History! How fascinating, and specializing in resistance. So I gather you studied slavery, Nazi Germany, Stalinist Russia and labor history among other things," Foley seemed genuinely impressed. Ed's respect for the man increased exponentially.

"You summed up a good deal of my studies right there. It's nice to know not everybody sees history as a way of copping out." The doctor's face took on a serious note.

"Don't ever let anyone put down your education," he said firmly. "I strongly believe that undergraduate studies should be devoted to as broad a scope as possible. Colleges and universities were originally designed to provide a liberal arts education, in order to teach about the world around and before you. Graduate studies should be devoted to specializing. You see too many engineers and scientists out there these days who may know how to build a bridge or isolate a gene, but can they recite Shakespeare and Tennyson, intelligently discuss Plato's allegory of the cave, appreciate Tchaikovsky and Vivaldi, or even identify Maslow's hierarchy of needs? And if not, what kind of lives are they really leading? Lives of quiet desperation no doubt. I admit ignorance is bliss but to paraphrase Aristotle, 'tis better to be a Socrates dissatisfied than a pig satisfied'. Today's college and university graduates are learning more and more about less and less until they know absolutely everything about nothing. Never be ashamed to tell anybody you have a history degree." Dr. Foley leaned back in his chair and smiled.

Ed was shocked. Foley had just summed up in two minutes everything he had ever felt about his degree but could never quite articulate to others or himself.

"I'm speechless," was all he could manage to get out.

"That must be a first, a speechless insurance salesman," Foley said. Just then, Barb's voice cut in over the intercom, "Doctor Miller is here to show Mister Morgan around."

"Well, looks like our time is up. It's a shame we couldn't continue our conversation. Doctor Miller will show you around the Clinic and explain to you what it is we do here, so if you have any questions, just ask her." Foley stood up and extended his hand. Ed rose out of his chair and took the doctor's hand for the second time.

"It's been a pleasure meeting you, and an even bigger one talking to you." Ed let go of the doctor's hand and headed for the door. "Perhaps we'll have a chance to speak again."

"If you're going to be here for two weeks you can count on it," Foley replied as he sat back down and reached for his pipe as Ed let himself out.

Chapter 12

Rachel was sitting in the same chair Ed had occupied just twenty minutes earlier. She now rose as Grant Foley's office door opened and the insurance agent she was supposed to accommodate stepped out. He stood at about five eleven, had a trim figure, short, wavy black hair, and a contagious smile. Rachel was taken aback. She was expecting to meet someone older and much less pleasing to the eye.

"You must be Edwin Morgan," Rachel said, holding out her hand.

"Yes, and you must be my tour guide. It's a pleasure," Ed said smiling as he shook Rachel's hand.

"Yes, Doctor Miller, but please call me Rachel. I'm just barely a doctor and you're probably older than I am."

"All right, but only if you call me Ed, only my mother calls me Edwin," Ed said sheepishly, "and I'm only twenty-eight," he added.

"It's a deal." Rachel opened the outer door leading to the hallway and stepped aside to let Ed out first. "After you."

Ed moved past Rachel into the hallway. Rachel joined him and closed the door behind her.

"If you want, you can leave your stuff in my office. It's just around the corner and down the hall." Rachel began walking down the hall before Ed had a chance to reply. He followed her.

Rachel stopped at the seventh door on the right and let herself in. Ed stepped in behind her and passed his attaché case and PC to Rachel who placed them on a smaller version of Foley's desk which sat in the middle of a smaller version of Foley's office. Rachel did not have a secretary nor did she have as impressive a "glory wall" as Foley had.

"Not as nice as Doctor Foley's office, I know, but at least I have a window." The single window overlooked the parking lot and Ed could see his truck from where he stood.

"It's very nice. Besides, don't you spend most of your time with patients?" Ed asked.

"Generally yes, but I imagine I'll be spending a lot of late nights up here burning the midnight oil working on case files and trying to get published. We have a saying in our world, 'Publish or Perish.' If you don't get published, you may as well kiss your career good-bye." Ed wondered how many articles Rachel had to her credit.

Rachel and Ed stepped back into the hall once more. The office door swung shut automatically behind them with an audible click. Heading towards the elevators, Rachel asked Ed, "So what kind of background do you have in psychiatry?"

"Very little, as I was just telling Doctor Foley. I took a first year psychology course and I've seen a few movies, but aside from that, not much."

"Well, I'll take you through step by step. I'll give you a tour of the building first and then I'll try to get you acquainted with the most common dissociative disorders. The top floor, as you can probably guess, is where all of the doctor's offices are and where we do most, if not all, of our paperwork," Rachel pressed the button for the lobby as they got into the elevator. "We'll start at the bottom and work our way up." Upon reaching the lobby, Rachel gave Ed the same tour she had received when she was hired by Grant Foley.

It was just before noon when Rachel finished showing Ed around the facility. They stopped in the Clinic cafeteria on the main level to grab lunch. Most of the tables were occupied by the Clinic's staff who were all in the midst of discussing their cases with as much enthusiasm as some people discussed sports. Sitting down at the only available table tucked away in a corner, Rachel asked Ed what he thought so far of the Clinic.

"Very impressive. I had no idea there was such a market in treating dissociative disorders."

"Actually, the Clinic is also designed to do a lot of research." Rachel said between bites of her tuna sandwich. "The International Society for the Study of Dissociation, or ISSD, is financing a longitudinal study on dissociative amnesia to determine its long term effects on both mental and physiological processes. I'll be contributing to that study when time permits, otherwise I'm here to treat those patients with any type of dissociative disorder."

"Why a study on dissociative amnesia? I thought the Clinic's main focus was on dissociative identity disorder."

"Oh, it is, don't get me wrong, but there have been large scale surveys done recently, I believe nineteen eighty-six and nineteen eighty-nine, which focused entirely on clinicians' case histories of dissociative identity disorder, or DID, from around the world. The information those two studies compiled has been incredibly useful in terms of diagnosing, predicting, and treating, DID, yet there is still a lot we don't know about the disorder. Meadowvale plans on conducting its own survey on DID once we have treated enough patients to make its results statistically significant. Hopefully this will happen within the next two or three years. Once we're done lunch, I'll take you to the courtyard and tell you all about the actual disorders we treat here." Rachel finished her sandwich and washed it down with a small carton of milk. Ed still had half a sandwich to eat and a full Dr. Pepper. Gulping both down quickly, he finished his lunch and expressed his anxiousness to resume.

Chapter 13

▼

"So how many patients can the Clinic cater to at a time?" Ed asked as he and Rachel made their way to the courtyard.

"Well it depends."

"On what?"

"The third floor is dedicated to the housing of long-term patients. Those patients who stay with us for an indefinite period of time. They essentially live here during their treatment. The third floor has forty-eight rooms."

"So not all patients actually live at the Clinic?"

"That's right. Most of our patients are what we call out-patients. That is, they lead a normal life outside the Clinic but come to us for treatment on a regular basis. Some come several times a week, others once or twice a month. Our schedules are individually tailored to meet specific patient requirements. This isn't a cookie-cutter institution. In another few months we'll probably have over three hundred out-patients."

"What determines the status of a patient? I mean why do some patients stay here while others live at home and walk in?"

"The Clinic treats both private patients and patients covered by insurance. That is, some patients, generally those who come in for appointments, pay for their own therapy or it's paid for by their family. Insurance covers the treatment for those patients who are fortunate enough to be covered by their employers. Having a dissociative disorder doesn't mean you have to spend your life in a padded room. Many people who suffer from dissociative disorders lead full, active, and rewarding lives. Unfortunately, some patients are sent here by their families to undergo treatment. It's like a private school in a sense where some parents send their kids away to get them out of their hair. In this case however, some families will send their own mothers, sisters, and daughters, to undergo treatment. For that reason it's a sad state of affairs, but with the level of treatment we can provide here at the Clinic, they're actually probably better off."

"You said mothers, sisters, and daughters, but not fathers, brothers, and sons. How come?"

"Studies have shown that on average, ninety percent of dissociative patients are female."

"Why is that?"

"Females are more commonly sexually and physically abused which are two of the major factors leading to dissociative disorders. Over three quarters of dissociative patients fall into those categories. Females also tend to repress and deny traumatic experiences more often than men. Repression and denial are the fountainhead of dissociative disorders."

"Is it really that prevalent?"

"You'd be surprised."

"You said three quarters. What other kind of factors can cause people to develop the disorders?"

"Stress, caused by any number of things ranging from school to work to relationships. Trauma, such as that experienced in Post-Traumatic Stress Disorder. During wartime, soldiers frequently experience dissociative fugue. Sometimes patients just seem to develop dissociative disorders with no apparent precursors. In the early twentieth century, a thirteen year old girl from Britain was found to have ten separate personalities following a bout with influenza. Prior to that she was a regular, healthy teenage girl."

"Isn't that a little young to get multiple personality disorder, or I mean, uh, what was it changed to again?"

"Dissociative Identity Disorder."

"That's right," Ed snapped his fingers, "so isn't thirteen years old pretty young?"

"Generally, yes, although it's not unheard of. The average age for our patients usually hovers around thirty-two years old. But that's only when they get diagnosed. Most personalities develop at a very young age."

"So getting back to the patient floors?"

"Oh, I'm sorry, I guess I got a little sidetracked there. There's so much to talk about when it comes to dissociative disorders that it's easy to go off on a tangent. The fifth floor is used for both patients who stay here and those who come in by appointment. We call it the TT floor. TT stands for Treatment and Therapy."

"You aren't conducting pre-frontal lobotomies or using electric shock therapy are you?" Ed asked half-serious.

"No, we've evolved somewhat in our methods," Rachel laughed, "though we still have our critics. Our treatment consists of drug therapy, regressive hypnosis, and a lot of one-on-one interaction between doctor and patient. Besides, the use and public financing of electric shock therapy was outlawed in San Francisco in nineteen ninety-one. We treat other disorders here as well however."

"Other disorders? I thought the Clinic was solely dedicated to the treatment of dissociative disorders? Hence the name."

"We are the Meadowvale Clinic for the Treatment of Dissociative Disorders, but the fact is that many of our patients also suffer from a variety of other psychological disorders."

"Really?"

"Really. Some of our patients are also being treated for depression, neuroticism, post-traumatic stress disorder, borderline personality disorder, and even schizophrenia. A lot of patients with dissociative disorders experience a vast array of symptoms such as depression, mood swings, suicidal tendencies, panic attacks and anxiety, phobias, alcohol and drug abuse, eating and sleeping disorders, compulsions and rituals and even psychotic like symptoms such as auditory and visual hallucinations. No one disorder or patient ever has all of these symptoms but they are still quite serious and sometimes need to be treated on their own before focusing on the dissociative disorder. Patients with dissociative disorders quite often undergo six to seven years of treatment for their symptoms before it's even discovered that they have a dissociative disorder."

"That's unbelievable. That's like going to see a chiropractor for seven years only to discover your shoes are causing your back problems."

"Not a bad analogy. You have to understand however that determining what is going on in someone's mind is a lot more difficult than finding out what's wrong with their body. At least if the problem is physical, objective tests can be done. If you have a broken leg, you have a broken leg. And if you have psoriasis, you have psoriasis. It's difficult to misdiagnose that type of phenomenon. In the case of psychological disorders, particularly dissociative disorders, there are no obvious telltale signs which indicate to a psychiatrist what the problem is. Diagnosis can, and often does take years, and can depend a lot on the patient. Reliving an abusive past isn't the easiest thing to do. Bodily scars heal with time. Psychological scars only heal with effort."

Rachel led Ed out into the courtyard through a glass door. The yard itself was about forty feet across and fifty feet wide. A man-made pond spanned by a small arched foot-bridge took up a sixth of the yard while the rest was dominated by trees, and flower gardens overflowing with red, deep blue, and yellow pansies, bluish-purple lavender, and white, yellow, and pink lilies. Tall pink and white rhododendron bushes lined the Clinic walls. The courtyard was deserted now except for two nurses who were sitting on a bench near the back wall under the shade of a cherry blossom.

Rachel and Ed found their own bench to sit on near the pond. Dozens of Japanese Koi fish swam aimlessly narrowly missing each other in the pond. They came in and out of view as they swam to the bottom of the pond and then just as quickly swam back up looking for food.

"This is gorgeous." Ed gave a low whistle as he looked around at the meticulously kept courtyard. "You must have a full time gardener working here."

"No, just a few knowledgeable staff and patients."

"Wow."

"It gives the patients a place to come to and relax. I like to come out here and have my lunch when it's nice."

"I can see why."

"The reason I brought you out here to tell you about the actual disorders we treat instead of going to the third floor is because all of our patients are treated with the utmost confidentiality."

"That's understandable, I wouldn't want to be put on display either."

"It wasn't too uncommon."

"How do you mean?"

"In the early thirteenth century, a priory was founded by the Sheriff of London. In fifteen forty-seven, it was turned into a hospital for the insane, although records show that it housed insane people since fourteen oh three. Unfortunately, back then, people believed that the mentally ill should be completely segregated from general society and treatment consisted of cold showers and severe isolation. The hospital was infamous for its brutal treatment of its patients.

"It was during the eighteenth century that the facility actually made money by putting these people on public display for a price. A small tip to the warder granted anyone access to the facility where you could walk around freely and look into patients' cells at your leisure. That place was officially called the Bethlehem Hospital, but is better known as the Bedlam Hospital."

"Is that where the expression 'bedlam' comes from?"

"That's exactly where it comes from and if you read the descriptions of it you'd understand why the name has become synonymous with the word 'madhouse'."

"So are dissociative patients prone to violence?"

"No, dissociative patients are well behaved, they're mostly just confused or depressed, they don't tend to lash out uncontrollably. They're more prone to hurt themselves though. Many dissociative patients attempt suicide, especially those who have had a really abusive past. That's why we have an observation room where patients can be monitored around the clock. It's called suicide watch. If a patient is particularly depressed it's a good idea to keep an eye on them."

"Have you had any suicide attempts yet?"

"No, thank God."

Before Ed could ask his next question, a high-pitched scream pierced the morning silence.

"What was that?" Ed asked in horror.

"Remember where you are. You get used to it," Rachel said, unfazed.

"Don't you have to check it out?" Ed asked, amazed at Rachel's calm.

"I'm sure the situation is under control."

Chapter 14

▼

The attack on Carl Sanford was swift, violent, and took him completely by surprise.

Lisa Parsons smiled cheerfully as Dr. Sanford entered her room and extended her hand to greet him. Sanford smiled back and gave her his hand. Without warning, Lisa yanked on his arm and used the doctor's stumbling momentum to send him sprawling headfirst into the wall behind her. She quickly withdrew several large wood chips she had collected from the courtyard garden and wedged them firmly under the door.

Sanford yelped as he was flung across the room and met the wall head on. He staggered to his feet but was kicked violently in the stomach before he could get off his hands and knees.

"Lisa, what in God's name…" Sanford panted in agony but was cut off by another well placed kick to the sternum taking his breath away. Lisa pounced on him and began tearing and scratching at his face. Sanford quickly abandoned the idea of reasoning with his patient and began screaming for his life. His screams echoed desperately in the small confines.

Lisa hesitated for only a second as she heard the banging at the door and just as quickly resumed her attack. Sanford tried to get up several times but was quickly knocked down after each attempt. The best he could do was crawl up in a defensive fetal mass and try to minimize the damage being done to him.

Lisa screamed as she attacked Sanford with all her animal strength. Outside, two attendants pushed with all their might in an effort to open the door. Sanford huddled even more as his attacker relentlessly punched and kicked him. His entire body was racked with pain. He focused on the attendants' efforts to gain entrance into the small patient room that had become his own personal purgatory.

Finally, after what seemed an eternity, the door flew open sending the wood chips flying across the room and the two attendants pulled Lisa off the badly mauled doctor.

Sanford pulled himself up off the floor only when Lisa was hauled roughly out of the room.

"Carl, what was all that screaming abou…, Good Christ man! What happened to you?" Grant Foley entered the room and kneeled beside his wounded colleague. He helped him to Lisa's bed.

Carl held his hands to his face, blood running through his ravaged fingers.

"Let's get you to the infirmary and get those cuts looked after." Grant pulled Carl to his feet and supported his colleague so that he could walk out of the room. Patients stared as the two doctors walked off the ward.

Carl didn't talk until he had his face looked at. Grant Foley tended to the wounds himself with a nurse looking on unsure of what to say or do. Carl's nose had been bloodied and his bottom lip split wide open. Several of the deeper scratches on his face drew blood but none would require stitches.

"I don't know what happened," Carl said in confusion. "When I came into the room, Lisa was all smiles and giving me her hand to shake, the next thing I knew she threw me into the wall and attacked me like some sort of wild animal."

Grant turned to the nurse and asked her to give him and Dr. Sanford a few minutes alone.

"I think we better talk to Walter about this. She was one of our project patients wasn't she?"

"Yes, she was. Although I have no idea what went wrong," Carl looked dumbly at the staggering number of scratches on his hands and the rags that his Polo shirt had been reduced to.

"Regardless, it's obvious something did or you wouldn't look like you had just lost a wrestling match with a lawnmower. I'll call Walter and have him meet us downstairs."

Walter was just as shocked to see Carl Sanford's bloodied appearance as Grant Foley had been. Carl and Grant arrived in the basement of the Clinic just a few minutes before Walter and were waiting in a large room that resembled an operating theatre.

"Jesus, Carl, what did she do to you?" he asked once he had taken stock of the damage done to his colleague.

"I'd rather not talk about it," Carl said. He was leaning against a counter still wearing his tattered clothing.

"She went apeshit on him, Walt. She snapped." Grant interjected from his perch on a plain hospital bed.

"Do you know why?"

"Given what we've put her through over the past few months, I'm not surprised but I don't think we'll ever really know why."

"Well, it's obvious she remembers me and what I've done to her," Carl added.

"I thought the hypnosis was supposed to prevent that?" Walter asked.

"It was but we need more time."

"Is she salvageable?" Walter asked, ignoring Carl's remark about needing more time.

"I don't think so. She was a heavy drug user before we ever went to work on her. Her brain's like a fried egg. Not everyone is going to make the perfect subject."

"I'll take another look at the drugs we're giving her," Grant said.

Walter leaned heavily on the medical monstrosity that dominated the center of the room. The piece of equipment looked like a cross between state-of-the-art medieval and modern technology.

"We have plenty of subjects and plenty of time, gentlemen. Let's not waste our efforts on those who don't react well."

"What should we do with Lisa Parsons?" Carl asked.

"What we would do with any patient who was beyond helping," Flemming said coldly. "Transfer her."

Chapter 15

▼

"So give me the lowdown, what is dissociation?" Ed asked

"You'll have to pardon the textbook definition, but here goes," Rachel began, "Dissociation is a psychological process which occurs in response to trauma such as physical or sexual abuse. It's the fragmentation of the mind. When a person dissociates, they experience a lack of connection in their thoughts, memories, feelings, activities, and most noticeably, their identity. Dissociation allows people to go on as if the trauma they have dissociated from never occurred.

"In a sense, dissociation is a highly creative survival technique resorted to when no other avenue of escape exists. When children have no way of protecting themselves using what's available in their external environment, they essentially turn inwards and retreat into the inner recesses of their minds. As a result of this mental dissociation, patients usually don't remember what happened to them while they were dissociated from themselves," Rachel said. "They are also often confused or completely unaware of their identity, and in many cases, as a result of their memory and identity lapses, consciousness suffers."

"How do you mean suffers?"

"Patients can lose hours, days, and even years at a time when they're in a dissociative state."

"Years?"

"Yes, they actually dissociate from themselves for long stretches at a time. That's why these types of disorders are so terrifying. You could be sitting at work one minute and the next thing you know you're in a shopping mall in a different city wearing clothes you never knew you owned and you have no idea as to how or why you're there. It's a very persistent and maladaptive condition."

"Okay, I think I've got you so far," Ed said trying to cram all of this new knowledge into his head.

"There are four major types of dissociative disorders," Rachel continued, "some of which you're probably already familiar with. Obviously dissociative identity disorder is one of them, made famous by written accounts such as *The Three Faces of Eve* and *Sybil*. It's probably the most well known and researched of the four. The other three are dissociative fugue, depersonalization disorder, and dissociative amnesia, which has three sub-types.

"People who have dissociative identity disorder possess two or more distinct personalities. These personalities can have different memories, different moods, and even different attitudes, tastes, skills, and ambitions. Each personality is completely separate from the others and may or may not be aware of the others' existence."

"So people with multiple personalities don't know they have other personalities?"

"For the most part, but eventually they figure it out, quite often during treatment. It's like having other people sharing your body and your life, but trying to carve a niche of their own out of your life. Generally the original personality is the one that doesn't know of the others' presence while the others can see everything the original personality does. The disorder is brought on by severe trauma such as sexual, physical, and even ritualistic abuse."

"Ritualistic?"

"As in Satanic rituals."

"That's horrible."

"Anything that can lead to someone withdrawing into themselves to such a degree that they develop new personalities usually is. Dissociation is quite often a person's last line of defense. Unfortunately, in more cases than not, that person is a child."

"So each personality deals with different things, right?"

"Generally, yes."

"So, the original personality doesn't remember anything that happened to them when another personality takes over?"

"Exactly, you catch on quick. That leads into the next disorder, dissociative amnesia."

"This is the one with the three sub-types?"

"Yes. Onset is usually quite sudden when it comes to amnesia and consists of the inability to remember lots of personal information. Important stuff like your name, age, address, and other things that exceed the scope of normal forgetfulness. Dissociative amnesia too is caused by trauma or extreme stress and not things like substance abuse and cognitive disorders, like Alzheimer's and head injuries. The recovery of memory is usually as sudden as the initial loss of memory.

"The three types of dissociative amnesia are retrograde amnesia where one forgets stuff that happened before the trauma; post-traumatic amnesia where one forgets events that happened after the trauma; and anterograde where one has difficulty learning new material.

"The final, and most common type of dissociative amnesia which incorporates the three sub-types is selective amnesia where a patient doesn't lose all their memory but only selected personal events and information. Studies have shown that upwards of three-quarters of dissociative patients have selective amnesia."

"I gather roll call doesn't go over very well here then?" Ed said.

Rachel groaned and rolled her eyes.

"Getting on with dissociative disorders," she said with a mock serious look on her face. "Dissociative fugue is one of the more interesting disorders. It's characterized by sudden, unplanned travel. The travel is often purposeful, but fugue sufferers have no recollection of their travels. People with fugue usually can't remember their own past, they get confused about their identity, and sometimes even assume a different identity. Dissociative fugue usually follows a traumatic event. There are a lot of documented cases of soldiers experiencing it after battles."

"So do fugue sufferers ever remember their past?" Ed asked.

"Oh yes, certainly. The problem is that the process of remembering everything can be quite lengthy. With dissociative fugue, it's essentially a waiting game.

"The last type of dissociative disorder, depersonalization disorder, is less dramatic than the other types of dissociative disorders. Sufferers complain of feelings of being detached from themselves. People who have it say it's like watching yourself from outside your own body, almost like being in a dream. Most people experience these feelings once in awhile, but it can cause a lot of distress if it occurs frequently. Its onset is usually attributed to new or disturbing experiences such as drug use."

Once she was done describing each type of dissociative disorder, Rachel then explained the layout of the patient floor.

"Are all of the rooms filled now?" Ed asked.

"No, only about three quarters of them are occupied right now, we expect to fill the rest within the next month or so once we all get adjusted and the Clinic gets going at full steam."

The patients were allowed to roam anywhere they wanted on the floor and were allowed access to the courtyard in the center of the Clinic after lunch. There, they could sit in the sun, play catch and exercise, or just walk around and grab some fresh air. With the exception of the main doors to the floor, there were no locks in the patient wing. All the rooms had doors but could not be locked shut. This was so that patients couldn't completely isolate themselves and also in case of an emergency such as a fire or if a patient had a seizure.

"Come on up to my office. You can grab your stuff and I also have something for you that you may find helpful."

"What is it?"

"You'll see." Ed followed Rachel up to her office almost disappointed to leave the beautiful courtyard.

Rachel quickly scanned the tall narrow bookshelf in her office and picked out what she was looking for. It was a thick, red, hard-covered book.

"What's that?" Ed asked.

"This is the Diagnostics and Statistical Manual number four, or DSM IV. It's the psychiatrists' bible in a sense." She flipped it open to show Ed.

"It lists every type of psychological disorder, including the four types of dissociative disorders I just told you about, as well as a comprehensive breakdown of all of their symptoms. This should help you sort each disorder out in your mind," she said, handing the book over to him.

"What's with the number four?" Ed asked looking at the Roman numeral printed on the cover.

"That's the fourth edition of the DSM."

"What was wrong with the first one?"

"The first one came out in nineteen fifty-two but wasn't very accurate in a lot of its information. So the APA put out a second one in nineteen sixty-eight when the World Health Organization developed a new classification system for mental disorders, then a third, then a revised edition of the third, and finally this one which came out in nineteen ninety-four. It was in the DSM IV that Multiple Personality Disorder was changed to Dissociative Identity Disorder."

"Why is that?"

"A lot of psychiatrists believed it was a both a misleading name as well as a self-fulfilling prophecy of sorts. When patients are told they have MPD, some psychiatrists believe they try to fulfill that diagnosis in order to please their therapist and in some cases it can lead to a patient giving up on themselves once they realize they can shift responsibility onto the disorder. That's why we don't say a patient is a disorder, but rather has a disorder. Like schizophrenia. It wasn't too long ago that we called people with the disorder schizophrenics. That type of labeling can be extremely detrimental to the healing and recovery process. Nowadays we prefer to say that people have or suffer from schizophrenia, just as they have or suffer from dissociative identity disorder."

"Were there any other major changes in this edition?"

"Yes. This is the first edition in which homosexuality isn't listed as a mental disorder."

"Are you serious?"

"Yes, until nineteen ninety-four, lesbians and homosexuals were considered mentally ill by professional standards."

"Wow, it must have looked like San Francisco had the highest proportion of mental disorders per capita in the world if the Castro was included," Ed said.

Rachel laughed. "I don't know about that, but unfortunately some psychiatrists as well as a lot of laypeople still believe that being gay is equivalent to having a mental disorder."

"We haven't come very far as a species in a lot of regards, have we?" Ed mused aloud.

"No, we haven't," Rachel replied thinking about her freshly slashed tires.

"Won't you need this?" Ed interrupted her thoughts holding up the DSM IV.

"No. There's a copy in every office on this floor, besides, I know the thing inside and out, cover to cover. I must have read it at least ten times over the past seven years. I also have a bunch of pamphlets on dissociative disorders and one on the Clinic itself which you may find helpful." Rachel reached into a drawer in her desk and fetched the pamphlets for Ed.

"Great, thanks, Rachel," Ed said as he stored the pamphlets and the DSM IV in his attaché case.

"No problem, you can keep the pamphlets but just make sure to get the DSM IV back to me. Now, I'll show you where you can find all the information you'll need." She led Ed out of the office and down the hall. A mid-sized room toward the back of the building housed all of the Clinic's patient files and records. Large steel filing cabinets adorned with locks, lined the walls and formed two passageways trisecting the room. Situated against the back wall underneath a small square window was a computer terminal. Rachel showed Ed this first.

"Our records are updated each week so you'll have access to the latest records. You won't have access to actual patient information but you will be able to determine the costs and length of treatment for each type of disorder. I don't have to tell you that everything you see in this room both on the computer and in the files is extremely confidential."

"Of course."

"These files," Rachel patted the top of one of the shoulder high filing cabinets, "only go back five years."

"Isn't the Clinic only two weeks old?" Ed asked, confused.

"Oh, I'm sorry. These files are copies from the San Francisco Psychiatric Hospital. Three of the six doctors who work here used to work there so they brought copies of all their files with them and quite a few of the patients we have are also originally from the San Francisco Psychiatric Hospital."

"Makes sense."

"Once in awhile we do." She added, "I'll show you how to use the computer to access the data we have here." The system itself was easy to use and Ed caught on quickly.

When they were finished, Ed asked, "What if I want to access and see data that dates back further than five years?"

"Why would you want to do that?"

"Well, to examine trends. For instance, how much has treatment time been reduced or expanded over the years? On average, how many people with DID do you treat per year? How long does it take to treat one disorder compared to another? That kind of stuff. I want to be able come up with enough numbers to extrapolate future figures so I can tell my boss what kind of rates we can charge now and what we can expect later on."

"Oh, okay, that makes sense."

"I sometimes do." Rachel rolled her eyes.

"For any data dating back more than five years, you'll have to go to the psychiatric hospital," Rachel told him.

"Will they let me look at their records?"

"Only the data sheets. And with permission from one of the Clinic doctors."

"Could you do that for me?"

"Sure, of course. Do you need anything else?"

"No, I think I've got everything I need."

"Well, if you need anything, I'll just be down the hall so feel free to stop by if you want to ask a question or need any help."

"Thanks. I think I'm just going to spend the rest of the day familiarizing myself with the computer."

"Have fun."

"I'll try."

Rachel left Ed to his work and went off to do some of her own.

It was two and a half hours later, when Rachel was leaving that she even thought about Ed again. She caught sight of him climbing into his truck at the far end of the parking lot. She waved as he approached and he pulled up beside her while she fumbled with her bike lock.

"Need a lift?" he asked leaning out the window.

"If you don't mind?"

"Not at all," he said. Rachel finally got her lock undone and helped Ed put her bike in the back of his truck.

"This is a nice truck you have."

"Thanks, it gets me around," he said as he drove off of the Meadowvale grounds.

"That's a good quality to have in a vehicle. Unfortunately, my car doesn't possess it."

"Oh? What do you drive?"

"A maroon VW Rabbit."

"Is that why you've resorted to two wheels instead of the usual four?" Ed asked, hiking his thumb backwards, pointing to the bike.

"Sort of. Some kids slashed my tires two nights ago. I was just going to bike down to the garage where it's getting fixed. They said they'd be done by this afternoon."

"Just tell me where to go and I'll drive you there." While Ed drove and Rachel navigated they talked about the weather, and other trivial things leaving their work behind them. She thanked him as he dropped her off promising to see him the next day. After paying for her newly tired car and stuffing her bike in the back seat, she drove home.

Chapter 16

▼

11:31 p.m.
99 Mission Street

"Go! Go! Go!" John Haskins yelled as he pressed himself against the prickly stucco wall to the left of the front door. The crack of splintering wood met his ears as two of his agents flew past him with a miniature battering-ram.

As soon as he saw the door was no longer an obstacle, John swiveled his athletic physique into the modest two story home motioning for the gate-crashers to hold back until he signaled otherwise.

With his arms outstretched and his Smith & Wesson 1056 grasped firmly in both hands, he quickly swept the living room to his right and the stairwell to his left. There was no one there.

"FBI! I'm armed!" he yelled up the darkened stairs.

There was no answer.

A hallway bisected the ground floor. Looking down the hallway through the kitchen in the rear of the house, John could see two more of his agents at the back door waiting to come in. He gave them the signal to do so and the door came crashing in with a minimum of resistance.

Once he was confident that the first floor of the house was secure, he motioned to the two agents flanking the front door to cover him as he proceeded cautiously up the stairs. He paused on a small landing three steps up to crane his neck around a corner.

"Carlos Hernandez? We know you're here. My name is John Haskins, I'm a Special Agent with the FBI. Can you hear me?" John paused to listen for a reply. Only silence greeted him from upstairs.

"We have the house surrounded. You cannot escape. You can make this very easy on yourself. Just come down the stairs, unarmed, with your hands on your head and your fingers interlaced." John continued up the stairs. He was pretty sure Carlos Hernandez wasn't going to make it easy. They virtually never did.

Nine hours ago, John had been called by the San Francisco Police Department. They had a kidnapping. A young boy had been taken from his home in the middle of the day while his parents were at work. The only other person in the house at the time was Juanita, the housekeeper, who also acted as a nanny three days of the week.

"Juanita, I want you to tell me exactly what happened," John asked her less than eight hours ago.

"I was in the kitchen making lunch when the doorbell rang. I answered it and a man from the gas company said he was there to read the meter and inspect the gas lines inside the house." Juanita told John. Her hands were clasped tightly in her lap and she sat on the edge of her seat.

"How do you know he was from the gas company?"

"That's what he told me. There was a blue van outside too."

"A gas company van?" John asked.

"I think so, I didn't get a good look."

"Then what happened?"

"I let him in and went back to the kitchen to finish making lunch for me and Richard. A few minutes later, I heard the front door open and close, I went to the door and saw the van driving away. I thought that the gas man had done what he had to do and left. I had no idea…" Juanita started crying.

"How long was it before you noticed Richard was no longer there?" John kept on.

"When I finished lunch, I called him to come downstairs but he didn't come. I called again a few minutes later thinking maybe he was in the bathroom but he still didn't come down. When I went to check, he wasn't in his room and I checked the whole house. When I still couldn't find him, I called his parents right away."

Mr. And Mrs. Connely immediately called the police who soon after called John at the FBI.

John had Juanita go over the events a couple of times and didn't notice any inconsistencies. But that in itself raised an alarm for John. All law enforcement officers knew that when conducting an interview, there were two things to look for: lack of consistency and too much consistency.

If someone could repeat verbatim, the same series of events, without changing a single thing, chances are it was rehearsed. Such was the case with the Connely's housekeeper.

Her story didn't change.

It was as if she had been reading from a script. John also noticed how increasingly nervous and agitated she became with each questioning.

He decided not to make her take a polygraph and let her go home. He had a good idea of what had happened. He had one of his agents do a background check on Mrs. Hernandez. By nightfall he was even more convinced about what had transpired.

Mrs. Hernandez's husband, one Carlos Hernandez, worked for a construction company driving a loader but had just recently been laid off for the rest of the season. John asked the Connely's how much they paid Juanita; the Fortune 500 had nothing to worry about.

He had a motive.

Before he could act on his hunch however, the Connely's received a phone call from the kidnapper. The caller was male and sounded nervous; he threatened the boy's life if a ransom of a quarter million dollars in small bills was not met. Mrs. Connely wrote down the kidnapper's instructions.

She was to bring the money to a downtown address at midnight the following night.

John had the address looked up.

Just as he expected it was a construction site. A thirty-six story skyscraper was being built at the location where the kidnapper had asked the money to be brought. John was able to get a hold of the construction site's foreman and sure enough, Carlos Hernandez had worked for him but had recently been laid off.

While John was talking to Carlos' ex-foreman, the call from the kidnapper was traced to a payphone just two blocks away from the Hernandez residence.

John wasted little time. He called Mrs. Hernandez and asked her to come down to the police station for more questioning but was sure to tell her that she was not a suspect so as not to tip off her husband. Next, he had four of his agents accompany him on a visit to Mrs. Hernandez's home. They wasted no time upon arriving at the house.

Now, looking up the stairs, John was at eye level with the second floor landing. There was a long hallway running perpendicular to the one downstairs. Straight ahead, fifteen feet away, John could see an open door; it was the bathroom. Moonlight cascaded in through a small window that provided the only source of light on the entire floor. It was enough to see without having to resort to the night-goggles perched atop John's head. Not only did they let him see in the dark by magnifying the smallest amounts of light, but when not in use, as they were now, they kept the sweat off his brow, and his thick wavy blond hair out of his eyes.

There were four other doors on the floor. All of them were closed. John asked Mrs. Hernandez to describe the layout of her house over his cell phone on his way to the Mission Street address. Since she was being safely held at the police station, he was no longer concerned about tipping her off.

She told him that the first door to the right was the hall closet. The two doors on the left were small bedrooms. One served as a storage room, the other as a sitting room. The Hernandez' had no children of their own. The second door on the right was the master bedroom which faced the front of the house. This is where John believed Carlos and young Richard to be.

John padded softly up the remaining few steps. The thick carpet on the stairs cushioned his ascent. The only sounds he could hear were the swishing of his jacket sleeves against his Kevlar flak jacket and the beating of his heart. He breathed through his mouth.

Without looking back, he knew two of his agents were close behind him, not so close that they would impede a retreat, but close enough to help him in a clutch. The other two agents would be watching the front and rear of the house to ensure no daring window escapes were attempted. Even though there were four other agents in and around the house, it was John's show.

This was just the way he liked it, alone, yet with backup.

He knew without a doubt that he could depend on the four men and women with his life, but he enjoyed leading the way, testing the ice. He started out just like them years ago, fresh out of Quantico, naive to the grim realities of field work. He once had the attitude that he could outsmart any adversary. In this regard, he idolized his former superior, special agent Sam Case.

In John's first year, his superior and mentor took a bullet to the chest and died of complications on the operating table. He had just made a successful bust on a crackhouse in the Haight-Ashbury. He didn't even think to keep his eye on the dealer's ten year old son. It was the last mistake he ever made.

From then on, John never underestimated anyone regardless of how smart he thought he was. Even Einstein couldn't outsmart a bullet. Consequently, John always went by the book, no matter how rigid the procedure; he firmly believed in the age old saying about being safe rather than sorry.

Reaching the top of the stairs, John slipped down the hallway with his body parallel to the walls so as not to make a target of himself should one of the doors fly open unexpectedly.

He passed the closet door and stood to its side. When he saw Susan Baxter, his most experienced agent, take position at the head of the stairs to cover him, he took hold of the closet doorknob which rattled in his grip, and eased the door open.

It was full of shelves packed tightly with linens and boxes. Closing the closet door as quietly as possible, he motioned to Susan that he was going to try the first spare bedroom next, the one that served as a storage room.

John stepped across the hallway keeping his eyes on the two doors at the other end of the hall as he did so. Susan crept up onto the landing and crouched with her arms outstretched pointing her firearm at the bedroom door. Her black Kevlar vest made her look daunting. All John could see of her, for lack of light, was a dark amorphous shape. He could also see her partner, Shane Pavletic, just over her shoulder, further down the stairs providing coverage for Susan and himself.

John opened the spare bedroom door and looked inside. With the exception of a pile of orderly boxes in the far corner of the room and a few suitcases, it was empty. There was no closet in the room. John followed the same procedure and checked the second bedroom.

It too was empty.

There was only the master bedroom left. He knew that Susan, Shane and the other agents were tense at this moment despite their experience. He was too. He knew how slow a search of a simple house could be. He also knew that nervous or not, he alone controlled the pace of the events to follow.

Double checking to make sure the two agents behind him were ready, John pointed to the master bedroom door. Standing to the side, he turned its handle expecting it to be locked but was surprised when it turned in his hand. No sooner did he push the door open that a shot rang out and a bullet lodged into the wall opposite the door. Flattening himself against the hallway wall, he spotted Susan dashing forward to take up position on the other side of the master bedroom doorway.

"Carlos Hernandez! The house is surrounded, we are armed, and we will shoot you if necessary. Throw out your gun and you will not be harmed!" John yelled over his left shoulder into the bedroom.

Carlos did not respond.

John strained to hear movement from within the bedroom but could not hear a sound. John was prepared to shout out again but stopped himself. He could hear a faint whimpering from inside the room. He looked across the doorway at Susan; she heard it too. It was the sound of a child crying. John's gut tensed. He was going to put an end to this.

He reached into a pocket located on his right shoulder and withdrew a small silver sphere with a ring in it. It was a flash grenade. Once the ring was pulled, it would let off an extremely bright flash that would temporarily blind anyone unlucky enough to be in its range. John lifted it up for Susan to see and held up three fingers. They would move on the count of three.

John nodded his head once. Twice. Three times.

He pulled the pin and lobbed the silver sphere into the bedroom. The grenade emitted a small popping sound as it burst open. Even though his eyes were closed, John could make out a network of veins in his eyelids and detect the movement of the blood within them. Carlos screamed, swearing in his native tongue, and the boy yelped in surprise.

John crouched and dived into the room landing in a roll. He saw two figures writhing about underneath the bedroom window. Quickly determining which was Carlos, John hurled himself on top of him. Wisely, Carlos, didn't put up a struggle. John knelt on something that dug painfully into his knee. Looking to the ground beside him, he saw Carlos' gun. He had dropped it when he raised his hands to cover his eyes.

Susan rushed into the room, turning on the lights once she saw Carlos was subdued. She helped John handcuff him. Richard was lying on the ground a few feet away. He was blindfolded, so the flash grenade hadn't affected him to the same extent it had Carlos. Susan went to him and removed the blindfold. Once Richard saw that he was safe, he gave Susan a ferocious hug.

"I'm not the one you should be hugging," Susan laughed, "he is," she said pointing to John.

"Thank you, mister," Richard said as he wrapped his arms around John's neck.

"No problem." John hugged the boy back. He wished all his cases turned out so well.

The rest of the evening passed quickly for John. Carlos was arrested, his wife collaborated his confession, and Richard was returned safely home to very relieved parents. John exchanged goodnights with his agents telling them he would see them the next day. It was past two in the morning when he arrived home. He chose to forego his report for the Assistant Director until he returned back to work in six hours.

John's wife was asleep when he returned home. Slipping off his shoes, he ascended the stairs in silence. He found his training came in handy in the weirdest situations. His wife, Cindy, never even stirred when he climbed into bed beside her. She was used to his coming and goings at all hours. Her job as a small bakery owner forced her to wake up early to supervise the morning shift but otherwise her schedule was rather normal, as far as normal goes in today's job market.

A combination of residual adrenaline and endorphins prevented John from falling asleep quickly. He lay on his back listening to the sounds of his wife's breathing and went over the evening's events in his head. He often mentally reviewed his work and his actions to make sure that he had done everything properly and without risking his or his agents' lives. The cases that went well, as tonight's did, required little review. Everything had gone relatively smoothly. Not for Carlos however; because of the shot he took at John, he would be charged with attempted murder and resisting arrest on top of his kidnapping charges.

John stared at the ceiling for what seemed like an eternity. He realized something was nagging at his subconscious and he knew exactly what it was.

A little less than six months ago, a distraught woman called the FBI reporting her husband missing. She had been in contact with the SFPD who told her to call the San Francisco Bureau. It wasn't long before John was called in on the case.

At first it appeared that her husband had simply left her, but upon further investigation John and his agents discovered that her husband was not the type to simply up and leave. He was a happily married man by all accounts, had two wonderful children, no massive debts, excellent paying job, he was a pillar of the community and of his field as a doctor, and as far as both the SFPD and the FBI could ascertain, he had no enemies.

The man had left home for work as usual at seven forty-five on a Monday morning and was never seen again. His wife was the last person to see him.

His car was found in his parking spot at work but according to the staff where he worked he never showed up that morning.

With the exception of a brief note from the kidnapper explaining that he wanted one million dollars in cash and that instructions were forthcoming, there was nothing to work with. Days turned into weeks and weeks into months but the kidnapper failed to send the promised instructions. The safe return of the kidnapped doctor was looking less and less likely.

Despite this, and partly because of his own obsessive-compulsive nature, John kept the case active. Until the man's body was found or until he showed up alive, preferably the latter, John would not let go. His track record was far too good to let one case spoil it. Aside from that however, John witnessed what the man's disappearance had done to his family; his wife and children were devastated. John could only imagine how his family would feel if he disappeared or how he would feel if his wife or only child, Julia, were to vanish. He doubted he could go on without them.

Five months of interviews, phone calls, forensics, profiling, and waiting turned up absolutely nothing. John was positive that a break would come in this case, he just didn't know when. He accepted the possibility that his query was already dead, but knew that neither he, nor the doctor's family would sleep restfully until they knew for sure. Not knowing was the most frustrating feeling.

All John could do now was wait. Hopefully the body would be found or someone involved would slip up by boasting or revealing the truth out of a sense of guilt. Either way, there was little John could do to speed up the process.

Just like Tom Petty said, the waiting is the hardest part.

Closing his eyes, and pulling the sheets up to his neck, John sighed in frustration; where the hell was Arthur Montgomery?

Chapter 17

Tucked away in the Meadowvale Clinic, Jim Wells could not fall asleep either.

He had spent at least two hours tossing and turning underneath his institution-issued sheets but to no avail. Sleep remained elusive.

The dark surroundings and lack of environmental stimuli should have been conducive to nodding off, but Jim remained restless. He tried counting sheep; it didn't work. He ran on the spot for a few minutes hoping to tire himself out; that didn't work either. Twenty minutes earlier, a nurse had come into his room.

"Evening, Mister Wells. I need to give you a small injection."

"Injection? What for?"

"Just a little something to help you sleep." The drugs didn't help.

The real problem was that he couldn't get to sleep because of the voices. At first he thought it was only the television across the hall intruding on his thoughts, but he realized the voices were much closer. He tried pressing his ear to the walls adjoining the other rooms on either side of his own but discovered the voices were even closer than that. The voices had no outside source. The voices were in his head.

Jim didn't know how he had ended up at the Meadowvale Clinic. One of the doctors had had to tell him when he first woke up a few days ago. He just remembered his own name yesterday. His past was as big a mystery to him as it was to the doctors taking care of him.

Today they told him that he suffered from post-traumatic amnesia; whatever that was. They tried to explain it to him but he figured it was more important to try and remember his past first then listen to their psycho-babble. With much reluctance they had convinced him to undergo regressive hypnosis. It was supposed to help him remember his past and maybe shed some light on how he had gotten here. The hypnosis hadn't helped him at all. Neither did all of the drugs they gave him. Modern science, huh! He should have made a break for it when they took him to the hospital to get the tests done on his head.

The voices had started up shortly after he came out of his hypnotic trance. Though he was still drowsy from all of the drugs. At first they were only whispers, easily ignored. Later they had competed for his attention all during dinner. They were still pretty quiet however. At times they sounded clear and distinct but then they would morph into each other like the mysterious gelatinous fluid found in lava lamps becoming entirely incoherent.

When it was finally time to watch TV for an hour or two before bed he found he could not concentrate properly. At the time, he figured perhaps the voices were a side affect of the hypnosis. He knew now they were not. They were here to stay. They were not going to simply fade away. And worst of all, they were getting louder.

Jim sat up in his bed and swung his legs over the side. Holding his head in his hands with his elbows resting on his flannel covered knees Jim tried to decipher what it was the voices were saying. He thought for a second that maybe it was his own thinking which was causing all the chaos in his head but dismissed this thought as quickly as it emerged.

Another, more shocking revelation suddenly came to him: maybe he was going crazy. *Wasn't the first sign of insanity hearing voices in your head?* Jim wasn't sure but it didn't sound too far off. Jim counted to twenty and recited the alphabet aloud hoping to prove to himself that he wasn't going crazy. Whether this proved he was still sane Jim did not know. It comforted him for the moment though.

Jim strained to hear what the voices were saying. Since they seemed to be speaking all at once it was virtually impossible to understand what each one was saying. Jim heard two male voices distinctly. One was high pitched and sounded insecure; the voice of a child. The second male voice was deep and gruff. It could have belonged to a macho type, someone who feared nothing and cared about less. The third voice, if Jim was hearing it properly, was that of another child. His voice was not as deep as the second male's, nor was it as lilted as the other's.

Jim focused all of his mental energies on the third voice. If he could hear what it was saying, he might be able to prove to himself that he was definitely not going crazy. On the other hand, if he did understand what the voice was saying, the words might prove that Jim was indeed out of his mind.

Either way, he had to find out. Sleep was obviously not going to come to him, chemical or otherwise, and TV, as he had discovered earlier, was out of the question. Jim was by nature a passive person and didn't like taking initiative, but in this case he had no choice.

He closed his eyes and blocked out all external sounds: the TV across the hall, the other patients, the opening and closing of the elevator doors, and even his own breathing.

The deep male voice began to take shape. He wasn't sure whether it was his imagination or not, but the two children's voices seemed to fade away as the man's became clearer.

The voice was confident. From what he could hear, it sounded to Jim as if its owner was in the process of building something. He was humming an unfamiliar tune and talking to himself. Jim strained to hear more but was interrupted by the first child's voice. It was yelling at somebody. Jim was pretty sure the voices weren't talking to him, they seemed to be talking to someone else; someone not present, either in his room or in his head. The child's voice drowned out the man's voice. He was telling someone that the pain didn't hurt, that he could take it, pretending to be tougher than he really was. He was challenging someone who Jim could neither hear nor see. The third voice joined in then. Jim could not tell what he was saying but it sounded like he was arguing with the man's voice. The deep male voice became agitated and he began arguing with the child. Soon, all three voices were competing for volume inside Jim's head.

Jim leaped out of bed with his hands clasped tightly to the side of his head covering his ears in a futile attempt to stop the voices. They were all yelling now. The first child was actually screaming in his head. The soprano screams seemed to threaten to burst his eardrums but Jim knew this would not happen since the voice was only in his head. The two other voices were arguing incessantly with each other. Neither seemed ready to back down. The second child's voice sounded like it was screaming through tears.

The simple act of thinking became more and more difficult as the voices increased their full scale attack on Jim's cerebrum. Jim was convinced beyond a shadow of a doubt that his mind had opened wide like a proverbial Pandora's Box and unleashed unspeakable horrors. His thoughts became tangled and he could hardly discern between what he was thinking and what the three voices in his head were saying. The inside of his head felt like a well tossed salad. His head began to throb.

Hardly cognizant of his environment, Jim noticed that he was standing in the brightly lit hallway outside his room. Somehow he must have opened the door and let himself out of his room without even being aware of doing so. He was not normally prone to black-outs, but then again he was not normally prone to voices in his head.

One of the floor attendants on duty, the one who had given him the injection, a well built Oriental man with a look of concern mixed with caution on his face, approached Jim and was now talking to him. Jim couldn't hear a word he was saying despite the attendant's moving lips. He felt his own mouth moving and realized that he must be talking himself but he couldn't hear his voice; the other three voices in his head were drowning him out. One sounded frightened while another sounded hostile. The third voice could barely be heard at all.

All of a sudden Jim was standing on the threshold of the TV room. He looked back into the hallway and saw the attendant who had been trying to communicate with him lying on the ground rubbing the back of his head. A second attendant, a tall redhead, was running down the hall, he had just stepped around the corner at the far end of the hall.

Jim quickly deduced that he must have knocked the first attendant over on his way to the TV room. How he did so was beyond his own comprehension. He must have blacked out again.

The redheaded attendant was helping his colleague to his feet.

Jim remained rooted in place.

A number of the other patients were now peering out of their rooms to see what all the commotion was about. The TV room was occupied as well. Five or six patients sat watching Jeopardy. Alex Trebek was talking to Jim.

Jim turned around to listen to the Jeopardy host. The voices in his head persisted. The hostile voice dominated conversation however. It was yelling obscenities at the TV using Jim's mouth.

One of the attendants was talking to him again. Jim could hear him this time. He was asking Jim to lie down on the floor. The hostile voice in his head using his mouth took on a different tone. It was screaming. The other voices began talking as well. Jim couldn't hear what they were saying though. All of a sudden, Jim's body was whipped around. He had no control over his own actions. His legs began pumping involuntarily and he sprinted into the TV room narrowly avoiding the attendants' outstretched hands as they attempted to grab him. His fellow patients stared at him wide eyed as he streaked past them and threw himself with all his might headfirst into the TV set. Jim Wells, along with the voices in his head, died instantly.

Chapter 18

▼

Wednesday
8:22 a.m.
Meadowvale Clinic

The last thing Rachel expected to find at work this morning was a flock of emergency vehicles and uniformed people scrambling all over one another just outside the Clinic. That however was just what greeted her as she pulled up to the Clinic's front entrance. Her usual reserved parking spot was currently being blocked by one of two SFPD cruisers so she drove behind the building into the visitor's parking spaces. She noticed Ed's truck was nowhere to be seen.

Rachel hurriedly grabbed her briefcase and strode purposefully to the main entrance to find out what was going on. She just missed being bowled over by an occupied gurney whose passenger was covered head to toe with a clean white sheet. One of the two men wheeling the gurney mumbled an apology but kept on his course.

Rachel noticed that the awaiting ambulance's lights were not turned on indicating that there was no need for anyone to hurry. Now she really wanted to find out what was going on. Who had that been on the stretcher? Hopefully not one of the patients. Before she let her imagination run wild, Rachel decided it would be best if she got inside and talked to one of the other doctors.

The lobby was filled with Clinic staff, emergency personnel, and a couple of reporters, all deeply in conversation. Rachel was just about to go to the sixth floor to look for Grant Foley when a tall policeman blocked the elevator doors easily with his body.

"Excuse me, miss?" he said in a deep voice that most law enforcement types would envy, "are you Doctor Rachel Miller?"

"Er, yes I am." Rachel replied a little shaken that the police knew her name and were obviously looking for her.

"Okay, you can go on up," he said.

"Uh, thank you." More apprehensive than ever, Rachel watched as the elevator doors closed shut on the hectic mass of people in the lobby.

The third floor was even busier if that was possible. Looking around, Rachel only recognized a few faces in the sea of uniforms. The patient's entertainment room seemed to be the focus of attention. Rachel tried to peer in to the room but was pulled brusquely aside by Kevin Cheung.

"You don't want to go in there, Rachel," he said with a grave look on his face. His bloodshot eyes carried matching luggage underneath them.

"Why? What's happened? Who was that being wheeled out of here on the stretcher?" the questions tumbled out of her mouth.

"You don't know? I mean no one has told you?"

"No, I just got here two minutes ago."

"Oh, God, I'm sorry, Rachel."

"Sorry? About what? Could you please just tell me what is going on here?"

"Of course, but let's get out of the way," Kevin led Rachel towards the elevator out of the way of the crowd. "I thought one of the other doctors would have told you what happened," his voice dropped a few decibels as it no longer had to compete with the voices coming out of the TV room.

"No, like I said, I just got here a few minutes ago but I saw them take a body out of the building. Who was it?"

"Last night, just before eleven o'clock, that new patient, Jim Wells, ran out of his room screaming. He was one of yours wasn't he?"

"Yes, he was admitted just this weekend. I saw him for the first time on Monday. He didn't kill anyone did he?"

"Only himself."

"What?" Rachel asked aghast.

"He committed suicide."

"Wha? How? Oh my god," Rachel leaned against the wall behind her in an attempt to steady herself. Her head was swimming.

"I'm sorry Rachel, I wish I wasn't the one who had to tell you."

"I can't believe it. Are you sure it was Jim Wells?"

"Positive, I was here myself when it happened. I was almost finished my shift when I saw him leave his room. He was heading for the TV room."

"Is that where it happened?" Rachel asked trying to understand how her patient could have done something so unexpected.

"Yeah."

"Did any of the other patients see him do it?"

"About seven of them did."

"Jesus."

"Doctor Foley, Doctor Flemming, and Doctor Sanford talked to all of them for an hour or so to calm them down."

"And you've been here all night?"

"Yeah, the cops wanted to talk to me and I had to give my statement about five times."

"They don't suspect foul play do they?"

"No, no, nothing like that. It was clearly a suicide. They just wanted to figure out exactly what happened and make sure no one was at risk."

"And you could tell them? I mean you saw the whole thing?"

"Unfortunately. He didn't choose the easiest way to go."

"How do you mean?"

"Well, Dean and I were just about to call lights out and make our final rounds of the shift when Jim came running out of his room looking lost or something."

"Did Dean see what happened too?"

"He didn't see Jim tear out of his room but he got there in time to pick me up and watch Jim kill himself."

"Pick you up?"

"Yeah, your patient might not look it, but he's a strong little bastard. I mean, was. He knocked me right off my feet and tore down the hall as if he was being chased by the four horsemen."

"And then what?"

"Well, Dean and I took off after him and almost had him but he bolted into the TV room just before we could grab him," Kevin nodded towards the TV room as he spoke.

"But how did he kill himself if you and Dean were right there?"

"We couldn't stop him, I mean he was fast, too," Kevin said without having to correct his tense this time. Rachel hung on Kevin's every word.

"I managed to get a piece of his night shirt but he tore free, ran into the TV room, and literally threw himself into the TV set. The medical examiner, who was here earlier, said he died instantly. Broken neck, severed spinal cord, the whole bit."

"What a horrible way to die. Have they figured out why he did it?"

"That's what they want to talk to you about, they hope that you can shed some light on the subject. And they also want to know if you can make any sense of his last words."

"His last words?"

"Yeah, he was screaming some pretty weird stuff just before he used his head as a remote control."

"Like what?"

"They told me not to tell anyone. Besides, I already told them what he said and they wrote it all down. I'm sure they'll let you see the report. After all, you were his doctor. In the meantime, I think Foley wants to see you before you talk to anyone, seeing as it was your patient and all."

"Of course," Rachel barely heard Kevin's last sentence. She was deep in thought about what Jim's last words could have been.

"Anyway, I'm outta here," Kevin said suppressing a yawn, "I'll see you tomorrow. Hopefully things will have calmed down by then."

"Okay, bye, Kev, and thanks." Rachel smiled wanly as he stepped into the elevator. She was still a little overwhelmed by the news she had just received. She looked around for Dr. Foley but couldn't see him among the people gathered in and just outside the TV room. She was just about to leave the floor in search of him when a policeman stepped out from in front of the television and allowed her to see what remained.

The picture tube itself was completely shattered and she could make out a variety of tubes and wires within. They all looked dead. Glass and dried blood on the carpeted floor in front of the TV formed a colorful mosaic like some morbid Rorschach ink blot. Rachel also noticed the lack of a chalk outline, or at least a tape outline. Obviously that was only done in murder cases. Presumably pictures had already been taken. Those people who remained in the room all looked tired and ready to leave. Their job was done. Rachel's day on the other hand had just begun. She left in search of Grant Foley.

The sixth floor was quiet as usual, the thick office doors were practically soundproof, blocked off from the horrors below. Rachel doubted that the offices themselves were quiet. She raised her hand to knock on Foley's door but it opened just as she did so and she almost punched him in the face as he stepped out.

"There you are, Rachel, I was just on my way out to find you. I imagine the morning's events haven't escaped your attention?"

"No, I was just talking to Kevin Cheung, he told me most of what had happened, but he said you wanted to talk to me and tell me the rest."

"That's right, but that can wait. Look, Rachel, I'm terribly sorry this happened, I just want to make sure that you don't blame yourself or beat yourself up over it. The self-destructive tendencies of dissociative patients are well documented as you know and there was little we could have done to prevent this. I'm just on my way to see Doctor Flemming and Doctor Sanford now, we're going to discuss a course of action in terms of dealing with the press, improving supervision, and most importantly how to prevent this sort of incident from ever occurring again. I want you however to take the day off and take it easy."

"Take the day off? But what about the rest of my patients?"

"Don't worry, they'll still be around when you come in tomorrow. What's most important now is that you take time to deal with Jim's suicide yourself. Tomorrow you're going to have to spend a lot of time with the other patients, and if you're up to it, perhaps talk to them as a group and help them deal with the incident. You can't do that if you haven't come to grips with it yourself. I know what it's like to lose a patient, especially your first one, believe me, taking the day off will do wonders. I see that look in your eye that tells me that you're going to be thinking about this all day."

"All right, Grant, but only because you insist."

"That's right, I do insist. Now go, try to make the most of your day, but remember, don't blame yourself. You couldn't have stopped it from happening."

"Thanks, Grant, I guess I'll see you tomorrow. Please call me if anything comes up."

"Will do, and you're welcome," Grant put his hand on Rachel's shoulders and squeezed gently, "We'll fill you in on what we discuss tomorrow."

"Sure," Rachel said. She watched as Foley walked down the hallway and let himself into Flemming's office. Running her fingers through her hair, Rachel sighed, flummoxed. She tried not to think about the morning's events but found it virtually impossible, like trying to get an annoying commercial jingle out of your head. She waited for the elevator. The jingle played on.

Chapter 19

"What are you doing here?" Hal Rosenberg asked surprised when he saw Ed working in his office.

"I work here," Ed said in mock indignation.

"No, I mean why aren't you at Meadowvale going over their records?"

"I came in early to grab some stuff from my office and got a call from Doctor Foley just as I was stepping out the door to head over there."

"What did he say?"

"One of the patients went Kamikaze so he asked me to stay away until tomorrow."

"Kamikaze?"

"Yeah, one of the patients committed suicide late last night."

"Good Lord. How?"

"I don't know. I'll ask Rachel tomorrow."

"Who's Rachel?"

"She's one of the doctors at the Clinic."

"Oh. Can you do any work on the Clinic portfolio from here?"

"Not from here, but I don't have to be at the Clinic either."

"How so?"

"Rachel, I mean Doctor Miller, the woman who gave me the tour said that if I needed any statistics five years or older, I would have to go to the San Francisco Psychiatric Hospital to get them."

"Why do they have them?"

"Three of the doctors at the Clinic used to work there and a bunch of the patients at the Clinic were transferred from there. I'll need those stats to establish patterns and trends in order to extrapolate future figures."

"Of course. So you're heading there now?"

"Yep. I just got off the phone with them to make sure they know who I am and let them know I was coming."

"Well keep me up to speed on how things go. And if you need more help than Bernard can give you give me a holler, I can spare a few people."

"Thanks, Hal, but I think I can handle it on my own. I just need Bernard to crunch numbers for me."

"Suit yourself. By the way, I was talking with Mister Wainfleet this morning. I think this assignment will turn out to be good for your career."

"I don't see what can go wrong."

Chapter 20

▼

Rachel left the Clinic as quickly as possible in her Rabbit and found herself driving aimlessly through the hilly streets of San Francisco. The death of Jim Wells hit closer to home than Rachel let on. It wasn't just the shock of losing a patient or the violent manner in which he had ended his life that affected her so much. It was the fact that the incident reminded her of something in her own past. Few people were aware of the true motivation behind Rachel's desire to become a psychiatrist, one that specialized in dissociative disorders, and even more narrowly, one that concentrated on dissociative identity disorder as much as possible. She intended to keep it that way.

When she was only three years old, Rachel's parents agreed to a mutual separation. The divorce was amicable and no one was hurt.

At first.

Years later, Rachel's mother would tell her that she and her father had simply grown apart and both had felt that it was best to go their separate ways. She stayed at home in Oakland with her mother while her father moved out taking Rachel's two year old sister, Theresa, with him to San Francisco. This had been agreed upon by both parents. They both deeply loved their children and felt that the two sisters wouldn't have forged a strong enough connection to seriously affect them by separating them. Hindsight being 20/20, Rachel knew, in light of future events, that keeping them together would have prevented the tragedy that shattered all of their lives.

Her mother never remarried but her father didn't take long to find a replacement. The woman he rumpled sheets with, one Becky Stockel, was a far cry from the woman he left behind. Her domestic talents left a lot to be desired, as did her attitude, but they seemed to suit each other. She smoked in the house constantly without consideration for young Theresa's tender lungs and when she wasn't high on some cheap household cleaner she had a bottle nearby. And it wasn't Theresa's. To Mr. Miller's credit, his new companion didn't enter his life in such a state but gradually deteriorated as their relationship wore on. Unfortunately, Mrs. Miller was totally unaware of the company her ex-husband was keeping and the conditions in which her youngest offspring was being raised. Had she known, she would have fought for custody of the child and taken her back.

All the while, Rachel's mother juggled responsibilities as only a single mother can. She worked days as a nurse at the Oakland Memorial Hospital sending Rachel to daycare and would spend every evening with her daughter, playing with her and reading to her. Rachel's upbringing couldn't have been more diametrically opposed to her sister's. Theresa was often left at home alone to fend for herself. Mr. Miller would leave to run his building company every morning at seven under the assumption that Becky would stay home all day and look after his daughter and home.

He remained in the dark in regards to his daughter's welfare. Becky would spend most of the day hanging out with deadbeat friends partaking in one mind-numbing, self-destructive behavior or another. It wasn't a rare occurrence that Becky would return in the middle of the day either by herself or with company, almost always under the influence, and take out her hostilities on the girl she was supposed to be taking care of. When Becky did have a friend over, most often male and in the same condition as she or worse, Theresa would be picked on and locked in a tiny room in a corner of the unfurnished basement that originally served as a fruit cellar while her father's live-in girlfriend satisfied her carnal needs upstairs.

When Becky's frequent and numerous lovers left, Theresa would be released from the tiny, unlit crawlspace she was forced into on a regular basis. The abuse didn't end there though. If Theresa was unfortunate enough to do something Becky didn't approve of, such as get in the way of the television, or in any way annoy her, she would be beaten, often severely. The bruises would always be covered up either by clothes or makeup by the time Mr. Miller returned home from work. Those that couldn't be hidden would be attributed by Becky to be 'accidents'. Rachel could never forgive her father for not becoming suspicious at the number of accidents Theresa seemed to have. Perhaps he just thought he had a klutz for a daughter.

The abuse, as it was later discovered, went on for a period of three years. It came to an end when Rachel's mother decided to drop in on Theresa to see how she was mending. A week earlier, according to Becky, Theresa had a spill down the stairs and broken her left arm and seriously bruised her face and back. This had been the second major incident. When Mrs. Miller rang the doorbell of her ex-husband's home there was no answer. This was unusual since she had called the day before to let him know she was coming. She almost left after the second ring went unanswered but was stopped short in her tracks when she heard her youngest daughter screaming from inside the house. She was unable to force the door open so she ran to the neighbor's house where the police were summoned.

Theresa was found crying in the basement. Becky and one of her lover's were apprehended as they tried to escape out the back door. Both were charged and sentenced to time in jail. Becky only ended up serving three years for the three years of neglect and abuse she had heaped upon Theresa. Her friend got away with two years. He was charged with both physical and sexual abuse of a minor.

Rachel was never told how extensive the abuse her sister suffered had been, nor did she really want to know. All she knew was that it was enough to send Theresa over the edge into the lonely and frightening world of dissociative identity disorder. Over the course of three years filled with neglect, physical, sexual, and verbal abuse, Theresa had withdrawn into herself and found a way to deal with her environment. She unconsciously developed five separate personalities.

With the exception of being withdrawn, which wasn't surprising, Theresa seemed to be on the road to recovery once she moved back in with her mother and sister who, like herself, were unaware of her proclivity for dissociation. It wasn't until her teens that people started to notice how oddly she was acting. Her moods would change frequently, her grades in school became erratic, sometimes excellent, sometimes so poor that her teachers wondered if it was the same person. She also complained about missing time. Time which she could not remember experiencing. Her sister and her mother would try to fill in the gaps but try as she may, Theresa couldn't remember a lot of the things people said she did.

After a few months of this eccentric behavior, Mrs. Miller took her youngest daughter to the family doctor. She couldn't find anything wrong with Theresa physically, and aware of her abusive past, she recommended a child psychologist. The child psychologist couldn't seem to find anything manifestly wrong with Theresa either. She knew that Theresa differed from other children, but she couldn't quite place her finger on the difference. It was during a regular session with the psychologist that all of the pieces seemed to fall together. When Mrs. Miller brought Theresa in to see the psychologist, she wasn't aware that the girl she brought in was not her daughter.

The young girl who came in claimed her name was Terri, not Theresa. With much patience and perseverance, the child psychologist discovered that Theresa had mentally dissociated from herself during the many instances of sexual and physical abuse. When informed that she was going to the doctor's again, Theresa switched to Terri in response. Having been to the hospital so many times as a child due to her frequent 'accidents', Theresa had developed an unmitigated fear of doctors.

Doctors who couldn't take away the pain.

Doctors who couldn't alleviate the fear she experienced daily.

Doctors who bandaged her contusions and told her everything would be all right.

Doctors who told her to be more careful, essentially blaming her for what was happening in her life.

Theresa spent the next several years in and out of hospitals undergoing extensive therapy. Unfortunately, each time it seemed as if she was on the road to recovery, one of her personalities would resist. Unlike traditional medical treatment, to cure a patient with numerous personalities, one had to work backwards before progress could be made. This method of treatment could be very taxing on psychoanalysts but even more so on the patient who had to relive the trauma which led to the development of the separate personalities in the first place. As well, individual personalities often misconstrued the re-integration process as a means of killing them off, thus making it exponentially more difficult to incorporate all of the personalities into one.

After a particularly emotionally draining week of therapy, Theresa seemed better than ever. At the age of twenty-two, after years of denial, Theresa was able to not only accept that there were others sharing her body but also came to value and trust them. Rachel visited her sister every weekend during her institutionalization, observing her progress. She couldn't wait for the day that the two of them would be together again free of the confines of the hospital and dissociative identity disorder.

That day never came.

Theresa died of a cerebral aneurysm three days short of her twenty-third birthday. Her father did not attend the funeral.

Now, seven years later, Rachel found herself driving along the car-paths of Woodlawn Cemetery where her sister was buried. She found Theresa's grave without difficulty and stood over it in silence.

She had not been out here in over a year.

She never came on her sister's birthday as her mother did every year. She didn't want to belittle her sister's life by turning it into a commemorative event, nor did she want to feel as if she had an obligation to visit the grave once a year. She came when she missed her sister the most. Now was one of those times. Those times didn't revolve around dates or events. She liked to share important news with her sister. Like her graduation, the completion of her doctorate, her new job. Over the past seven years, Rachel had made the trip about twenty times. The weather and bloom of the trees were always different when she came but the tombstone remained the same. It read simply:

Theresa Anne Miller

Beloved Daughter & Sister

1979-1998

Rachel stared at the tombstone for fifteen minutes trying to recall memories of her sister as a child when they had lived under the same roof. As usual, she could not. The only memories she had were of her sister in the psychiatric hospital. Regretting not having brought flowers for her sister, Rachel reached into her purse and pulled out one of her cards, she kneeled down and placed it on the ground.

"I wish you were here to share this with me." Tears ran down her face as she stood up.

Rachel drove out of the cemetery without looking back. Driving less aimlessly now, Rachel had a destination in mind; she would visit her mother in Oakland. She felt her mother was the only person she could talk to about what she was feeling. The grayness of the sky complemented her mood. The low celestial ceiling did not dissipate on her way, rather it seemed to close in around her, becoming more and more foreboding making the road seem like an endless tunnel.

Chapter 21

▼

Rachel wasn't the only one to react negatively to Jim Well's death. As soon as the police had left and Jim's body was removed, Walter Flemming summoned his colleagues Grant Foley and Carl Sanford to his office.

"How the hell did this happen?" Flemming asked both of them at the same time. He was livid.

It was Foley who braved a response first, "Well, to be honest, we can't be sure exactly," he said.

"What do you mean we can't be sure? This is a matter in which we cannot afford uncertainty."

"Walter, with the exception of your first serious attempt over at San Francisco Psychiatric, the project has been tremendously successful up until now. The same thing happened to Jim Wells. We just have to move past this, learn from our mistakes and carry on," Foley said.

"I think we're moving too fast," Sanford piped up, "after all, we're not even one hundred percent sure what kind of effects the project is having on the other subjects. We should abandon this phase of the project and return to the original plan."

"Carl, this is part of the original plan," Flemming fumed. "When you were asked to join us you had no qualms about what we were doing and you knew what it was you were getting into. You knew the risks. We cannot afford to stop now, we've come too bloody far." Carl Sanford shut up. After what had happened to Arthur Montgomery, Carl knew he didn't dare oppose the project.

"So what do you propose we do, Walt?" Foley asked.

"First off, we have to make sure your young Doctor Miller doesn't try to find out exactly what caused her patient to terminate himself. We'll have to come up with some plausible reason for Mister Wells' unfortunate demise to satisfy her before she goes off digging on her own. Once we have a cover story, the next thing we have to do is notify the press. The kind of coverage this story may get could scare away many potential patients. Grant, you take care of Miller and the press. Carl, I want you to personally examine the rest of the project patients and make sure they're not at risk of following Jim's lead like a herd of lemmings. Also, make arrangements to have another subject brought in to replace Wells. Try to get a female this time if you can, preferably late twenties, early thirties, and one with a cleaner history than Lisa Parsons. Do a little research this time. We have to get back to work on this as soon as possible. Is that understood?" Both Foley and Sanford nodded in agreement, Sanford less enthusiastically than Foley.

"Good, then let's get the damage control under way and start anew. Let's also take another look at the dosages we're giving. Once we get things running smoothly again, we'll all be very rich men."

"Walter, what are you going to be doing?" Sanford asked wondering if he and Foley were going to get stuck with all the grunt work.

Flemming looked at his watch and said, "In fifteen minutes, I have a Tele-conference with several potential government clients who are interested in procuring our services. We can't let this minor incident get in the way of our day to day operations. So if you'll excuse me gentlemen, or should I say partners, I have a meeting to prepare for."

Foley and Sanford left Flemming's office together.

"Do you think we should slow down a little? I mean at least until we get settled in and develop a larger client base?" Sanford asked Foley as soon as they were out of earshot of Flemming's office. One of the scratches on his face was still bleeding through the bandage. He played with the edge of the bandage threatening to tear it off entirely.

"I agree with Walter. I think we should just get on with it. There's no reason we should stop now after all the work we've put in. I think once this Jim Wells business dies down, as I'm sure it will within a couple of days, things will return back to normal and we can look forward to a prosperous future. You've seen the numbers haven't you?"

"Yes, I just went over them again with Walter last week. Hard to argue against that kind of revenue."

"Exactly. Look where arguing got Arthur Montgomery."

"Huh, yeah, look what happened to Arthur," Sanford said putting a hand to his face, hoping Foley wouldn't detect the despondency and hint of fear in his voice.

"Well, I'd better prepare a statement for the press. Good luck with the patients."

"Thanks, I'll see you at lunch." Sanford watched as Foley took the elevator downstairs and then locked himself away in his office for the rest of the morning.

Chapter 22

The drive to Oakland went slowly.

Rachel hadn't talked to her mom in over two weeks and hadn't called in advance to let her know she was coming. She hoped her mom had the day off and would be at home. She desperately needed to tell someone what was going through her head. She hated to admit it but she needed a shoulder to cry on.

Turning off the freeway, Rachel drove without thinking. The route was so familiar to her. She looked about as she pulled into her old neighborhood. There was the playground she used to play on with the other kids on the block. There was the corner where she had fallen off her bike and landed on her face. The left side of her face had been a hideous scab for the entire summer. There was old Mr. Kurdle's house which all of the neighborhood kids thought was haunted. She did too eons ago. She noticed its appearance hadn't changed. If anything it was even more decrepit than she remembered.

The neighborhood itself was old yet still seemed like a typical suburban development. Large clapboard houses sat on raised lawns all equidistant from the street. On many of the houses, vinyl and aluminum siding now replaced the ornate brickwork, lovely pebble-dash, and plain, yet appealing stucco which had decorated the neighborhood of her youth.

Rachel couldn't stop looking around. She passed the same houses dozens of times in the last several years but she had never seen them as she was seeing them now. As memories. There comes a time in one's life when what happened in the past makes the transition from simple memories to sentiments. Rachel was practically overcome by her emotions, so clean and pure, like the white picket fences that surrounded several of the homes in the area. Including her mother's.

The house where she grew up seemed to loom brighter than any of the other houses on the street. The driveway had recently been resealed and two shirtless young men were mowing the front lawn and trimming the thick hedges that hugged the house. She pulled into the driveway behind her mother's Taurus. Checking her hair in the rearview and checking her emotions, Rachel got out of her car, struggled to close the warped door to her Rabbit, and looked up to the house. Home.

She waved to the two boys working on the lawn. They waved back, shyly yet enthusiastically as only young adolescents can do. Rachel felt their eyes on her back, and her behind, as she made her way up the wide porch steps. She was flattered, but not in the mood to talk with them. She couldn't tell if they were neighborhood kids or not. They obviously recognized her, or wished they did.

The front door chimes rang throughout the house as she pushed the doorbell button. The wide porch seemed smaller now as she looked up and down its length. Countless hours had been spent on this porch in the form of mornings waiting for the bus; meals when it was warm enough to eat outside; talking on the phone to high school girlfriends; her sister's wake. The last thought was thankfully pushed out of her mind as the front door was opened wide.

"Rachel? What in heaven's name are you doing here?" Deborah Miller said, wiping pastry dough off of her hands onto the large apron she had on. Emblazoned across the front in tightly stitched embroidery it read, *Best Cook in the World*. Rachel had given it to her on Mother's Day ages ago.

"Hi, Mom, I needed someone to talk to. Can I come in?"

"Of course you can honey. This is still your home, no need to ring the doorbell everytime you visit. Come in, come in." Her mother ushered her into the house. The smell of fresh baking pervaded the bright foyer. Rachel took off her shoes as she had been instructed to do so many times as a child. Her stockinged feet sunk into the plush, broadloom carpet.

Deborah Miller's face was fraught with worry at the sight of her daughter.

"Are you okay Rachel? You look upset. What's going on? Did you and Marty break up?"

Rachel held up her hands defensively, "Mom, slow down. Could we get a drink first and then sit down and talk?"

"Sure, honey, I'm sorry, but I haven't heard from you in two weeks and you know how worried I get about you living in the city by yourself with a new job and driving around in that death trap on wheels you call transportation."

"Yes, Mom, I know."

"Well then, let's get you into the kitchen and fix you up with a drink. I just baked some apple turnovers as well. We can nibble on those if you like."

"I'd like that, Mom," Rachel said, meaning it.

"Good," Deborah moved about effortlessly in the kitchen. Rachel had always envied her mother's efficient nature and culinary skills. Leaning against the refrigerator, careful not to jar loose any of the magnets stuck to the door, she watched quietly as her mother made a pot of tea and prepared a small tray of snacks. Once the turnovers were sufficiently cool enough, they were added to the tray as well. Rachel wondered if such ease in the kitchen skipped a generation. It had certainly skipped over her.

The living room had not changed in over ten years. The walls were painted a cheerful daffodil yellow which, in conjunction with the white stucco ceiling and white carpet, made the room seem twice as large as it really was. Overlooking the freshly mowed front lawn, expansive bay windows offered a clear view of the street. Rachel and Deborah both took a seat on the room's long, soft sofa. Two matching chairs stared vacantly from across the room. The hearth in the brick fireplace was cold but the room was warm. For the first time in a long time, Rachel felt truly relaxed. She wished she could just curl up into a corner of the sofa, wrap herself in one the afghans which were draped over its back, sip her hot Orange Pekoe and let her mind, along with her worries, drift away.

Deborah got comfortable as well. She placed the tray of snacks on the long glass coffee table in front of herself and Rachel. A large coffee table book on flowers was edged off the table and fell to the ground with a soft thud. Rachel went to retrieve it but her mother told her to leave it, she would get it later.

"Now what's on your mind dear? Is it the new job?" her mother asked anxiously.

Rachel surveyed the room nostalgically. Her eyes swept across the mantelpiece. Numerous framed pictures competed for space upon it. Six were of herself and two were of her sister. If Theresa had still been alive, she too would have graduation photos up there among Rachel's. Turning now to look at her mother, a single tear rolled down her cheek. She had so much she wanted to say yet didn't know where to start.

"What is it dear?" her mother asked when she saw her daughter was having difficulty finding the words. "Go on honey, tell me what's wrong, I'm your mother, you can tell me anything."

Rachel sniffled and wiped away the solitary tear and the streak it had made on its journey down her face. She took a deep breath and told her mother everything. She told her about her and Marty breaking up, or rather his dumping her.

She told her about her slashed tires and the constant reminders about her student loan. She told her of the superhuman effort it took to deal with people with dissociative disorders and how taxing it could be physically, mentally, and particularly emotionally. She finished by telling her of Jim Wells' death and how she felt responsible and how it had reminded her of Theresa. Despite earlier assurances to herself that she would not cry, the tears flowed freely while she poured out her frustrations to her mother. Although draining, both physically and mentally, crying also served as a release. It was a way of purging her mind and prioritizing her emotions. Telling her mother all the things that had upset her in the past week not only revealed what was on her mind but also allowed her to put them in perspective.

"I just feel I have no one to talk to, to unload on, that's why I came here."

"That's what I'm here for, honey. I have to admit I'm sorry to hear that you and Marty are no longer seeing each other but if he can't love you the way you are now, for who and what you are, you can't change your nature to appease him. I think you two made a fine couple, but sometimes that's not enough. There has to be a fundamental connection there for a relationship to really work.

"I think that's why your father and I eventually separated. While he preferred sports and other macho activities, I would much rather spend an evening in discussing politics or philosophy over a glass of wine. That arrangement worked out fine for the first half of our marriage, but soon it became obvious that we couldn't wait to be away from each other to enjoy our own interests. It got to a point where we literally wouldn't see each other for days, and when we did, we hardly spoke to one another. The divorce wasn't a messy one, thank God. We both agreed that we wouldn't upset you and Theresa with our problems. You'll know when the right one comes along honey," she said, steering the conversation back to Rachel's problem. "As for your student loan, I wouldn't worry about that. If you want, I can help pay it off and you can pay me back at your leisure, no interest."

"Thanks, Mom, I really appreciate it, but I think I can manage it on my own. I just get so frustrated when they keep calling me as if I'm going to forget I borrowed money from them."

"Is Marty gone for good then?"

"I think so," Rachel said, wondering to herself if she would ever call him back. "Breaking up over the phone lacked dignity. He hasn't called since and he didn't make it sound like he really wanted me to call him."

"His loss," Deborah said as she pinched her daughter's cheek. She smoothed out Rachel's hair with an open hand as she used to do when Rachel was younger.

Rachel looked up and brushed her mother's hand aside. "Stop it," she said embarrassed, though there was no one there to see mother and daughter bonding.

"Yeah, his loss. Although I'm not getting any younger, Mom."

"You're plenty young dear," Deborah admonished, "besides, aren't there any cute doctors working with you at that clinic." Rachel laughed.

"No," she said almost too quickly, "most of them are twice my age and I think they're all married. Besides, I wouldn't want to work at the same place as someone I was dating."

"It was just a thought."

"There is one cute guy there, but he doesn't really work there."

"Don't tell me he's a patient?" Deborah asked horrified.

"Of course not, mother, that would *slightly* breach the doctor-patient relationship. No, he's been sent over by an insurance company to assess the Clinic's needs. He's working on our malpractice insurance. He's going to be around for the next two weeks going over our files and stuff. I gave him a tour of the Clinic yesterday. He's a really sweet guy."

"So this guy, does he have a name?"

"Of course he does, it's Edwin Morgan, but only his mother calls him Edwin."

"And you."

"He insists I call him Ed."

"That's a nice name, kind of like the horse."

"Mom," Rachel groaned.

"I'm sorry honey, I was just teasing you. So what's he like?"

"I said he's cute and sweet, what more do you want?"

"Is he single?"

"I'm not sure."

"Well did he have a wedding band?"

"I don't think so. Mom, I don't look at a man's hand every time I meet someone new. Besides, I've only spent a few hours with him so far."

"Will you see him again?"

"Probably. I'm supposed to make myself available if he needs help or has any questions."

"Well that's good, I'm happy for you." Her mother always had a way of making her life seem so much more exciting than it really was. Every time she met someone new her mother thought there was a serious relationship underway already. When she told her mother of her first date with Marty two and a half years ago, the first thing her mother said was to be sure to use protection. Perhaps that was the thrill of living vicariously through others. You could take the good parts and in your mind make them better while completely ignoring the bad parts.

"Thanks for talking with me, Mom. I guess I just came down with a case of 'Me Against the World' syndrome and started feeling sorry for myself."

"That's alright dear. Everyone gets down at some point in their lives. Just be glad you don't have the same problems as those people you treat. Ever since you're sister was first diagnosed with multiple personality disorder, I've been reading books about it. First hand accounts mostly, like *The Three Faces of Eve, Silencing The Voices, Suffer The Child*, and *Sybil*. After reading what those poor women have gone through and how they were able to get better through faith and perseverance, I can never feel sorry for myself again. You would do well to learn from your patients. They know what true pain and suffering is all about."

"I guess you're right, Mom."

"Of course I'm right honey. I've been down before. Everybody has. It's just a matter of having something to believe in. Something to carry your faith. I know you're not a churchgoer and will never turn to God like I do in my times of need, but there are other things to which you can turn. Whether you believe it or not, faith in the human spirit and the kindness of your fellow men can be enough to carry you through the hard times. Everyone needs a rock to brace themselves against once in awhile. Did I ever tell you about your grandfather's near death experience?" Rachel shook her head.

"It happened back in London when I was just a child, I think I was six...or was it seven? It was during the height of the German air raids over Britain. The entire city was blacked out. There were no streetlights. No car lights. No lights in storefronts. We couldn't even turn on the lights in the house without the use of black-out curtains for fear of revealing our location to Hitler's Luftwaffe.

"Well, on a particularly bad night, bombs were dropping so closely that the house shook with every explosion. I remember the next door neighbor's house was hit and old Mister Friedman had been taking a bath. He was found the next day two streets over still in his bathtub. He was scared and hurt but alive. Lucky for him the bathtub was one of those huge porcelain tubs, the ones with stubby claws for legs. We had a good laugh over that for years.

"Anyway, that same night, while my mother and I huddled underneath the stairs, your grandfather busied himself around the house battening down the hatches so to speak. Your grandmother and I heard a loud crash from the living room and went to see what had happened. My poor father had tried to move a large china cabinet by himself into a corner so that it wouldn't be damaged. As he was moving it, his hand slipped and went through the glass front. He fell down and the china cabinet came crashing down on him. His face and hands were badly cut up by the broken glass and the cabinet pinned him to the ground. My mother and I were just barely able to shift the cabinet off of him. It was then that we realized how badly his arm had been cut. He couldn't even move it and blood was everywhere. He must have been in such agony.

"We called for an ambulance to come get him but it took them over two hours to get there. Not only did they have to drive in the complete dark, but the hospitals were packed because of the war you see. When we got to the hospital, Grandma and I were told to sit in the waiting room while my dad was waiting to be operated on. A nurse came in to tell us that your grandfather was prepped and that the doctors were just about to start operating on him when two bombs hit the hospital at the same time. Mom literally threw me to the ground and lay on top of me using her own body as a shield to protect me. Fortunately, the waiting room wasn't hit and we weren't injured. The ceiling and walls were cracked but intact. The entire hospital was in chaos. We went to see if your grandfather was all right but when we got to the wing where he had been taken to have his operation, it was gone. There was literally nothing left but a heap of rubble.

"We stood there in shock not knowing what to do. Mom cried the whole time they dug up the broken building. It took them several hours before they got down to the level where they could find your grandfather's body. A police officer came over and talked to my mother for a minute. I didn't hear what he told her then, but she told me years later that he said she shouldn't be there because if they found Dad he would most likely be unidentifiable.

"We stayed.

"We looked on oblivious to the planes overhead and the explosions all around us. Dad just couldn't be gone. Your grandmother couldn't take it anymore and was just about to take me home when shouts could be heard from the diggers. Someone was yelling that they had found someone still alive underneath the debris. My mother rushed me over so we could get a better look. After digging for over four hours, the rescue crew had uncovered a group of people who looked as if they had died worshipping some strange altar. It was the operating room where your grandfather had been taken. Just before the explosion, he was placed on the operating table and the operation had begun. When the bombs dropped and the hospital started collapsing, the four doctors and nurses in the operating room had thrown themselves on top of your grandfather to protect him. He lived, while they were all killed by the blast. He was rushed to another hospital, received his operation, and after two months of recovery, made the walk home on his own two legs. The night he came home, Churchill was making a speech on the radio about the British airmen who had fought so valiantly against the Germans. I'll never forget that speech. He said, *'Never in the field of human conflict was so much owed by so many to so few.'* People help each other in a crisis. Four perfect strangers sacrificed their own lives, their futures, to save someone they had never even spoken to; my father, your grandfather. No matter how bad things may seem, there will always be someone to turn to and someone to look after you even if you can't see them.

"When I first found out about the abuse your sister underwent I didn't know what to do but somehow I got by. Then when she was diagnosed nine years later with multiple personality disorder I was crushed even further. I forced myself to go on for your sister's sake. Finally, when she was found dead, I about gave up. I fell into the greatest depths of despair and depression. I thought the scars would never heal and that the pain would go on forever infinitely increasing. During my blackest moments, I was able to rely on the support of my friends, what family I had left, including you dear, and of course my faith in God. Without those pillars of stability to hold me up during my greatest times of need, I don't believe I could have gone on.

"This is why I say to you now dear, that no matter what life throws at you, you're equipped to deal with it as long as you know where to place your faith." Deborah reached out and took her daughter's hands into her own.

They talked more about Rachel's past few days and how much they each missed Theresa. Rachel left the house in which she grew up in much higher spirits than when she had first despondently showed up on the porch looking for a shoulder to cry on. The adolescent lawn crew was gone by this time, leaving no hint of their presence except for a neatly manicured lawn. The sun tentatively poked its way through narrow crevices between the receding clouds.

The ride home was a lot more enjoyable. Rachel ruminated over what she and her mother had talked about and realized she had nothing to fret over. After all, she still had her health. She looked forward to spending a quiet evening at home. Thinking back over the last couple of days, one thought kept on popping up in her mind: at least things couldn't get any worse.

Chapter 23

▼

Thursday
10:49 a.m.
Meadowvale Clinic

The next morning things got a lot worse.

Rachel spent the first half of the day talking with the police and seeing patients. Once her fifth appointment left, the rest of her day was clear to get some much needed paperwork out of the way. Before she had a chance to delve into her work however, Walter Flemming burst into her office unannounced. Striding purposefully to her desk he slapped a copy of the *San Francisco Globe* squarely in the center of the desk.

"Have you seen this?" Flemming yelled.

Rachel looked down at the paper curiously; she didn't see anything of interest. "No I haven't. Why?"

Flemming looked at the paper and turned it over in disgust so that the lower portion of the front page was now facing upwards.

Rachel's eye immediately caught the article on Jim Well's death. She looked up at Flemming unsure of how to react. Why was he angry at her? She said nothing.

"Go on, read it!" Flemming said.

Rachel slid the paper closer to her and quickly read the article in its entirety. It was not flattering. It also brought up the issue of Dr. Arthur Montgomery's disappearance again. When she was finished she remained silent.

"Do you have any idea how bad this looks for the Clinic?" Flemming fumed.

"Well, I guess…"

"You guess? Is that what you did when you diagnosed this poor man as well? You guessed? I see by his chart that you diagnosed him with post-traumatic amnesia while all the evidence, a little too late to help Jim Wells I might add, would point to dissociative identity disorder."

"Dissociative identity disorder?" Rachel asked incredulous.

"Yes, dissociative identity disorder. As for the Clinic's reputation, let's hope this misdiagnosis of yours is not picked up by the papers. The last thing I need is for my Clinic to become the laughingstock of California. You're extremely fortunate that this patient of yours didn't have any relatives to bring a lawsuit against the Clinic and yourself." Rachel had tried to remain calm throughout Flemming's tirade but her reserve quickly vanished when he accused her of misdiagnosis and professional misconduct.

"Now hold on just a minute," Rachel rose to her full five feet eight inches prepared to lock horns with Flemming. "First of all, I did not misdiagnose Jim Wells. He suffered from post-traumatic amnesia, plain and simple. Doctor Foley even concurred with my diagnosis. He was there when I made it. As for being sued, even if Jim Wells did have a family, his death can't be blamed on the Clinic, nor myself. Granted I don't know why Jim committed suicide, but I assure you that it wasn't due to any misdiagnosis on my part. I did what I was trained to do and carried out my responsibilities to the best of my ability."

"Regardless," Flemming said as if she hadn't spoken at all. "Despite your claims, the death of Jim Wells is a black mark on this Clinic's otherwise spotless reputation. You had just better hope, for your sake and the sake of your future here at this Clinic that this incident doesn't have any further consequences. As for your patient roster, I think it would be best if we lightened your caseload both quantitatively as well as qualitatively. I'll be keeping a close eye on you, Doctor Miller. As for the Jim Wells incident, I'll handle it. I've already taken the liberty of pulling the file you started on him. Good day." With that, Flemming marched out of Rachel's office and closed the door behind him none too softly.

Rachel slumped into her chair and put her head in her hands supporting herself with her elbows. She could scarcely believe what had just transpired. Reading over the article in the *Globe* once again, she admitted that it did not put the Clinic in a positive light. Still, she did not think she deserved to be reamed out by Flemming the way she had been.

She did not understand how she could have misdiagnosed Jim Wells. Grant Foley had been right there when she assessed him and he even agreed with her findings. And what was Flemming talking about when he said Jim Wells had dissociative identity disorder? How could he know that Jim Wells had dissociative identity disorder? Rachel had seen nothing to indicate that Jim Wells had multiple personalities so how could Flemming posit such a thing?

Rachel was further aghast at Flemming's not so subtle reference to the precarious nature of her future at the Clinic. She wasn't entirely sure if he was threatening her or not. Either way, she was going to avoid Walter Flemming for awhile. One thing was certain, she was going to see Dr. Foley as soon as she could.

Chapter 24

▼

Marjorie Newman was instructed by her boss that he was not to be disturbed for the next hour. Flemming had returned to his office not sure of whether to be proud of his performance or still angry at the fact that the article on Jim Wells' death had brought up the subject of Arthur Montgomery again.

While he was quite pleased with himself for having put the fear of God into Rachel Miller and was sure that he had convinced her not to pursue the Jim Wells' matter any further he was still upset that Montgomery's disappearance still made the news and that the search for his colleague continued. The constant coverage and reminders of the Montgomery disappearance reminded Flemming of an Edgar Allen Poe story; The Telltale Heart. Unlike Poe's protagonist however, Flemming was certain he would not succumb to a guilty conscience.

Picking up the phone, Flemming dialed the San Francisco branch of the FBI. When the receptionist politely asked what extension he wanted, he informed her he wished to speak with Special Agent John Haskins.

John Haskins arrived at work ten minutes late. He checked his watch for the tenth time in the last ten minutes like a kid in detention and hurried towards a formidable modern skyscraper located on Golden Gate Avenue. His trenchcoat billowed out behind him like a cape as he bounded up the front steps and his red conservative tie flopped over his shoulder. His first priority of the morning was to write up a report on the Hernandez case of the previous evening and see Assistant Director, Julie Spracken.

John hurried up to his office on the thirteenth floor where the San Francisco Bureau was housed and made a beeline for his office. He hoped to get the report out of the way early so that he could devote some more time to other matters. The report itself would only take half an hour to write up. John had written so many of the things over the past decade that he could practically do them in his sleep. It had taken him awhile to get used to what Assistant Director Spracken wanted in a report, but once he had found out, report writing became a whole lot easier.

Assistant Director Spracken had joined the San Francisco Bureau just under two years ago. Her arrival caused many heads to turn and ruffled many feathers. At least three agents of the San Francisco Bureau had been anxiously awaiting and expecting their promotion once the news was leaked that the current Assistant Director was being promoted to Washington. When it was announced that not only an outsider but a woman was to be filling the void, tensions rose.

John had no problem working under a woman, but apparently, many of his colleagues did. An uncomfortable and perpetual tension pervaded the Bureau's walls for days after Spracken's name replaced her predecessor's on the Assistant Director's office door. Harsh words were spoken behind her back, cruel rumors were spread about her, and she had a difficult time earning her agents' respect. At first.

Few people were aware of Spracken's background. None of the San Francisco agents were. If they were, the incident which forever changed their opinion of her would not have had the impact that it had. In a single afternoon, in the time it takes to have a cup of coffee, Assistant Director Spracken proved that she was not a person to be taken lightly, nor under any circumstances to be underestimated.

Just over a month after her arrival, on a day like any other, one of the FBI's Top Ten Most Wanted was cornered in a busy shopping mall by the SFPD.

His name was Paul Razowski.

He had a hostage. A K-Mart employee.

The Bureau was called the moment one of the officers recognized the wanted man. Ten agents were dispatched to apprehend him. When they arrived, the police told them their suspect was hiding in the aisles of the K-Mart store. When asked if the suspect was armed, the police told them he was. Two of the agents, Pembroke and Hailey, went in to determine his location and hopefully flush him out into the awaiting arms of the other agents and police officers. Aside from the hostage, all K-Mart employees and customers had been cleared from the store.

Spracken was unaware of the situation at the shopping mall until things turned bloody. What happened next prompted her into action.

The two agents who had gone in to find Razowski were aware that Razowski was armed and had taken precautions. Both wore thick Kevlar flak jackets.

What they were not aware of was the caliber of Razowski's firepower.

He had a .38 Special with KTW bullets.

Otherwise known as Cop Killers.

Originally designed for police forces in nineteen sixty-seven to pierce car doors and windshields, the Cop Killer was an agent's worst nightmare; made of a super hard metal alloy, sheathed with a Teflon coating and specially shaped to maximize penetration, Cop Killer bullets could pierce law enforcement body armor.

Later reports indicated that the two agents followed the sound of a whimpering woman's voice. This turned out to be a decoy to lure them into a quickly improvised ambush set up by Razowski. They found the female K-Mart worker tied up in a display rack and were in the process of freeing her when agent Pembroke went down. Hailey himself was shot in the shoulder. He would later recount how he had turned around to face the gunman but he was nowhere to be seen. He went to the aid of his partner but it was already too late. Both Pembroke and the woman Razowski had used as bait were dead.

Hailey had time to radio in the situation and request backup but was cut off by an audible click. It was the cocking of a very large caliber gun. Razowski had managed to sneak up behind agent Hailey. Surrendering his firearm, Hailey became Razowski's new hostage. As a federal agent, he made a much better bargaining chip.

When Spracken was notified that one of her agents was dead and another wounded and taken hostage, she arrived at the mall within minutes. While she was being briefed on the situation by the Special Agent in Charge, several more agents arrived on the scene to take down Razowski. In all, seventeen FBI agents and twelve police officers awaited Spracken's orders. Most were expecting her to send everyone in guns ablazing. What she did next took them all by surprise.

She ordered her agents and the police officers present to form a tighter perimeter around the K-Mart. When asked how many agents were going to go in, she replied none. She would go in alone. Many of the agents balked at this and the police told her it was a suicide mission. To that she replied, "exactly." She would rather risk her own life than that of another one of her agents'.

Razowski was one of the nation's most wanted men. He faced the death penalty in three states. He had killed over eleven people in his past and would not hesitate to take down as many law enforcement agents as he could if he knew he was trapped. Spracken knew all this because she herself, as a former member of the Special Investigative Unit, had drawn up the profile on him which had led to his first conviction seven years previously.

Aware of the Cop Killer bullets, Spracken went in to the K-Mart without a flack jacket armed only with a Sig Sauer 9mm. The agents and officers on the scene would all later say that the next fifteen minutes were the most tense they had ever experienced.

Not a sound could be heard from within the vast expanse of the K-Mart store. Seconds ticked by like minutes, minutes felt like hours.

Eight minutes after Spracken went in armed only with a handgun, a single shot rang out. Only silence followed.

Seven more minutes passed. Nothing happened.

Just as the tension outside became unbearable and tentative decisions were being made to rush the store en masse, Spracken emerged with agent Hailey. He was wounded but would live. Spracken was sweating.

Razowski was still inside. A heavily armed armada of vehicles escorted the ambulance he rode in to the hospital. With the one shot heard by the agents outside the store, Assistant Director Spracken had ensured that none of Razowski's progeny would ever walk the earth. This was all explained in the hospital reports. What was not explained was the origin of the bruises Razowski had all over his body, the internal bleeding, and the two broken ribs.

Hailey could remember very little of what had happened in aisle seven that day and Razowski, who lived, only after sixteen hours on the operating table, refused to talk about it. No one dared ask Spracken herself. The matter was dropped; but the stories persisted. Within a day, Spracken's status, like David, St. George, and Beowulf before her was elevated to heroic proportions within the Bureau and the SFPD.

No one ever knew for sure what transpired in aisle seven that day, and with the exception of Hailey, Spracken, and Razowski, it was doubtful that anyone ever would.

John Haskins had a pretty good idea of what had gone on but he kept it to himself. Finishing up his report in record time despite only five hours of sleep the previous eve, John printed up his report and got up from his desk. Just as he reached the doorway on his way out of his office, the phone on his desk rang.

He paused momentarily debating whether he should bother answering it or not. Curiosity won out and he picked up the receiver.

"John Haskins."

"Agent Haskins, good morning," Haskins recognized the voice, "it's Walter Flemming from the Meadowvale Clinic. How are you today?"

"Hi doc, what can I do for you?"

"Well, I was just calling to see if any further progress had been made in the matter of Doctor Montgomery's kidnapping."

"Not since you called last week, Doctor Flemming," John replied impatiently.

"Oh," he sounded disappointed and relieved at the same time. "Nothing at all?"

"Nil. I've checked every lead twice and my agents and I have conducted more interviews than Larry King."

"So is that it then? Is the case considered closed after only six months?"

"I didn't say that. However, legally, nothing can be done until seven years have passed at which time Doctor Montgomery can be declared officially dead. Until that time, or until he returns or his body is found, the case will remain open. I myself intend to continue working on it."

"For how long?"

"As long as it takes, Doctor Flemming, as long as it takes."

"Well that's good to hear, I wish you all the best. You'll keep me posted if anything comes up?" Flemming asked.

"Sure, doc."

"Great, thank you, Agent Haskins."

"You're welcome, have a good day, bye now."

"Good-bye."

John put the phone down annoyed. Walter Flemming had called at least once a week for the past twenty-four weeks. Each time asking about John's progress on the Montgomery case. John had told him six months ago that he would call him if anything surfaced yet the calls persisted. If Flemming's own background hadn't been so impeccable, Haskins would have considered him a suspect for his intense interest in the case. It was a well documented phenomenon that many killers attempted to become involved in the investigation in some capacity or another in order to keep tabs on the authorities' progress. Despite the fact that Flemming wasn't a suspect, John's "spidey-senses" went off each time he talked to the man.

John put Flemming out of his mind and went to see Assistant Director Spracken.

Julie Spracken was sitting at her desk when John entered her office upon her secretary's insistence. If John were not happily married and if she was not his superior, John would have asked Julie Spracken out a long time ago. She was in her late thirties, just as John was, yet standing at five foot nine she had the figure of a curvaceous twenty-five year old. Her hair was a silver blond which contrasted against her dark eyebrows. Her eyes were a steely gray flecked with hints of emerald green. She had an almost stoic appearance due to her square jaw and full lips.

It wasn't only her appearance that John, and most of the other agents found attractive. She was also extremely intelligent. Recruited straight out of Princeton, she had no problem keeping her performance up at Quantico, the FBI's training ground for new recruits. What John admired most of all however was her professionalism. John had never seen her lose her cool, get stressed out, or treat anyone unfairly. In that regard, she was the perfect superior.

"Good morning, John, congratulations on your performance last night," she said as John took a seat opposite her desk. John could feel his cheeks glow.

"Thank you. Here's my report, sorry it's a little late," John placed a folder onto her desk with the file name and a number written across the top.

"Don't worry about it. You could use a break. Speaking of which, when are you going to take that vacation time of yours?"

"No time soon," John answered, "I've a few cases I'm working on right now that I'd like to close while they're still fresh."

"Still working on the Montgomery case?"

"Of course, although it's been cold for awhile now and all the leads I've turned up have proven less than useful."

"Have you seen the paper this morning?"

"No, why?"

Spracken reached underneath a pile of folders leaning precariously on her desk and skillfully removed the morning copy of the *San Francisco Globe* without sending the entire mass of paper sprawling. She tossed it on John's lap.

"Bottom, right hand corner," she said. John unfolded the paper to reveal the entire front page. In the bottom right hand corner was a picture of an ambulance gurney wheeling a body out of a building John didn't recognize. The caption read; Bizarre Death at New Clinic Raises Concerns. There was four inches of print devoted to the story on the front page and it was continued further on within the paper.

John looked up at Spracken with raised eyebrows.

"Read it," she said.

John read the article;

> *A middle-aged male died early yesterday morning at The Meadowvale Clinic. The patient, whose name cannot be disclosed until the next of kin are contacted, ran out of his room, yelling incoherently according to several witnesses. Although attendants attempted to subdue the patient, he managed to overpower them. Death appeared to be self-inflicted.*
>
> *Witnesses report that the patient brought his life to an end by throwing himself headfirst into a television set. The patient suffered fatal injuries to his neck.*

According to the medical examiner on scene, death was instantaneous and no foul play is suspected.

The incident could not come at a worst time for the recently opened Meadowvale Clinic for the Treatment of Dissociative Disorders and its Chief of Psychiatry, Doctor Walter Flemming. Flemming and his colleagues at the Clinic have come under fire of late due to their heavily criticized methods in treating patients with dissociative disorders. Using a combination of drug therapy and hypno-therapy, patients are made to relive their abusive pasts in order to come to grips with their present condition. Although the method of treatment has drawn much criticism from many corners, its continued success has converted a lot of critics. None of the doctors or Clinic staff were available for comment yesterday.

With the exception of its official opening, this is the second time the Meadowvale Clinic has made the news. It was just over six months ago that Doctor Arthur Montgomery, one of the men responsible for the creation of the Clinic, mysteriously disappeared. According to Julie Spracken, Assistant Director at the FBI, no new leads have been made in the case, which is still widely believed to be a kidnapping case despite the fact that no further contact has been made with the kidnapper. The search for Doctor Arthur Montgomery continues.

"Now that is interesting reading," John said when he finished the article and placed the *Globe* back on Spracken's desk.

"I thought that might be of interest to you. Does it give you any new ideas?"

"Not right off, but it makes one wonder. I was thinking about Montgomery again last night and it struck me that I haven't looked very closely at his involvement with this new Clinic." John pointed to the newspaper, "Perhaps there's some connection there that I've overlooked."

"I wasn't even aware that he was involved with it until I read that article. There's no mention of it within any of your reports on the subject."

"You're right, there isn't, but I wasn't aware of his involvement until after the initial investigation myself. Do you know Walter Flemming?"

"The doctor who keeps calling you asking about Montgomery?"

"That's the one. Shortly after Montgomery disappeared, Flemming mentioned that he had to find a replacement for him to start work at the Clinic. I think it might be worthwhile to check him out once more."

"I thought he came up spotless the first time?"

"He did, but that's what worries me. Besides, I've exhausted all other possibilities. I can't think of a single thing to do with this case any more. If I can't dig up anything new this time, I may have to shelf the case."

"I don't think it will come to that, John."

"I certainly hope it doesn't, but if it does, at least I'll know that I did everything in my power."

"So what kind of approach are you going to take?"

"I think I'll start at the psychiatric hospital he worked at before Meadowvale opened."

"Well, keep me posted on whatever you do and whatever you turn up."

"Sure. Who knows, with a little luck, maybe he'll just turn up at the Clinic."

Chapter 25

Rachel saw two more patients before lunch. She felt a little guilty because while they were recounting their problems to her, she was busy ruminating about her own while trying to listen at the same time. One of her patients had even asked if she was listening to her. Now that she had her mind to herself once again, she devoted her thoughts to the death of Jim Wells. She wanted to figure out how and why Flemming believed Jim had DID. She was still convinced that her diagnosis of post-traumatic amnesia was accurate but now that Jim Wells was dead, there was really no way to prove it.

Checking her schedule to ensure that she had enough time to grab a late lunch in the cafeteria, Rachel left her office to see if Ed had come to the Clinic this morning. The door to the records room was open and a figure was hunched over the computer.

"Hi, Ed, want to join me for lunch?"

The figure wheeled around surprised. It was Kevin Cheung.

"Doctor Miller, you scared the bejabbers out of me. You shouldn't sneak up on people like that."

"I'm sorry, Kevin, I thought you were someone else. Have you seen a tall, dark haired guy around? He's an insurance agent."

"You mean Ed? Yeah he was just here, he went downstairs to get something for lunch. Did you see the paper this morning?" Kevin asked.

"Doctor Flemming made sure I did."

"Ouch, I can't imagine he was too happy about it."

"There's the understatement of the year. I'd stay out of his way for the next day or two. He's on the warpath."

"Thanks for the tip, I gotta go." Kevin quickly turned off the computer station he was working at and left Rachel by herself.

"Hey Rachel. How's it going?" A voice from behind Rachel asked.

Rachel wheeled around and found herself looking up into the freckled face of Dean Campbell.

"Oh, hi, Dean, I didn't realize you were up here as well."

"I just got here, Doctor Henderson asked me to come and get a file for him. I hate talking to that guy, I can never understand a word he's saying. I just hope I get the right file this time."

Rachel laughed. "I'll trade you. If you want to talk to Flemming for me I'd be glad to talk to Henderson."

"Did you two actually talk about what happened then, or did he just bite your head off?"

"He pretty much just chewed me out."

"So he didn't tell you what Jim Wells said when he came tearing out of his room?"

"No," Rachel's eyebrows drew close together as a look of perplexion shadowed her face, "what did he say?"

"I can't believe nobody's told you. It was really weird, Doctor Miller. When Jim Wells came out of his room he had a bunch of different expressions on his face as if he wasn't sure what to feel. I know that sounds weird but it was the same with what he was saying. One second he's yelling about how he wants to get out of the hospital, I think he yelled something like 'get me out of here', and then he started screaming as if someone was beating him up and his voice changed. It went really high, not just because he was screaming but as if he was trying to sound like a kid. Then as soon as he started screaming, he stopped and started yelling, this time he was yelling about killing the demons within. Whatever that means. I only spoke to him briefly earlier on in the day but when he was yelling about demons and voices in his head, that was the voice that I remembered from earlier on in the day. It was Jim Wells screaming about voices and demons but I couldn't tell you who the other voices belonged to.

"I've seen several DID patients switching from personality to personality but what was happening to Jim was frightening. It was as if he had DID and his personalities were on fast forward. I know that's not the case though because I remember when I checked his chart earlier in the evening to see if he was getting any new drugs I saw that you had diagnosed him with post-traumatic amnesia earlier in the day. I'm surprised Flemming didn't tell you all this. Doctor Sanford told me yesterday that he or Doctor Flemming would fill you in," Dean finished.

"I guess they just forgot or wanted to spare me the gory details," Rachel said although she didn't believe her own words. She herself believed that something was being purposefully kept from her and Dr. Flemming did not want her to find out what. Knowing that details about Jim's death were being kept secret from her only intrigued her more. She wanted to find out why this relatively healthy, both physically and mentally, patient of hers had suddenly killed himself with no apparent precursors. She would start looking for answers right after lunch. First things first though, she was starving.

She found Ed sitting in the same corner the two of them had occupied two days ago.

"Mind if I join you?" she asked as she approached him with her tray.

"Oh, hi, Rachel, not at all, have a seat," Ed said, clearing the table so there was room for Rachel to put her tray down.

"I went by the records room to see if you wanted to come down for lunch."

"I thought you would have already eaten. I got here early this morning and lost track of time. Staring at numbers on a computer monitor for hours on end can be somewhat hypnotic."

"I know what you mean. So what happened to you yesterday? I didn't see your truck in the parking lot when I got here."

"Doctor Foley called me. He told me to take the day off. I don't blame him though. So I spent the day at the psychiatric hospital. That guy who killed himself, was he one of your patients?"

"Yes, but I can hardly call him a patient. I only met with him once and that was for an initial evaluation."

"I'm sorry, Rachel."

"It's not your fault."

"I feel guilty for having taken up your entire day the day before yesterday when you could have been with your patients. Maybe you could have prevented it."

"A one hour meeting with him wouldn't have made a difference. Besides, one of the other doctors saw him yesterday, in my absence. I would like to find out why he did it though."

"Looks like you have some detective work to do," Ed said between bites of a tuna sandwich.

"That's me, Nancy Drew," Rachel said.

Ed laughed. "Need any help? I can be Frank Hardy." This time Rachel laughed.

"I don't think so, I just have to take a look at his admission sheet and find out why he was sent here and who brought him here. How's your work coming?" she asked switching the focus on to him so she could eat her lunch.

"Not too bad. I've been going through all of the demographic data available on the patients the Clinic is treating right now. I stayed up late last night reading those pamphlets you gave me to get a better grasp on dissociative disorders. I think I'm catching on. The DSM IV is immensely helpful, thanks again for lending that to me. The next thing I have to do is check out the San Francisco Psychiatric Hospital again and go through their numbers some more. Do you need anything while I'm over there?"

"No thanks."

"All right. Hey, are you going to be in your office all afternoon?"

"I might not be in my office, but I'll be around until about six. Why?"

"Once I'm done at the psychiatric hospital I might have some questions. I just wanted to know if you'd be around."

"If I'm not in my office, just have me paged."

"Thanks. I guess I'll see you later," Ed picked up his tray leaving Rachel to finish her lunch alone.

Rachel finished the rest of her lunch in silence hoping no one would ask to join her. She was disappointed that Ed had left so abruptly but was glad for the silence it brought and the opportunity it afforded her to collect her thoughts. The first thing she had to do was talk to Grant Foley and then she wanted to find out under what circumstances Jim Wells was brought in to the Clinic.

Foley was in his office reading some files and smoking a pipe when his secretary let Rachel in.

"Oh, good afternoon, Rachel. How are you today?"

"I'm not quite sure," Rachel replied taking a seat.

"What a strange response. You sound like one of my patients."

"What I mean is that the death of Jim Wells doesn't upset me per se, but I am puzzled about a few things."

"Such as?"

"Well, I had a talk with Doctor Flemming this morning and he was somewhat agitated. He seemed under the impression that I misdiagnosed Jim Wells and as a result my misdiagnosis somehow led to his suicide."

"I hardly..."

"And then, he told me that my caseload should be lightened and that the Jim Wells matter is no longer my concern. He said he would take care of it."

"I do agree that it would be best if you let Doctor Flemming take care of it, and as for his accusing you of misdiagnosis, I'll talk to him this afternoon. I'm sure he didn't mean it. After all, I was there and still think you were right. It did appear as if Jim Wells had non-dissociative post-traumatic amnesia as a result of a blow to the right temple. It's too bad we didn't get the CT scan results before he did himself in. I wouldn't worry about Flemming though, he's just an old bear. If you hadn't noticed he's also a little overprotective of the Clinic, as am I, but not to the same obsessive degree. The *Globe's* coverage of the incident didn't rest well with him. While it is unfortunate that Jim Wells killed himself and that he did it while under our supervision, it is hardly a reflection of the people this Clinic employs." Foley smiled reassuringly at Rachel.

"Thank you for your vote of confidence. I wish Doctor Flemming were as understanding."

"He'll come around. He just has to let off some steam. He's under enormous pressure of late. If I were you I'd steer clear for a day or two until he cools down. In the meantime, I'll speak with him."

Rachel forgot to tell Foley of her talk with Dean Campbell but when she realized it, she was glad of it. She wasn't sure why, but she thought she should go about her investigation into Jim Wells' death quietly. The last thing she wanted to do was irk Flemming again.

Returning to the records room, Rachel felt a pang of disappointment when she discovered Ed had already left for the psychiatric hospital. Going through both the filing cabinets and the computer, she was unable to locate Jim Wells' admission report. Obviously it hadn't been filed yet. She went downstairs to the reception desk to see if they had it amongst their papers to be filed. Daniella and another young buxomy girl were on shift.

"Hi, Daniella, I was wondering if you have Jim Wells' admission records down here? They haven't been filed in the record room yet," Rachel said.

"Let me check," Daniella said. She searched several trays designated for holding files and searched all behind the desk but came up empty-handed.

"It's not back here," she reported.

"Could you check the computer to at least let me know who checked him in?" Rachel asked. Daniella quickly typed in the patient's name but the screen came up blank.

"I'm sorry, Doctor Miller, there's no information here on your patient. We either didn't receive the file here at the desk, or, oh, hold on a second..." Daniella's eyes went back to the screen.

"It says here that that patient's file has been classified until further notice. It was classified by Doctor Flemming the morning of your patient's death. Doctor Flemming himself must have the file." Although disappointed, Rachel thanked Daniella and headed upstairs to her office. Without that file there wasn't much else Rachel could do in terms of getting to the bottom of Jim's death and she was not about to ask Dr. Flemming for it.

Chapter 26

Grant Foley went straight to Walter Flemming's office once Rachel had left his own.

"Why did you accuse Rachel of misdiagnosing Jim Wells?" he asked Flemming.

"How was I to know you were there agreeing with everything she said?"

"Well I couldn't deny what she saw. Doctor Miller is not to be your personal scapegoat. Hell, if I was the one who diagnosed Jim Wells I probably would have come up with non-dissociative post-traumatic amnesia as well under the circumstances. That man did not appear to have dissociative identity disorder. And until you brought it up to Rachel, she was none the wiser."

"I don't think she'll be giving us any problems."

"And what makes you so sure of that?"

"I had a talk with her this morning about her future here at the Clinic."

"You threatened her?"

"Not exactly. I just reminded her of the hierarchy."

"You threatened her."

"Threaten is such a harsh word," Flemming said casually.

"Not as harsh as APA investigation."

"I assure you it won't come to that."

"I certainly hope not."

"So what else did your little protégé have to say?"

"She was upset that you took the matter out of her hands but I was able to convince her that it was for the best. I think she was almost relieved."

"At least we won't have to worry about her digging around."

"Speaking of which, what about Wells' admission sheet? Have you taken care of that?" Foley asked.

"It's taken care of." Flemming was about to continue when a knock sounded on the door.

"That would be Carl," he said as Carl Sanford let himself into the office.

"Afternoon, Walt, Grant," he nodded to his colleagues and took a seat beside Foley.

"Grant and I were just discussing the Wells matter," Flemming informed Sanford.

"I thought that was taken care of?" Carl said.

"It has been. The medical examiner has all the information he needs already. Jim Wells had no family, no criminal record, and no history of mental illness so it should be an open and shut case."

"Won't he do an autopsy?"

"Probably, it's standard procedure to conduct autopsies on all suicide victims. But even if he does, what would he find except traces of sodium amytal and muscle relaxants which we're well within our right to administer. He can't tell what dosages we were using."

"I suppose you're right." Sanford admitted

"Of course I'm right." Flemming said confidently.

"How's the new subject coming along, Carl?" Foley asked Sanford, changing the topic. He removed a pipe from his coat pocket and began packing it with tobacco.

"She's doing fine, much better than Lisa Parsons. I think she'll make an excellent test subject."

"I hope so," Flemming said.

"Do you want me to work on her again tonight, Walter?" Sanford asked.

"You might as well. There's no sense in wasting time. We're already a little behind because of this Wells fiasco."

"Speaking of which, how many patients do we have undergoing treatment right now?" Sanford asked.

"Twenty-three. But only half of them are undergoing electro-shock therapy," Flemming said.

"And we're limiting the next phase to ten patients?"

"For the time being," Flemming said. Then added, "At least until we perfect our methods. If we bring in two new subjects a month for the next four months, that should give us enough time to do our work."

"Then we can step into the final phase which is where the real money will be." Foley added, lighting his pipe. Thick clouds of rich-scented smoke filled the air.

"Absolutely, Grant. Then maybe you can trade in that mini-van for a real car," Flemming quipped. The three doctors laughed.

"That reminds me, Walt, how did your teleconference go yesterday?" Foley asked.

"Very well indeed. We will soon have two additional sources of income."

"Which are?" Foley asked impatiently.

"The CIA and the U.S. Army, off the record of course."

"Why are the CIA and the Army so interested in what we're doing?" Sanford asked.

"I assume that's a rhetorical question?"

"I'd like to know the details, Walter," Foley interjected.

"The CIA has been interested in any kind of research on the brain and mind control since its inception, full access to the human brain allows it to be manipulated with ease," Flemming began, lapsing into the speech he had been given over the phone by his CIA contact. "Why torture people for information when you can have them willingly tell you everything you want to know? The Russians and Chinese have been trying to gain access to the inner secrets of the human brain since before World War Two, with mixed results, I've been informed. Nothing they've discovered comes close to what we ourselves can do at this very moment. They've pretty much abandoned conventional methods of looking into mind control and are now looking to technology to save them. Already they have created highly sophisticated microchips that can be embedded into the brain itself which rival our own advances in the same field. All that this does is give them external access to a computer they still don't fully comprehend. The human brain is nothing more than a gray, wrinkly piece of software. It can be programmed and reprogrammed. All they've done is hook up a modem, what we're doing is rewriting the software."

"What exactly does the CIA want from us?" Foley asked.

"Just the detailed notes of all our experiments and their results. That's the beauty of it, we just keep on doing what we've been planning all along and all we have to do is share our notes and results."

"They're not going to start sending us their own patients are they?"

"No, of course not, it may come down to one of us going to them to explain what we've done and help them duplicate our results, but aside from that our obligation to them is simple: prove our methods work and pass on the information."

"Okay, I can see why the CIA would be so interested in our work, but what about the Army? What's in it for them?" Foley asked.

"This is the interesting part," Flemming began. "Imagine if you will a soldier who doesn't experience stress. As we all know, dissociation occurs due to unbearable levels of stress. When the individual can no longer tolerate the pressures of external stimuli whether they be physical or mental, he turns inward to escape and disassociates from his present state. What if you could create the dissociation *before* the stress and channel that stress into a dissociated state of your own creation. Not only would you prevent mental breakdowns but these people could live normal lives. No more Post Traumatic Stress Disorder."

"From a mental health standpoint, you would have the perfect soldier," Foley said in awe. "One who could be programmed to do anything you want him to, feel nothing, and kill without guilt or remorse and go home the next day to his family and enjoy a day in the park."

"That's only the beginning. Once we perfect our techniques, the possibilities are endless."

"So what will the contract with the Army entail then?"

"The same as our agreement with the CIA. Create the technique and share our knowledge. Our plans will go on as we originally intended but once we have Uncle Sam's financial backing, we can speed up our research."

"God bless the American taxpayer," Foley chuckled.

Sanford left Flemming's office as soon as he could. He breathed deeply out his own office window in an attempt to purge Foley's tobacco smoke from his lungs. He hated tobacco in all its forms. He couldn't comprehend how people could willingly inhale and chew the vile plant even when they were more than aware of its harmful effects. Sitting down at his desk, he reached into a lower drawer and withdrew a bottle of Pepto Bismol. He untwisted the childproof cap and chugged from the small pink bottle. His ulcer was acting up again. His own doctor had started him on a triple regimen of drugs two weeks earlier but Sanford didn't think they were having any effect. Not a noticeable one anyway. The other doctors at the Clinic didn't know of his ailment and he had no intention of letting them find out. Unfortunately, despite the drugs he had access to and used frequently at the Clinic, he was still under a lot of stress.

He tried to relax as much as possible when at home by reading or exercising but his children were at an age where everything they did was annoying and his wife seemed to be nagging him more than usual. He needed a vacation.

He thought for sure the entire project was going to be exposed, as well as his involvement in it, when Jim Wells committed suicide. Fortunately, his fears did not come true. He was still extremely anxious about phase two however. When Flemming had first recruited him as a member of the project just over four years ago, he had only been introduced to the first phase. He never realized how much further they were going to take it. But now that he was in so deep there was no turning back. He was in for keeps. The second phase seemed the riskiest phase of all, even more so than the final phase. Sanford hoped the pressure would not be as intense once phase three began. He didn't think he could take much more. Either mentally or physically.

Immediately after the attack, Sanford seriously considered leaving the Clinic and abandoning the project. As much as he wanted to quit the project, there were too many factors keeping him tied to it. The freedom he was granted at the Clinic to carry out his own research was unlimited. The pay was extremely good and only promised to get better. Not only that, but with the work they were doing, as unethical as it may be, they were learning at a rapid pace. Similar to animal testing, the benefits accrued overshadowed both the risk involved and any ethical considerations.

Sanford wasn't morally opposed to the project, he couldn't care less about ethics, but he thought Flemming was moving things a little too quickly. He couldn't argue with the results though. There was one other factor keeping Sanford involved in the project. It was something that Flemming seemed to almost enjoy holding over his head like the *Sword of Damocles'*. Arthur Montgomery had once opposed Flemming and his work. Flemming assured Sanford that if he chose the path Montgomery had, it would lead to the same end. Unlike Montgomery, Carl Sanford intended to live a long and relatively healthy life.

Chapter 27

The San Francisco Psychiatric Hospital was situated in the middle of a fifty-acre plot of land off Potrero Avenue. Surrounded by lush green lawns and tall black iron gates, a single winding drive granted passage to the front of the imposing building. It was one of the few buildings in San Francisco that had not been seriously compromised by the nineteen oh-six earthquake. Massive oak trees, all within the fence's perimeter, served as mute testament to the institution's age and durability. A small John Deere tractor lawnmower made its way up and down the length of the sprawling lawn. Its rider waved lazily to John Haskins as he passed him on the way up the drive. John waved back.

A wide set of stone steps led the way up to an arched double-doorway set a few feet into the building. Layer upon layer of dark forest green paint prevented the doors from swinging open easily. The four-story red-brick structure seemed more like an Ivy League dormitory than a psychiatric hospital. Despite the archaic appearance of the exterior of the building, the interior was relatively modern. Everything was white, or close to it.

John walked over to a small kiosk which served as a reception desk. It resembled a movie theater's ticket wicket. A short stocky woman with a severe bun of dyed black hair manned the kiosk. Her ample bosom stretched the cotton fabric of her starched uniform. The skin around her eyes wasn't nearly as tight. A nebulae of wrinkles stemmed from the outer corner of her eyes.

"Good morning, can I help you?" she asked John in a husky, almost baritone voice. Her eyes were cold like those of a long dead sturgeon fish and her hands played impatiently on the desk in front of her. A clear sheet of Plexiglas extending from the top of the desk to the low plaster ceiling above separated John from the woman. A small baseball sized hole cut out from the middle of the glass at mouth level allowed John's voice to be heard. He had to restrain himself from saying 'one for the nine o'clock show please'.

"Good afternoon, I'm Special Agent John Haskins, with the FBI." John pressed his badge wallet flat and open against the glass so the receptionist could see it clearly. She looked like the type who would ask him to recite his badge number to ensure he was the real McCoy.

"Could you tell me your badge number, sir?" she asked. John rhymed it off for her while trying not to smirk.

"And what is it you want here, Agent Hasking?" John didn't bother to correct her.

"I called earlier. I have an appointment to see Doctor Winslow."

"Hold on one second, sir," she said. She reached for her phone and punched one of the numerous buttons on the machine. She rolled her eyes at John as she waited for someone at the other end to pick up. John hazarded a guess that this woman did not wake up excited every morning eager to get to work for another fun-filled day.

A voice on the other end of the line finally picked up after what seemed an eternity. The receptionist exchanged a few words with the individual on the other end. John watched as her face went from a look of intense boredom to the look of a child who has just been caught reading his father's dirty magazines. She hastily hung up the phone and looked up at John. Her eyes were much warmer and her cheeks flushed a deep scarlet.

"I'm sorry, Agent Haskins, you can go right in. Doctor Winslow is waiting for you downstairs. Just go through that door behind you to your left and walk down two flights."

"Thank you." John turned his back, and with a swish of his black trenchcoat, pushed his way through a large steel door leading to the stairs. The stairwell reminded him of a scene from '*Silence of the Lambs*'. Fortunately the purpose of his visit was much less innocuous.

The basement of the hospital had a dank texture and smelled like a wet sleeping bag. Dark, unlit corners made the hallway seem narrower than it in reality was. John could hear two people conversing in hushed tones at the end of the long hall. It was more of an alley really. Dark gray asbestos sheathed pipes ran down the length of the corridor directly overhead. John kept expecting a rat or two to emerge from underneath one of the ancient radiators that lined the walls at sporadic intervals.

Several caged lights lit the way.

Barely.

Following the source of the voices, John turned left at the end of the hall and found himself in another hallway. This one branched off into three more. John called out Dr. Winslow's name for fear of becoming hopelessly lost in the subterranean labyrinth if he ventured any further unaccompanied.

John heard a filing cabinet drawer close shut on squeaky rails followed closely by the sounds of high heel shoes striking the bare floor. John peered into the darkness of one of the hallways and saw a woman emerging from out of the darkness. Short black hair framed a youthful face, although John guessed she was in her fifties. Wafer thin lenses framed by blue plastic made her eyes seem wide open and combined with a high forehead, she looked as if she was in a perpetual state of surprise. Her heels added two to three inches to her five foot four frame and her rigid military style posture made her seem taller than she was. She carried a clipboard protectively under the crook of one arm. Her tightly tailored suit made her look like a research scientist in a television commercial for cold medication.

The last time John had seen the woman was over five months ago. He met her for the first time just two days after Arthur Montgomery's disappearance. Approaching quickly, Taryn Winslow held out her hand for John to shake. Her grip was firm and dry.

"Hello, Agent Haskins. I thought I'd seen the last of you." John shrugged his shoulders noncommittally. "Sorry about the lighting down here, budget cuts have been rough on us this year and the first thing to be cut back on is always maintenance. So, as a result, I have to put up with these conditions." She swept a thin arm upwards.

"Thank you for letting me see you again, Doctor Winslow. I hope I'm not interrupting anything." John glanced back towards the hallway from which the doctor had emerged.

"Oh, no, not at all. It seems the hospital is a very popular place these days. Usually we have people begging to be let out. But this week we've been opening our doors to a variety of people. What can I do for you?" Dr. Winslow looked up into John's face with keen interest.

"Well, unfortunately I bring no news regarding Doctor Montgomery." The muscles in Taryn's face slackened when she heard this. She was visibly disappointed.

"I was hoping you wouldn't say that but had a strong feeling that you would. I'm beginning to wonder if he's ever going to reappear. Alive or dead."

"Frankly, so am I. That's why I came to see you again. I just wanted to go over everything we've already talked about and ask you a few more questions. I've seen the pain Doctor Montgomery's disappearance has caused amongst his friends, family, and colleagues and I can't help but think there must be something more that I can do."

"I'm sure you've done everything in your power and I'm not sure if talking to me again is going to accomplish much but if you think it will help I'm perfectly willing to do so."

"I appreciate that. One of the reasons I wanted to talk to you again is because I just recently found out, six months late via the *San Francisco Globe*, of Doctor Montgomery's strong affiliation with the Meadowvale Clinic. An article appeared this morning on the front page about the Clinic. Have you seen it?"

"Yes, isn't that tragic. We've been exceedingly fortunate here at the hospital. We've been here since the turn of the century and despite numerous attempts, only a few patients have ever committed suicide while here. The most recent was five years ago. I certainly hope the incident doesn't negatively affect the Clinic."

"I'm not sure what it will do for the Clinic, but the incident has given me a new lead to pursue and made me think of a few questions I'd like to ask of you."

"Such as?"

"How involved with the Meadowvale Clinic was Doctor Montgomery?"

"Very. He, Doctor Flemming, and Doctor Foley were going to run and administer it together. All three of them were extremely gifted intellectually and all tireless workers. Unfortunately, Arthur didn't even get to see the Clinic open. As you know, he disappeared not soon after construction began on it."

"Would you know if he and the other two doctors, Flemming and Foley had any disagreements about anything, the Clinic in particular?"

"Not to my knowledge, but then again I wasn't around them all the time. They stayed late many lights working on their research. Those three men have done more for the field of dissociative disorders…" She left the sentence hang. "They tended to focus on dissociative identity disorder more than the rest but that's only because it's the most difficult to properly diagnose and treat. They were constantly challenging themselves. Pushing themselves to the limit."

"Wasn't there another doctor that worked here that was affiliated with the Clinic?"

"Oh, Doctor Sanford? He was here for eight years but he preferred working with schizophrenics and border-line personalities. It wasn't until Doctor Foley came that Doctor Sanford showed an interest in dissociative disorders."

"When did Doctor Foley come to this hospital?"

"I think it was about four years ago, maybe five. I'm not positive but I can check for you later and find out for sure. He and Doctor Flemming went to medical school together. It was actually Doctor Flemming who convinced Doctor Foley to leave his practice in New York."

"He moved from a private practice to a post at a state psychiatric hospital?"

"I thought it was kind of a bad career move as well, but hey, look where he is now. It obviously worked out for him."

"Do the doctors at the Clinic make a lot of money?"

"I couldn't give you numbers but they certainly make more than they would have had they stayed on here."

"Do you think somehow Doctor Montgomery might have threatened the creation of the Clinic in any way?"

"Definitely not. What are you suggesting?"

"I'm not suggesting anything, I'm just trying to figure out why someone would kidnap him."

"It sounds like you're trying to say one of the other doctors might have had something to do with his disappearance."

"I assure you that that's not what I meant. All I'm trying to do is find out why someone would want Arthur Montgomery removed. It obviously wasn't for ransom, there have been no further demands since the first note. I just want to find out what his relationship was with the other doctors. Those involved with the Meadowvale Clinic in particular."

"As far as I know his relationship with the other doctors was strictly professional. I don't think looking into his professional past is going to help you. I think you should look into his personal history. You know for things like jilted lovers or unpaid debts." Dr. Winslow half-turned glancing toward the hall which led back upstairs. A stolen peek at her watch indicated to John that the conversation was over.

"Well, thank you very much for talking with me again, Doctor Winslow. It's much appreciated." John shook her hand once more. Her grip felt distant and John felt as if she had already left despite the physical contact.

John had no intention of looking into Arthur Montgomery's personal life again. The first time he had checked, the only skeletons he had found in Montgomery's closet were a few parking tickets and an overdue library book. It was overdue by three years, but John doubted that was justification for kidnapping or murder. John was left alone in the recesses of the hospital's basement. The sound of a filing cabinet drawer slamming shut further in the basement reminded him that he had more work to do back at his own office.

Running his fingers absently along the cinder-block walls, John heard footsteps behind him. A tall, dark-haired man rushed towards him. His nose was buried in a sheaf of papers and his lips moved as he read their contents silently to himself. John was barely able to move out his way. A briefcase swung dangerously close to his right knee.

"Oops, terribly sorry," the man apologized, "I didn't realize anyone else was down here." John muttered something to the effect that it was no problem and kept on his way. The other man had already finished climbing the steps when John reached the stairwell entrance. John waved to the groundskeeper again as he pulled away from the hospital disappointed that he hadn't turned up anything new. Not only that but he didn't think Dr. Winslow would greet him with open arms again.

Chapter 28

Ed rushed out of the psychiatric hospital with a dozen questions on his mind. He had been so deeply involved in reading the notes he had taken from the files he had been leafing through that he had almost collided into some guy with a dark trenchcoat in the basement. It had startled him quite a bit actually.

Now, sitting behind the wheel of his truck, Ed left the hospital grounds and turned right on Potrero Avenue with the intention of seeing Rachel at the Meadowvale Clinic. He wanted to ask her a few questions about what he had just read, and what he had just heard.

Unbeknownst to Dr. Winslow and the man she had been talking to, Ed had overheard snippets of their conversation. He hadn't eavesdropped intentionally, but he couldn't help but overhear them talking while he punched numbers into his calculator in the next room.

Ed wanted to know who Dr. Montgomery was.

Contrary to what he had originally thought of this assignment, working on the Meadowvale portfolio once again was far from uninteresting. Although the first trip to the San Francisco Psychiatric Hospital the day before had been rather tedious, today's excursion had proved quite rewarding in terms of the amount of work he had accomplished and what he had learned.

Looking at the truck's digital clock, Ed saw that it was approaching six o'clock. He had spent over four hours in the psychiatric hospital poring over photocopied material. Yesterday, he was able to gather the information he needed from the computer but today the computers were down. A virus, Dr. Winslow told him. As a result, Ed was forced, with the approval of Dr. Winslow, to go over photocopies of the original files' stat sheets which provided basic information on each patient but not the patients' names. Unfortunately he wasn't allowed to read the actual files, but having read the pertinent sections of the DSM IV and the pamphlets Rachel had given him, Ed could imagine to some degree what the patients were going through. Although he was sure that no one could truly appreciate what they lived with every day. Not even those who treated them.

Having looked at hundreds of stat sheets, both on the computer and photocopies, all on different patients, treated by different doctors and at different times, spanning a time period of roughly nine years, Ed felt that he had enough statistics and information to begin forecasting. He just had a few questions to ask Rachel and then he could start number crunching. Playing with the numbers would be the longest and most tedious part of the entire process; he wasn't looking forward to it. He was however, looking forward to seeing Rachel again.

There were a couple of things Ed had found that he didn't entirely understand, and it was because of these things that he wanted to talk to Rachel. Not that he needed a reason to want to see her again.

Weaving in and out of rush-hour traffic, Ed pushed a *Def Lepard* CD into the requisite slot in his dashboard and put all things psychiatric out of his mind. The road was meant for driving and listening to tunes. He slammed on the brakes momentarily as a Lexus careened out in front of him, its driver obviously too impatient to wait for traffic to thin to turn the corner, and continued on his way in too good a mood to let the reckless behavior of others spoil his day.

Chapter 29

▼

Not paying attention, and perhaps driving a little too quickly, Walter Flemming narrowly avoided being sideswiped by a half-ton pickup truck. Fortunately the driver had braked and allowed Walter just enough space to squeak by without damaging the paint job on his two year old Lexus.

His driving reflected the inner turmoil of his mind. He had left the Clinic earlier than usual this evening to sort out his thoughts. He also had plans for the evening. He was still somewhat concerned about the Jim Wells incident although he had no real reason to be. He knew it would be declared a suicide by the medical examiner and that would be that. Just like five years ago. No one had ever suspected that Sanford's patient Emily Jenkins was anything but the victim of her own internal struggles.

The only individual he had to concern himself with now was Rachel Miller. He had resented her right from the first time he met her. He especially resented the fact that Foley had hired her without consulting him. He couldn't deny that she was well qualified for the job, but she was too ambitious and headstrong. Flemming imagined that she had firm scruples and was ethical in all aspects of her life. Not the type who would be easily convinced that what he, Foley, and Sanford were doing was morally acceptable. That could always change however. Leopards might never change their spots but people certainly re-evaluated their beliefs when vast sums of money were at stake. Anyone could be bought. Sanford had been. Unfortunately, he still went on about such abstract concepts as implications and ramifications, and consequences. But Flemming knew he wouldn't take it any further. Not like Montgomery had intended to.

Despite Sanford's hypochondrial paranoia, Flemming wondered briefly if Foley too was getting a little worried. The last thing he needed now was for everyone around him to fall apart. He knew he didn't really have to worry about Sanford. All he had to do if Sanford expressed doubt again was remind him of the tragic fate of Arthur Montgomery. It seemed to work in the past and he couldn't imagine why it wouldn't keep on working. Sanford was in as deep as the rest of them and therefore had no way out. That is unless Flemming granted him escape but that was unlikely. Despite his misgivings, Sanford was invaluable to the project, particularly to the second phase due to his skill in hypnosis and his extensive knowledge of the properties of sodium amytal and sodium brevital.

Along the same lines, Flemming wondered how Sanford's new patient was coming along. He had not met her yet, but Sanford had assured him that she would make the perfect subject: young, insecure, easily influenced, and, given the right conditions, highly susceptible to suggestion.

It was too bad that Jim Wells had not worked out. Flemming had had great things in store for him. It was also rather unfortunate that he had no idea why the man had chosen to kill himself. He wondered if had undergone too many electro-shock treatments. Or perhaps not enough? Like so many other branches of science, working with the human mind was often a game of trial and error. In this case however, the trials cost nothing but time and effort, and the errors cost less. Flemming held little regard for the value of another human's life. That had been made sufficiently clear to him when he had disposed of his friend and colleague Arthur Montgomery.

He had always wondered if he had it in him to kill another person. Death had always fascinated him. Few people seemed to truly grasp the concept of death. For if they did, the number of suicides would radically decline as would the astronomical number of murders which took place each year all over the world. Death was forever. Not being a religious man, Flemming believed that there was nothing after death. How could people honestly believe that there was something better awaiting them? When you die, there is no more. People often claimed that they just couldn't accept that there was nothing afterwards. How soon they forget however that there was nothing beforehand either.

Flemming had had no qualms about putting an early and unnatural end to Montgomery's life. It was one of the few memories in his life that he recalled quite vividly. The rush had lasted for days. He had even experienced to a certain degree what authorities on the subject call post-homicidal depression, the feeling of emptiness serial killers often get once they have killed their victim and the thrill of killing dissipates. It's their drive to combat this depression that leads them to kill again and again. He could even recall what the weather had been like that Monday morning...

It was a crisp, cool morning. The warm rays from the sun quickly evaporated the dew that had formed overnight. Despite its brilliance however, the sun failed to warm the air. The lack of cloud cover revealed a cerulean blue sky and prevented the sun's heat from being held within the atmosphere. Traffic was unusually light for a Monday morning and Flemming found himself at work earlier than usual.

He pulled his car into his reserved spot located behind the San Francisco Psychiatric Hospital within seconds of Arthur Montgomery's doing the same. Flemming waved across the passenger side of his car. The two doctors exchanged good mornings once they had each stepped out of their vehicles.

"What's your schedule like this morning, Walter?" Arthur asked.

"Busy, but not overly so. What's on your mind?"

"I was wondering if you felt like making a run up to the Clinic and check on their progress."

"And I thought I was the impatient one."

"You can't blame me for wanting to take a peek."

Flemming smiled. "You're right on that count."

"I can't believe it's going to be done in less than six months. I can hardly wait to move in and get started."

"Neither can I. Should we bother letting them know inside where we're going?"

"I don't see why. We shouldn't be more than an hour. If need be we'll tell them traffic was bad."

"I don't know if they'll buy that. I only live fifteen minutes away."

"I'm sure you can come up with something," Arthur assured him. "We'll take your car. I don't have a leather interior," Arthur gestured to his Corolla.

With Flemming at the wheel and Arthur strapped in beside him, the two doctors left the hospital. No one saw them together in the parking lot and no one saw them leave. It was seven fifty-eight a.m.

The skeletal framework of the Meadowvale Clinic could be seen from the highway. Thick red iron I-Beams made up the majority of what could be seen. Several large earth moving vehicles were visible as well; dumptrucks, loaders, excavators, and a cement mixer. They sat motionless, unoccupied. The construction crew started at nine o'clock in the morning and worked ten to twelve hour days.

Flemming drove his car carefully up a muddy, unfinished drive. The ground made a sound like slowly tearing cardboard under the weight of the car. He parked between two portable trailers which served as offices and changerooms for the foremen and workers. Both men stepped out into the cool air and looked up at the hollow structure. Neither said a word for at least a full minute. They walked through the structure looking up through its welded beams. Arthur was picturing himself seated in his own private office up on the sixth floor. Flemming looked up as well but his mind was elsewhere. The previous evening he and Foley had decided to tell Arthur what they had been doing over the past four years and ask him to join them. Neither of them had anticipated Arthur's reaction when Flemming told him the next morning.

Like a paper cut, Arthur's response was sharp and intensely painful.

"You've been doing what?" he shouted into the still air. "How dare the two of you. How could you even come up with such a despicable plan?"

"Now, Arthur, calm down and listen to me. Hear me out. I think you'll come to appreciate what we're doing."

"Appreciate what you're doing? You're violating every ethical and moral principle known to the profession. I simply cannot believe what you're doing. I especially can't believe Grant is involved. He must be…"

"Carl is too." Flemming interrupted him.

"Sanford's in on this as well? Has the whole world gone crazy or is this the most depraved thing I've ever heard?"

"Arthur, I think you should at least listen to what I have to say. I think you might even want to join us once you know more."

"I don't want to know more and I certainly have no intention of joining you. The only thing I'm going to do is drive right back to that hospital, inform them of what you and your two psychotic colleagues are up to and then put in a call to the APA." Arthur pushed Flemming rudely aside as he walked past him and headed back for the Lexus.

Flemming clenched his fists and ran after him.

Grabbing his shoulder, Flemming spun Arthur around.

"Let go of me, you monster! You're worse than Victor Frankenstein," Arthur shouted, "And Carl and Grant are your Igors. Thoughtless minions doing your bidding no matter how depraved the request. And like Victor Frankenstein your experiments will bring you down. I'll make sure of that. Stay away from me!" Arthur yelled, lashing out blindly in rage. His face was livid and his thinning hair flew up in disarray. At that moment it was he who looked like the quintessential mad scientist.

"Arthur I think you should reconsider."

"Reconsider what? My value system? That little thing called the law? All society's morals and ethics? What? What should I reconsider?"

"Why don't we go talk with Grant and Carl. They'll convince you."

"I don't want to be convinced. The only people I'm talking with are the authorities. Now give me your keys." He stuck out his hand. It was trembling.

"I can't do that, Arthur."

"Oh no?" Arthur lunged. Flemming raised his hands in defense but was slammed hard against the hood of his car. His skull made contact with the hood's smooth surface and his teeth rattled in his head. Arthur Montgomery was a whirling dervish on top of him. Arms flailed, legs kicked, he even tried to bite him.

Flemming managed to pull up one of his legs and slide it between himself and his attacker. With a tremendous amount of effort, he was able to shove Arthur back, giving himself time to rub the back of his head and get back on his feet.

Stumbling on the uneven terrain behind him, Arthur quickly regained his balance and pressed on with his assault. Flemming sidestepped out of the way this time. Sticking his leg out and using Arthur's momentum against him, Flemming threw him roughly to the ground. It was a simple but effective move.

Arthur clawed at the ground around him. His breathing was labored. A savage look crossed his face. His searching hands came upon a cylindrical object. Raising the two foot length of lead pipe in his right hand, Arthur pushed himself up with his left.

His left hand out in front of him, fingers curling like one hand clapping, Arthur shouted "Give me the Goddamn keys or I swear to God I'll bash your head in! If you think I'm bluffing try me."

Flemming knew he wasn't bluffing but he also knew that he couldn't hand over his car keys. To do so would end not only his career and land him in jail but would do the same to Foley and Sanford as well. Flemming did what anyone in his situation would have done.

He ran.

The unfinished Clinic provided few hiding spots but was suitable for dodging pursuers. Arthur raced after him screaming, referring obscenely to both his origins and personal habits.

Leaping over tools and unused construction material; steel girders, boxes of rivets and bolts, spools of high tensile wire, and rusty oil drums used as garbage bins, Flemming realized he couldn't keep on avoiding Arthur indefinitely.

Swinging the pipe like a caveman on PCP, Arthur continued the pursuit. Flemming looked up and realized his only chance of escape might lay skyward.

There was no way he could make it back to his car and Arthur would catch him eventually if they kept running around in circles. At least if he could climb his way to safety, he could wait perched up on the girders for the construction crew to arrive and come to his rescue. The only drawback to that was that Arthur would then be free to do whatever he pleased. Including telling the APA what was happening within the bowels of the San Francisco Psychiatric Hospital. Against his better judgment, Flemming found a girder with an aluminum extension ladder leaning against it and began climbing up.

One of the ladder's legs shifted and sunk an inch or two into the ground below causing the entire ladder to shift a foot to the left just as Flemming neared the top. Reaching up for the steel girder, he was able to steady himself and prevent the ladder from sliding any further to the side. He had barely pulled himself up onto the beam when Arthur began climbing the ladder himself. The man was in a rage.

Looking down at his colleague and regretting what he was about to do, Flemming waited until Arthur reached the tenth rung, about three-quarters of the way up and pushed the ladder backwards with Arthur on it.

The ladder paused for a moment as it came to be perpendicular to the ground and in slow motion continued on its trajectory. Arthur screamed as he realized what was happening and actually climbed two more rungs even as the ladder fell backwards. Flemming watched helpless as both Arthur and the ladder hit the ground.

Arthur released his grip moments before he made contact with the ground. The ladder slammed into him with a hollow ring, each rung hitting him individually yet all at once. Flemming cringed. He looked for a way to get down but couldn't see one. He looked at his watch. It was eight-thirty-seven. The first members of the construction crew would be arriving shortly.

Flemming got down onto his hands and knees and in super slow motion, lowered himself over the edge of the girder. It was at least twelve feet to the ground.

His left leg dangled over the edge and he carefully brought his right leg down after it. The girder dug into his solar plexus as his forearms and chest took up all of the pressure. He grasped the edge of the girder with sweat soaked hands and lost his grip. Clawing desperately at the girder, Flemming fell to the ground rather ungracefully.

When he hit the surface below him, he heard a crunch and a snap. The force of the fall was unevenly distributed across his back and legs. He had fallen directly onto the ladder. After assuring himself that it wasn't his body that had snapped and crunched, he rolled himself off of the ladder and brushed himself off.

He looked at his fallen comrade upon whom he had fallen. The ladder remained on top of him pinning him down. In his right hand, seized by a cadaveric spasm, was the heavy lead pipe. Also known as the Death Grip, the muscles in Arthur's hands had tightened involuntarily. His left arm protruded between two rungs at an unnatural angle. That must have been what made the snapping sound when Flemming fell. What had made the crunching sound became immediately apparent as well.

What remained of Arthur's skull lay beyond recognition underneath one of the rungs. Supported by a stray steel girder, Arthur's head had been the last part of his body that hit the ground. The ladder must have then fallen upon him causing further damage to his head. One of the rungs rested where his nose normally would have been. Finally, with Flemming falling on top of the ladder, and Arthur's head being higher than the rest of his body due to the girder underneath it, the added sudden impact had surely been the straw that broke the camel's back. Or in this case Arthur's face.

Flemming gasped at the gruesome sight before him. Barely unaware of his own actions, Flemming's instincts for survival kicked in. He returned the ladder to its upright position and dragged Arthur's limp body towards one of the many empty oil drums. He found one that wasn't full and tipped it over to empty its contents.

Looking at his watch, Flemming noticed it was eight-forty-three.

Sliding his arms under Arthur's armpits, Flemming could just manage to dump the deceased doctor into the barrel head first. He attempted to remove the pipe from Arthur's grip but his hand was like a vise so Flemming left it. He pushed Arthur's legs in as well and then filled the drum to the top with the garbage he had tipped out. He was breathing hard and sweating.

A truck's engine broke the morning silence. Flemming looked up and saw a beat up GMC pick-up truck ambling up the drive approaching his car. He was just about to walk out but saw the blood on his coat. The red juice of life and pieces of Arthur's brain were smeared into his jacket. Quickly tearing it off and wiping his hands clean on it, he stuffed his four-hundred dollar jacket down into the depths of the drum. Arthur didn't mind.

Fortunately no other traces of blood could be seen upon his person. Flemming composed himself and walked out towards his car.

"Hey, what are you doing here?" A hardy, unshaven giant of a man yelled across the site as he climbed out of his truck and saw Flemming walking towards him.

"Oh, sorry, Doctor Flemming, I didn't know it was you." The burly man apologized when he recognized the doctor coming closer.

"I just wanted to see how things were coming," Flemming said hoping his voice didn't betray the fear that was building up inside of him.

"Great so far," the other man exclaimed oblivious to what Flemming was going through. "We're a week ahead of schedule and should be able to keep it that way if not get further ahead."

"Good to hear that. I'll leave you to your work."

"Oh, we won't be here long. We're just pouring the foundation for the auditorium and then packing up for the day. I'm giving the guys a half holiday as a kind of reward."

"Well that's awfully nice of you." Flemming grew excited at the prospect that he would be able to return later in the day to do something with Arthur's mangled corpse. "So there won't be anyone around after noon?"

"That's right, we're just pouring the concrete and getting out of here."

"I wish I could have a half day sometime."

"Don't we all."

After rushing home to change into a fresh set of clothes, Flemming drove into work and spent the morning seeing patients and telling the hospital's staff that, no, he did not know where Dr. Montgomery was. He tried not to think of his colleague crumpled inside the oil drum as he kept himself busy so that the day would go by faster.

Waiting until one o'clock to give the construction crew extra time to leave, Flemming jumped into his Lexus under the pretense of going to lunch. He headed straight for the unbuilt Clinic. When he arrived, the oil drum was no longer where he had left it.

Flemming looked around frantically. He was overcome with a wave of relief when he saw that all of the drums had been rounded up and deposited side by side. He had no time to waste. He didn't know if a truck was on its way right now to pick them up.

Rooting through each one, he finally came across the drum with the morbid contents. He looked around. No one else was in sight. That in itself was good but it didn't help him any. Although he knew he had to get rid of the body, he never had any thoughts on how to do so. He had driven to the Clinic like a Nascar driver. Unfortunately he had thought like one as well and thus had no plan when he arrived.

Surveying the grounds again, a thought struck him. A plan was hatched.

He dumped Arthur's body and his own blood and brain stained coat onto the ground. Dirt, dust, and bits and pieces of building materials had collected in the concave surface of Arthur's head. Flemming threw his coat over top of the mangled countenance careful not to get any more blood on him and looked away.

Dragging the body through the dirt was not as easy as it looked on TV and in the movies. It took Flemming a full five minutes to haul Arthur's corpse to the edge of what would, in less than half a year, be the auditorium.

Flemming peered over the edge of a three foot high retaining wall. The freshly poured cement was still wet. He heaved Arthur's body up onto the narrow wall and unceremoniously dumped him in. The body sunk slowly, taking Flemming's blood-soaked coat with it as it did so.

Once it had completely submerged, Flemming found a broom and pushed the body down even further ensuring that it would not be discovered. He wiped off the broom handle on a trowel he picked up and quickly smoothed out the surface of the wet cement. It didn't look very smooth.

Flemming played with the cement some more but it refused to be shaped as he wanted it to be. He developed a new respect for masonists. He pitched the trowel aside after doing what he could and stuck his index finger into the mix. He outlined a large, crude heart and wrote in it "Stanley loves Jeanine". He traced the day's date underneath and wrote beside it "Chris Was Here." He then scraped the cement off his finger on a rag he found nearby. Hopefully when the crew came in the next morning, they would assume some kids had been poking around, spotted the wet cement and couldn't resist. The workers would smooth out the surface or perhaps even leave it.

Flemming got back into his car, drove to the psychiatric hospital, prepared the bogus ransom note he would drop off in the mail later that day and feigned ignorance the rest of the day.

He had committed the perfect crime.

Flemming smiled as he recalled the detailed memory. Turning off Van Ness Avenue, he drove up Sacramento Street for several blocks until he reached a small side street which ended in a court. Only seven houses were situated within the court. The front lawn of each home stretched on for at least forty yards from front door to curb. There were no sidewalks. In the center of the court was a well-tended garden and an old fashioned street lamp planted in the middle. A single viny plant dangled from a macramé basket which hung loosely from the lamp.

Flemming drove halfway around the garden and pulled up to his house, an ornate two-story affair. Reddish-brown bricks made up the outside of the home framed by dark green eaves, soffits, and trim. The window frames and front door were of the same shade of green. A narrow walkway made up of dusty rose pink and light gray stones led to three wide curving steps which in turn led to the front door. Black iron hand railings curved with the steps.

With a push of a button, one of three garage doors smoothly and silently rose to an open position. Flemming eased the luxury car up the inclined interlocking brick driveway and parked the vehicle beside a dusty land rover. The garage door descended automatically as he got out of the Lexus and a piercing beep proved the car was now secure.

Punching a five-numbered code into the pad of numbers located to the right of the door which led into his house, Flemming stepped inside. He loosened his tie, and removed his shoes with his toes. The interior of the house was austere and sterile just like the facilities he was used to working in. Decorations were sparse, while the parsimonious furniture was utilitarian in nature.

Flemming tossed his jacket onto a leather bench near the front door and headed for the phone in the kitchen to check his messages. There was only one. It was from Tanya, the red headed pyschology student from Berkeley, to remind him they were meeting at eight that evening for dinner at the Acquarello, a romantic little Italian restaurant on Sacramento Street.

Loosening his tie, he headed for his study. He would have to brush up on his Freudian terminology.

Chapter 30

▼

Ed found the parking lot at the Meadowvale Clinic practically deserted. Aside from a large white van, Rachel's VW Rabbit, and his own truck, Ed surveyed only five other vehicles, presumably those of the janitorial staff and the attendants on the night shift. Ed pulled up beside Rachel's car in a reserved spot, confident that Dr. Tanner wouldn't be returning within the next half an hour.

The sun hung low and bright on the horizon casting a golden hue on the Clinic. Ed had to shield his eyes as he walked towards the front entrance.

Rachel was standing at her bookcase running a finger along the spines of her reference books when Ed found her in her office.

"Exciting day in the belly of the beast?" she asked, referring to the catacomb-like basement of the psychiatric hospital.

"Ha, Ha. *Tres Drole*. Actually, I got a lot of work done and as I thought I might, I do have a number of questions for you."

"Quick and easy questions or questions that may require long and complex answers?"

"A little of both and some I'm not so sure."

"All right, why don't you give me a few minutes to finish up here and then we'll go grab something to eat. We might as well feed ourselves. I'm starving."

Ed rubbed his stomach in agreement. "I'll wait for you downstairs. Hey, do you know if Doctor Foley is in?" he asked.

"I think he is. His secretary probably won't be though, so if the door to the outer office is closed just walk in and knock on the inner office door."

"Okay, if I'm not downstairs then I'll be with him, I just want to let him know how things are coming."

The door to Grant Foley's outer office was ajar so Ed let himself in. He knocked three times on the inner office door and waited. It swung open within seconds.

"Mister Morgan," Foley seemed genuinely pleased, "what a pleasant surprise. Come in, come in." He ushered Ed into his office and pointed to a seat for him to take.

"So how are things coming along?" he asked sitting at his desk.

"Just great Doctor Foley. That's actually why I dropped by. Rachel and I are going to talk about some questions I have over dinner but I wanted to see you before we left."

Foley paused before answering; he wondered if he should comment on Ed's dinner plans and the fact that he was on a first name basis with Rachel. Something in the back of his mind told him not to so he let it pass. "And what did you want to see me about?" he asked instead.

"Well, as you know, I've been going over old data at the San Francisco Psychiatric Hospital and I've come across something which I'm afraid I don't understand. That in itself isn't surprising given my limited knowledge of all things psychiatric, but I was wondering if you could help me out?"

"Of course, of course. Now what is it you found?"

"I found several of a Doctor Sanford's statistics, all on patients being treated primarily for dissociative identity disorder dating back five years or so." Foley sat up straight. Ed had his complete attention.

"Anyway," Ed continued, "what I found was that on each one, Doctor Sanford wrote beside the number of personalities two numbers separated by a backslash. Now, does that mean the patient was originally thought to have the first number of personalities but then later discovered to have the second number? It doesn't make a difference to my work, but I was curious what the numbers meant."

"I couldn't speak on Doctor Sanford's behalf, but as I'm sure you're aware, everybody has their unique way of doing things. I'm afraid only Doctor Sanford could tell you why he wrote down two numbers. Your hypothesis seems as reasonable as any. And as you say, if it doesn't apply to your work, it doesn't really matter, does it?"

"I suppose not," Ed said. He decided to let the matter drop. The man across from him seemed agitated and gave the distinct impression that he did not want to talk about it anymore. Ed changed the subject.

"One thing I have noticed is that psychiatrists have some of the most organized records I've ever encountered." Dr. Foley seemed visibly relieved when he realized Ed was not going to pursue the numbers issue any further. "The data base you have here and the one they have at the psychiatric hospital are excellent. I'll tell you, it's made my job a lot easier."

"So are you almost done then?" Foley asked.

"Almost. I just want to go back to the psychiatric hospital one or two more times to make sure I have everything I need. Aside from that, all I have left to do is a lot of data crunching and comparative analysis. That should take a week or so."

"Well, I'm glad everything's coming along so well," Foley stood up and started walking around his desk, "I don't want to keep you from dinner, I myself have to get home soon, too. My wife and I are celebrating our anniversary this evening."

"Really? Congratulations. I hope you have a great night. I'll keep you posted on my progress. 'Bye Doctor Foley."

"Good-bye Ed, and thanks."

Grant wondered what his wife would think if she knew what he, Carl, and Walter were doing at the Clinic. She would no doubt strongly object but what she didn't know couldn't possibly do her harm. Besides, the money was good and she had never complained about that. Grant wanted to give her anything and everything she wanted.

When Walter Flemming had called him up out of the blue five years ago and asked him if he wanted to quit his lucrative private practice and come work with him at a State psychiatric hospital, Grant had almost laughed out loud and hung up the phone. It wasn't until Walter had started discussing the amounts of money to be made that Grant began seriously considering the move. The money was practically non-existent for the first two years after Grant and Gillian moved from New York to San Francisco, and it could hardly compare to what he had been earning as a private practitioner.

Once he, Walter, and Carl had the first stage of their project underway however, the amount of money involved looked more promising. With the help of Arthur Montgomery, he and Walter had also initiated the development of the Meadowvale Clinic, which unbeknownst to Montgomery, would serve as a base of operations for stage two and three of the project. Grant sometimes wondered whatever happened between Arthur Montgomery and Walter that morning six months ago but he wasn't that inclined to find out. The less he knew the better. The last thing he wanted to be was an accessory to murder. Grant was certain that that had been Arthur's fate but again, didn't see the need to find out. If

Arthur had threatened the project as Walter said he had, then it was better that he was out of the picture.

Why was he risking everything? His career, his reputation, his family. He supposed it was for the money. He knew Walter was doing it primarily for the prestige, money being his secondary purpose. He didn't know why exactly Carl was doing it. He knew that Carl sometimes feared Walter, but he wondered if that was enough to keep him in the thick of things. Grant himself had plans to quit the project in five or six years once he had made enough money to provide his family with the lifestyle they deserved. By that time, they should be able to find another doctor willing to join their staff and take over his work with the project. Although he had mentioned it in passing to Walter earlier in the week, Grant didn't want Rachel getting involved in what they were doing.

He had hired Rachel on because she reminded him of himself in his youth; bright, full of potential, idealistic, eager to take on the world. Now he wondered where that former self had gone. He felt that he was still the same man, but somehow, something fundamental had changed about him. He couldn't put his finger on it, but he suspected that age and a growing indifference had something to with it. The last thing he wanted was the same thing happening to Rachel.

Foley closed the door to his office and stared at the pictures on the back of his door. Their random simplicity was very soothing. Deep in thought, Foley sighed aloud and absently scratched his temple. He lit his pipe and then made three phone calls. The first was to the Fleur De Lys restaurant on Sutter Street. He informed the Maitre'd that he and his wife would be about an hour later than originally planned. The second was to his wife. He told her he had to stay at the Clinic for at least another hour. She was not impressed, but like most doctors' spouses, she was not surprised either. The third, and longest call was to Walter Flemming. He answered after three tries. He had been in the shower. They talked for just over thirty minutes.

Both agreed on what had to be done.

Chapter 31

▼

Rachel gave Ed directions to the restaurant she suggested they go to and told him she would meet him there.

It was the same restaurant that Rachel had ordered from countless times. Family owned and operated, the small Chinese restaurant turned over a brisk business and served a steady, loyal clientele. Inside, hushed pink walls met with a red ceiling and dark red and green carpets. Two dozen tables, all covered with tablecloths the same shade of red as the ceiling and carpet, took up most of the floor space. Four well-stocked banquet tables and bain maries lined an entire wall overlooked by Chinese paintings and a quaint Chinese scrolled calendar. All the tables were set but few were occupied. A local radio station played a muffled Alanis Morrisette song.

The smell of fried rice and chicken hung thickly in the air. Rachel found a table for the two of them off to one wall next to a forty-gallon aquarium. Hungry bottom-eaters roamed the uneven, artificial terrain. Numerous giant goldfish swam around lethargically. Somewhat alarmed, Ed noticed one of them had no eyes. The glow from the tank's light augmented that which came from the dim lights sunken into the ceiling.

The restaurant was owned by a third generation Chinese couple, Mr. and Mrs. Liu. Rachel had come to know them quite well over the past few years and tried to bring them as much business as she could. She herself was one of their steady and loyal customers.

It was Mrs. Liu who emerged from the kitchen, pen and pad in hand ready to take their order. With hunched shoulders and a fragile appearance, the casual observer might describe her as timid, perhaps even weak, but she was neither. A soft voice and pleasing warm countenance greeted Ed and Rachel. Although heavily accented, she spoke superb English. Standing between the two of them, Mrs. Liu spoke.

"Hello, Rachel. I was wondering when you would come in again. I see you brought a friend." She smiled at Ed.

"This is my friend Ed Morgan, Missus Liu. Ed, Missus Liu." The two exchanged a nod.

"What would you like?" Mrs. Liu asked.

"I think we'll take the buffet," Rachel looked across the table at Ed, "if that's all right with you? They have an excellent selection."

"That's fine with me. Oh, and a Dr. Pepper please," Ed said.

"Okay, just wave if you need anything." Mrs. Liu tucked her pen and pad into a large pocket and went back to the kitchen.

Just as Ed and Rachel stood for the buffet, Bryan, the delivery boy, walked into the restaurant with an empty delivery bag. He spotted Rachel and smiled and waved, but a look of disappointment, maybe jealousy, swept across his face as he saw Ed. He stepped through a set of swinging doors into the kitchen without a word. Rachel had seen the look on his face and was amused to note that she felt guilty. Ed had not noticed the silent interaction. His gaze was intent on the buffet.

The row of bain maries boasted a wide assortment of Chinese fare. Shrimp fried rice, chicken fried rice, vegetable fried rice, and plain fried rice took up half of one table. A variety of seafood dishes crowded for room, along with deep silver shaving dishes of chow mein, chop suey, won ton soup, foo yung, honey garlic ribs, moo goo guy pan, and chicken balls. Two huge pans at the far end of the tables held plum sauce and sweet and sour sauce. For dessert there were fortune cookies and a bowl full of lichee nuts. Rachel filled her plate sparingly with the intention of making a second trip. Ed loaded his plate up to the outer edges intent on getting his money's worth.

"So are you buying?" Ed asked as he sat down, setting his stacked plate down in front of him.

"I wish. I can barely afford to pay for my own meal never mind for both of ours." Rachel said.

"What are you talking about?" Ed asked jokingly. "You're a doctor, aren't you raking in the big bucks?"

"Once I pay back my student loans and finish paying for my car, then, maybe I'll have enough to buy dinner for two. As it stands right now, I'm a poor doctor."

"A poor doctor? Isn't that an oxymoron?"

"As much as an honest salesman is."

"What about Army intelligence?"

"Or postal service," Rachel said.

"Airline food."

"Peace force."

"Passive aggression."

"Clearly misunderstood."

"Act naturally."

"Alone together."

"Pretty ugly."

"Exact estimate."

"Microsoft Works."

"Soft rock."

"Rap music."

"Stop, I've run out, I can't think of any more," Rachel almost fell off her chair laughing.

"A psychiatrist who can't think? Isn't that…"

"Good grief," Rachel said and they both doubled over in laughter. The small restaurant's other patrons looked over at Ed and Rachel.

Once they had finally composed themselves they began eating.

"So how did you get into insurance anyway, Ed?" Rachel asked between bites of her shrimp fried rice.

"It seemed like a fun thing to do at the time."

"No, seriously."

"I guess I like the sales aspect of it. I'm comfortable with people and I enjoy providing them with something that can make a difference in their lives. I would hate to have to sell an inferior product. I don't think I would have it in me to lie about something just to sell it. That's why I like selling insurance, I've seen how much people appreciate it. Also, as an insurance agent, I make commission on my sales which means I only get paid what I'm worth. The harder I work, the more money I make and vice-versa. I think all jobs should be set up that way. And that in a nutshell, is why I became an insurance agent. Also I had no idea what I wanted to do with my life after university." Ed then told Rachel of his first encounter with Hal Rosenberg and how he won fifty dollars on a bet while Rachel ate. "How about you Doctor Miller, what made you want to go into psychiatry?"

"No reason in particular," Rachel said, pushing her food around her plate absently, "I just always found the field interesting and I too wanted to make a difference. You know how idealistic people can be in their youth. I thought if I became a psychiatrist I would be able to see the fruits of my labors and know that I was truly helping people who needed help." Rachel hoped her answer would satisfy Ed, she felt awful avoiding the truth but she didn't want to reveal her true motivation for going into psychiatry. Someday she might tell him, but not here and not now. Fortunately he seemed to accept her explanation without question and asked her another, less personal, question.

"So who is this Doctor Montgomery I keep hearing about?"

"Where did you hear that name?" Rachel asked surprised.

"I overheard some people talking about him today at the psychiatric hospital and noticed the auditorium at Meadowvale was named after him, and I thought I read his name in the newspaper article about your patient who committed suicide earlier this week. I was just curious to know who he was."

"Oh. He was a doctor at the psychiatric hospital who disappeared about six months ago. A ransom note was mailed to his home but after that the kidnappers never tried to make contact again. He was a colleague of several of the doctors at Meadowvale and was one of the founding members of the Clinic. It was partly under his guidance that the Clinic was transformed from an idea to a tangible reality. Unfortunately he never even got to see it completed. As horrible as it may sound, his disappearance was to my advantage, although I didn't know it at the time. I met Doctor Foley shortly after Arthur Montgomery disappeared and was hired in his place. They needed another doctor who would specialize in dissociative disorders and I just happened to fit the bill. To this day, nobody knows what became of Doctor Montgomery. He hasn't reappeared, there have been no further ransom demands, and his body hasn't been found anywhere. For all intents and purposes, Doctor Montgomery has vanished off of the face of the earth."

"Wow!" Ed exclaimed, when Rachel finished her story. "Did he have a family?"

"That's the tragic part. Not only was he at the pinnacle of his career, but he left behind a wife and two young children. It's really quite sad."

"That's horrible."

At that moment, Mrs. Liu stopped by the table to ask how everything was so far. Both Ed and Rachel let her know everything was fine and she left.

"So what were these questions you wanted to ask me?" Rachel asked.

"Well, who Doctor Montgomery was, was one of them. But I also came across a couple of things today in the stat sheets at the psychiatric hospital that I couldn't understand. I asked Doctor Foley about one of them but he wasn't very helpful. It seemed he was trying to dodge the question so I didn't pursue it."

Rachel's curiosity was piqued. "What was the question?" she asked.

"Well, I came across a few stat sheets, not the originals but photocopies, all on dissociative identity disorder patients of Doctor Sanford's. He's one of the doctors at the Clinic, isn't he?"

"Yes."

"I thought so. Doctor Foley got all tense when I mentioned his name. Anyway, on each of the stat sheets I found, beside the space left for the doctor to fill in how many personalities the patient has, there were two numbers with a backslash in between them."

"Two numbers? Are you sure?"

"Positive. I even wrote them down and copied the patient numbers down so that I could show you." Ed reached into the breast pocket of his ash-gray single breasted blazer and removed a folded piece of paper. He spread it out on the table upside-down so that Rachel could see what he had written on it. There were four sets of numbers, and beside each set were two more numbers separated by a backslash:

00176859—4/9

00374775—7/15

01849254—6/12

01964783—2/7

Ed chewed on a chopstick while Rachel studied the numbers he had placed in front of her.

"Any idea what they mean?" Ed asked removing the chopstick and shoveling a forkful of chicken fried rice into his mouth.

"Well the first numbers all represent patients and I recognize the second one as one of the patients at Meadowvale. But I don't understand why he would have written two sets of numbers under the number of personalities heading. Are you sure that's how you found them?"

"Like I said, I'm absolutely positive. That's why I wrote them down. I'd seen so many other stat sheets that I immediately noticed something was off kilter with these. When I asked Doctor Foley what he thought the two numbers might mean, he just said everyone has their own little way of doing things and that he didn't know."

Rachel peered at the numbers again. The second number, 00374775, represented Amanda Rutherford, the DID patient who had hidden herself in the kitchen freight elevator. Rachel didn't know for sure but she remembered Dr. Sanford mentioning to her that same day that Amanda had over ten personalities. In which case, the first number, seven, had no business being on the chart.

"That's very strange. And you said these stat sheets are all at the psychiatric hospital?"

"Sitting there collecting dust mites even as we speak."

"You don't have the photocopies with you?" Rachel asked.

"No, Doctor Winslow was quite adamant about that. I had to return them to her before I left."

"I think I might have to drop by and take a look for myself. Maybe there's something else on the stat sheets that might shed some light on this mystery."

"Suit yourself."

"Okay, let's leave that question 'til later. What else did you want to ask me?"

"I wanted to ask you about this new treatment Doctor Flemming and his colleagues have come up with for treating dissociative disorders. I've read about it in the papers and seen it mentioned on a few stat sheets, but I've no idea what it entails. I'd like to know so that I can compare it to other methods of treatment in terms of cost, duration, and recidivism rates. I've also heard it's quite controversial so naturally I'm curious."

"That's an easy question to answer. Essentially Doctor Flemming uses what is known as an individual modality approach, that is, a one-on-one approach, as opposed to a family or group approach. Most psychotherapists use this method in treating DID so that in itself isn't so unique. What is unique is the aggressive nature of his approach."

"Aggressive nature?" Ed asked wondering what Rachel could possibly mean by aggressive. Images of Iron Maidens and gimps immediately sprung to mind.

"Through the use of regressive hypnosis, Doctor Flemming forces patients to confront their pasts. It's a no-holds barred approach to psychotherapy. Although the treatment can be emotionally draining, it's been shown to be very effective. It's like ripping an old Band-Aid off. The slower you do it, the longer the pain is dragged out. If you tear it off quickly, the pain can be intense but at least it's short-lived."

"Are the patients put on any type of medication at all during the treatment?"

"Yes, but only to aid in the hypnosis. Medication is generally not recommended for DID patients."

"Why not? Is there nothing out there that can help them?"

"It's not that there's no medications out there which could prove useful, the problem lies in the fact that a prescription drug must be taken consistently and given the multiple personality states which our patients experience, that consistency can be difficult, if not impossible, to attain."

"Oh, okay, I never thought about it that way. People with DID must miss a lot of appointments too."

"Unfortunately, yes. Not all of a DID patient's personalities are willing to undergo therapy. Some drugs can be helpful. Neuroleptics, for instance, are used to decrease anxiety caused by conflicts between alters in DID patients. High dose Benzodiazapine strategies have been shown to be effective in some cases, but they're often abused and dependence is a problem. Other drugs, like anti-depressants, while suitable for many other disorders, have proven to be less than effective when taken by DID patients."

"So the only part of Doctor Flemming's treatment protocol which could be construed as negative would be his aggressive approach which the patients understand and agree to?"

"That's it."

"Well, that's not as bad as the press makes it out to be."

"No, definitely not. The press can make anything look bad. Unfortunately it's not only the method of treatment that's being criticized."

"How do you mean?"

"The timing of this new method of treatment couldn't be any worse."

"Why? Is it expensive?"

"No, it has nothing to do with the cost, directly anyway. Although DID has been widely accepted and classified within the DSM IV, its always been treated like psychiatry's illegitimate child."

"You're losing me."

"Sorry. Unlike most psychological disorders, DID has had its critics from day one. Its only been within the last twenty years that the disorder has received the recognition it has come to deserve. But now, just at the peak of its acceptance, at a time where great progress is being made in its diagnosis and treatment, there is a lot of pressure within the psychiatric community to take it out of the DSM IV."

"Why would they want to do that?"

"Because there are many people out there who believe that the disorder does not exist."

"Doesn't exist?"

"That's right. The debate has essentially been ongoing for the past century and has only become more intense within the last two decades. The scary thing is that there may come a time when the naysayers have their way."

Chapter 32

"So wait a second," Ed interrupted in an attempt to clarify Rachel's last point, "there are people out there, psychiatrists, who don't believe that DID exists?" he asked incredulously.

"Yes."

"How is that possible? I mean isn't it obvious that the disorder exists? How could there even be a debate?"

"There are numerous reasons why actually. There is very compelling evidence on both sides of the debate which makes it difficult to come down on one side or the other unless of course you're biased or extremely well informed. I'm both."

"What kind of evidence could there be which could be used to suggest the disorder doesn't exist?"

"Fortunately for those of us who believe in it, not a lot. They don't even really have any empirical evidence to speak of as the pro-side does, but they do have something which can often enough be more damning than solid proof."

"What's that?"

"Wild accusations, which by nature are so fantastic, that they attract all sorts of attention."

"And to think, psychiatry always seemed boring to me. I thought the only thing you people did was analyze people's dreams as they lay on couches."

Rachel laughed, "Sometimes I wish."

"So what are these accusations the naysayers make?" Ed asked.

"They like to point out the effects of the media, the sheer increase in the number of cases since the discovery of the disorder, and the attention seekers. In North America, DID is generally well-known and understood. Over the last few decades, the disorder has been described and portrayed in books like the *Three Faces of Eve* and *Sybil*, in movies based on those and other books of their kind, and in television documentaries. As a result of all this exposure the disorder has received, it has become well known, and thus quite exploitable."

"Exploitable?"

"Yep, by attention seekers. Since the disorder is one of the most fascinating to mental health workers, people seeking attention often pretend to have multiple personalities. This not only wastes the time and effort of many mental health workers but it also takes away from those individuals who genuinely need the care that those attention seekers are receiving. Do you remember the case of the Hillside Strangler in Los Angeles?"

"I'm aware of it but not entirely familiar with the details."

"For two years, starting in nineteen seventy-seven, the Hillside Strangler roamed LA torturing, raping and strangling prostitutes. Ten young women ranging in age from twelve to twenty-eight were killed." Rachel paused before continuing, "At first the police thought it was the work of one man but soon they discovered it was the work of two. Two cousins to be exact. Kenneth Bianchi and Angelo Buono. They stopped for awhile and may have gotten away if Bianchi hadn't raped two more women. The police brought him in and his cousin soon afterwards.

"In desperation, Bianchi adopted an alter personality he named Steve Walker in hopes that he could plead insanity and essentially blame all of his actions on this violent alter ego. The Bianchi case was extremely controversial at the time, and is still often referred to, because it called into question whether or not DID was a true disorder. The Kenneth Bianchi case is a watershed event in the history of the disorder. From that point on, attacks on the integrity of those who studied DID and those who claimed to suffer from it were renewed. The widely published interview with Bianchi supposedly demonstrates that people under hypnosis can be convinced that they have alter personalities and can be easily encouraged to develop these 'personalities'. The negative publicity the disorder received due to that case was extremely damaging."

"I'm not surprised. So aside from the media and attention seekers, what other proof does the opposition have?"

Rachel smiled. "The opposition. I like that."

"I thought it seemed appropriate."

"Rightly so. But to answer your question, critics of DID often charge that the number of reported cases have increased exponentially. When the disorder was first discovered, it was thought to be rare. It is now being diagnosed much more frequently which critics attribute to fakery."

"Couldn't that be attributed to better diagnostic criteria and increased awareness in general?"

"Exactly. You are catching on." Rachel said impressed with Ed's observation. "There are those who refuse to see the other side. Over the years, other disorders such as Lyme Disease, Obsessive-Compulsive Disorder and Chronic Fatigue Syndrome, also known as 'Yuppie Flu,' have shown equal or faster rises in their number of cases as well. Another major criticism aimed at the credibility of DID is that over time, the symptomatology has changed. Although this is true, it doesn't prove anything."

"What kind of changes are we talking about here?"

"Well, for instance, prior to the twentieth century, patients with DID rarely exhibited more than two or three personalities whereas today the numbers are much higher. Back then, there was also a definite demarcation in switching between personalities such as sleep or convulsions. Nowadays, patients can switch in front of your eyes from personality to personality, in some cases at will."

"You said the evidence in support of DID was stronger."

"Much stronger. The disorder's symptoms have been studied to death and have been found to be quite valid and reliable. Psychiatric overkill if you ask me, but with the controversy that surrounds the disorder, it's to be expected."

"So in all of the studies they've conducted, what have they found?"

"A lot. Patients with DID when compared to the general population have been found to have different Electroencephalograph readings for each personality they manifest while the subjects without DID, when asked to fake DID had consistent EEG readings. Other tests reveal that DID patients display a change in their optical functioning, transient microstrabismus, which is the involuntary lateral movement of the eye, in particular. Transient microstrabismus cannot be faked. Patients with DID often experience discrepancies between personalities as well. For instance, some patients' personalities can demonstrate differences in visual acuity, that is some alters may suffer from myopia while others have 20/20 vision. Handedness can change from left to right between alters in one individual. Even a person's handwriting style can change dramatically as they switch from personality to personality. One of the most compelling findings is that some personalities can have allergies which don't affect the other personalities whatsoever."

"Those sound like pretty convincing arguments to me."

"They are. Not only that though. DID has been diagnosed in over twenty-one different countries and one territory. So it's not only a prevalent disorder in North America, it's a cross-cultural phenomenon as well."

"And yet some people still believe that it doesn't exist?"

"Unfortunately, yes."

"That's incredible. So what's going to happen? I mean will it ever be proved or disproved?"

"It's hard to tell. There may come a time when health management and insurance companies refuse to treat it and cover it any longer. It's a shame that it may come to that all because there are people out there who fake it and would use it to their own advantage. The impact that that sort of behavior has right now and may have in the future on those patients who do suffer from the disorder is significant. Not only because it affects what sort of treatment they receive, but just imagine how you would feel if you had a severe mental disorder and nobody believed you."

"I know what you mean. It's like insurance in a way. The reason insurance rates are so high is largely because of all the insurance fraud going on. It's unfair that we have to pay for the selfish behavior of others."

"No one ever said the world was a fair place," Rachel said. Ed and Rachel finished eating the rest of their meal in silence, both deep in thought. When Mrs. Liu brought the bill, Ed reached for it.

"This one's on me," he said.

"Why thank you, kind sir." Rachel said.

"When are you going to go to the psychiatric hospital tomorrow?" Ed asked, withdrawing his wallet.

"First thing in the morning. And I expect you to meet me there."

"Me?"

"Of course. It was you who initially discovered the anomalous files, besides, I may need an objective observer."

"You mean inexperienced don't you?"

"Well, yes, but you said it, not I."

"What time shall we meet then?"

"How does eight sound?"

"Early."

"Good, I'll see you then."

Chapter 33

▼

Agent Haskins sat in an unmarked sedan gazing out the windshield. A yellow projectile whizzed past his windshield and over the top of his car. Two kids on rollerblades streaked by in hot pursuit. The shot had gone just over the net. John longed for the days when one's only concern was scoring a goal in an inconsequential game of road hockey and what was being served for dinner that night. Skating past him again, the kids glanced into the car at John. He smiled and waved. His eyes settled back on the goalie of the closest net. He was ten years old and wore a Felix Potvin jersey which came down to his knees. It was the only kid John recognized of the dozen or so youths in the game.

He was glad that the kid was outside. That way there wouldn't be a chance of him overhearing the conversation soon to take place.

Summoning up his courage, John pocketed the single car key, and slowly lifted himself out of the blue metal frame. Ambling across the street, he noticed that some of the kids were watching his every move. A young girl with pigtails and braces pointed at him and whispered something to one of her playmates. Potvin pretended not to see him.

The two-story house looked quiet. The grass in the front yard was longer than the neighbors' yet just as green. A myriad of sports equipment lay haphazardly around the front step and in front of the two-car garage. A brand new basketball net and backboard were placed directly over and between the two open doors.

John rang the doorbell almost hoping no one would answer but the Explorer in the garage suggested that his trip would not be in vain.

The door opened inward revealing a tall, dark haired woman, with a stunning figure and facial features to match. Although in her mid-forties, Eileen Montgomery, could have avoided widowhood with ease. She possessed the same faith that John did that her husband's fate would be discovered. Until that time she would neither mourn nor accept what the press had already hinted at.

"Agent Haskins," Eileen beamed, "what a pleasant surprise. Would you like to come in?"

"I'd like that," John said softly, "how are you, Eileen?" he asked watching her face. It was fraught with weariness. Just as he remembered it from his previous meetings with her.

She looked down the street to where her eldest child was shouting encouragement at his teammates.

"We're doing all right I guess. Mark seems to be coping."

"I was watching him play, he's good."

"He likes being goalie." The two of them watched the game unfold on the asphalt. One of the bigger kids on the court was weaving in and out of the other players deftly handling the ragged tennis ball with his stick. He outskated most of the other skaters and was soon alone on his path for the net. He wound up raising his stick high in the air and brought it down with full force in a sweeping trajectory. The ball made a hollow thumping sound as contact was made and it rocketed towards the net Mark Montgomery was tending.

With one quick movement, Mark's left arm swept up and plucked the ball out of the air as if it was a languidly floating soap bubble.

Eileen Montgomery smiled.

"Won't you come in, Agent Haskins?" she asked.

"Sure, thank you."

John had been inside the house on three previous occasions. The first time was the day after Arthur Montgomery's disappearance. The second and third times were simply to keep Eileen up to date on his progress. Such was the purpose of his present visit as well.

"It's been over three weeks since I last heard from you. Anything new yet?" Eileen asked hopefully sitting at an oval table in the kitchen across from John. She played absently with a pepper shaker.

John reached across the table and took her hands in both of his. She let go of the ceramic shaker.

"I'm afraid not, Eileen. I've checked all leads twice and my team has been putting all their spare time into searching for your husband but we're not making any progress."

"So why did you come here tonight?" she asked withdrawing her hands. Her eyes had become moist at the news John brought, or lack thereof.

"I wanted to ask you about your husband's involvement with the Meadowvale Clinic."

"The Clinic?" she asked surprised. "Why?"

"It's the only connection we haven't thoroughly checked yet and I don't intend to give up looking for your husband."

"But what are you saying? Do you think my husband was taken because of his work with the Clinic?"

"I don't know what I think yet. All I know is that your husband was heavily involved in its development and someone for some reason may have had his reasons for…" John let his voice fade.

"For killing my husband. You can say it, Agent Haskins. I know that Arthur did not run away, and I know that I'll probably never see him again. I also know that I will not be able to sleep comfortably or stop worrying about my children until I find out what happened to him."

"I know. I know." John said in as sympathetic a voice as possible.

"So what do you want to know about Arthur's work with the Clinic?" Eileen asked sitting up straight. She sniffled and reached for a napkin from a pile in the center of the table.

"Whatever you can tell me. I don't know much about the Clinic myself so that's why I wanted to talk to you first."

"Have you ever been there?"

"No, I'm afraid I haven't."

"It's a cold, sterile place, Agent Haskins. It's not what Arthur would have wanted at all. The way he talked about it I envisioned a warm, inviting building. Now that he's gone though, I just can't see it in that light. It's probably because I see the place through gray-tinted glasses. Everything has lost its flavor to me. Everything except the children. I seem to be living vicariously through their young, naive view of life."

"Who was your husband working with on the Clinic? I assume it wasn't all his doing."

"Heavens no, although with the amount of time and effort he put into that place one would have thought so. No, he worked with three other doctors. All were originally from the San Francisco Psychiatric Hospital. That's how he knew them. There was Walter Flemming who has been extremely supportive over the last six months. He calls regularly and he bought and installed a new basketball net for Mark the other night. I don't what I would have done without Walter's support. There was also Grant Foley. I don't know him as well but he seems like a nice fellow. And the third doctor was, um, hold on a sec. I can never remember his name. He's a fidgety little man." Eileen pursed her lips and drew her eyebrows downwards wrestling with her memory to remember the third doctor's name.

"Carl Sanford!" Eileen practically shouted. "That's it! Carl Sanford was the third doctor." John wrote down the three names in a small black notebook. He left it open for further notes.

"Did you ever meet him?"

"No, I never did."

"Are all three of those doctors working at the Clinic now?"

"Yes they are, and I believe they will all be very well off once that Clinic gets established. There's a lot of money in treating mental disorders."

"Do you know how many other doctors are working at the Clinic, Eileen?"

"I think only three others, six in total. Arthur wanted to keep the Clinic relatively small and he wanted the patients to receive the best care they could. He didn't want too many doctors there, otherwise politics become an issue and the patients are usually the first to suffer when that happens. Look at the larger hospitals and the HMOs and you'll understand what I'm talking about."

"So Arthur would have been the seventh doctor?"

"No, he would have been one of the six."

"He was replaced?" John asked trying to contain his excitement. If another doctor was filling his shoes and making a profit at it, there was a motive. Had someone kidnapped Arthur just to get a position at the Clinic? The idea seemed ridiculous but John didn't completely disregard it.

"Yes," Eileen said with a slight bitter hiss in answer to John's question, "Grant Foley took it upon himself to hire a cute young thing from the local university to replace my husband less than a month after he disappeared."

"Do you know her name?" John asked ready to write it down.

"Rachel Miller. I've never met her and frankly I never want to. I heard she was responsible for the death of a patient over there."

"Where did you hear that?" John scribbled a few more words beside Rachel's name in his pad.

"Walter isn't fond of her either and is still upset with Grant for hiring her without informing the other doctors at the Clinic."

"What about the other two doctors? Can you tell me anything about them?"

"I knew their names and actually met one of them before but I can't remember now. One's a nice black man and the other's a woman. She's not very friendly. I think they're both new, that is not originally from the psychiatric hospital. I don't recall Arthur ever really talking about them."

"I'll check them out."

"So does any of what I've told you help?"

"It's hard to say just yet. Maybe. I'm going back to my office now to check on some things. In the meantime, can I call you if I have any additional questions, Eileen?"

"Of course." John stood up to go and began saying good-bye to Eileen when he was interrupted by a child's crying voice emanating down the stairwell.

"That would be Claire, she's teething. Can you see yourself out, Agent Haskins?"

"Sure."

John let himself out the front door pulling it shut behind him. He stepped gingerly over a discarded pair of goalie pads left on the walkway. The hockey nets were lying on their mesh-covered backs on the front lawn. The kids' energies had been transferred from the street to the driveway where a fast-paced game of basketball ensued. John walked down the length of the drive on the grass careful not to step on a heap of rollerblades.

He peered down the length of the street just before crossing and was halfway across when something bounced off his ankle.

"Sorry, mister," a short Dennis-The-Menace lookalike yelled. The Spalding which had hit him rolled underneath his car. John knelt down and fished it out. He dribbled it across the road to the edge of the driveway. The blonde kid waved his hands in the air signaling for a pass. John stopped dribbling, looked up at the net over thirty feet away, and with one fluid motion, hurled the ball towards the backboard in a high arc. Without touching the backboard, the ball dropped straight through the net barely touching it.

Swish.

Larry Bird, eat your heart out.

John smiled, winked at the awestruck kids and got in his car.

When he got back to the Bureau, the offices around his own were desolate and empty. The phones had ceased their intermittent ringing, fax machines no longer spewed out their endless stream of information, and the normal hushed insistence of the day seemed thankfully past. John sauntered over to the coffee machine and went about making a new pot for himself. He would need it, he intended on burning a little midnight oil, and his own stamina could only carry him so far.

Calling his wife to let her know that he would be in late this evening, John reclined in his desk chair and breathed deeply. He talked briefly to his daughter Julia, wished her good night and replaced the phone in its cradle.

John reviewed the conversation he had with Eileen Montgomery in his mind. There was one thing that had stuck in his craw about the whole thing. He wasn't entirely sure he agreed with Eileen's interpretation of Dr. Walter Flemming's behavior. While on the surface it seemed supportive and generous, John was accustomed to thinking and expecting the worst when it came to human behavior. He didn't believe there was any romantic involvement between Walter Flemming and Eileen Montgomery but he couldn't shake the feeling that something was amiss and it was inextricably linked to Walter Flemming's acts of kindness.

Coming up to the Montgomery's house earlier that evening, John had noticed the numerous pieces of sports equipment lying around the yard, but it was not until he left the house that he observed just how much equipment there was. And most of it seemed new.

There were only two possible motivations John could think of which would drive a man to be so generous and supportive of another man's family: love and guilt. Having talked with Eileen Montgomery numerous times, John was convinced it wasn't love. Unfortunately he had nothing but a gut feeling that told him it was guilt. Fortunately, his gut had an excellent track record. He didn't want to make the obvious assumption that Walter Flemming had killed Arthur Montgomery, but the way he was acting would at least suggest he perhaps knew something which could lead to the capture of the real perpetrator. Either way, it was one of the few promising leads that John had had in awhile and he intended to pursue it to its logical conclusion.

Pulling out his notepad in which he had recorded the late Arthur Montgomery's colleagues' names, John adopted a scribe's pose and began jotting down page after page of notes and questions.

First thing the next morning, he would take it upon himself to make an appointment with the doctors at the Meadowvale Clinic. He would interview all six of them. He was especially looking forward to talking with Dr. Walter Flemming and Dr. Rachel Miller.

Chapter 34

▼

In nineteen-seventy-three, a psychological experiment was conducted.

Eight normal people, in five different US states, made hospital appointments and complained of hearing voices. Seven of the eight people were admitted, with a diagnosis of schizophrenia. Not one of them actually suffered from the disorder.

Once admitted, the seven subjects halted their claims about hearing voices, and proceeded to behave in a normal manner. Despite the fact that they were sane and didn't actually have schizophrenia, they were never discovered by the hospitals' staff. Eventually, all seven *"patients"* were discharged, since their *"schizophrenia"* was apparently in remission. The average stay lasted nineteen days. The longest was fifty-two.

The reason that none of the *"patients"* were detected, is that everything they did within the confines of the mental hospitals in which they were admitted, was construed as the behavior of an individual suffering from a psychological disorder. Activities such as pacing the halls, staring out the windows, talking to themselves, and counting floor and ceiling tiles were all interpreted as signs of insanity. All of these behaviors, under any other circumstances, would be taken as signs of boredom, not mental illness.

If Sandra Hillock knew of the study, she could have related to the pseudo-patients' predicament.

"I don't belong here," she said.

"Sorry?"

"I said I don't belong here. There's been some kind of terrible mistake."

"I'm afraid there's been no mistake."

"That's not true. I've never seen this place before. I don't even know what this place is."

"You're in the Meadowvale Clinic for the Treatment of Dissociative Disorders."

"Clinic? Dissociative Disorders? What am I doing here?"

"You were brought in yesterday and have been a patient ever since."

"But I don't remember being brought in. Why am I here?"

"That question alone should answer your question."

"What do you mean?"

"You're here because you're not always yourself."

"Not always myself? Then who else am I?"

"That's what we're trying to find out here at the Clinic."

"Hold on! Stop the world, I want to get off. Would you please tell me what is going on!"

"My name is Doctor Sanford. I'm a doctor here at the Clinic. Your doctor actually. You appear to have Dissociative Identity Disorder, also known as Multiple Personality Disorder."

"That's impossible," the patient said flatly.

"Is it?"

"Of course it is"

"Do you remember anything from the past few days?"

"No I don't. But that doesn't mean that I have Multiple Personality Disorder."

"That in itself doesn't, but the manifestation of at least three other personalities would strongly suggest that possibility."

"Three other personalities?"

"At least."

"At least? How is that possible?"

"Most people with Dissociative Ident…"

"Could you please call it Multiple Personality Disorder?"

"Of course," Dr. Sanford said apologetically. "Most people with Multiple Personality Disorder don't realize they have the disorder for years after its onset."

"And that's why I can't remember anything from the past few days? Because somebody else was living my life for me?"

"Essentially yes, although it's a little more complicated than that."

"How much more complicated?"

"That question can only be answered over time. You may have other personalities, or alters as some people call them, which we don't yet know about."

"This isn't a prison of some sort is it?"

"Definitely not."

"What I mean is, I didn't do something stupid like kill somebody did I?"

"No, you did nothing of the kind."

"Thank God. So when can I get out of here?"

"As soon as you like, provided you know where you live."

"Of course I know where I live. I live at…Ohmygod, I can't remember where I live."

"Can you remember your name?"

"No, no I can't. Oh God, Oh God, Oh God. This isn't happening." The patient began weeping.

"Unfortunately when you were brought in you had no identification on you so we're at a loss to identify you as well. Don't worry though, we'll find out who you are and get you back to your life. What you have is exactly what we specialize in at this Clinic. I assure you, you're in the best of hands."

The patient stood up and looked into a large mirror affixed to one of the walls in the cramped room. She stared at the reflection measuring herself up against the image that was cast back. She reached out and touched her own hand. There wasn't even a hint of recognition. She had no idea who the woman in the looking glass was.

"If you'll come back to the chair here, we can get to work on figuring out who you are." The patient reluctantly shuffled back to the inclined chair and pulled herself up onto it.

"What are you going to do?"

"First I'm going to give you something to help you relax." Sanford quickly put a needle in her arm and injected its contents "We're going to try what's called regressive hypnosis."

"What does that do?"

"It will allow us to explore your past and perhaps find out who you are and where you came from."

"Will you talk to the other personalities?"

"Most likely yes."

"Have you talked to the others before?"

"Yes I have. But we'll talk about that later."

"Are they nice?"

"I don't think we should talk about that right now. What I want you to do right now is close your eyes and listen to the sound of my voice. That's it, concentrate on nothing but the sound of my voice. Relax your entire body and just concentrate on my voice. Good. I would like to speak to the others in you. So just relax and let those others come to me. Focus on what I'm saying, don't let anything else distract you. Excellent. We'll take care of you here.

"We'll take care of all of you."

Chapter 35

▼

Friday
8:02 a.m.
San Francisco Psychiatric Hospital

"They're gone!" Ed cried out in disbelief when Rachel joined him in the basement records room of the psychiatric hospital. He had come early to get some more work out of the way as well as to find all the stat sheets he wanted to show Rachel.

He had talked with Dr. Winslow but she told him they were missing. All of the stat sheets he had told Rachel about, those of Dr. Sanford's dissociative identity disorder patients with two numbers where there should have only been one, were nowhere to be found. Ed and Dr. Winslow searched all over the dim, low-ceilinged room but the records were simply not there.

"What do you mean they're gone?" Rachel asked incredulously wondering briefly if Ed was playing a bizarre prank on her.

"I mean they're gone." He repeated. "Not here. They've disappeared. Doctor Winslow and I checked all of the cabinets twice and each and every data sheet that I was telling you about is gone."

"That's not possible."

"I assure you it is."

"Let's check upstairs and see if they know where the files could be. Maybe someone has them up there."

"I don't see why," Ed said, "they were all inactive. None of the patients in those records are here at this hospital."

"Not one of them?" Rachel asked.

"No. When I first came here, Doctor Winslow, told me that all the data sheets down here are inactive. None of them are on the patients that are currently being treated here. Those are all kept upstairs for convenience' sake."

"So why wouldn't the stat sheets that Doctor Winslow photocopied for you and that you saw yesterday be here today?"

"That's exactly what I mean. There's no reason they shouldn't be. I can understand if maybe one or at the most two of them were taken, but all of them? It doesn't make any sense."

"Who else, aside from me, did you talk to about those stat sheets?"

"Just Doctor Foley. I was going to ask Doctor Winslow about them when I was here yesterday but she had to take off and meet with some guy from the FBI."

"FBI? What do they want?"

"I overheard them talking about that Doctor Montgomery guy. He was just asking her questions about him."

"So only you, Doctor Foley, and I know what you saw on those stat sheets?"

"As far as I know, yes."

"Well, let's go upstairs and check to see if they're on the computer system. Maybe that'll give us some answers."

"Do you think Doctor Foley took them for some reason?" Ed asked as he and Rachel left the basement and headed up the stairs for the main level.

"I don't know but something about this is very odd. Let's wait until we see what we can find on the computer before we start forming conspiracy theories."

Arriving upstairs with Ed in tow, Rachel approached the main reception desk and asked the woman sitting behind it if she could check on some records for her.

"And you are?" the woman asked in a bored, condescending tone.

"Doctor Miller, from the Meadowvale Clinic. I need to check on four patients in particular."

"Well, I'm kind of busy right now. Can you come back later?"

"No, I need to see them as soon as possible. We need to check a few things," she nodded her head towards Ed, "for insurance purposes."

The woman behind the desk recognized Ed from previous visits and remembered Dr. Winslow's instructions to grant him whatever he wanted. She made a sigh as if it was an infringement upon her own personal liberty and said to Rachel, "If you really have to, you can come back here and check for yourselves. Do you know what you're looking for?"

"Yes, we have the patient numbers and there's only four of them."

"All right, come on back." She disappeared into the back of the reception area around a corner and within seconds, a door to the left of the kiosk opened. She waved them in. Once they were in, she pointed to a solitary computer against the back wall.

"Make yourselves at home. If you could keep an eye on the desk as well, I'd appreciate it. I just have to make a quick trip to the bathroom."

"Sure," Rachel said.

When she had gone, Ed turned to Rachel, "That was easy."

"Well, we're not doing anything illegal. We're just checking the stat sheets which you have permission to do. Besides, we only have the patient numbers. We need a password to find out who those patient numbers belong to."

"Well, we know they were all Doctor Sanford's patients."

"That's a start." Rachel turned her attention to the monitor in front of her. A busy menu occupied the screen. Scrolling downwards. Rachel found a search command. She hit enter and a blank space popped up where she typed the first patient number in: 00176859.

The screen immediately changed and was filled with a patient's file cover sheet. Ed looked over Rachel's shoulder, and saw that beside the line labeled personalities, there was only one number: nine.

Looking down at the crumpled sheet where Ed had written the four sets of numbers, they noticed that only the second number had been entered under number of personalities. Where the written copy of the file had read four/nine, the computer version only showed the number nine.

"Curiouser and curiouser." Rachel muttered under her breath.

"What? What does it mean?" Ed asked.

"I'm not sure yet. Let's check the other numbers."

"Wait a second, hold on!" Ed grabbed Rachel's wrist before she could move the computer's mouse any further.

"What?"

"Look down there." Ed pointed to the bottom of the screen.

Under the heading Current Status, someone had typed in, in capitalized letters, 'DECEASED/S.I.' There was a date next to it. The patient had died just over five years ago.

"What does the SI mean?" Ed asked Rachel.

"Self-Inflicted. It means the patient committed suicide." Rachel paused wondering what it was she was getting herself into.

Before she let her imagination get the better of her, she scrolled the screen back up and typed in the second patient number. It was Amanda Rutherford's file.

Once again, beside the line left for filling in the number of personalities, someone had entered fifteen. The first number which appeared on the written record Ed had come across, seven, was not there.

Rachel scrolled the screen downwards and noticed that someone had made a note that patient number 00374775, Amanda Rutherford, was to be watched closely. She had attempted suicide five times during her four years at the psychiatric hospital. Rachel wondered whether Amanda had been looking for a way to kill herself when she had hidden in the dumbwaiter. She hit the "Print Screen" button to make a copy of Amanda's file.

"Let's check the other two files before that lady comes back. She gives me the creeps," Ed said, interrupting Rachel's thoughts. The next two patient numbers, 01849254 and 01964783 were both of more recent patients and under Current Status, someone had typed in: RE-INTEGRATED/STABLE.

"What does that mean?" Ed asked when the first record revealed RE-INTEGRATED/STABLE.

"It means that the patient's personalities were successfully unified into one and that no relapse's have occurred. Yet."

"Do relapses occur often?"

"It depends. If a patient faces a situation in which he or she finds it difficult to cope, one of the personalities can easily emerge. If however the re-integration process is done well, the patient will learn to cope with whatever happens without resorting to dissociation."

"Did you find what you were looking for?" the receptionist's husky voice asked from behind them as she returned from the bathroom, wiping her hands on her generous midsection.

"Yes, we did thank you." Rachel quickly returned the screen back to the original menu and got up out of her chair. She managed to remove the print-out she had made without the receptionist seeing her. She folded it behind her back and stuffed it into her pocket.

On her way out she turned around and asked the receptionist, "Oh, by the way. Has anyone from outside the psychiatric hospital been downstairs in the records room in the last day or so?"

"Not that I know of."

"All right, thank you, you've been a great help."

"Whatever. Just make sure the door stays shut when you close it. Damn thing hasn't shut properly since I started working here." Rachel pulled the door shut tightly and exited the hospital with Ed by her side.

"Do you think Doctor Foley came here and took the files because of what I told him yesterday?" Ed asked once they reached their vehicles in the full parking lot.

"I'm beginning to wonder. Although I still can't figure out why he would do such a thing. It seems they're hiding something but I don't know what. One thing I know for sure is that one of Doctor Sanford's patients is a part of whatever's going on and her life may be in danger."

"Why do you say that?"

"Well you saw the first set of stats. One of his DID patients committed suicide five years ago, another one, the second file we looked at, has tried to kill herself several times but fortunately hasn't succeeded. I think that the second patient whose file we just looked at may be at risk."

"So what are we going to do?"

"The first thing I'm going to do is try to find out who the third and fourth patients are. Did you grab the piece of paper with the numbers on it?"

"Right here." Ed patted his breast pocket.

"Good, I'll need a copy. While I do that, why don't you try to find out who the first patient was."

"How am I supposed to do that? I don't have access to that kind of information."

"The first patient committed suicide right?"

"Yes?"

"The city library keeps all of the major local newspapers on microfilm. I'm sure one of the city's papers would have reported the incident. Even if it's just a brief clipping buried in the back page, there must be some kind of record of it out there. Why don't you try to find out who that patient was."

"At least that doesn't sound too hard. How are you going to find out who the other two patients are though?"

"I have an idea about that." Rachel said with a smile.

"I don't like that look in your eye."

"You just find out who the first patient was and I'll do the rest. Can you meet me back at the Clinic later this afternoon?"

"Sure, when?"

"Say around four o'clock?"

"That should give me enough time."

Rachel and Ed left the hospital together through the front doors where they witnessed a very bizarre scene indeed. A man wearing hospital clothing was standing in the shade of an enormous oak tree and looked to be having an animated conversation with the tree itself.

"Is that man talking to the tree?" Ed asked.

"It would appear so." Rachel confirmed.

"Wonder what they're talking about?" Ed mused.

"Are you as curious as I am?"

"Probably more so," Ed said and they walked over towards the patient and the tree.

The patient saw them approaching and stepped out from the shade of the tree to greet them.

"Hi," Ed announced in greeting, "from where we were standing, it looked like you were talking to the tree."

"I was," the patient answered casually.

"I see," Ed said, he looked at Rachel, "I think this is your field."

"Oh, um, sorry to have interrupted your conversation, we'll be going now." Rachel grabbed Ed's arm and began pulling him away.

"Do you think they'll ever find him?" the patient called after them. Rachel and Ed turned in unison.

"Find who?" Rachel asked.

"Doctor Montgomery, who else?"

"Why do you ask?"

"The FBI made another visit yesterday but I think you already know that," he nodded his head in Ed's direction.

"You saw me here yesterday?" Ed asked.

"I was the one driving the lawnmower.

"You certainly seem to know a lot about the comings and goings of the hospital." Rachel pointed out.

"I should, I'm the groundskeeper here, name's Chad."

"I'm sorry, we were under the impression that you were, um…" Rachel faltered.

"A patient," the groundskeeper offered, "I am," he explained no further.

"Do you have any idea where Doctor Montgomery went?" Ed asked.

"None, that's the biggest mystery about this place. That, and why those other three doctors just picked up and left for that new clinic, Meadowvale."

"Those three doctors and Doctor Montgomery created the Meadowvale Clinic, what's the big mystery behind that?" Rachel asked, confused.

"They were up to something big here just before they all left. It just seems odd, to me."

"How do you mean something 'big'?"

"Just that. Those doctors that are at the Clinic now, spent pretty much all of their time here working the oddest hours."

"What's so odd about that, don't most doctors work irregular hours?" Ed asked looking to Rachel for confirmation.

"Not like these guys. Most of the time they spent in the basement, a lot of the time with patients too."

"What were they doing?"

"I could never figure that out. But whatever it was, they kept it awfully secret. Real Cloak and Dagger stuff. Whatever it was, they didn't want anyone else knowing about it."

"And you have no idea what went on down there?" Ed asked.

"Nope, but I know their work isn't over yet."

"How do you know that?" Ed asked.

"Because if it was, Doctor Flemming wouldn't have the need to visit the basement in the dead of night as he did last night."

Chapter 36

▼

As Rachel headed towards the Meadowvale Clinic, Ed drove off in the opposite direction and took the Central Skyway on his way to the San Francisco Public Library. The three year old facility was located right downtown near the Civic Center on Larkin Street. Ed parked his truck behind the modernized version of the old Beaux Arts library located less than a block away. His quest to find information on Sanford's patient's suicide loomed larger after what he and Rachel were told by the groundskeeper at the Psychiatric Hospital.

The library's interior was bright and quiet. Hushed conversations, padded footsteps, and the rustling of pages filled the air. The sounds were at once overwhelming yet at the same time barely perceptible. Having never set foot in the new library, Ed surveyed his surroundings in search of an information desk. It didn't take long to find. Approaching the desk and its only occupant, a petite, frail looking older woman, Ed put on his warmest smile.

"Good morning, young man. Can I help you?" the woman asked in a tone that Ed was sure his smile was responsible for. He found his boyish good looks and easy charm especially useful when he was looking for information. He would have made a good reporter or lawyer.

"Yes, good morning." He smiled even more, "I need to look at some old newspapers."

"Those would be in the morgue."

"The morgue?" Ed asked.

"Oh, I'm sorry, I meant to say the Archives. We call it the morgue around here. Library jargon. The Archives is where we keep all the old records such as back issues of periodicals, newspapers, government surveys, and even city plans and records, hence the reason we call it the morgue. Also, the Archives are located in the basement which gives it a certain atmosphere."

"I see," Ed said, "and how do I get to the morgue?" Ed asked.

"If you take the elevator downstairs and turn to your left you can't miss it."

"Thank you very much."

"You're welcome. But unfortunately sir, we don't open the Archives until eleven o'clock on Fridays."

"Eleven o'clock?"

"That's right."

Ed looked at his watch. It was barely nine o'clock. He had just over two hours to kill.

"If you want," the librarian broke into his thoughts, "the library does have an art gallery, a cafe, a rooftop garden and terrace and a five-story atrium to keep you occupied."

"Thank you, I might just take advantage of those." Ed left the information desk and began wandering around taking in his surroundings as he did so. He decided he may as well stay at the library and get some paperwork out of the way. Two hours wasn't that long a period of time. Besides, as the librarian had mentioned, there were plenty of things to keep him occupied within the building.

Serving as his own tour guide, Ed went from floor to floor studying the architecture of the building itself and the numerous murals adorning the walls, all painted by local artists. Arriving at the cafe, he asked the young woman behind the counter for a Dr. Pepper.

"We don't have Dr. Pepper, sir. Will Pepsi be alright?"

Ed looked skyward and asked, "Is there a machine in the building that sells Dr. Pepper?"

"There is a machine on the top floor just as you enter the rooftop garden but I don't know if they carry Dr. Pepper."

"I'll push my luck, thanks." Bypassing the elevator, Ed took the grand staircase up to the rooftop garden, where, much to his surprise, there was a soft drink machine that sold Dr. Pepper. With his drink in one hand and briefcase in the other, Ed found a bench in a quiet shaded corner of the garden. Only a few other people occupied the terrace, making it a perfect place to get some work done.

Ed spread a pile of papers out before him and started going over the materials he had accumulated so far. Although he wasn't finished, the figures he had calculated roughly looked promising. For five million dollar malpractice liability insurance, the Meadowvale Clinic would have to pay an increasing amount of money per year per doctor. All six of them. The estimated figures looked like this;

Year One—$2,428.00 per doctor

Year Two—$3,875.00 per doctor

Year Three—$4,879.00 per doctor

Year Four—$5,442.00 per doctor

Although not as high as what Hal Rosenberg may have expected, the figures were still impressive. Now, going over the numbers for the hundredth time, Ed thought, if Rachel Miller was indicative of the quality of staff they employed at the Clinic, they would never have to use any of it.

Chapter 37

▼

The two hours passed quickly and it was a quarter after eleven before Ed realized how long he had been in the garden. He regretted having to leave the peaceful solitude he had discovered high atop the concrete structure located in the middle of one of the world's busiest cities.

Ed made his way to the basement via the elevator. Two middle-aged men sat behind a large wooden counter. The first, short, portly, and with dark, close-cropped hair was intent on a computer screen. He didn't even acknowledge Ed's presence. The second, a few inches taller and a few inches slimmer, caught sight of Ed with friendly eyes behind silver-framed bifocals. He wore dark flannel pants and a tweed coat with large patches covering the elbows. He seemed a lot more affable than the first.

"Good morning, sir. May I help you?" he asked, standing up.

"Yes, you could open the Archives earlier next Friday," Ed joked. The man smiled loosely, apparently not accustomed to humor in the basement of the library.

"Actually, I need to find some information in a newspaper."

"Any newspaper in particular?"

"I'll try the *Globe* first. I'm looking for an article on a person who died about five years ago."

"Anybody I would know?"

"Extremely unlikely."

"So it's not a famous person?"

"No, afraid not. Nothing as glamorous as that."

"Newspapers go crazy when a celebrity dies."

"That's not surprising," Ed said.

"It's especially annoying to them when a young celebrity dies."

"What difference does it make whether the person is young or old?"

"Preparedness."

"Preparedness? What's that supposed to mean?"

"It means that a lot of the bigger papers around the world carry on file ready made obituaries for old famous people. That way they can get to press a lot quicker than if they had to compile everything quickly everytime someone keeled over unexpectedly."

"That's sick."

"But it makes sense. Did you know the British papers had the Queen Mother's obituary on file for thirty years? They had to keep updating it every couple of years. Who knew she would kick around for as long as she did. If you read the papers the first couple of days after Diana died you'll see a lot of confusion. No one was prepared for her death. Least of all the tabloids. That's why I asked if you were looking for a famous person, because depending how old they were when they died, you might be better served to check the papers dated a few days after their death."

"I'd be surprised if there was one article on this person I'm looking for, never mind dozens of inaccurate ones."

"Just thought you should know. Besides, I need to dispense with some of this useless trivia I've accumulated over thirty-five years of working in a library. If you'll come this way, I'll show you where we keep the microfilm. That's what we keep all of the local newspapers on. It takes up a lot less room than keeping the actual papers themselves."

"No doubt," Ed said.

The gentleman led Ed down a series of narrow corridors walled by endless rows of miniature filing cabinets, immediately bringing forth to Ed's mind memories of the Dewey Decimal system. He shuddered at the thought.

Stopping so suddenly that Ed almost walked right into him, the archivist pointed to a wall of miniature filing drawers.

"The *Globe* takes up these twenty rows from floor to ceiling. The papers date back to the eighteen-nineties but the records are spotty at best until about nineteen-oh-three. The microfilm machines are located at the end of this hall and the copiers are there as well if you need to copy anything. Is there anything else you need?"

"Bread crumbs," Ed said only half-jokingly. The archivist chuckled when he saw the look on Ed's face.

"There are arrows which lead the way out and numerous staircases to lead you upstairs if you get lost. I shouldn't laugh. It took me a few weeks to figure out the layout of this place. If you need anything else though just come back to the desk. My name's Frank."

"Thank you, Frank." Ed watched the archivist walk away. Turning to the wall of drawers Ed scanned the years. It only took a minute to find three drawers labeled nineteen-ninety-five. He pulled out the sheet of paper from his breast pocket upon which he had written the date that the first patient had committed suicide. It had been on the seventeenth of June. A Thursday. Finding the June eighteenth, nineteen-ninety-five edition of the *Globe* was a lot easier than Ed would have ever thought possible. It seemed every time he had had to do research for a paper in college it took eons to drag up the material he was looking for.

Pulling the small roll of film out of the drawer and leaving the drawer slightly open so that he could easily find it once he was done, Ed walked back towards the entrance of the archives and sat down in front of one of the ten microfilm machines. Only four of them were occupied.

Scrolling through the film even for a short period of time was hard on the eyes but fortunately Ed didn't have to do so for long. The passage he was looking for was buried near the back of the paper just as Rachel had guessed it would be. The story was only a few paragraphs long. It identified the patient who had killed herself as Emily Jenkins. She had been thirty-five years old and had been receiving treatment at the hospital as an in-patient for over four years. The article didn't mention what she was being treated for or who was treating her.

Ed quickly copied the page he wanted, returned the roll of film to its drawer, and left the library, thanking Frank on his way out. It was only just before noon so Ed decided to drive to his office and do some more work on the Meadowvale folio. He didn't know how Rachel intended to obtain the information she said she would get her hands on but he thought he should give her until at least four o'clock.

The air-conditioned interior of the Steinbeck and Wainfleet building served as a nice contrast to the humid day it had become outside. Ed purchased a Dr. Pepper from one of several soda machines located in the building and headed for his office. There were over a dozen post-it notes affixed to his desk and computer monitor. The majority were from Bernard. Ed quickly read all of them, tapping his pencil on his knee as he did so, and came to the conclusion that Bernard was paranoid, insecure, and in desperate need of a female companion. All of the notes Bernard had left were questions in reference to the work he was doing on the Meadowvale portfolio and from Ed's standpoint they were all overtly obvious or so trivial in nature that only someone as compulsive as Bernard would think to ask them.

Throwing his pencil skyward, Ed stepped out of his office in search of Bernard. A slightly open door revealed that Bernard's office was unoccupied. Ed noticed that Bernard's desk was perfectly organized yet the floor was awash in papers and folders. Heading back to his own office, Ed was stopped by one of his fellow agents, Joe Green. He was at least six inches taller than Ed and had as much on him across the shoulders and chest as well. Ed was glad he was on good terms with the massive insurance agent.

"Hey, Ed. Hal's been looking for you all morning, he wants to talk to you right away," Joe said.

"Thanks, Joe. I'll go see him right now. Hey, have you seen Bernard anywhere?"

"Yeah, he just stepped out for lunch."

"Thanks."

"How's that Meadowvale folio coming along?"

"So far, so good. I'm almost done. I just need Bernard to finish crunching numbers for me."

"Well, when he's done your dirty work, send him over to see me. I need him ASAP."

"You can have him soon."

"Thanks, Ed. I appreciate it."

"No problem, catch you later."

"Sure."

Hal was standing at his window, hands clasped behind his back when he called Ed into his office. Ed stepped in, closing the door behind him.

"You wanted to see me, Hal?"

"Yes, Ed, I did. I looked at some of the numbers Bernard was working on this morning. Very impressive. Can we expect those numbers to remain consistent?"

"I think so, yes."

"Good. So are you almost done over at the Clinic then?" Hal had still not turned around to face Ed yet.

"Almost. I just have a few more things I want to check out and then I just have to wait for Bernard to crunch all the numbers for me."

"Will that take long?" Hal asked finally turning around.

"No, I shouldn't thinks so," Ed said looking Hal in the eye, "a couple of days at the most. If need be I'll have Bernard put in some overtime to make sure he gets it done."

"Excellent."

"Has Doctor Foley talked to you lately, Hal?"

"Just yesterday as a matter of fact. He was telling me you seem to be getting a grasp on things over there. I got a message early this morning to call him this afternoon. Will you be in around three-thirty?"

"No, unfortunately not. I've got to be at the Clinic by four and I still have a whole lot of running around to do if I'm going to get everything in order for Bernard."

"Very well. Keep up the good work and have a good weekend. I'll see you Monday morning?"

"For sure. I should have a solid preliminary report ready for you by then."

"Good. Don't work too hard."

"No such thing," Ed said with a smile as he left the office. Ed hurried down to his own office and noticed with satisfaction that his pencil was still firmly lodged in the ceiling tile. He jumped up and grabbed it. It could only mean one thing; lady luck was smiling and the next hand she dealt would be in Ed's favor. He still had over an hour before he had to meet Rachel so he drove downtown to grab a bite to eat. He smiled the entire way.

Chapter 38

Rachel sat at her desk deep in concentration. She had no idea how she was going to find out who those patient numbers belonged to. She couldn't just walk up to Carl Sanford and ask him. Nor could she sneak into his office and look the numbers up on his computer. Rachel tapped her foot incessantly, straining to come up with a plan. Suddenly she stopped tapping and smiled. She had an idea. And it just might work.

The door to Sanford's outer office was open and his secretary informed Rachel that he was in. Rachel knocked lightly and entered the inner office. It was as large as Foley's and Flemming's offices but not as well lived-in.

Everything was in perfect order. Every surface in the room was spotless, all the books on the shelves were arranged in order by height and were all placed exactly one inch from the edge of their shelves. If not for her knowledge of abnormal psychology, Rachel would have scarcely believed anyone could be so fastidious. Several Freudian terms came to mind.

In direct contrast to the room itself was its occupant, Carl Sanford. Rachel took one look at him hunched slovenly behind his desk and felt repulsed. His eyes darted nervously as Rachel entered the office, they seemed unwilling to focus on anything. He fidgeted uncontrollably and large stains of sweat had accumulated underneath each of his armpits, easily visible through his blue collared-shirt. She wondered briefly if Jim Wells' suicide had anything to do with his present state.

"Good afternoon, Doctor Sanford." Though Rachel didn't think the word good could be applied to Sanford's day. His physical appearance left a lot to be desired.

"Hello, Doctor Miller, to what do I owe this visit?" he asked tersely.

"Well, I've got a patient with multiple personalities that I'm treating right now and I'm having a hard time determining what type of approach I should take," Rachel began.

"The reason that I've come to see you is that I was going through some old files over at the psychiatric hospital and came across two of yours from about four years back. File numbers…" Rachel withdrew a piece of paper from her pants pocket and read off the numbers she had written down, "01849254 and 01964783. Both seemed strikingly similar to my patient in terms of the onset of the disorder. I took the liberty of reading through both files and noticed that once you had diagnosed DID for patients 01849254 and 01964783, and identified the numerous alters, your treatment progressed very rapidly and you had integrated both patients' personalities within less than a year. I also observed that patients 01849254 and 01964783 have remained stable since their re-integration. So, I was wondering if you could share with me your treatment protocol that you used on patients 01849254 and 01964783."

"Rachel, Rachel, Rachel, slow down. Why don't we find names for these patients before we go any further. We can't go on referring to them as numbers. Hold on one moment while I check my computer. What were those numbers again?" Sanford asked.

Rachel repeated the two numbers.

Sanford started typing commands into his computer and guided his mouse to the appropriate icons.

"Ah, here's the first one, Shelley Bockrath. And the second patient is, let's see here, ah here we go, Barbara Tusane." He quickly read his own summaries on both patients.

Rachel repeated the two names to herself in her head over and over.

"Now that we have names for these patients of mine and I've refreshed my memory on the subjects why don't you start by telling me about your patient." Sanford's posture and appearance had improved markedly since Rachel first came into his office. He seemed to enjoy the teacher's role. The fact that Rachel appealed to his ego probably helped matters as well. Now she just had to sit through a half hour of Sanford discussing his methods of treatment. Oh well, Rachel thought, it was a small price to pay for the information she had guilefully obtained.

Chapter 39

Leaving Sanford's office an hour later, Rachel hoped that Ed's search for the first name on their list had not been as torturous as her own. Carl Sanford had to be one of the dullest people alive. Not only that but Rachel could have sworn he was flirting with her in his own awkward fashion. The mere thought sent shivers of revulsion to the ends of her appendages. She shuddered involuntarily.

Closing the door to her office did wonders for her peace of mind. Looking out her window, she couldn't see Ed's red pick-up truck. She looked at her ancient Timex and noticed that he still had twenty minutes before their agreed upon meeting time of four o'clock.

When he did arrive fifteen minutes later, he was wearing a black suit and a broad grin and held up a sheet of paper with a photocopied newspaper article on it.

"Bingo!" Ed exclaimed waving the paper triumphantly, "we have a winner. Well, actually, that's a poor choice of words all things considering. Her name is Miss Emily Jenkins." Ed surrendered the sheet to Rachel who read it twice before placing it on her desk.

"Did you find out who the other two were?" Ed asked.

"Yes I did. Barbara Tusane and Shelley Bockrath."

"How did you get their names?"

"I appealed to the ego of a depraved man."

"I hope that didn't involve any depravity on your part."

"No, but I did have to stoop a little. Now that I've told you their names, forget I ever told you."

"Told me what?" Ed said with a mischievous grin. "Now that we know who these people are, what are we going to do about it?" he asked becoming serious.

"We let our fingers do the walking."

"Huh?"

"We'll call them."

"Just call them out of the blue?"

"Do you have a better idea?"

"Uh…No. No, I do not."

"Alright then. Pass me the phone book on the top shelf of my bookcase and we'll get started."

Ed reached up to the top of the bookcase, pulled down the San Francisco directory and handed it to Rachel. She immediately flipped it open and started scanning the B's for Shelley Bockrath.

"Good, there's only two of them listed."

"What if she moved, or married, or divorced?"

"We'll find out soon enough Mister Glass-Is-Half-Empty." Rachel punched in the first Bockrath number. It was listed under Peter J.

"Hello," a tired male voice answered. It sounded like he had just woken up.

"Yes, hello. Is there a Shelley Bockrath there please?"

"Who wants to know?" the voice asked grumpily, suspicious. No doubt wary of the thousands of telephone solicitors eager to sell their wares via fiber optics.

"This is Doctor Miller from the Meadowvale Clinic."

"Hold on a sec." Rachel heard the phone being put down and the male's voice shouting to Shelley Bockrath.

"Hello?" a woman's voice asked.

"Hi, Shelley Bockrath?"

"Speaking."

"Hi, Missus Bockrath. My name is Doctor Miller. I'm from the Meadowvale Clinic. Are you familiar with the Clinic?"

"Yes I am. What do you want?" she asked guardedly.

"Were you treated by Doctor Carl Sanford three years ago?"

"Yes I was. I'm sorry, who are you again?"

"Doctor Miller from the Meadowvale Clinic for the Treatment of Dissociative Disorders. I'm calling to check on your present state. Kind of a progress check if you will."

"Oh, okay," Shelley Bockrath's voice lost its edge. "What do you want to know?"

"Well, first of all have you maintained integration since you ended treatment with Doctor Sanford?"

"Yes, surprisingly, I have."

"How do you mean surprisingly?"

"Well, I had DID for over twenty-five years with over seventeen personalities. Up until my mid-thirties I only discovered seven of my alters with help from my first doctor. Once I began seeing Doctor Sanford though, he discovered ten more alters residing inside of me."

"Why did you stop seeing your first doctor?"

"She was a rich ivy-leaguer. Very well-to-do. She was very personable but I could tell that she was repulsed by me. I don't think she had any idea what she was getting into when she chose psychiatry as a discipline. She also didn't hypnotize me. That's what I liked about Doctor Sanford, we did a lot of what he called regressive hypnosis sessions. That's how he uncovered all my other alters and that's how he eventually cured me. I'm a whole woman again thanks to Doctor Sanford."

"Well, it definitely sounds that way. I appreciate your candor Missus Bockrath. Thank you for talking with me."

"No problem, I hope I was of some help."

"You were, Missus Bockrath, thank you and good night."

"Good-bye."

"Phew!" Rachel hung up the phone and wiped her brow. Ed stood up from the chair he was sitting in and began clapping.

"Bravo! That was an excellent performance. I think you missed your calling."

"I don't think so. If I had to do that all day, I'd develop ulcers."

"You didn't even have to fib."

"Thank God. I feel bad enough as it is. I did learn a few things however." Rachel recounted her conversation with Shelley Bockrath. The parts he hadn't overheard.

"So what does that mean? Another dead end?"

"I don't know. There's something gnawing at the back of my mind but I don't know what it is. I'm sure I'll think of it eventually."

"Well, let's call the other one now. Now that you've warmed up to it."

"Sure."

Ed slid the phone book across the desk and began thumbing through the thin gray pages.

"What did you say that other name was again?" he asked.

"Barbara Tusane."

"How do you spell that?"

Rachel spelled it out loud for him.

"Tusane. Tusane," he muttered to himself, "Terwilliger, Thomson, Toslanki, Trepanier, Tupper, here we go, Tusane. Oh boy," Ed groaned.

"What?" Rachel asked in alarm.

"There are over twenty Tusanes living in the San Francisco area."

"None of them listed under B. Or Barbara?"

"Not that I can see. So what do we do? Call each one?"

"I guess we don't have much choice. Read out the first one for me."

Ed read out the first Tusane phone number. It took them fifteen minutes to get the right number. Of course it was the second last phone number.

"Hello?" a woman's voice asked on the other end of the line. It sounded like she had the speaker phone on.

"Yes, hello. Is Barbara Tusane there please?"

"This is she. Who is this?"

"This is Doctor Miller from the Meadowvale Clinic calling."

"The Meadowvale Clinic?"

"Yes it's the new Clinic devoted to the treatment of dissociative disorders."

"Why are you calling?" Barbara Tusane's voice instantly changed from curious to hostile.

"I'm calling past patients of those doctors who work here at the Clinic to ask them how they're managing several years after integration."

"You know I have DID?"

"Yes, Ma'am, but I assure you this phone call and the conversation we have is strictly confidential."

"It's also over thank you very much. If I'm going to talk to anybody about my disorder it will be with Doctor Sanford. Please don't call me again or I'll report you and have you charged with harassment." The phone slammed down in Rachel's ear.

"Ouch." Rachel said putting the phone down.

"No luck?" Ed asked unaware of what had transpired on the other end of the line.

"Let's just say she wasn't very cooperative. I can't really blame her though. I think we were extremely lucky that Shelley Bockrath was so cooperative."

"So now what?" Ed asked disappointed that the phone calls hadn't proved entirely useful.

"I don't know. I'm kind of at a loss. Unless…"

"Unless what? I can hear the gears in your head shifting, come on share with me this idea of yours."

"Why don't we meet here at the Clinic at ten o'clock tomorrow morning?"

"That sounds a little better than eight o'clock. But for what?"

"I'm going to ask Doctor Sanford right now if we can bring one of his patients, Amanda, to the park."

"To the park? Why?"

"Trust me."

"Do I have a choice?"

"No."

"I didn't think so. Alright, ten o'clock it is."

Rachel saw Ed to the elevator and marched back up the hallway to Sanford's office for the second time that afternoon.

"Doctor Sanford?" Rachel called through the narrow crack of the slightly open office door. His secretary wasn't at her desk.

"Yes, Rachel what is it?" he replied waving her in.

"Sorry to bother you again, but I wanted to run an idea by you."

"No bother, what's this idea of yours?"

"Well, I noticed one of your patients, Amanda Rutherford, has been acting pretty withdrawn of late and…"

"Well, she does have DID." Sanford retorted.

"Oh I realize that, and that's actually why I came to see you. You see I have the day off tomorrow and I was hoping that you would give me permission to take Amanda with me to Golden Gate Park for the day."

"Why would you want to do that?" Sanford asked defensively.

"Well, I thought it would be a nice change for her. She's obviously very eager to be outside as her behavior has indicated in the past."

"A little too eager if you ask me. What would prevent her from taking off tomorrow once you get to the park?"

"Well, I could take Ed with me. You know, the insurance guy from Steinbeck and Wainfleet?"

"Is he still here?"

"Yes he is. Doctor Foley kind of assigned him to me. I'm supposed to explain to him what it is we do here and help in any way I can."

"Is he in good shape?"

"I guess, yes. Why do you ask?"

"Because he might be doing a lot of running tomorrow."

"Does that mean I can bring Amanda to the park then?"

"Let's go talk to her right now and then I'll make up my mind. As long as Amanda feels up to it though, I don't see any problem with it."

Chapter 40

The lock on the front door of the shoddy Brownstone required more exertion on Rachel's part than usual. This after the day had gone relatively well. Her apartment door opened more easily.

Spooky squinted lazily across the living room from atop his perch on the narrow windowsill. Warm rays of sunlight bathed his thick coat.

"And how is Spooky doing today?" Rachel asked. She received another lethargic turn of the head in response.

"Oh, I'm sorry, I didn't mean to interrupt your catnap." Spooky closed his eyes and returned to his peaceful, gravity defying, slumber. Rachel decided to cook for herself that night. A person could only eat so much Chinese food in one week. Unless of course that person was Chinese.

There were two messages on the machine. Rachel listened to them as she began making preparations for her solo pasta festival. Spooky looked over in annoyance at the banging of pots and pans.

"Hi Rachel, it's Marty," Rachel was surprised he called. She had not called him since he had dumped her over the phone.

"Look, I'm really sorry I broke up with you over the phone. I realize it wasn't the classiest thing I could have done," there was the understatement of the year, "anyway, I've been doing a lot of thinking this past week and I was hoping I could take you out to dinner and a movie some time soon. You know, to make it up to you and to give me a chance to talk to you. That new John Malkovich movie begins tonight at the Cineplex. I remember you saying you wanted to see it when it came out. So how about it? I'll try calling again later tonight so I hope you're in. Talk to you soon. I miss you."

Rachel's movements in the kitchen slowed as she tried to perform the physical task of cooking pasta and sauce in conjunction with the mental and emotional task of what to do about Marty's phone call. The beginning of the second message put her thoughts on hold.

"Hello, Doctor Miller. My name is Detective Sawatsky," Rachel's heart somersaulted at the sound of the man's voice and how he identified himself. Had Barbara Tusane followed up on her threat and called the police? Would they notify Dr. Sanford? Or had Mrs. Tusane already done so herself?

"I just wanted to let you know that we have in our custody two teens who have confessed to slashing your tires the other day. They were caught this afternoon stealing a stereo from a car in the parking lot next to yours. We're keeping them down here until their parents come to get them, so if you'd like to come down and press charges, now would be a good time. I'm sure we could probably convince the parents to pay for your tires as well. You can reach me at five-five-five-oh-six-seven-two extension three-oh-five."

Rachel heaved a sigh of relief once she realized the call was not related to her actions that afternoon. She jotted down the Detective's number and extension and called him. She let him know that she wouldn't be pressing charges but if the kids' parents were willing to repay her for the tires, she would be more than grateful.

The kids who had slashed her tires were already going to get punished. There was no need for her to charge them as well. She was glad that they had been caught and there was a chance that her tires would be paid for, but she saw no point in adding to their troubles.

Spooky supped from a bowl of Tender Vittles Rachel placed on the floor for him as she ate in the living room. She left the TV off and turned her thoughts to the men in her life. All two of them. She was sure that she didn't want to rekindle her relationship with Marty but not as sure what to make of Ed. He was sweet, funny, charming, and quirky in a down-to-earth way. Marty had always been so serious. Ed also had Marty licked in the looks department. Marty was no slouch himself but Ed seemed to hold himself with a certain confidence that Rachel admired.

"What to do? What to do? Huh, Spooky? What's your take on my situation?" Rachel asked her cat. Spooky looked up from his bowl and bounded into Rachel's lap. He curled up on her legs and began purring contentedly.

"What are you saying? I shouldn't stress myself out over it? Life is too short to be constantly worrying? Sounds like good advice." Rachel stroked Spooky's soft fur and rubbed the underside of his chin and behind his ears. His long thin tail undulated through the air in satisfaction.

From the hallway, Rachel heard the sound of keys jangling and a door being opened and closed. Her neighbor Ted Harpingham was home. Just the man she had to see.

After talking to Barbara Tusane and Shelley Bockrath over the phone, Rachel realized that the only way to find out more about what Dr. Sanford was doing to his patients was to get inside one of his patient's heads. Getting Amanda Rutherford out of the Clinic tomorrow was the first step towards that goal. Talking to Ted Harpingham was the second.

Rachel had known Ted ever since she first moved into her apartment. He had helped her move the heavier pieces of furniture she had in her possession. He asked her why her boyfriend wasn't helping her. She didn't have a boyfriend at the time, but joked that he was in a particularly heavy trunk that she and Ted were carrying down the hall. His face became serious for a moment and then he burst out in gales of laughter.

Although they weren't close friends, she and Ted got along quite well over the years. They often asked for and granted favors for each other. As far as she could remember, Ted had never turned her down. She hoped he didn't tonight. Rachel had to ask him for a huge favor.

When the door to Ted's apartment opened, Rachel was greeted by Handel's *Water Music* and the smell of brandy. Ted held the door in one hand and a crystal snifter in the other.

"Rachel? What a surprise. To what do I owe this unexpected yet pleasant visit?"

"I was wondering if I could talk to you for a bit?"

"Of course, come on in." Ted stepped aside and ushered Rachel into his apartment. Although of the same dimensions as her own, that was where the similarities between the two apartments ended.

The living room was painted in balsam green and the kitchen in antique wine, the ceilings, baseboards, wainscotting, window and doorframes were painted in a satin off-white so as not to contrast too starkly with the dark hues of the walls. Slick hardwood floors were punctuated by several Persian rugs of varying sizes and black leather furniture dominated the living room. Their arrangement seemed to augment the size of the living area despite the low lighting and color of the walls.

"Have a seat, Rachel," Ted aimed his snifter at one of two leather loveseats. He walked into the kitchen where the stove light provided just enough illumination to cast a shadow over the black Formica counters.

"Can I get you a drink?" he called from the kitchen.

"Sure, that would be lovely."

"What would you like?"

"Do you have any wine?"

"Red or white?"

"Red please."

"Anything's fine really, Ted. I'm not much of a connoisseur."

"Red it is." Ted handed Rachel a glass half-filled with a rich looking wine when he came back into the living room.

"Hmmm, it's delicious." Rachel said after taking a sip and exposing her mouth to its full aroma.

"Thank you. It's nice to watch someone enjoy a fine wine. Do you like Handel?"

"Handle?"

"Handel. The composer."

"Oh, I'm sorry," Rachel laughed at herself, "I'm not familiar with his music."

"This is called *Water Music*. Beautiful isn't it?"

Rachel cocked her head and listened as numerous high-pitched trumpets responded echoically to the French horns reverberating in the background. The acoustics provided by several small speakers placed strategically around the apartment enabled Rachel to actually feel the music. Each note had a tangible quality to it.

"It's nice. I would expect something that was called *Water Music* to sound different, though."

"It wasn't titled *Water Music* because it sounded like water, it was actually written for a river party on the Thames in the early eighteenth century. Legend has it that King George, the host of the party, was so impressed by the piece that he forgave Handel for walking out of his court and leaving his position as chief musician when the King had been Elector of Hanover."

"I can see, or rather, hear why." Rachel leaned back and sunk into the soft leather cushions of the loveseat listening to the multisonant piece. The wine slowly made its way from her stomach to her head and filled her with a full warm sensation. She sat up with effort and cleared her mind, wishing she could just lie back, drink, and listen to classical music for the rest of the night.

She took a large sip of wine and drained her glass.

Liquid courage.

"I have a favor to ask you, Ted."

"What can I do for you?" Ted asked. He too appeared to have been nodding off.

"It's a big favor, Ted." Rachel said, the tone of her voice leaving no room for misinterpretation. Ted sat up, took another drink from his glass, and put it down on the small wooden table beside the loveseat he occupied. Several magazines covered the top of the table. *GQ. Details. Esquire. George.*

"Oh." He said. "What kind of favor?"

"Well, it's funny. I've known you for a number of years but this is the first time I've ever seen the inside of your apartment. It's a side of you I've never seen before. What I do know on the other hand, is that as an ex-police officer you have a lot of connections as you've indicated numerous times."

"Are you in trouble, Rachel?" Ted asked, easily seeing Rachel's true motives.

"No, no, of course not. But I do need some help."

"What kind of help? And where do my connections fit into this?"

"I need a hypnotist."

"A hypnotist?" Ted asked puzzled.

"A good one. Someone who you can trust to keep quiet."

Ted put his elbows on his knees, crossed his hands and rested his chin in the bridge they formed. His brow furrowed deeply.

"Why do you want a hypnotist?" he finally asked after what seemed an eternity.

"I can't say. Only that it's important."

"Is it legal?"

"It's not illegal," Rachel answered hopefully.

Ted looked like he was deep in concentration. Finally, he looked at Rachel.

"I can't help you, Rachel. I'm sorry." He stood up and began walking to the door.

Rachel took that as her cue to leave although it felt more like she was getting the bum's rush. She placed her empty glass on a coffee table and stood up as well.

"Thank you for the wine, Ted."

"You're welcome, Rachel," he opened the door, "stop by anytime. Good night."

Rachel skulked back to her apartment and filled one of her own glasses with red wine. It tasted bitter in her mouth. She wasn't sure if it was because she was comparing it to Ted's or if it was because she was in a despondent mood. She felt like getting drunk and going to bed.

She had hoped Ted would come through for her. She wanted to have Amanda hypnotized to see if they could uncover something about Dr. Sanford. Unfortunately the only doctor at the Clinic who was truly proficient at hypnotizing was Dr. Sanford himself and Rachel didn't know if she could trust any of the other doctors to do what she wanted done. She looked at her watch. It was too late to call Ed and change plans. She hoped he wouldn't be mad. It looked like they really were going to spend the day in the park.

Chapter 41

Ted Harpingham stood in his darkened kitchen alone. He had refilled his snifter twice in the last ten minutes. Handel was no longer emanating from the speakers. Ted desperately needed the silence.

He hadn't thought of Sherman Myers for over seven years. That was one demon he was hoping to erase from his memory completely. Now, with Rachel coming into his apartment and asking if he knew anyone who could hypnotize, his mind was flooded with a torrent of memories.

Sherman Myers was the reason Ted no longer served on the force.

It was eight long years ago that Ted Harpingham had made San Francisco Homicide. It seemed much longer though. It took him ten years of department hopping to finally reach his goal. He couldn't believe so much time had passed. It felt like yesterday and twenty years ago at the same time. He'd only worked a dozen or so homicide cases when the case that would change his life, in more ways than one, landed on his desk.

The victims' names were Nathan Canungo, Hank Shenter, and Max Freeburn. All were shot execution style in a public bathroom at the San Francisco International Airport. No witnesses were found. A fourth man, an innocent bystander who had gone into the bathroom to relieve himself, had been shot as well but not killed. A bullet had grazed his skull.

Under normal circumstances, the incident would have received low priority. Ted was already involved in three other investigations, one of which had the markings of a serial killer. When it came to homicide though, as Ted quickly learned, there was no such thing as normal circumstances. Particularly not in this case.

Canungo had been killed in the custody of the U.S. State Department. Four agents from the State Department were responsible for the safe passage of Canungo from Lahore, Pakistan to San Francisco. Hank Shenter and Max Freeburn were two of those agents.

Nathan Canungo worked for the Pakistani equivalent of the U.S. Department of Defense. Under the guise of a physicist working on cold fusion, his government had him developing nuclear technology. Once the purpose of his work dawned on him and he realized what his government intended to do with the technology he developed, Canungo decided to defect, knowing full well that if he quit he would be putting his safety, and that of his family, at risk.

Sending his family over before him on the pretense of visiting relatives, Canungo began making preparations for his own departure. In so doing, he contacted the U.S. Embassy in Pakistan and apprised them of his situation. That was how the U.S. State Department became involved.

With the combined manpower of the San Francisco Police Department, U.S. State Department, and FBI, it didn't take long to discover that Canungo's travel plans had been leaked. The leak originated in the U.S. and flowed all the way back to Pakistan. Once the possibility of foreign intervention seemed likely, the last of the letter organizations reared its ugly head: the Central Intelligence Agency.

That was when Ted met Sherman Myers for the first time. Sherman was introduced to Ted as a CIA Specialist. What he specialized in wasn't mentioned at the time of their introduction. It was only later that Ted would find out.

After three days of intense investigation all the parties involved were still in the dark as to what had transpired in the airport washroom. They still didn't know how Canungo's assassins had learned about his travel plans either. The only avenue of hope lay with the man who had been shot in the head in the bathroom. Brett Constance, a traveling hotel inspector, fluttered in and out of consciousness. Every time he awoke, someone from the State Department would turn on a tape recorder and try to ask him questions about his involvement in the shooting. Before he could answer however, Brett would lose consciousness once more.

Even when he did regain consciousness almost a full week after the incident, he couldn't remember what had happened. He was unable to remember a single thing about the shooting. For all intents and purposes, as a witness, Brett Constance was useless.

Enter Sherman Myers.

A lifer with the CIA, Myers specialized in witness interviewing and interrogation. If someone had seen or heard something but couldn't, or wouldn't, consciously recall it, Sherman Myers could bring that information to the surface using a wide array of techniques. Some more effective than others.

He used simple regressive-hypnosis on Brett Constance. Although not always reliable, hypnosis could be used to take a person back to the scene of a crime and coaxed into remembering specific details. The problem with using hypnotism though, is that it heightens the subject's susceptibility to suggestion. Therefore, when asking questions, it is crucial not to ask leading questions.

Sherman Myers was well aware of all the potential problems with hypnotism. He knew better than anybody the negative effects of hypnotism. During the investigation, Myers held over ten sessions with Brett Constance. His fellow spooks nicknamed him Sherman Svengali.

Myers had the information he needed after only three sessions but persisted for another two weeks to make sure what Brett Constance was telling him was accurate. As far as Myers could tell, it was. Not only was Brett able to remember what had happened in the airport washroom, he was also able to recall what the shooter looked like.

Brett had gone in to wash his face and brush his teeth after a long red-eye flight from Geneva. He noticed one man at the urinals and two other men standing around looking as if they were waiting for the man relieving himself. He didn't notice the fourth man come in until he looked up from the sink into the mirror. A gun equipped with a silencer was pointed at his head. The gunman coldly said, "Wrong place at the wrong time, buddy," and fired the gun. That was all Brett could remember. That and the fact that the shooter was a San Francisco police officer.

Once the identity of the shooter was revealed, the wheels of justice, as greased by the Internal Affairs Department of the SFPD, moved very quickly. Aided by Internal Affairs, Brett Constance was able to identify the gunman by looking through the SFPD computer system which held a picture of every police officer on the force. His name was Lou Galvano. Galvano's confession, obtained over the course of two grueling days of grilling by Internal Affairs, should have been the end of the affair.

He admitted to the triple homicide and one attempted murder. Twenty-thousand dollars, recently deposited, were found in a cousin's bank account. Galvano didn't deny that it was his pay off for the job. His share for the killing of three innocent people: just over six and a half thousand bucks a head.

Galvano revealed everything. And then he revealed more. In his confessions, he made reference to a little black book kept by someone high up in the SFPD. A little black book that was being used for a lot of black mail.

Recorded within the book, so Galvano said, was the name of every cop on the take. It listed who was paying off who and how much they were paying. The book itself was never found, but the search for it escalated into a witch hunt within the SFPD and by the time IA was done conducting its massive investigation, over seventy officers were facing charges. Layer upon layer of corruption was discovered and it spanned the entire department, from the rookies on up. The media had a field day comparing it to the purges of Stalinist Russia.

For a period of two months, Ted Harpingham watched, partly in awe, partly in anger, but mostly in disbelief, as the men and women around him, those people whom he trusted with his life, were systematically revealed to be no better, and in some cases worse, than the scum that resided on the other side of the bars. Ted became so disillusioned that he turned in his gun and badge to an empty desk. His superior's office was already empty.

Now, thinking back, though wishing he hadn't, Ted wondered if maybe he should give Rachel Sherman Myers' number. The havoc that Myers' initiated eight years ago was not his fault, and in the end, it was for the better. Not only for the SFPD and the residents of San Francisco, but also for Ted himself. He loved the work he was doing now, and wouldn't give it up for the world. He just hoped Rachel knew what she was doing.

Chapter 42

▼

Rachel left her empty wine glass and dirty pasta dishes on the edge of the sink with good intentions of cleaning them up in the morning. Her mind was set on climbing into bed and crawling underneath her thick duvet. Just the thought of sleep made her emit a long, anticipatory sigh. She turned off the lights in her apartment, shucked off her shoes, and walked down the short hall to her bedroom.

Three knocks on the door forced her to turn around. Very reluctantly. Ted was standing in the hall when Rachel opened the door.

"Ted?" she said surprised upon seeing who her visitor was.

"Can I come in for a moment, Rachel?" he asked.

"Of course."

"I apologize for being curt with you earlier this evening. It's just that your question brought back a lot of memories for me. Some I haven't wanted to think about for a long time. Actually I was hoping to forget them entirely."

"Oh God, I'm sorry, Ted, I didn't mean to…"

"It's not your fault Rachel, there's no way you could have known. What I wanted to tell you is that I do know someone who's good with hypnosis. I haven't talked to him for over seven years but I can tell you where to reach him. Do you have a pen and some paper?"

"Yeah, hold on a sec." Rachel rushed to her bedroom, glanced longingly at her bed, and scooped a pen and sheet of paper off her desk. She gave both to Ted who jotted down a name, phone number and what looked like an address. He handed it to Rachel.

"Sherman Myers?" Rachel read the name printed neatly on the paper.

"Sherman Myers. He's trustworthy. He's good at what he does. And I have to warn you, he's a little quirky."

"Quirky? In what way?"

"Let's just say he's eccentric. Tell him I gave you his name and number, he'll talk to you."

"Thank you Ted, I really appreciate this."

"You're welcome. I hope he can help you. Good luck."

"Thanks. Good night, Ted."

"'Night, Rachel." Rachel slid the deadbolt and attached the chain on her door and picked up her phone. She might as well call Sherman Myers now, especially since she wanted to see him late tomorrow morning.

"Hullo?" an elderly man's voice answered. He didn't sound as if he'd been sleeping despite the late hour.

"Hello, is this Sherman Myers?"

"It is. Who is this?"

"Mister Myers, my name is Rachel Miller, Doctor Rachel Miller. I got your name from a friend of mine, Ted Harpingham."

"Did you say Harpingham?"

"Yes sir, Ted Harpingham."

"I haven't heard that name for quite some time." The line on Myers' end was quiet for a long time.

"Mister Myers?" Rachel asked checking to see if he was still on the line.

"I'm still here. I was just thinking. Now what can I do for you?"

"Well, Mister Myers, Ted told me that you're good at hypnosis."

"That I am, that I am."

"I was hoping to retain your services if that's possible."

"You want me to hypnotize you?"

"No, not me, someone else."

"Why do you need a hypnotist?"

"It's a long story Mister Myers, one which I would be happy to tell you later but I need to know if I can bring this person to you and if you can hypnotize her for me."

"I don't see why not. I don't get out much anymore and I certainly could use the company. When did you want to do this?"

"Would tomorrow before noon be too soon?"

"No, I suppose not. Do you need my address?"

"No sir, Ted already gave it to me."

"I figured he would have. Alright I'll see you before noon tomorrow."

"Thank you very much, Mister Myers."

"Oh, Rachel, one more thing."

"Yes?"

"Call me Sherman."

"Okay, Sherman." Rachel hung up the phone and smiled. She climbed into her bed and turned off the light. She briefly considered finishing her Oliver Sacks book but chose to lie in the dark and think happy thoughts before drifting off to sleep. With any luck, such a train of thought would ward off the unknown stalker who pursued her in her dreams.

With any luck.

She had dreamt again the night before of being chased by the shadowy figure. This time she was running through the wide halls of the Meadowvale Clinic and could hear the pounding footsteps behind her, sounding closer and closer. The figure's face was cloaked in darkness and an immense, swirling cape flowing behind him ate up everything in its path, leaving nothing but darkness in its wake.

Her sister's voice echoed through the halls but no matter how hard she looked, Rachel couldn't find her. It was as if Theresa was running away at the same speed that Rachel was running towards her.

The opaque silhouette which hounded her more nights than not almost caught her the previous night. As he did every time he appeared in her dreams.

Rachel was sprinting down the halls but they were growing increasingly narrower making it more and more difficult for her to run. The walls clamped down on her shoulders and the ceiling brushed up against her head, forcing her to run sideways and crouched at the same time. She woke up when she felt the blackness swarm around her like a million silent, unstinging hornets.

She'd begun to notice several common themes in all the dreams she had involving the threatening figure. First of all, she could never see his face and therefore she had no idea who or what she was running from. Second, she was always alone in her dreams. Aside from her pursuer, there was never anybody else in her nightmares. The last similarity she observed in her dreams was that she was always cornered by the menacing figure. It seemed she was never given the opportunity to escape. Her mother always told her as a child that nightmares were brought on by a guilty conscience. Rachel wondered how much truth there was in her mother's admonishments.

Rachel pushed the memories of last night's dream out of her mind and wrapped herself up like a fajita in the thick, fluffy duvet. Sleep came quickly and dreamless.

Chapter 43

Saturday
9:00 a.m.
Meadowvale Clinic

John Haskins had never set eyes on the Meadowvale Clinic and was not particularly impressed when he did. It was one of the ugliest buildings he'd ever seen despite its modern appointments. Eileen Montgomery was right in her assertion that it was a cold and sterile place. He'd talked to Walter Flemming the previous night shortly after his visit with Eileen Montgomery. Flemming assured him that all six of the doctors who worked at the Clinic, would be present. John wanted to interview all of them. He thought he would start with Flemming himself.

John ignored Margaret Newman's insistent pleas to stop and walked right into the doctor's office. "Good morning, Walter. How's it going?" He loved walking in unannounced and talking to people on a first name basis. It really threw them off. He didn't like it when the people he wanted to question were prepared.

"Oh, hello, yes, good morning to you, too, Agent Haskins," Flemming sputtered, surprised by the FBI agent's unannounced entrance. He excused himself to go to the bathroom.

John looked around the office trying to get a feel for what type of man Walter Flemming was. He saw no personal momentoes, and no pictures whatsoever. The only thing personal about the room at all were the degrees and citations affixed to one wall. They made the room seem colder somehow.

Sunlight filtered in through cracks in the venetian blinds and a musky odor seemed to linger in the air.

Flemming re-emerged from the washroom a little more composed than when he had first entered.

"Sorry about that, Agent Haskins. I didn't realize you were coming in so early."

"The last time I visited my doctor, I must have waited for over two hours. So, the way I see it, if I intend to see six doctors in one day, I'd better get an early start."

Flemming smiled, "Fair enough. Now what did you want to ask me?" Flemming was relatively certain that Agent Haskins was at the end of his rope and was simply going to ask the same questions he'd been asking since the beginning of his investigation. That was why his jaw almost dropped when Haskins asked his first question.

"How exactly was Arthur Montgomery involved with the Meadowvale Clinic and why would someone have wanted that involvement to come to a premature end?"

"Along with myself and Grant Foley, one of the doctors you'll meet later in the day, Arthur was responsible for the creation of this Clinic. Though I can't imagine why someone would want to get rid of him because of it."

"How's the money in treating dissociative disorders, doctor? Pretty good, I would assume, huh?" John asked.

"Relatively good, yes. Most of our patients are covered by insurance, and the treatment of dissociative disorders can be a lengthy process."

"So you and this Doctor Foley aren't hurting financially then?"

"No, I suppose not. What does this have to do with Arthur Montgomery?"

"Nothing I suppose. What did you and Doctor Foley do when you discovered Arthur Montgomery had disappeared and was probably not coming back?"

"Well, we were in shock at first, but we realized that the creation of the Clinic had to go on without him. We hired a replacement."

"Doctor Rachel Miller?" Haskins knew a lot more than he was letting on. Rule number one in interrogation: always know more than your adversary.

"Yes, Doctor Rachel Miller. Doctor Foley was the one who actually hired her, I only met her when she first arrived here."

"So you had nothing to do with her hiring? Did you even know who she was before Doctor Foley hired her?"

"No, I didn't. Foley met her at the university where he was briefly conducting lectures."

"I know I've asked you this question before, Walter, but when was the absolute last time you saw Arthur Montgomery?"

Flemming sighed, "As I've told you countless times, the last time I saw Arthur Montgomery was the night before his disappearance as I was leaving the Psychiatric Hospital. Around six-o'clock."

"Thank you for your time, Walt. Could you tell me where Doctor Henderson's office is?" John stood up to leave.

"Take a left when you leave my office, his name is on the door, you can't miss it."

"Thanks," John opened the door and paused. "If Arthur Montgomery were to walk in to your office this afternoon, what would you tell him?" John asked over his shoulder in an attempt to catch Flemming off guard.

"That he's got a lot of patients to see. Good morning, Agent Haskins."

"Catch you later."

Ten minutes with Clyde Henderson turned up absolutely no new information. John was pretty certain that Henderson wasn't involved. The scholarly looking doctor had only been at the Clinic for two weeks and had not known any of his colleagues prior to his being hired. John had cut the interview short because he wanted to talk to Grant Foley and Dr. Rachel Miller. That, and because Clyde Henderson's thick accent made it impossible to talk with him for any longer. John hadn't concentrated so hard in such a short period of time since reading Hegel in college. A minor headache began to unfold within the confines of his head.

John made his way to Foley's office next. His secretary, Barb, was somewhat more gracious than Flemming's secretary.

"Agent Haskins, welcome." Foley stood up from behind his desk as John let himself into the office. Taking in every detail in a matter of seconds, John felt more at ease in Foley's office. Here was a family man who took pride in his work.

"Thank you for seeing me on such short notice, Doctor Foley." John decided to take a garrulous approach with Foley. He seemed the chatty type. The two of them chatted for awhile about the weather, their families, and Foley's work at the Clinic.

"I assume you didn't come just to chat with me, Agent Haskins," Foley said after they had talked for over ten minutes. "Unless of course you're working up a profile on me."

"No, not at all. I just wanted to ask you a few questions about Arthur Montgomery. You were acquaintances, were you not?"

"More than just acquaintances. We were close colleagues and good friends. We took our families out to the lake together every Labor Day for the last four years. This was the first year we didn't do so."

"That's too bad. Can you think of any reason why someone would want Arthur's work with the Clinic to stop?"

Foley didn't answer for almost a full minute. He appeared deep in thought.

"I can't think of a single thing," he finally said. "If someone was hoping to prevent the Clinic from opening, they would have had to remove Walt Flemming and myself as well. Even after Arthur's disappearance, there was no question that the Clinic would open."

"You're sure?"

"Positive. Arthur Montgomery was a straight arrow. I can't imagine he would ever be involved in something that would lead to his removal."

"What about this Doctor Miller you hired to replace Doctor Montgomery?"

"Rachel? I met her at the University where I was conducting a lecture series shortly after Arthur's disappearance and got to know her quite well. She's an extremely bright and competent young woman and when it comes to dissociative disorders, she knows her stuff. I hired her because of her zeal and qualifications. If not for Arthur's disappearance, she wouldn't be working here."

"So she was just in the right place at the right time, so to speak?"

"So to speak. Yes." Foley didn't like the intonation in the FBI man's voice.

"So how did you get involved with the Clinic?"

"Walter Flemming and I went to medical school together at Columbia. I started my own private practice on the East Coast while he came out here to work on the West Coast. He was working at the San Francisco Psychiatric Hospital when he called me four and a half years ago with a proposal."

"What proposal was that?"

"To come join him here and build the Meadowvale Clinic. He and Arthur Montgomery had been working on the idea for a year or two and decided they needed a third man. I was he."

"So you didn't know Doctor Montgomery before you came out East?"

"That's right. I met him for the first time at the hospital where he and Walter Flemming worked," Foley said.

"And the three of you got along alright?"

"We worked very well together. This Clinic is testament to that."

"Well, thanks again for seeing me this morning, I hope I didn't take up too much of your time, Doctor Foley."

"No, I had to come in this morning to do some paper work anyway. Have a good day, Agent Haskins."

"Same to you." John wondered if there was more to Foley's and Miller's relationship than Foley let on. Could they be having an affair? Did Arthur Montgomery somehow discover their little secret? Was he killed for what he knew? Was Rachel Miller hired in his place as a tragic, ironic postscript to the whole sordid affair? John was really looking forward to talking to Dr. Miller now. He would see her last. He still had to drop in on Dr. Tanner and Dr. Sanford.

Ruth Tanner was of even less help than Clyde Henderson had been. She was hired at the same time as Henderson and had never even heard of Arthur Montgomery until the Clinic had officially opened. John only spent five minutes with her. She wasn't the most amiable person he had ever met. John imagined she spent more time poring over books than she did in the company of other people.

John spent over half an hour with Carl Sanford. It took him that long just to answer a few questions. Everytime John asked him a question, the doctor would answer back with a question of his own.

"When was the last time you saw Arthur Montgomery?"

"Why? Am I under suspicion?"

Or, "Can you think of anyone who had a grudge against Doctor Montgomery?"

"Why would someone have a grudge against him?"

The overall impression John left with was that Carl Sanford knew something. He didn't think he knew exactly what happened to Montgomery, but he sure as hell knew someone who did. If ever he found some hard evidence, John knew he could always come back and exert pressure on Sanford. He also knew that the doctor wouldn't last longer than five minutes. The man was a nervous breakdown waiting to happen. The little pink bottle that Sanford had tried to keep hidden from view spoke volumes. He reminded John of an old Stones song, *Nineteenth Nervous Breakdown*.

The door to Dr. Rachel Miller's office was locked and John's knocks went unanswered.

John walked back to Flemming's office. "Where can I find Doctor Miller?" he asked.

"In her office I would assume. If you go down the hall..."

"I checked her office. There's nobody there and the door is locked."

"Well, she should be there. Let's go ask Doctor Foley." Grant Foley didn't know where she was either.

"She took one of my patient's to the park," Carl Sanford said when they approached him.

"I guess I'll talk to her on Monday." John left the three doctors as they headed back to their respective offices.

After leaving a message on Dr. Miller's voice mail informing her he would see her on Monday, John left the Clinic in a somber mood. Not only hadn't he learned anything new, but he now had more questions than ever. He was sure Walter Flemming was hiding something but he didn't know what to make of Grant Foley. Foley had said to him, *"I can't imagine Arthur would be involved in anything that would lead to his removal."* That seemed an odd thing to say. Was there something going on at the Clinic? Maybe that's where he should start digging next. His wife would love it. Plotting doctors, medical conspiracies, missing colleagues. It all sounded like something out of a Robin Cook novel, one of his wife's favorite authors.

For now though, he had other things to think about. He wanted a background check done on all six doctors and he wanted to find out who benefited monetarily from Arthur Montgomery's death. John didn't harbor any suspicions toward Eileen. After all, if Arthur's body never turned up, his wife wouldn't see a penny until seven years had passed. John wanted to see who else may have found advantage in Montgomery's disappearance. Someone he may have looked over the first time. Most importantly however, he wanted to talk to Dr. Miller. She could be the key to the whole mystery.

Chapter 44

Rachel pulled out of the Meadowvale parking lot at the same time that John Haskins was talking to Ruth Henderson. Amanda Rutherford was sitting in the passenger seat.

"What a great day for the park, huh, Amanda?" Rachel said as she turned onto the highway. There were few other cars in sight.

"It's gorgeous. I wish they would let me out more often." The windows on both sides of the small VW Rabbit were open. Amanda's long blond hair whipped in and out of the window on her side.

"I think they would if you didn't always try to run away."

"I know." Amanda's eyes were closed as she savored the feel of the wind on her face. She was as content as a dog with its head out the window.

"You're not going to pull that on me today, are you?" Rachel asked seriously.

"No, Doctor Miller, I won't," Amanda said sheepishly.

"Promise?"

"Promise."

Rachel hadn't told Amanda yet of her plans to take her to see Sherman Myers. She wanted to hypnotize Amanda to see what, if anything, Carl Sanford had done to her. Rachel thought there might be another reason for Amanda's desire to escape aside from her penchant for freedom. She suspected that some of the patients were being abused by the doctors at the Clinic. Carl Sanford and Walter Flemming in particular. Once she had proof, she would go to Grant Foley with it. She trusted him.

She wished Ed was around to bounce some of her theories off, but he hadn't shown up at the Clinic this morning and didn't answer his mobile. He hadn't even left voice mail for her to let her know why he hadn't come. She wondered if he was a reliable person at all. The first time she met him at the beginning of the week, she found herself attracted to him based solely on his looks and physique. After spending more time with him though, she found him to be warm, sweet, and smart. She had hoped they could see more of each other after his work at the Clinic was done. Now she wasn't so sure. What she was doing now was important and Ed had let her down. That was the problem with depending on others for help. It seemed they let you down more often than not. It also seemed to be a recurring theme in her life if past boyfriends were indicative of anything.

A blast from a horn behind startled Rachel out of her thoughts. She checked her speed to make sure she wasn't holding up traffic and pulled her car as far to the right as it would go, giving the vehicle behind her plenty of room to pass on her left.

The horn sounded again, this time closer and louder. Rachel cursed and looked into her rearview expecting to see some prick in a sports car. Instead, she was surprised to see Ed smiling behind the wheel of his pick-up truck. He signaled to Rachel to pull over.

Ed got out of his truck and walked over to Rachel's car. "Where have you been?" Rachel asked as Ed leaned into her window. The question came out harsher than she had intended. In actuality, she was relieved to see him. Almost giddy, really.

"Sorry I'm late. I'll explain later," Ed said. He extended his hand across the interior of the car, "Hi, I'm Ed," he introduced himself to Amanda.

Amanda took his hand and shook it lightly, "I'm Amanda, it's nice to meet you."

"Where do you want to meet?" Ed asked Rachel after exchanging pleasantries with Amanda.

Rachel gave him Sherman Myers' address. "We'll go to the park right afterwards."

"Okay, I'll meet you there." Ed got back into his truck and pulled out ahead of Rachel.

"Where are we going before the park, Doctor Miller?" Amanda asked.

"Amanda. The reason I brought you out here wasn't to take you to the park."

"What?" Amanda asked, puzzled.

"I want to take you to someone who can hypnotize you."

"What for?"

"Are you afraid of any of the doctors at the Meadowvale Clinic, Amanda?"

"What do you mean?"

"What I mean is, do any of the doctors at the Clinic hurt you or touch you in inappropriate ways?"

Amanda didn't reply.

"I want to help you, Amanda. I know we don't know each other very well but you can trust me. I won't hurt you. What I want to know is if you'll let someone hypnotize you. I want to find out if the doctors are hurting you. I can't do that without your help. You have to want to do it. If you don't, that's okay, but I sense you want help, that you need help."

The Lord helps those who help themselves. The words sprung into Amanda's mind without warning. She didn't know where she knew them from, but she had heard them before. Dr. Miller sounded like she really wanted to help her but could she trust her? She didn't know who to trust anymore. She knew something was being done to her at the Clinic and at the Psychiatric Hospital before that, but she didn't know what. All she knew was that she wanted it to end and she wanted to be a whole person again. If the doctors were hurting her or touching her, or both, that meant that she would never get better. She'd heard of cases where people with dissociative identity disorder were taken advantage of precisely because they were so vulnerable. Was that what the doctors at the Clinic were doing to her? There was only one way to find out. *The Lord helps those who help themselves.*

"I'll do it," she told Rachel.

"Great, thank you, Amanda. And don't worry, I'll be with you the whole time." Rachel reached out and took Amanda's hand into her own. She gave it a gentle squeeze.

Chapter 45

Carl Sanford didn't like the way Flemming's voice sounded over the phone. Images of volatile liquids in flimsy containers sprung to mind. Sanford didn't think he had done anything wrong, but the tone in Flemming's voice moments ago suggested he had.

The door to Flemming's outer office was ajar. His secretary wasn't at her desk. Sanford could hear voices from inside. They sounded like they were having a heated discussion. One of the voices belonged to Flemming. Sanford recognized the other as belonging to Grant Foley. He heard Foley say, "Let's just wait until we talk to him, before we start jumping to conclusions."

Against his ulcer's better judgment, Carl Sanford knocked lightly on the door and walked in. He could have used a machete to cut through the tension.

"Walt, Grant. What's up?"

"What's up?" Flemming mimicked back. "What's up is that you are this close to ruining everything." Flemming held two fingers a hairwidth apart. "That's 'What's up'."

"What are you talking about?" Sanford asked defensively.

"Hold on a second, Walt, let's hear what Carl has to say first." Foley broke in before Flemming could continue his outburst. He looked longingly at his unlit pipe in one hand but never lit it. His wife wanted him to quit. If he could make it through the scene he imagined was about to take place, he knew he could quit for good.

"Say about what?" Sanford asked.

"About letting Rachel Miller take our best project patient out for a day in the park by herself."

"She's not by herself. She's with that insurance guy from Steinbeck and Wainfleet."

"What!?" Flemming screamed across his desk and stood bolt upright. Every muscle in his body tensed as his rage increased.

"Oh, shit." Foley slumped back into his chair. He tamped down on his pipe, then lit it.

"What? What did I say?" Sanford asked.

"Walt, sit down, I'll handle this," Foley interjected. "Carl, I talked to Hal Rosenberg last night, Ed Morgan's boss. I told him that his agent was involving himself in matters that didn't concern him and that he was hitting on one of the doctors here, Rachel. Ed Morgan will no longer be working on the Meadowvale portfolio. We don't know if he knew anything, but he was asking questions which seemed a little too close to the project. We think that he and Rachel might be on to us. We don't believe they know exactly what's going on, but we're sure they're suspicious."

"Tell him why we think they're suspicious," Flemming interjected. His words were laced with acid.

"I talked to Ed Morgan two days ago," Foley began, "and he asked me why some patient stat sheets he found in the basement of the Psychiatric Hospital had two numbers written underneath the number of personalities heading. He said he found several of these sheets. All of them were your patients. All had DID, and all were subjects of the earlier stages of the project."

A look of terror and guilt swept across Sanford's face. How was he supposed to know some nosy insurance agent would be poking around his old files?

"What did you tell him?" Sanford asked.

"I made up some cock and bull story and Walter has since removed the files in question."

"So if the files aren't there anymore, what's the problem?"

"If they find out the files aren't there anymore, then they'll really become suspicious, but obviously we couldn't just leave them there either to be browsed through at anyone's leisure."

"So what do we do?"

"About the files? There's not that much that we can do anymore. We've already taken care of Ed. So he won't be snooping around here or at the hospital anymore. Our next problem is taking care of Miller."

"Can't we just fire her?" Sanford asked.

"Without a reason? Not a chance. We'd be hit with a wrongful termination suit so fast we wouldn't know what hit us. No, there has to be another way."

Foley rested his chin on top of folded hands and closed his eyes, thinking. None of the doctors said a word for over a full minute.

"Let me take care of our young Doctor Miller." Flemming finally said.

"What are you going to do?" Foley asked.

"Let me worry about that. In the meantime, Carl should concentrate on our latest subject, the Hillock woman. She should be almost ready by now. Grant, you get our insurance coverage sorted out. We can't proceed with the project until that's all taken care of."

"What about Henderson and Tanner?" Sanford asked.

"What about them?" Flemming said.

"Are we ever going to approach them? Do you think they have any idea what's going on?"

"No, we are not going to involve them in the project, and I'm positive that they have absolutely no clue as to what we're doing. That's exactly why I hired them. They're excellent psychiatrists, and Ruth is an excellent researcher, but truth be told, they're idiots. They're our legitimate front."

"Speaking of which," Foley spoke up, "why is the FBI still looking for Montgomery?"

"The FBI is not looking for Montgomery," Flemming said, "one FBI agent is looking for him. I wouldn't worry about him."

Chapter 46

Ed's truck was already parked on Clayton Street in front of the shoddy pre-war brownstone where Sherman Myers lived when Rachel and Amanda arrived. Clayton Street was in the middle of the Haight-Ashbury. Back in the seventies, the area was overrun by deadheads and hippies. Now it catered to a yuppie crowd. Sherman Myers was neither.

Five minutes later, Rachel, Ed, and Amanda were all cramped inside his small, dimly lit, third floor apartment. It didn't look like he had redecorated since the early seventies. Wallpaper the color of coffee with cream covered walls that met vaulted, smoke-stained ceilings and thick, faded yellow carpets. The three guests occupied a dull orange chesterfield which was in surprisingly good shape. Ed stretched his legs onto one of several mustard yellow and olive green hassocks. Words like opulent, modern, and refined would never be used to describe Sherman Myers abode. *Home and Garden* wouldn't be knocking anytime soon.

Sherman Myers himself sat across from them in a burgundy, leather La-Z-Boy. A coffee table to his right was littered with dog-eared magazines with titles like *Fate, Soldier of Fortune, UFO Magazine,* and *Fortean Times*. Although he was only sixty-two, he looked eighty-five. At the youngest. Everything about him was old. His posture. His pale, wrinkled flesh. His sunken features. Everything except his eyes. They were a deep brown, almost on the verge of black. They traveled over his guests methodically, sizing them up. Once he ascertained that they weren't a threat or practical jokers, his gaze became less piercing, but remained intense nonetheless.

"Thank you for seeing us, Sherman," Rachel began, "this is Amanda, the person I told you about over the phone. She's agreed to go through with the hypnosis. And this is Ed, a friend of mine."

"Hello," Ed waved. Sherman raised a veiny hand in response. His movements were slow and deliberate. Economical. He reminded Ed of a grown-up version of Yoda.

"Amanda is a patient at the Clinic where I work and I think her doctor may be doing something to her without her knowing it," Rachel said when she realized Myers wasn't going to speak. "So we were hoping you could hypnotize her to find out what, if anything, they are doing to her."

"Do you think they're sexually abusing her?" Myers finally spoke up.

"That is a possibility." Rachel admitted, happy that the man was obviously on the same wavelength as she was. Or at least on the same radio.

"Well, let's get on with it." Sherman Myers got up out of his chair and waved Amanda over. She climbed into the chair and Myers tilted it back so that she was almost parallel to the floor.

"How long have you been hypnotizing people?" Ed asked Sherman as Amanda got comfortable.

"Since nineteen-forty-five. The government had me doing a lot of rehabilitation work with all the vets coming home. You kids are lucky you've never had to live through a war. You couldn't imagine how god-awful it is. Anyway, after the war was over and I became a specialist of sorts helping people with shell shock, I had built up a reputation as a man who could make people forget. That made me a first rate candidate for Spooksville, the CIA. They recruited me, and had me literally brainwashing people."

"You weren't party to the brainwashing experiments the CIA was involved in Montreal, Canada, were you?" Rachel asked feeling queasy. She had just read a book called *In the Sleep Room* a month or two ago which recounted how the CIA funded the brainwashing of innocent people to the point of insanity.

"No, fortunately not. My work was less experimental. Do you know of a place called Roswell and of a certain incident that happened there?"

"Yes," Ed answered.

"You wouldn't if I had spent some time with you."

"Are you saying you were at Roswell when The Crash happened?" Ed asked dubiously.

"July fourth, nineteen-forty-seven. I was the one who made sure those who witnessed it, didn't witness it."

"You didn't do a very good job. No offense." Ed said.

"None taken, Major Jesse Marcel was a strong-willed individual. He somehow broke through the block I implanted in him, long enough to come forward with his story. Fortunately, the CIA's spin doctors did a relatively decent job of making sure no one believed him."

"So you were one of the original Men In Black?" Ed asked, pseudo-excitedly. Although no one would ever suspect, he was a closet UFOlogist.

"I've been known to set trends," Sherman said modestly.

Rachel laughed at Sherman's response. She was glad for the break in conversation. She had no clue what the two men were talking about.

"So you can hypnotize Amanda, is what you're saying?" Rachel broke in.

"Of course, I'm sorry. We got sidetracked there," he winked conspiratorially at Ed. He was beginning to like the young man. "Amanda?" Sherman said turning his attention to the figure in his recliner. "I want you to lean back in this chair as far as you can. Make sure your head is comfortable and put your hands to your sides. Good. Now stretch out and get as comfortable as possible. That's it." Amanda did everything Sherman told her to.

"Now I want you to close your eyes and relax. Think about going to sleep. Concentrate on your breathing. Take a deep breath…and release. Just breathe naturally. Listen to everything I say and concentrate on nothing but your own breathing and the sound of my voice." Sherman's voice was soft and reassuring yet eerily persuasive at the same time. Rachel found herself getting a little drowsy and had to struggle to stay alert.

"Soon you will find yourself in a deep, restful sleep. Don't let your eyes open, keep them shut. Not too tight. Just relax. You're doing well, Amanda. Now I want you to relax every muscle in your body starting with your forehead…now your jaw…your shoulders. Your arms are getting very heavy, now your legs are getting heavy. Your whole body is so relaxed. Every muscle in your body is at rest.

"You are getting sleepier and sleepier. Soon you will be deep asleep. You are going to sleep…by the time I count to twenty you are going to be fast asleep. One…Two…Three…" Sherman continued counting until he reached twenty.

"You are now sound asleep," Sherman continued, "so very, very asleep. I'm going to count to five and then you will be even deeper asleep. Deeper than you are right now. One…Two…Three…Four…Five. You are sound asleep, dead asleep, you will stay asleep until I tell you to wake up.

"You are now sound asleep, and falling deeper and deeper asleep with every passing second. You will not feel, or hear, or be aware of anything except what I tell you and what Rachel asks you to recall. Sleep deeper until I tell you to wake up." Sherman looked up at Rachel and Ed and nodded, "She's under. You can ask her anything you want."

"Amanda?" Rachel asked. This is Doctor Rachel Miller from the Meadowvale Clinic. Are you ready to answer some questions?"

"Yes, Doctor Miller."

"Okay, I want you to think back to the earliest instance you can remember in which you were abused."

Amanda's face was a mask of concentration. She looked like she was having an unpleasant dream.

"I'm in a dark place. I can feel him on top of me. He's hitting me and tearing my clothes off." Amanda's voice became childlike. She curled up in the chair in a fetal position.

"Where are you, Amanda?"

"Amanda isn't here. I'm in the basement."

"Who's in the basement?"

"Me. I'm Mandy."

"How old are you, Mandy?"

"Seven."

"Who's hitting you, Mandy?"

"My daddy. My daddy is hitting me. Make him stop."

"All right, Mandy, I want to talk to Amanda again. Can I speak with Amanda? I want Amanda to think back more recently, let's go back to when you first met Doctor Sanford. Can you do that for me Amanda?"

"I think so. I'm in a forest." Her voice was still childlike.

"A forest?" Rachel asked not sure that she had heard correctly.

"Yes, a forest. It's real dark and there are people all around me."

"Is Doctor Sanford one of those people?"

"I can't tell. They're all wearing some kind of robes with big hoods. There's a fire nearby. I can see the light from it."

"What else can you see, Amanda?"

"I'm Mandy. Amanda's not here right now. A baby. I see a baby being cut with a knife."

"Who's cutting the baby?"

"I don't know. They're on me now. Holding me down. Tying my arms and legs. I can't move. They're all over me chanting." Mandy was no longer in a fetal position. Her body thrashed about on the recliner.

"Amanda, you're safe. No one is going to hurt you."

"Oh God, it hurts. Please stop. Please make them stop. I don't want to die."

"Sherman, can you wake her up?" Rachel cast a worried glance at Sherman.

"Certainly. Amanda? It's Sherman. I want you to think about a sunny day in the park. Think about the trees, the birds, the soft grass on your bare feet." Amanda stopped writhing in the chair and her body went limp.

"I am going to count to three and you are going to wake up feeling fine. You are going to feel awake and refreshed as if you just had a nice long sleep. You will not remember anything that happened here today, but you will be glad you came. When I count to three you will wake up. One…Two…Three…Wake up!"

Amanda's eyes fluttered open. She looked up at the three faces peering down at her.

"Did it work?" she asked.

"Yes, it worked, Amanda. We talked to one of your alters, Mandy."

"What about the doctors? Did you find out anything about them?"

"No, I don't think so. You talked about people in robes surrounded by fires. But there was nothing about doctors."

"You mean the cult?"

"What cult, Amanda?"

"Doctor Sanford says that Mandy is my way of repressing memories about the cult. He hypnotized me a bunch of times and he found out that I had been abused in a Satanic cult."

"When was this?" Rachel asked concerned.

Amanda looked at Ed and Sherman self-consciously. "We still don't know for sure. We're working on it right now in treatment."

"What else did he tell you?"

"He told me that I have a bunch of other personalities in me and some we probably haven't even met yet."

"How many alters has he counted so far?"

"Fifteen, but he says more will come as my treatment progresses. He said people with MPD often get worse before they get better. That's the truth. The last couple of years have been horrible," Amanda said with a pained look on her face.

"Thank you for being so open, Amanda."

"I'm sorry we didn't find out anything."

"It's not your fault. If you want, we can try it again sometime. Only when you're ready though."

"Whatever. Can we go to the park now?"

"Sure. Why don't you wait here for a few minutes. I just want to talk to Ed and Sherman for a bit, okay?"

"Okay."

"What do you think?" Rachel asked the two men in the hallway just outside Sherman's apartment door.

"It looks like she has more serious problems than doctors abusing her," Ed offered.

"My thoughts exactly," Sherman agreed.

"So what's the next step?" Ed asked.

"Well if it was possible, I wouldn't mind checking out this cult where she claims she was abused."

"Fat chance of that," Ed said.

"Hold on a second," Sherman said, "I don't know if it's the same cult that abused your friend in there, but I can tell you how you can see one."

"What?" Ed asked, "Are you serious?"

"Dead serious."

"How?" Rachel asked. The seriousness in her voice matched that of Sherman Myers'. Sherman Myers withdrew a pad of paper and a stubby pencil from his brown, faded corduroy pants and started writing. Within minutes, Rachel and Ed had the time and place of a satanic ritual. And directions to get there.

"You've got to be kidding me! I think we should just go to the police and tell them what we know so far." Ed groaned as he saw that Rachel was serious about the matter.

"No, I think we should check this ritual out. Besides, we don't really know anything so far. If it can help us figure out what's going on at the Clinic, I think it's worth checking this ritual stuff out. I'm going to grab Amanda." Rachel stepped back into the apartment leaving Ed alone with Sherman Myers.

"Hi," Ed said to Sherman, unsure of what else to say.

"You strike me as a rather impatient man," Sherman leaned into Ed.

"Only when I want to be," Ed responded.

"I think you should listen to your lady friend. She's got a good head on her shoulders. I don't know what you three are involved in but it sounds complicated. I've spent enough time working in complicated situations to know that the more complex a situation, the more caution one should proceed with. Slow and steady win the race."

"I just want to find out what's going on at that Clinic," Ed rebutted.

"So does Rachel. She's going about it the right way though. You need proof of whatever it is your searching for. You know what a Bull moose is?"

"Of course, it's a male moose, and a cow is a female," Ed said wondering where the conversation was headed.

"Good, now pay attention. An old Bull moose and a young Bull moose are standing at the top of a mountain. Down below them is a field full of cow moose. The young Bull moose says to the old Bull moose, 'Let's run down the mountain and screw us a cow,' to which the old Bull moose replies, 'How about we walk down the mountain and screw 'em all.'" Sherman Myers doubled over in laughter. Ed had to laugh as well.

"You understand what I'm telling you?" Sherman asked.

"Yeah, I get it." Aesop would be rolling in his grave.

"You just take your time with whatever it is you're doing. Good things come to those who wait."

"What's so funny?" Rachel asked as she and Amanda came out of the apartment.

"Nothing much, just guy stuff," Sherman winked at Ed.

"Are you ready to go?" Ed asked Rachel.

"Yep, we're ready. Thank you very much for seeing us on such short notice, Sherman."

"No skin off my back, just wish I could have been of more use to you."

Ed, Rachel, and Amanda walked down the three flights of steps together and squinted in the bright morning sun outside. Rachel took off the cable-knit sweater she was wearing. The temperature had risen at least five degrees since they arrived.

"Why don't we meet at the park since we have two vehicles?" Rachel suggested.

"Lead on, MacDuff."

Chapter 47

Over a thousand acres of prime land offered a myriad of things to see and do in Golden Gate Park. Ed, Rachel, and Amanda walked down one of the many winding pathways which dissected the vast expanse of lush green grass. The pale azure sky was void of clouds and the noonday sun cast a bright, warm blanket over the earth. Cyclists, pedestrians, runners, rollerbladers, and parents with strollers competed for room on the pathways. College students studied under trees, frolicked on the grass playing Ultimate Frisbee and soccer, and picnicked in secluded spots.

The park seemed ready to burst with all the activity going on within. Rachel's head felt the same way. She had hoped the session with Sherman Myers would have revealed something tangible. Evidence of some sort that the patients at the Clinic were being mistreated. She learned as much from the session as she knew prior to it; practically nothing.

"Doctor Miller?" Amanda asked.

"Call me Rachel here, Amanda," Rachel replied.

"Rachel? Would you mind if I kind of walked around on my own and explored? I've never been to the park." The voice was childlike and the eyes puppylike. Amanda had switched to Mandy.

"Sure, just keep in sight of Ed and I. You don't want me to get in trouble with Doctor Sanford, do you?"

"No."

"If you need anything, just holler," Rachel called as Mandy bounded off exuberantly.

"You're good with her," Ed observed of Rachel's treatment of Amanda.

"It's not hard. I enjoy it, I guess that makes it easier."

"So what's on your mind? I saw you thinking back there when we first came in. Penny for your thoughts?" Ed asked as he and Rachel watched Mandy running through the park. Her high-spirited laughter fell upon their ears.

"They're not worth that much. I was just thinking about what we just saw at Sherman's place with Amanda. I don't know exactly what I thought would happen, but I guess I kind of expected something solid to come out of the hypnosis."

"You were hoping that Amanda would tell us about her doctor abusing her?"

"In a way, yes. I mean, we know there's something going on at the Clinic, but what? Or am I just being paranoid?"

"You are definitely not being paranoid."

"How do you know that?"

"Because I was fired this morning."

"What!?" Rachel stopped in her tracks and was almost bowled over from behind by a rollerblading youth who hadn't anticipated her sudden stop. He gave Ed and Rachel a dirty look as he weaved in between them.

"I stopped by my office this morning to drop off some papers I had been working on last night and my boss said he wanted to talk to me. So, we went up to his office, and he told me outright that I could pack up my stuff and get out. At first I thought he was kidding.

"I asked him why and he said that Grant Foley had called him and told him that Doctor Flemming complained about me. He said I was putting my nose in where it didn't belong, that I was wasting time and not getting any work done, and that I was hitting on you."

"You've hardly been hitting on me," Rachel said, "And how can Flemming say you haven't been getting any work done? You're almost done, aren't you?"

"Another few days of paperwork, and yeah, I'll be done two to three days ahead of my deadline. It was an impossible deadline to begin with."

"Did you tell your boss that?"

"He didn't want to hear it. He kept on going on about how disappointed he was in me, and how he couldn't believe I would behave in such an unprofessional manner. I tried telling him my side of the story, but he wouldn't hear it. Unfortunately, as in a lot of businesses, the customer is always right."

"That's bull."

"My boss doesn't think so. I think there was also some politics involved. If I wasn't fired, the Clinic might have switched over to another insurance company and my boss would have been left to answer to his superiors. Firing me was an easy way out for him. Not only does he save face, but he saved the Meadowvale portfolio."

"So who's going to take over for you?"

"Some guy named Bernard."

"I'm sorry, Ed," Rachel said.

"It's not your fault."

"I know but I still feel like I got you involved in all this."

"I got myself involved. No one put a gun to my head. So tell me, why do you want to check out a Satanic ritual? Are you hurting that much for things to do?" Ed quipped. He didn't want to talk about his termination any more.

"Nothing like that," although it wasn't far from the truth given her limited spending power and lack of time in which to do anything.

"Then why?"

"Honestly, because I'm at a loss for what to do next. I can't think of anything else to do. I would make a pretty lousy detective."

"You've done all right so far. You must have some theories about this cult though. Come on, tell me what's on that enigmatic little mind of yours."

Rachel smiled, "If you must know, I was thinking that maybe, and bear in mind that this is a long shot, that maybe some of the doctors at the Clinic are involved with the rituals themselves. Maybe the patients are being abused by the doctors at these rituals. Maybe that's why when I asked Amanda to remember when she first met Doctor Sanford, she recalled a cult gathering. It's the only thing that makes sense to me right now."

"That's not bad. You're right though, it does sound a little bit farfetched."

"It's the best I can come up with. What I don't understand is how those files you found with the two entries for personalities has anything to do with this."

"And what about Emily Jenkins and that patient of yours who just killed himself?"

"Exactly, none of this is coming together. Unless maybe they were abused by this cult as well? I wonder if we've seen too many conspiracy flicks and we're seeing hidden plots where there aren't any."

"No, I believe you that something is definitely going on. I think my being fired is related. Maybe I was getting too close to discovering something."

"That's another thing, we seem to be stumbling along in the dark here, just finding things by accident."

"Hey don't knock it, lots of things were discovered by accident."

"Like what?" Rachel asked.

"Like the stethoscope, X-rays, Teflon, vulcanized rubber, penicillin, Classical Conditioning, bubble gum, and all sorts of other things."

"How do you know all that?"

"I'm working on a book," Ed admitted, "I'm going to call it '*History by Accident*', and it's going to chronicle all the major discoveries that were made by accident."

"Really?"

"I'm serious. I've already done all of the research for it and I've written half of it. In another month or two, I'll be ready to go to a publisher with it."

"That's incredible."

"Thank you. Now that I don't have a job anymore, I might be able to finish it sooner than I'd planned."

"Good for you."

"Did you ever find out what happened to those files that disappeared from the psychiatric hospital?"

"No, I didn't. I checked again but they still weren't there and according to the log, no one checked them out."

"Strange."

"That's for sure. I just wish something would fall into place and we could figure out what's going on."

"Well, maybe we'll learn something at the ritual tonight."

"You mean you'll come with me?"

"Of course. I want to find out what's going on as badly as you do. And when it comes to entertainment, if it's free, it can't be bad. The one thing I want to know is how Sherman knew where we could go and check out a Satanic ritual."

"He's an odd duck, isn't he," Rachel said. It was a statement, not a question.

"And people call me weird. Hey, can you go grab Amanda and wait here for awhile?" Ed suddenly asked.

"I suppose so. Where are you going?"

"It's a surprise. You'll see. I'll be right back." Ed dashed off in the direction of the parking lot where they had parked their vehicles and returned within minutes with a large wicker basket.

"What's in the basket?" Amanda asked when Ed returned.

"Lunch for three." Amanda's eyes lit up. Rachel herself was surprised at Ed's considerate gesture. She watched fascinated as Ed spread a red and white checkered table cloth in the shade of a massive oak tree and began laying out the food he had packed into the basket. There was potato salad, a loaf of bread, trays of cold meats, cheeses, and fruits and vegetables, condiments and cutlery, chocolate cake for dessert and a choice of orange juice, apple juice, water, and Dr. Pepper.

Rachel felt guilty for doubting Ed's reliability. With a dramatic wave of his arms, Ed announced, "Lunch is served."

Chapter 48

450 Golden Gate Avenue
13th Floor
3:34 p.m.

Susan Baxter and Shane Pavletic sat across from each other in the hallway outside of John Haskin's office. Their boss had asked them earlier in the day to meet with him to discuss the Arthur Montgomery case. He was ten minutes late.

"Do you think he found something?" Shane asked Susan, the younger of the two.

"I wouldn't be surprised. If there's a lead to be found, that man will find it," Susan shook her head in admiration.

"I know what you mean. Anyone else would have given up this case a long time ago."

"Except for maybe Spracken."

"True. Do you think he'll ever turn up?"

"Montgomery? Yeah, I think he will. And if we stick close to Haskins, I bet you we'll be there when he does."

"I wouldn't be surprised," Shane said.

"What wouldn't you be surprised about?" John Haskins asked as he walked around the corner into the hall where Shane and Susan were talking. His blond hair was windblown and his trenchcoat was folded over one arm. A slight smile played on his lips.

"We wouldn't be surprised if you had Arthur Montgomery in your car right now, alive and well, with his kidnappers bound and gagged in the trunk of your car," Shane said.

John laughed, "I wish. No, unfortunately things aren't going that well. Come on into my office." The three FBI agents made themselves comfortable in John's small office. Ceiling high bookshelves packed with books on famous kidnapping cases, criminal profiling, forensic science, and psychology lined a wall and a half. The office was sparsely decorated, moderately appointed, and very utilitarian.

"I talked with five of the six doctors at the Meadowvale Clinic this morning," John began, "One of them was unavailable, Montgomery's replacement. I'll talk to her on Monday. I think there might be something going on between her and one of the other doctors, Grant Foley. He's the one that hired her."

"You mean you think they might be having an affair?" Susan asked.

"It's a possibility. I also think that Flemming knows more than he's letting on, and this other doctor, Carl Sanford knows something too. He's a nervous wreck, so I'm going to have a car follow him and hang around outside his house. No taps or anything. I just want him to know he's being watched. I think he'll crack for us when the time comes."

"What about the other two doctors?" Shane asked.

"They seem clean, they both just started with the Clinic when it first opened and didn't even know who Montgomery was before they started working there. I want background checks done on all six doctors though. Where they got their degrees, their training, how they know each other, any past brushes with the law, lovers, debts, I want everything. Can you handle that Susan?"

"Yes, sir."

"Good. Shane, I want you to dig up anything and everything you can on the Meadowvale Clinic. I mean everything. Talk to the architects who designed it, the bank that financed it, the contractor that built it. Everybody. I think whatever happened to Arthur Montgomery, is tied to that Clinic. Any questions?"

"No, sir," Susan and Shane said in unison.

"Good, then let's find that man."

Chapter 49

9:30 p.m.
Mt. Diablo State Park

The old man's instructions to Mt. Diablo State Park were relatively easy to follow. After a half hour of driving in comfortable silence, Rachel pointed out the turnoff they were meant to take. Ed turned off onto a narrow gravel road slowing down considerably. Rocks popped off into the forest on either side of the vehicle as the truck's tires slowly crunched over them. Ed turned off his lights so as not to attract attention. The running lights provided enough light for him to see the winding road ahead. Hundreds of airborne insects danced in their incandescent glow.

"If he was accurate in his directions, we have about two miles to go before we reach the site," Rachel said. "We should find someplace to hide your truck and walk the rest of the way. I don't want to be caught sneaking up on a bunch of cultists."

"Good idea," Ed concurred, "the last thing I want to do tonight is end up being sacrificed to some unholy Pagan god. Keep your eye on the right and I'll check out the left, if you see somewhere where I can pull in let me know." Ed and Rachel looked out their respective sides of the truck, straining their eyes in an attempt to get them adjusted to the dark. The trees on either side of the road towered upwards making the night even darker. The night seemed impossibly black. There were no street lights within thirty miles and even the distant glow from the city could not penetrate the darkness surrounding Ed's truck.

They had driven about a mile when Rachel pointed out a small, natural cul de sac on her side of the road. Ed backed up and easily maneuvered the truck into it. It went deep enough into the forest to provide ample protection. Ed made a three point turn once inside so that the nose of the truck faced the road. If necessary they could make a speedy getaway. Ed turned off the engine and lights and they were plunged into an inky darkness. It was so dark that Ed and Rachel couldn't even see each other across the bench seat of the truck.

"Let's get outside and let our eyes adjust to the darkness," Ed said, "hopefully the moon and stars will provide enough light to see where we're going." They both emerged from the truck and closed the doors, unlocked, as quietly as possible. It was even darker now that the running lights and dashboard console were turned off. It took a few minutes for Rachel to be able to make out shapes but soon she could see Ed and made her way towards him.

"After you," she poked Ed in the arm as she held out her hand into the darkness, "I think it's this way," she said nudging him, taking his hand in hers.

"Let's follow the road until we can make out the gathering. I imagine we would get lost pretty quickly if we attempted to cut through the woods, and I didn't bring any bread crumbs." Ed left the safety of the cul de sac with Rachel in tow and began walking down the washboard road. Rocks crunched under their feet but nowhere near as loudly as they had underneath the truck.

"How far do you think it is?" Ed queried.

"Depending on the accuracy of Sherman's instructions, we should be able to reach them in about ten to fifteen minutes. Why? Are you in a rush?"

"Oh, God no." Ed continued to lead the way trying not to walk off the road, which led them downhill and through numerous twists. With the exception of the many potholes, the going wasn't all that bad. Both Ed and Rachel stumbled once in awhile but managed to keep on their feet, catching each other when they tripped. The hardest part of their journey still lay ahead.

Rachel was walking with her head up admiring the millions of stars overhead when Ed suddenly stopped.

"What?" Rachel asked.

"Shhhh!" Ed held his index finger to his lips and with his other hand pointed off into the night. "Look over there."

Rachel strained to see what he was pointing at and could just make out a faint amber glow through the trees. It appeared to be the glow of a fire. Ed crouched down and Rachel did the same.

"I think we should stop talking from here on in," Ed said to Rachel.

"Sounds good to me," she could barely make out the features of his face even though they were crouched less than three feet away from each other. "It looks like we're going to have to make the rest of the trip through the trees. If we follow the road, we'll just be increasing our chances of getting caught. Also, their cars are probably parked up the road." Rachel stood up looking into the forest for a suitable place to enter.

"Cars? I thought maybe they rode brooms out here." Ed quipped.

"Who knows how they got here."

"I wonder what kind of insurance rates they get, I would imagine being allies with the Devil must have some benefits."

"Hopefully we won't be around long enough to find out. Let's go." Rachel ended the conversation and stepped off the road into the forest.

The soft forest floor was a remarkable contrast to the hard gravel road. With each step they took, they sunk an inch or two. Small twigs snapped underneath their shoes but not loudly enough to reach the ears of those who were undoubtedly surrounding the fire. Thick underbrush impeded their progress as they had to push branches out of their way with every step. Ed was slapped in the face a number of times as Rachel pushed branches forward and let them snap back. He dropped back a few feet.

The fire itself became visible once they had traveled through the woods for about ten minutes. The trees were still too many however, and the underbrush too dense to make out any figures. Pushing on, they reached the edge of a large clearing and crouched down.

"I don't think we should go any further" Rachel whispered, "we should just get comfortable here and see what there is to see."

"I was just going to suggest the same thing." Ed whispered and sat down on a fallen tree behind him and tried in vain to make himself comfortable. Rachel did the same. The tree was damp, making sitting uncomfortable.

Peering through the underbrush into the clearing before them, Rachel and Ed could make out a rough circle of a couple dozen figures.

"How many do you think there are?" Ed asked Rachel as he inserted a Lolli-Pop into his mouth.

"I was just counting them, I think there's twenty four, including one that looks like the leader." The figures all wore the same nondescript long brown wool robes with thin ropes tied around their waists. Each robe had a large hood affixed to it and these were all being worn. From their vantage point, and because of the robes, it was impossible for Ed and Rachel to determine the age, sex, or anything else about the mysterious figures who stood around the large blazing fire. A dozen of them held long dark candles despite the fire's far-reaching glow.

"Do you figure they've been here very long?" Rachel asked.

"Hard to tell," Ed replied, "the fire's going pretty well and they seem to be in the middle of something so I would guess they've been here at least half an hour."

Rachel was about to ask another question when one of the cultists spoke. The voice was deep and low like a foghorn and spoke in a foreign tongue.

"What language is that?" Rachel whispered to Ed being careful not to shift her body.

"I'm not sure. My first guess would be Greek or Latin, but from what I can tell its neither. It may be Celtic or some bizarre satanic verses." The leader continued talking. The size and voice of the leader led Rachel and Ed to believe it was a man. He was standing in front of a makeshift altar made of a thin layer of slate balanced on two old tree stumps. His hands were outstretched and his body gyrated as he began to chant. The rest of the figures followed his lead and began chanting as well. Ed noticed that some of them were holding pages in front of them apparently reading what they were chanting.

"Looks like some of our cultists didn't do their homework for this evening's ritual. I wonder what their punishment will be?" Ed whispered to Rachel who was watching the ceremony transfixed.

"The leader is about to do something," she said, nodding toward the ritual. Ed looked back and saw the leader reaching down to grab something underneath the altar. It was a bag. It looked like a pillowcase. It was a bag with something very alive inside it. Ed began to feel nauseous.

The leader raised the violently thrashing bag above his head and yelled something incoherent. All of the other figures continued to chant. Their voices were rising in both pitch and volume. He lowered the bag and reached inside with his free hand. He pulled out a chicken which continued to thrash about. His entire arm was shaking. Ignoring the chicken's movement, he reached into his robe and pulled out a long knife. Its handle wasn't visible but its blade was. It was about a foot long and even from thirty feet away, looked incredibly sharp. The chanting voices had reached a frenzied pitch. The zenith was near.

With one swift movement, the leader slammed the chicken down onto the altar and deftly lopped off its head with one sweeping arc of the knife.

Chapter 50

"Well, that was about the most gruesome thing I've ever seen." Ed looked away from the disturbing scene. Rachel tried desperately to hold her dinner down.

"Oh, my God. What are we doing here?" Rachel asked rhetorically, not particularly wanting an answer.

Peering through the trees once more, Ed and Rachel saw that the chicken had been disposed of by the leader. The knife was no longer in his hand. In its place was a large cup. He held it up for all to see.

"Please tell me that isn't what I think it is." Rachel squirmed on the fallen tree.

"If you're thinking what I'm thinking, and I'm thinking that cup is full of fresh chicken blood, I think you may be right."

"I told you not to tell me."

"Sorry." At that moment, the leader passed the cup to his left to the robed figure nearest him. The cultist took the cup in both hands as if it were the Holy Grail itself and raised it to unseen lips.

"I am definitely going to be sick," it was Ed's turn to squirm. The cup was passed again to the left and again was drunken from. It took about five minutes for the cup to make its way around the entire circle. Every member took a sip. The leader took the empty cup from the last member and placed it underneath the altar. Raising his hands once again, the leader spoke to his disciples, apparently giving them instructions. Those holding the candles approached the altar and placed them in the ground where they stood upright. Once they returned to their proper places within the circle, every member kneeled down and held out their forearms parallel to the ground. Their elbows were tucked into their sides.

Their palms faced the ground. The leader spoke once more. He extinguished the candles one by one squishing the flames between thumb and forefinger.

The cultists all rose and, following the lead of the member to the right of the leader, proceeded to disperse.

"Let's wait until they're long gone. I don't want to chance being caught." Ed looked to Rachel for approval. She nodded her consent.

They watched in silence as the cultists left the clearing. They couldn't see where they were parked but they saw headlights coming on and heard the idle hum of numerous engines. The crunching of gravel indicated the departure of one vehicle after another. Ed wondered where one went to unwind after a Satanic ritual.

The leader had remained to put out the main fire and to ensure that there was no incriminating evidence left at the scene. He dragged the slate which was used as the altar into the forest. Soon he left too. Ed and Rachel let five minutes pass. They dared not even breathe.

"Okay, I think it's safe to leave." Rachel said as she stood up. Both of her legs had cramped up and pins and needles tingled in her feet. Her bottom was wet due to the damp tree they had been sitting on. Rachel watched Ed as he stood up. The look on his face proved that he felt no better.

"Thank God. My butt is killing me. I was sitting on a knot the whole time." Ed massaged his posterior with one hand.

"Let's just be thankful they didn't know we were here. Who knows what they might have done to us. I can't imagine that a sip or two of chicken blood quenched their Satanic thirsts." Rachel walked out into the clearing.

Ed called out to her, "what are you doing?"

"Don't worry. They're all gone." She called back over her shoulder. "Besides, the walk back will be much easier if we take the road this time."

Ed shrugged his shoulders realizing she was right and stepped into the clearing. They both made a wide pass of the fire's remains and the two tree stumps. Without the light from the fire, the night was pitch black once again. Ed and Rachel found the road and began the upward climb back toward Ed's truck.

"Let's just get out of here and not talk about what we just saw for awhile," said Rachel hoping Ed would agree.

"Definitely," Ed said with obvious relief in his voice. He wished he could erase the entire evening from his memory. They walked the rest of the way in silence. The trip back was significantly shorter since there was no underbrush to slow them down nor did they have to worry about making noise as they walked. They passed the cul de sac when they reached it but quickly realized their mistake and turned back.

Ed's Ford was still parked where they left it.

"Well, safe and sound. Now let's go get something to eat." Ed moved towards his truck as Rachel went around to the passenger side. Ed opened his door at the same time Rachel opened hers.

Sitting in the middle of the truck's bench seat was the cult leader.

Chapter 51

▼

Rachel screamed.

Ed screamed.

The figure didn't move.

"I've been waiting for you." The robed figure spoke. It was definitely the cult leader.

Rachel slammed her door and ran to Ed's side of the truck as he did the same. They bolted for the road. A voice behind them boomed, "Wait! I won't harm you."

Ed and Rachel stopped in their tracks nearly falling over each other. They looked back. The cult leader had stepped out of the truck and was leaning against the cab.

"Come back here." He spoke again.

"Why should we?" Ed asked trying to mask the fear in his voice with a confidence he did not feel. He looked around trying to determine if there were any other members hiding in the bushes waiting to jump out.

"Well, first of all, it's a long walk back to the city and secondly, I think you may have misconstrued what you just saw."

"How do you know we saw anything?" Rachel asked.

"The tree you were sitting on was a big one. Every time you moved, its crown bobbed up and down. I would have to be blind to have missed it." The leader let out a small mirthful laugh.

"So why didn't you just send your Satan worshippers after us?" Ed's courage was returning, although he continued to glance around for fear of an ambush.

"There was no need. And besides, they're not Satan worshippers. And neither am I." The cult leader stepped away from the truck and removed his hood. The face revealed could have been anybody's. He was a white middle aged male with a widow's peak and dark hair. His smooth complexion and friendly eyes betrayed his position as a Satanic cult leader.

"What?" Rachel and Ed cried in unison.

"What you just saw was not a Satanic ritual. Technically." The gentleman before them untied his waist rope and revealed a collared denim shirt tucked loosely into a pair of Khakis; a small paunch was noticeable.

Ed approached the man leaning against his truck. He inspected him from head to foot. "If that wasn't a Satanic ritual, and those people aren't Satan worshippers, and you're not a Satanic cult leader, then pray tell what the hairy heck is going on around here?"

"Allow me to introduce myself. My name is Jack Tavender." He held out his hand which Ed shook reluctantly introducing himself and Rachel.

"Alright, Mister Tavender. Maybe you can explain just what it was that you and your bloodthirsty friends were doing then."

"Certainly. What you just witnessed was a mock Satanic ritual."

"But we saw you decapitate a live chicken and drink its blood." Rachel said.

"Actually, the chicken was already dead. I just shook it around a lot to make it appear alive. What you saw us drinking was actually red wine, not blood." Jack replied.

"Why would anyone want to perform a mock Satanic ritual? Never mind attend one?" Rachel couldn't believe what she was hearing. Ed was having a hard time believing it himself.

"I provide a service. I have a Web site on the internet which explains what it is I do."

"What exactly is it that you do?" Ed asked.

"I perform mock Satanic rituals for a price. Anyone who wants to know what a Satanic ritual is like can find out by attending one. A mock one that is. For only three hundred dollars, I send each customer a script outlining the ritual and what is expected of them. That way, when the ritual is underway, everyone knows what to do and what to say, or in some cases, chant. They are given a date and time and directions to the site. I provide the props such as candles and robes."

"You mean people actually pay money to take part in a Satanic ritual?" Rachel could barely comprehend what she was hearing. She was aghast.

"That's right, three hundred dollars, and…"

"Wait, wait, wait. Hold on a second," Ed interrupted Jack, "do you mean to tell me that each person out there tonight paid three hundred dollars to listen to you chant gibberish and cut the head off of a dead chicken?"

"That's not how I describe it on my Web site, but essentially, yes." Ed reeled back.

"That means you made…" Ed paused a moment as he quickly did the math in his head, "that means you made six thousand and nine hundred dollars tonight?"

"Correct. Sometimes there are more customers and sometimes there are less. The maximum I allow is thirty-five. Believe it or not, I even have several repeat customers," Jack beamed.

"I can't believe this. I simply cannot believe this. This is incredible." Ed paced up and down the side of his truck. "Can you believe this?" he asked Rachel waving his hands in the air. Rachel was flabbergasted as well.

"Why were you sitting in my truck?" Ed asked regaining his composure.

"It was chilly outside," Jack replied innocently.

"No, I mean why were you waiting for us?" Ed continued, "We thought you were going to kill us." Ed glanced over at Rachel for confirmation. She nodded her head.

"I wanted to find out who you were and what you were doing." Jack wrapped his robe around himself and tied the waistcord. "I thought you might be reporters or someone hoping to shut me down."

"Why? Is what you're doing illegal?" Rachel asked.

"Not that I know of, but I don't want it getting leaked to the press. To avoid publicity, I have all my customers sign non-disclosure forms."

"What about your Web site?" Ed said, "isn't there a risk that some reporter or animal rights activist may find out about what you do?"

"I don't list my name or phone number, just a post office box where interested people can write to for more information. I screen as best as I can. Obviously, word has gotten out however." Jack looked at Ed and Rachel with a question in his eyes.

"I guess you're probably wondering what it is we're doing out here." Rachel said to Jack.

"It was on my mind," he said casually, "I figure you're too old to be necking out in the woods. You don't look or act like the press or the fuzz. And you certainly aren't out here on a nature walk. So yeah, I guess I was wondering what you two were doing out here."

"We were told by someone that we could see Satanic rituals being performed out here on Saturday nights." Rachel offered.

Jack looked at Ed and said, "This is where you take your girlfriend on a date? This is how you show her a good time? Traipsing through the woods in the pitch black hoping to take in a Satanic ritual? I tell you, dinner and a movie worked fine back in my day."

"We're not on a date. We did come out to see a Satanic ritual but not to satisfy any perverse thrill," Ed shot back. "I work for an insurance company and she," Ed pointed to Rachel, "is a psychiatrist at the new clinic outside of town. Perhaps you heard of it. The Meadowvale Clinic?"

"Yeah, I've heard of it. It's where they're shipping all the crazies isn't it?" Jack said.

"People with dissociative disorders actually," Rachel said, a little annoyed at having to defend the Clinic's purpose everytime it came up in conversation. "Anyway, the reason we're out here is that one of the patients revealed to us under hypnosis that she was ritually abused by members of a Satanic cult operating in the area. We were hoping that we might be able to discover something ourselves by witnessing a real ritual."

"And did you?"

"Well, her account seems to loosely parallel what we saw you and your group doing minus the abuse," Rachel said. "Is that how most Satanic rituals are performed? Is there a standard version or anything?"

"Not to the last detail, but essentially yes, I guess what you saw me and my customers doing could be considered standard, with the exception that we don't kill live animals or actually believe in what we're doing."

"Have you heard of any cults abusing children ritually?" Rachel asked. She noticed that Ed had tuned out of the conversation, apparently lost in his own thoughts.

"No and I wouldn't dream of reproducing that kind of thing. I can't imagine it would be good for business."

"Well, I guess our trip was kind of a bust. I'm sorry we spied on you. At least no one else noticed."

"That's alright. I wish I could help you more. Just promise me you won't tell a soul about what you saw here."

"Sure, no problem. Our lips are sealed," Rachel said.

"Thanks, I appreciate it. Hey, if you're ever in the mood, I can give you and your friend here a good deal, kind of a two for one thing, whaddya say?"

"I don't think so, I think we've seen enough, thanks. We'll just rent a movie next time."

"Well, you know where to find me if you change your mind." Jack shifted his weight off the truck and headed for the road. He waved a quick good-bye as he pulled up his cloak and melted into the night.

"Well, that was about one of the weirdest encounters I've ever had," Ed said.

"You can say that again."

"Well, that was about one of the…"

"Stuff it."

"Sorry, I was possessed" Ed joked.

"Speaking of possessed, what happened to you back there?"

"Huh? When?"

"We were talking to Jack, and you just tuned out."

"Oh, sorry. I was thinking of something he said."

"What's that?"

"Well, remember when you asked him if his version was standard and he said not to the last detail?"

"Yeah. So what?"

"Well, that got me thinking."

"Uh, oh"

"No, no, no, hear me out, I think I have something. What was it about Amanda's story that seemed odd?"

"You mean aside from the fact that she was ritually abused by Satanic cultists?"

"Yes, aside from that. Come on, I'm being serious."

"I don't know."

"What I noticed but couldn't put my finger on until just now, was the lack of detail in her story," Ed said.

"Lack of detail? I thought it was incredibly vivid."

"Vivid, yes, detailed, no. She painted a decent picture, but with too wide a brush, if you'll pardon the metaphor. She never mentioned anything about texture, smell, sounds, anything. She went on and on about how much it hurt, but not about what hurt."

"Actually, now that I think about it, you're right. I guess I got so swept away by her emotional state that I didn't notice how vague she was being. Anyone who watched Hard Copy could have described what she did."

"Exactly!"

"It is a good point, but what does it mean?"

"That…I don't know."

"I think I do," Rachel said.

"What?"

"We have to bring Amanda back to see Sherman Myers again."

"I was afraid you were going to say that."

"Frankly, so was I."

"You weren't thinking of doing it tonight though were you?"

"Are you kidding? I've had enough excitement for one night. We'll do it tomorrow night."

"Thank Heaven for small miracles. Now get in the truck and let's go get something to eat."

"Good idea, as long as it's not chicken."

Chapter 52

Sandra Hillock's tongue felt like it was wrapped in a work sock, her mouth was so dry. Her joints ached and she had pain in muscles which she never knew existed. Her eyes opened slowly, revealing a blurry world around her. After a few minutes of intense focusing, she was able to see that she was in a small, bare room. In it was a dresser, a plastic mirror affixed to the wall over the dresser, and a single bed. Although the bed was quite comfortable, Sandra had never felt worse in her life.

Sitting up in bed required a Herculean effort and revealed even more sore muscles. Sandra briefly wondered if she was a somnambulistic marathon runner. She couldn't imagine how else she got into such rough shape. On top of all her bodily aches, pains, and discomforts, she also had a splitting headache. It actually felt like she had three headaches, each one competing for recognition.

Sandra stood up and began stretching. She hoped to get some of the kinks out of her system and then figure out where she was and how she had gotten here. She vaguely recalled, like a distant memory, talking to a doctor. She couldn't remember if it was yesterday, the day before, or even as long as two weeks ago. Her concept of time was shattered. She had no idea how long she had been at the hospital. No, wait, it was a clinic of some sort.

What had the doctor told her? That she had Multiple Personality Disorder? How was that possible? Everything seemed so unreal to Sandra. She felt like she was living in a dream, as if any moment now, she would wake up and return to her normal life.

Stretching her stiff muscles did a world of good and actually seemed to ease one of the three headaches. The other two seemed to intensify. Did she have a migraine? She couldn't tell.

A small window in the door enmeshed with thin wires enabled Sandra to look out into a hallway. Sandra tried the door to her room. It was open. She couldn't believe it. She thought for sure she would be locked up.

Voices drifted down from the far end of the corridor. Sandra could hear a TV playing. She walked down the hallway in a pair of slippers she had found at the end of her bed and made her way into a common room. Half a dozen other people, she assumed they were patients because they all wore the same non-descript clothes as she had on, were sitting down watching an old M*A*S*H re-run on a brand new thirty-two inch TV set.

None of the room's occupants seemed to notice Sandra as she came into the room. She was about to sit down herself and strike up a conversation with one of her fellow patients when a flash of pain raced through her brain. Headache number three was making a comeback. Sandra's knees buckled at the intense pain and she let out a gasp of surprise.

She felt a pair of strong arms reach under her armpits and lift her to her feet. She heard a volley of voices around her. Some of them actually seemed to be coming from within her own head.

The strong arms were helping her back to her room. Her own legs seemed to be moving on their own volition and aiding the journey. Her hamstrings cried out at the exertion.

She lay in bed once more. Her vision was coming back but it hurt to open her eyes. She still heard the voices, but eventually she was left with only the ones inside her head. It sounded like she had just stepped into a convention of some sort. She couldn't distinguish one voice from the others.

What's happening to me? Sandra wondered to herself. Her entire body still ached, her head was killing her, and she could barely think her mind was in such a turmoil. Dante would have needed another level to incorporate the level of pain Sandra was experiencing right now. Is this what Hell is like? Could it be any worse?

CHAPTER 53

▼

Sunday
10:55 p.m.
Meadowvale Clinic

Rachel looked up to the plain Bulova clock hung over her doorway, and saw that it was five minutes to eleven. Most of the patients would be in their rooms by now and the night shift would soon be coming on duty. Unaware of the utter despair Sandra Hillock was experiencing at that very moment, Rachel grabbed her coat, car keys and her copy of Amanda's file and left her office making sure to turn off the lights behind her. The rest of the floor was deserted. Rachel couldn't see any light seeping out from underneath any of the other doorways in the hall. Flemming and Foley often stayed late, but even they went home before ten most nights. Unlike the other doctors, Rachel didn't have to worry about a family waiting for her at home.

The day had passed slowly, every minute dragging on like the interim between final exams. Only one message had been left for her the day before. Some FBI guy wanted to talk to her. Supposedly she had missed an appointment with him yesterday. He would drop in on Monday morning. Rachel wondered if it had anything to do with the disappearance of Arthur Montgomery. If it did, why on earth would the FBI want to talk with her?

Rachel had called Ed during the day to devise a plan. She would sneak Amanda out of the Clinic just after eleven during the shift change and drive to Sherman Myers' where she would meet Ed. She had a good idea on how to get Amanda out of the building but getting her back in wouldn't be so easy.

The bell on the elevator signaling its arrival on the third floor seemed especially loud in the tomb-like silence of the Clinic after hours. Rachel stepped out of the elevator and was immediately greeted by Dean Campbell, his red hair and lanky build always brought images of Ronald McDonald to Rachel's mind.

"Hi, Doctor Miller, what are you doing here so late, and on the weekend?" he seemed a little surprised.

"I just have to check on Amanda quickly if that's alright?"

"Of course it is, Kevin's just making the rounds now. He's already checked her room."

"Thanks, Dean, I won't be too long."

"Take your time. Just let the next shift know when you leave."

"Oh, I should be gone before they get here."

"They'll be here anytime now."

"Like I said, I'll just be a minute."

"Okay." Dean said. He seemed a little perplexed and Rachel hoped she hadn't made him suspicious. She walked down the hall towards Amanda's room and entered her room after knocking softly. Amanda was sitting on the edge of her bed fluffing up her pillows. A single beam of moonlight shone in through the window and cast a radiant glow on the back of her head. Rachel immediately thought of a halo and her heart went out to the woman sitting on the bed.

"Hi, Amanda, I know its late, but would you like to go see Mister Myers again?"

"I should sleep, Doctor Miller." Rachel hadn't counted on Amanda saying no, she had just assumed she would come along willingly.

"I know it's late Amanda, but if you come to see Mister Myers again with me, Ed and I will take you to the park, how about it?"

"I like Ed. He's funny."

"He likes you too, Amanda. And I think he would like it if you came with us tonight."

"Really?"

"Really. And if you do come, I'll arrange it so that you can go to the park more often. Would you like that?"

"Yes." Amanda raised herself up and placed her pillow at the head of the bed. She reached underneath the bed and pulled out a pair of slippers. Rachel glanced at her watch and saw that it was almost eleven. They would be cutting it close if they wanted to avoid being caught by the night attendants.

Rachel led Amanda out into the hallway after ensuring the coast was clear and headed for the dining room. Kevin would be on the other side of the building checking the remaining rooms. They had to hurry. Amanda's slippers rustled softly across the glazed concrete floor while Rachel's sneakers issued a sharp squeak every third or fourth step.

"Do you remember when you hid in the elevator the other day Amanda?" Rachel asked as she and Amanda entered the dining room.

"Yeah," Amanda said in a soft voice.

"Would you like to go for a ride in it?"

"In the elevator?" she asked surprised.

"Yes, in the elevator."

"But it won't go."

"It will if I push the button."

"Where will I go?"

"Downstairs to the kitchen where they prepare your food."

"Will you come too?"

"Not in the elevator with you, we can't both fit. I'll meet you downstairs. You'll have to wait for me. Can you do that?"

"I guess so. Why don't we both take the real elevator?"

"Because the nurses don't like when patients leave at night. They get jealous because they have to stay inside all night." Amanda smiled at this. Rachel pushed the button to bring the elevator up when they reached the back of the dining room. The light that fell through the windows from outside was sufficient to see by.

"Okay, we have to do this quickly. Get in and I'll send you down." Amanda climbed into the small space without a fuss and waved to Rachel as Rachel closed the door behind her. She pushed the down button and left the dining room. She felt a pang of guilt at the thought of having sent Amanda downstairs in a space no bigger than a large oven.

Rachel found Kevin and Dean waiting for the real elevator. It was just past eleven.

"Long day huh?" Kevin asked Rachel.

"Too long," she replied.

"Is Amanda alright?" Dean inquired.

"Yep, she's fine, I just wanted to ask her something. Nothing important. But you know how it is when you think of something and can't rest until you satisfy your curiosity?"

"Yeah, yeah, like when you see an actor on TV and you spend all day trying to remember their name. Your head feels like it's going to pop unless you remember."

"That's exactly what I mean," Rachel smiled, "so where're the other guys who come on to replace you?" Rachel asked.

"We meet them in the lobby when we change shifts. It saves having to set the alarms to the front entrance twice."

"Oh," Rachel said. When the three of them arrived in the lobby they saw a stout solitary figure standing by the main entrance.

"Hey, Eric, where's Jesse?" Dean shouted across the lobby.

"He went to the kitchen to grab some coffee bags for the machine. You guys never leave us any," Eric called back. His round bald head seemed to accentuate his pudgy midsection.

"The kitchen?" Rachel asked, her heartbeat quickened at the thought of Amanda alone in the elevator.

"Yeah, that's where us lowly staffers keep the coffee, Doctor Miller."

"Of course, I didn't mean it like that, I just meant..." Rachel was interrupted by a set of swinging doors and another voice.

"I got the coffee," it was Jesse, a young psychology grad student who worked part-time at the Clinic, "man is it creepy back there. I couldn't find the lights so it I had to find my way in the pitch black and the elevator kept going up and down. It must be busted or something." Rachel sighed inwardly when she realized Amanda had not been discovered.

"We'll tell maintenance in the morning, they can have a look at it. We're outta here," Dean said as he and Kevin headed for the doors.

"Any problems on the floors tonight?" Eric yelled at their backs.

"Nope, quiet as a whorehouse in Haiti."

"Nice, haven't heard that one before." Eric shouted.

"Charming," Rachel said.

"Aw, come on doc, lighten up."

"Good night, Eric."

"Good night, doc," Eric said when he saw Rachel would not be baited, "You get the alarms alright, Doctor Miller?"

"I'll take care of them."

"Great, thanks." Rachel took her time resetting the alarm system and slowly walked towards the front entrance but turned on her heels as soon as Eric and Jesse got into the elevator. The kitchen was indeed pitch black and Rachel had a difficult time finding her way to the freight elevator. Its door was still closed and Rachel was relieved to see Amanda crouched patiently inside. Her nose scrunched up as she smelled the kitchen. A bitter lemon scent with a hint of ammonia hung in the air.

"I thought maybe you forgot about me, Doctor Miller," she said as she clambered out.

"I would never forget you Amanda. Let's go." Rachel held out her hand and the two of them exited the building via the small door next to the larger kitchen delivery door.

Rachel had parked towards the back of the building to facilitate escape. She had Amanda climb into the back seat and hide under a blanket she had brought from home. Bright halogen lights carefully hidden among the tree branches lit the drive. The security guard in the booth at the end of the drive didn't give Rachel a second glance as she drove through. He was more concerned with vehicles coming onto the grounds and his Arthur Hailey novel.

"All right, Amanda, you can sit in the front with me if you want." Amanda whipped off the blanket and climbed over the seats to the front. Rachel looked at her and laughed. The blanket had turned her head into a frizzy mass of static electricity. Amanda's long blonde hair was floating in every direction. It was clinging to the soft ceiling of the car, her seat, her nightshirt, and even her face. Amanda reached up to her head and tried to brush her hair back into place with her fingers. It resisted at first but after a few attempts, she was able to return it to some semblance of order.

It took just over twenty minutes for Rachel to reach Sherman Myers' apartment building. Ed's truck was parked across the street from the building and Rachel pulled in behind him. She flashed her highbeams twice to let him know it was her. He waved in his rearview, and got out of the truck humming the *Tears For Fears* song he had been listening to. He had a can of Dr. Pepper in his hand.

"You're drinking Dr. Pepper at this time of night?" Rachel asked Ed as she helped Amanda out of the car, "your teeth are going to rot right out of your head."

"Dr. Pepper will rot my teeth. Kraft Dinner will give me tapeworms. It takes seven years to digest gum. Gummi bears will hibernate in my colon. I've heard them all. I'm not too concerned," Ed said.

"Your dentist bill, not mine."

"Thanks for your concern. Speaking of which, I was getting a little worried about you guys. I was beginning to think maybe you got caught."

"No, it was a clean getaway. Right, Amanda?"

"Right," Amanda replied, then "hi, Ed."

"Good evening, Amanda. And how are you tonight?" Ed said in his best Belagosi imitation.

"Good, but a little tired," she smiled.

"I'm not surprised, I'm up past my bedtime too."

"Well, we should go see Sherman before he decides he's tired as well," Rachel interjected.

"Always the party pooper, huh, Amanda?" Ed said, giving Rachel a sidewards glance.

Mounting the narrow hallway stairs in single file for the second time that weekend gave Ed a sense of Deja Vu, only this time he hoped the hypnosis would be more revealing. Sherman Myers opened the door to his apartment just as his three visitors reached the landing outside his door. He was wearing a pair of gray flannels and a thick maroon cardigan. He ushered them in and offered them drinks. Ed showed him his soft drink, Rachel asked for water, and Amanda declined.

"Thank you for seeing us on such short notice, Sherman," Rachel said as the old man maneuvered around the kitchen getting the drinks.

"Oh, it's no bother, dear. I don't get out much these days. You people have been the most excitement I've had in years. Now what's this you were telling me on the phone? You say your patient here has memories that we didn't get to the first time?"

"That's what we think," Rachel said. Sherman listened with fascination as Rachel went on to describe the previous night's excursion and their suspicion that Amanda's recollections were rather vague and lacked detail. She then told him that she suspected that Amanda's true memories were being hampered by false memories.

"Very interesting," Sherman said when Rachel was done, "although I suspect you've been reading too many Dean Koontz novels."

"Can you at least humor me?"

"Sure, why not."

Chapter 54

"Amanda, can you hear me?" Rachel asked once Sherman Myers hypnotized her for the second time that weekend. She had gone under a lot quicker this time and seemed even more at ease than she had the first time, despite the late hour. Sherman and Ed looked on, silently.

"Yes, Doctor Miller," Amanda replied in monotone. She was reclined in the La-Z-Boy once more.

"I want you to think back to the first time you met Doctor Sanford again. But before you do, I want you to know that he is not really there, and no one can hurt you, no matter what you see or feel. Ed, Sherman, and myself are right here to protect you and we won't let anyone harm you. Do you understand? No one can hurt you."

"No one can hurt me," Amanda echoed, her voice sounded like it was drifting.

"Okay, now think back to your first encounter with Doctor Sanford."

As had happened the first time Rachel asked the same question the day before, Amanda became uncomfortable and a grimace settled on her face.

"Remember, Amanda, no one can hurt you. Just tell us what's going on."

"I see several people around me, they're holding me down. They're tying ropes to my wrists and ankles and…and…no…they have a knife. They're going to cut me!"

"Relax, Amanda, no one can hurt you, you're perfectly safe. You're doing great." Rachel said in her softest voice.

"They're cutting my arm, oh God…it hurts…make them stop."

"Amanda, I want you to concentrate on the faces around you. Look right into the faces."

"I can't, they're all wearing dark hoods of some kind."

"Look past the hoods, Amanda, look through them," Rachel insisted.

"I don't see anything, they're too dark. Wait!" Amanda's face brightened, "I can see one of them. It's Doctor Sanford, Omigod, it's Doctor Sanford. Why is he doing this to me? Why?"

Ed, Rachel, and Sherman all looked up in surprise. So Dr. Sanford was involved in some sort of cult. It looked like one of their hunches may be proven correct. Before they could share their enthusiasm, Amanda went on.

"I can see one of the others too. It's Doctor Flemming, he's there too. He's the one with the knife."

Ed looked over to Rachel who was sporting a satisfied grin, he was thinking the same thing as she was: *We've got you, you bastards.*

"Amanda, is there anyone else there with you aside from Doctor Sanford and Doctor Flemming?" Rachel asked.

"Yes, there's one other person but he's too far away. I can't see him. He never turns his face towards me. I can't tell who it is."

"Is it Doctor Foley?"

"No."

Rachel sighed in relief. "Amanda? I'm going to have Sherman wake you up…" Rachel began saying but was interrupted by Amanda's shrill, insistent scream.

"Wait!"

Ed and Sherman both jumped.

"What is it, Amanda?" Rachel asked leaning over Amanda.

"Everything is becoming brighter. The more I think about it, the more the darkness goes away."

"What do you see?"

"I'm in a room. It looks like a hospital room. Doctor Sanford and Doctor Flemming are still there but they're wearing regular clothes now. They're not in robes any more. I still can't see the third person though. I can see myself in a large mirror on a wall. I'm in some sort of chair, like a dentist's chair."

Rachel could barely contain her excitement at the new revelations.

"What can you see in the mirror, Amanda?" she asked.

"I can see myself tied down, not with ropes, but with straps." *Restraining straps*, Rachel thought. Commonly used in mental hospitals.

"What else?" Rachel probed.

"Doctor Flemming isn't holding a knife. It's not a knife at all. It's a needle, he's putting something in my arm. They're talking to each other."

"Can you hear what they're saying?" Rachel asked, she didn't want to progress too quickly, although she had a million and one questions she desperately wanted to ask.

"No, I can't. They're behind me."

Rachel gulped, and in her head, went over the words she would use to phrase the next question. She didn't want to frighten Amanda, but at the same time, she had to get a definite, clear, response from her.

"Amanda?"

"Yes, Doctor Miller."

"Are the doctors touching you in any way? I mean aside from the needle and the straps, are they hurting you?" Rachel watched Amanda's face as she answered.

"No, they aren't touching me at all. Not like that." Rachel's shoulder's slumped. Of course she was relieved that they weren't sexually or physically abusing her, but she was also disappointed. If they weren't sexually or physically abusing Amanda, what were they doing?

Rachel thought of something else to ask Amanda.

"Amanda, do either of the doctors ever talk to you?"

"No. Wait, yes. Doctor Sanford does. He's behind me though. I can't see anyone else. The chair's been turned so I can't even see myself in the mirror."

"Can you tell what he's saying?"

"Uh...I can barely hear him. Hold on." Amanda's nose and forehead wrinkled as she strained to hear what Dr. Sanford was saying behind her.

"He's talking about there being others." Rachel looked at Ed and Sherman. Ed mouthed the word 'others'. He was thinking the same thing that Rachel was. Emily Jenkins. Barbara Tusane. Shelley Bockrath. Were they the others?

"What else, Amanda?" Rachel continued.

"He's saying that he'll take care of us. That he only wants to talk to us and meet us all."

Rachel wasn't sure what that meant. But she was sure that if those others Amanda mentioned were indeed patients of Dr. Sanford and if Dr. Flemming was involved in what was going on as well, she and Ed had been right in their suspicions that something sinister had transpired at the San Francisco Psychiatric Hospital while Sanford and Flemming worked there. Perhaps they were continuing their work at the Meadowvale Clinic.

"Sherman?" Rachel looked towards the old man and nodded her head at Amanda. It was time for her to wake up. Following the same procedure he had used the first time, Sherman skillfully and gently, brought Amanda out of her trance-like state.

Amanda sat up in her chair and smiled at the three people seated around her. She didn't seem to recall what she had just recounted in her hypnotized state and actually seemed quite buoyant.

"Well?" she asked.

"You did very well, Amanda." Rachel told her. Then added, "We actually learned a lot more than we thought we would." She told Amanda what they had learned.

"What does it mean though?" Ed asked.

"I'm not sure yet," Rachel said, "But we will figure it out."

Chapter 55

▼

Monday
9:06 a.m.
Meadowvale Clinic

The next morning, Rachel sat at her desk waiting for her first patient to come in for her appointment. She was five minutes late.

Hearing footsteps outside in the hallway, approaching her office, Rachel cleared her desk of the papers she was sorting out and withdrew a blank pad of yellow legal paper on which to take notes of the forthcoming session.

Her office door was slightly ajar, and opened further when it was knocked upon.

"Come on in, Hillary," Rachel called to the door.

The door swung open, but Hillary was not standing on the other side.

"Who are you?" Rachel asked. Standing in the doorway, was a tall, well-built, man with a shock of unruly blond hair. He wore a dark suit and carried a black trenchcoat over one arm. His facial features looked like they were carved out of stone and his eyes were direct and penetrating. A slight smile softened his chiseled features.

"Doctor Miller, I presume?" John couldn't resist.

"Yes. And who might you be?" Rachel asked.

"Agent John Haskins, from the FBI. I left a message on your voicemail the other day saying I would drop by."

Rachel mentally slapped herself in the forehead, she had completely forgotten about the message Agent Haskins had left. She had been too busy thinking about what she and Ed had learned from Amanda last night trying in vain to piece it together with what little other information they had.

"I have a patient coming in soon, Agent Haskins," Rachel informed him, not trying to be rude, but she sensed that was the impression he was probably getting.

"Actually, Doctor Foley called your patient and canceled the appointment. He and Doctor Flemming felt that my talking with you was more important. May I come in?" The smile was still there, and Rachel couldn't tell if it was condescending or just boyish.

"Uh, sure. I'm sorry to have gotten off on the wrong foot, but I was expecting someone else."

"That's alright, Doctor Miller. I assure you I won't take up too much of your time." John studied the young doctor sitting across from him. Short brown hair framed a plain, yet appealing face. She wore no makeup and didn't have to. John didn't see any jewelry either. Soft features contrasted with a sharp jawline and high cheeks. Although her blue suit wasn't form-fitting, John could tell she had a firm body by her posture. All in all, a pretty package. She looked innocent enough, but looks could be deceiving. John thought of a line by Milton *"Wisest men have erred, and by bad women been deceived; And shall again, pretend they ne'er so wise."* John was not about to let himself be taken in by a pretty face.

"What can I do for you, Mister Haskins?"

"Call me agent, and I'll call you doctor." They both deserved it.

"Fair enough."

"In case you're not aware, Doctor Miller, I talked to the rest of your colleagues this weekend regarding the disappearance of Doctor Arthur Montgomery. Are you familiar with that name?"

"Yes, of course. I was hired in his place by Grant Foley." John smiled inwardly. At least she didn't deny it.

"That was a piece of luck for you then, wasn't it? I mean Montgomery's disappearance."

"I suppose. What are you implying?" Rachel didn't like the way the FBI agent put his words.

"I'm not implying anything, just that it was rather convenient, for you, that a position opened up here at the Clinic. Can I ask you a question, Doctor Miller?"

"Certainly. That's why we're here, isn't it?"

John ignored the last remark. "Are you involved with any of the doctors here at the Clinic? I don't mean professionally."

Rachel understood precisely what he meant, she wasn't sure whether to laugh out loud or scream in outrage. She chose to remain composed. She wanted to figure out what Agent Haskins suspected of her as it was becoming increasingly apparent that he did suspect something.

"No, I am not," she answered coolly.

"Do you have any thoughts on Arthur Montgomery's fate?"

"What exactly was his fate?"

"He has been missing for the past six months, supposedly kidnapped, and probably dead. That is his fate, Doctor Miller." John was becoming annoyed with the young doctor and wondered if she too was hiding something. Just like he was sure doctors Flemming and Sanford were.

"So he still hasn't been found and no one knows what happened to him yet?" Rachel asked. John sensed genuine concern in her voice. Either that or she was an extremely good actress. Perhaps she had missed her vocation.

"No, I'm afraid not."

A terrible thought suddenly occurred to Rachel. "You don't think I had anything to do with it, do you?"

In a moment of unguarded frankness, John answered, "Actually, I don't know what to think."

"Well, I didn't even know about the whole affair until I was hired."

"I apologize, Doctor Miller, I didn't mean to suggest..."

"No, don't apologize," Rachel found herself saying in Haskin's defense. "Obviously you must suspect everyone or else you wouldn't be doing your job, but I can tell you one thing; I am not involved in anything going on at this Clinic and I don't know what happened to Arthur Montgomery."

"As it stands, I have several theories of my own, but I was wondering if you had any ideas?"

For the briefest of moments, Rachel considered telling Haskins all that she and Ed knew, or thought they knew, regarding the Clinic. She decided not to. She didn't see how any of it could be related to the disappearance of Arthur Montgomery. Besides, what she and Ed knew amounted to very little. They had suspicions and theories, they even had evidence, of what, they didn't know. The problem, and it seemed an insurmountable one, was that they couldn't for the life of them piece everything together. Before they had left Sherman's apartment the night before, the ex-CIA man quoted for them a phrase by Oliver Wendell Holmes, *"Have faith and pursue the unknown end."* How appropriate.

Now, sitting in her office with Agent Haskins, Rachel thought she knew how he felt. At least he knew what he was looking for. In answer to his question, she replied, "No, I'm sorry I don't. I've never given the matter much thought, and until now have never had any reason to."

"Thanks for being honest, and I apologize for the entry."

"And I, for the cold reception."

"If you think of anything, anything, please give me a call." John withdrew a card with his name and office number on it and handed it to Rachel. It was an open invitation to her to call him. John remembered her saying *"I am not involved with anything going at this Clinic."* He also remembered Grant Foley's words from Saturday morning, *"I can't imagine Arthur would be involved in anything that would lead to his removal."*

John believed Dr. Miller's assertion that she wasn't involved in anything going on at the Clinic, but the fact that she made such a claim bolstered his confidence that there was indeed something going on here. It seemed that she too was harboring suspicions. Perhaps he had found a potential ally in young Dr. Miller as well. Despite his earlier doubts, he was willing to give her the benefit of the doubt. Something about her had an impact on John. He'd read up on her the day before, everything Susan Baxter could turn up on her anyway, and one word kept popping up in his mind when he thought of her: idealist.

Now, as he left her office, he hoped that she would call him. After the numerous dead-ends he had run into with the other doctors, it would be nice to have someone on the inside with whom to talk.

Chapter 56

Rachel sighed in relief as Agent Haskins left her office.

She was sure that he suspected her for some reason or other. Did he think she was having an affair with one of the other doctors? The mere thought was ridiculous. He also mentioned that it was quite a coincidence that she had been hired shortly after Montgomery's disappearance. Could it be possible he suspected her of having something to do with that in order to further her own selfish desires? She supposed she couldn't blame Agent Haskins. As she had told him during their conversation, his job involved suspecting everyone.

She wondered now if she should have mentioned anything to Agent Haskins regarding what she and Ed had discovered thus far. With all that they knew: Carl Sanford's discrepant files, the disappearance of those same files, the death of Emily Jenkins, the false memories of Amanda Rutherford, and Ed's termination, Rachel grew increasingly frustrated that they couldn't see what was happening. It felt like they were given a new game without the dice and not instructed how to play. One more piece was all they needed. One piece which would bring all the others together. She was sure it existed. Or was she?

Before she could engage in any further mental gymnastics, the phone on her desk rang bringing her back to the here and now. It also reminded her that she had patients to see starting in half an hour.

A green light on her phone indicated to Rachel that the phone call was internal.

"Doctor Miller's office," Rachel answered.

"Good morning, Doctor Miller. This is Daniella down at the reception desk. A gentleman from the General Hospital just dropped off a large envelope for you. Do you want me to bring it up?"

Her curiosity piqued, Rachel said, "No, I'll come down and get it myself. Thanks Daniella."

"You're welcome, Doctor Miller."

The envelope that Daniella signed for had been dropped off by a local delivery firm. The envelope was the size of a gameboard and printed across it in bright red capitalized letters, it read: DO NOT FOLD: Computerized Topography Films. After picking it up, Rachel set it upon her desk and tore open one end with a letter opener.

Inside, there were several large films and a ream of folded printout paper accompanied by a note from a Doctor Herschmann at the San Francisco General Hospital. The note read simply;

> Dr. Miller. Here are the EEG and CT scan results from the tests conducted on your patient Jim Wells. As the CT scan films indicate, there does not appear to be any physical intracranial damage. As for the EEG printout, I have enclosed a report.
>
> Gary Herschmann

Rachel felt a pang of sorrow as she looked through the computer readouts and glanced at the CT films. She had forgotten all about the tests that she had had run on Jim Wells the previous week. Now the results were in but the patient was no longer around to benefit from whatever wisdom they imparted to the therapist. Rachel would have tossed them away, but her curiosity got the better of her. Although the information would never prove useful to Jim, Rachel thought maybe she could learn something from the test results. Whatever she discovered though would be pure speculation since she couldn't prove anything without Jim's physical presence.

Contrary to what she had anticipated, the CT scan revealed no trauma whatsoever to the left side of the brain. Not even the most marginal of bruising. Whatever had caused the lump on the side of Jim's skull had not been responsible for his mental condition.

What she did notice, when leafing through the Electroencephalograph readouts, was a few minor discrepancies. The wavy jagged lines weren't as consistent as they should have been. Something gnawed at Rachel.

She knew there was something wrong with the EEG readout but she couldn't put her finger on it. The report that Gary Herschmann had included revealed little. Rachel considered asking one of the other Clinic's doctors for an opinion but realized that if anyone could interpret the anomalous data, it was her.

As part of the research for her doctorate thesis, conducted less than a year ago, Rachel had to pore over miles and miles of computer printouts filled with the exact same type of graphs on them. She had scanned over hundreds of EEG readouts taken from dozens of subjects, many who suffered from dissociative identity disorder, and numerous 'normal' subjects who served as controls. What she had found in her research, and postulated in her thesis, was that patients with DID manifested different EEG readings for each separate personality. Basically, that each personality had its own unique brain patterns. On the other hand, the normal subjects who served as the control for the study, even when asked to 'fake' having separate personalities, demonstrated consistent EEG readings. That is, they did not show different readings for each faked personality.

Then it occurred to Rachel what was so strange about Jim Wells' EEG results. Why she hadn't thought of it before she couldn't imagine. The more she thought about it, the more sense it made. Everything seemed to click at once. The two different numbers of personalities on Carl Sanford's anomalous files; the deaths of Emily Jenkins and Jim Wells, and the false memories of Amanda Rutherford. It was as if all the fog surrounding the mystery were lifted all at once. It reminded her of what Churchill said about Russia. *It is a riddle wrapped in a mystery inside an enigma.* Well, now here it was, naked and unraveled, in plain sight, no longer shrouded in secrecy.

How could she have been so blind?

She had to call Ed.

Chapter 57

"It was good talking to you again Doug, thank you for your help." Walter Flemming returned the phone back to its cradle and smiled.

Although he had promised Carl Sanford and Grant Foley that he would take care of Rachel and her meddling, he had no idea how he intended to do so at the time. As a result, he spent the rest of the weekend and a large portion of this morning digging up as much as he could on young Dr. Miller.

What he had learned would bore anyone to tears. With the possible exception of a few ex-boyfriends and her parents' divorce, Flemming couldn't find anything that would prove even remotely useful in getting rid of her. As he had told Sanford Saturday afternoon, he couldn't just fire her straight out, there had to be a reason. The death of her first pro-bono patient Jim Wells would have done nicely, but the incident was too long past. If possible, Flemming wanted Wells' death to be forgotten as quickly as possible. A call from the medical examiner's office that morning had confirmed what Flemming already knew and wanted others to think; that Jim Wells' death was a suicide, plain and simple. Since there was no next of kin to speak of and no foul play detected, as far as the medical examiner's office was concerned, the matter was over. Jim Wells' body was cremated and that was that.

The last thing Flemming did in his quest to dig up Rachel's past was talk to all of her professors, both at UCLA and Berkeley, most of whom he knew on a first name basis.

The third person he called, Doug Carpenter, was an old colleague from Berkeley where Flemming had lectured for a year before moving on to the San Francisco Psychiatric Hospital. The conversation started off predictably enough with the usual catching up people engage in when they haven't spoken with each other for more than two years. Once caught up, Flemming brought up the subject of Rachel Miller. To his dismay, Doug Carpenter remembered her with fondness.

"One of my brightest students. She was always questioning me. Once in awhile she actually bested me, much to my embarrassment. Why do you ask?"

"Well, she's working out here at Meadowvale under Grant Foley's supervision. I just wanted to find out more about her."

"I'm not surprised she ended up working out there."

"Why is that?"

"Not only is it a status symbol to be employed at the very institute Walter Flemming heads, but given what happened to her sister, it's understandable that she would gravitate towards dissociative disorders. Let me guess, she specializes with Dissociative Identity Disorder, or at least wants to?"

"She does. But how did you know?"

"Like I said, it's no big surprise. All things considered."

"How do you mean, 'all things considered'? And what's this about her sister? I didn't realize she had one."

"*Had* being the operative word there. It's quite sad really. When she and her sister were very young, her parents divorced. Mom got Rachel, dad got Theresa. For three years, Rachel's father's girlfriend physically and sexually abused Theresa. She was caught by Rachel's mom but by then it was too late. The damage had been done. Years later, when Theresa was in her teens, she was diagnosed with a host of ailments including DID. She died after a few years of treatment. Aneurism."

"That's awful," Flemming said. His mind was processing the new information as quickly as possible.

"Isn't it? Anyway, that's why Rachel began studying psychiatry and turned to dissociative disorders. We talked about it at length a couple of times. She beats herself up over it, too. Always asking why it couldn't have been her that went with her father. I think she still carries a truckload of guilt around with her. She feels like she should have been able to do something and punishes herself for not having done so. That's why she pushes herself so hard. Let me tell you, you won't find a harder worker. I think she feels that by helping others with DID she can alleviate some of the guilt. We're all motivated by something, right?"

"Right," Flemming replied, but his mind was elsewhere. He talked for a few more minutes about how things were coming along at the Clinic and wished Doug and his family the best.

Doug was absolutely right. Everyone had their motivations, and Flemming was motivated by money and prestige. With Foley's help, he had successfully ousted that pesky insurance agent, Ed Morgan, and now, all that remained was silencing Rachel Miller. He didn't think she would have to meet the same fate as Arthur Montgomery had but she couldn't be allowed to continue working at the Clinic either. No, she wouldn't be killed or fired despite all her meddling.

Flemming equated Rachel Miller with the reporters he had to put up with. A minor annoyance and nothing more. They were all sharks, living off the backs of others. Flemming had no intention of letting them steal his trophy as had happened to the Old Man of Hemmingway lore.

What he had learned from Doug Carpenter was the most useful item of information he had managed to come across in three days: Rachel had a sister named Theresa who suffered from, and ultimately perished because of, dissociative identity disorder. That information was very useful indeed and Flemming knew just how it could be used when the time came.

Chapter 58

Pulling his Bureau issued car in between a yellow Caterpillar loader and a black International dumptruck, Shane Pavletic found himself assaulted by clouds of dust, the cataclysmic noise of over a dozen earth-moving vehicles, the yelling between foremen and ground crew, and the general clatter of a construction site.

The sign tacked up to the perimeter fence proudly announced another quality job by Gable & Sons Builders Inc., an Oakland based construction company. The foundation for their current project, a thirty six-story office building was currently being prepared.

Choking on the dust in the air and shielding his eyes as best as he could, Shane scanned the construction site for a few seconds before he found what he was looking for; a white hat.

"Are you the foreman on site?" Shane asked as he approached the white hat. He was a short Italian man with muscular forearms and a stocky build. A loaded toolbelt hung low on one side of his hips and seemed to pull his entire body in that direction. To compensate for the weight, the foreman leaned to the right.

"Yeah. Whaddyawant?"

Shane had to yell over the din just to make himself heard. "I need to talk to Harry Gable."

"What for?" the foreman asked keeping an eye on the men working in front of him.

"I need to ask him a few questions about a building he put up awhile ago." Shane held out his badge while he informed the foreman what he needed to see his boss about.

"FBI?" The foreman seemed surprised for a moment but then went back to watching his crew. He pointed across the site to a row of trailers surrounded by port-a-potties. "He should be in the second trailer to the left. Just knock on the door and walk in. Grab a hard-hat on your way." The foreman pointed to a pile of hard-hats and safety glasses lying in the back of a well used pick-up truck. Shane helped himself to a hat and pair of glasses.

A large sewage truck blocked the quickest way to the trailer the foreman had indicated. Once a week, the portable toilets had to be emptied and cleaned by their supplier. Today was the day. The combined stench of human waste and ammonia was overpowering and Shane thought he would pass out from the fumes. Unfortunately, the smell pervaded the interior of the trailers as well.

Several benches lined the walls of the trailer, a row of closed-circuit TV's sat on a solid oak desk, coveralls, raincoats, safety masks and visors, and gasmasks took up most of one wall.

Three burly men were standing over a beat up metal table looking down at a set of blueprints and building plans. Shane had to tap one of them on the shoulder to get their attention.

"Who are you?" one of them asked.

"Agent Shane Pavletic. FBI." He held up his badge for the second time in five minutes. The novelty still hadn't worn off. "I'm looking for Harry Gable."

Two of the men immediately looked at the man standing between them, the smallest of the group, but by no means a small man.

"I'm Harry Gable. What can I do for you?" Harry Gable spoke slowly and clearly and his bright green eyes reflected an intelligence which his dirty coveralls often betrayed.

"I was wondering if I could speak to you in private?" Shane asked glancing at the other two men.

"Of course. Ted, Hank? Tell Marty what we just discussed and make sure he knows about the extra rebar. Also, have that new guy he was having problems with come and see me. I won't tolerate messing around on my site. If the guy wants to know what a cut-off saw can really do, I'll be happy to show him." Ted and Hank laughed as they stepped out of the trailer.

"Now what can I do for you, Agent Pavletic? You'll have to pardon the smell. I told them to come in on Fridays but they said Monday was the best they could do. Not the best way to start your first morning of the week is it?" Harry asked referring to the portable toilet cleaners. He had a friendly manner about him but Shane suspected he could be a hard-ass in a given situation.

"You put up the Meadowvale Clinic correct?"

"Yes, sir. We finished that two months ago. What seems to be the problem?"

"Oh, there's no problem with the building itself. I'm part of a team conducting a search for a missing person. A Doctor Arthur Montgomery."

"They're still looking for him?"

"You know him?"

"Not personally, but from what I've seen, heard, and read in the news. What does he have to do with me?"

"Nothing directly, but he was one of the men responsible for the creation of the Clinic and was supposed to work there. We're talking to anyone and everyone involved with the Meadowvale Clinic, so don't worry, you're not under suspicion or anything."

"Well that's a good thing I guess. I can only take so much bad news a day, and I've about reached my limit for today. I had a guy using an industrial cut-off saw to cut his submarine sandwich this morning. Can you believe it? Those things are used to cut through steel and concrete, not lettuce and whole wheat. I hope the bastard chokes on the thing. Unbeknownst to him, today's his last day. That's not even the worst of it. Just last week, a guy I laid off the week before tried to kidnap some rich family's kid. Idiot got caught the same day. Supposedly, he was going to use this very site as the drop-off point for the ransom. I didn't think I paid him that little." Harry laughed at his own joke. "Anyway, enough of my woes, what do you want from me?"

"I need everything you have on the Meadowvale contract," Shane said matter-of-factly.

"That's a tall order. Can you be a little more specific?"

"I wish I could, but frankly, I have no idea what I'm looking for. We believe Doctor Montgomery's disappearance is somehow linked to the Clinic but we're not sure how yet, hence the broad sweeping nature of my request."

"We keep all our old contract records in our office downtown. If you go there and speak with my wife Jane, I'm sure she'd be glad to help you."

"Thank you, Harry. By the way, when you were working on the Meadowvale contract, did anything out of the ordinary happen, did you notice any suspicious looking characters hanging around, anything that struck you as odd." Shane ran the usual private eye gamut.

"Nope, that job was as straightforward as they come."

"Thanks," Shane shook Harry's callused hand and turned to go when he spotted the close-circuit TV sets for the second time. Each set displayed a different view of the construction site.

"Hey, Harry?"

"Yeah?" Harry looked up from the blueprints he had returned his attention to.

"Do those cameras record?" Shane asked pointing to the TV sets.

"Only when there's nobody on site. We bought them to keep an eye on our equipment at night. Last year we had over two hundred thousand dollars worth of equipment stolen from our sites. From protective clothing, to materials, to tools. We almost lost a rig once but the thief couldn't drive it, obviously didn't have his A-Z. Someone even ripped off the thumb to our excavator last year." Harry said.

"What do you do with the old tapes?"

"We keep 'em for awhile, but if nothing turns up missing, we use them again and just record over the old footage. Damn set-up cost a fortune, but a lot less than what we've been losing in equipment. The excavator thumb alone costs close to a hundred grand."

Shane whistled. "Where would those tapes be if you still had them?"

Harry looked over his shoulder at a waist high cabinet. "In that cabinet right there."

Acting on a hunch, Shane asked, "Do you think there's a possibility that you might still have tapes of the Meadowvale Clinic?"

"We might. Do you want me to check?"

"Yes, please."

"They don't all have dates on them so it might take awhile."

"I have all day."

"I was afraid you might say that."

Two hours of playing and fast-forwarding the more than eighty tapes in the cabinet turned up seven tapes which showed the Clinic in varying stages of completion. To the best of Harry's knowledge, the site revealed in three of those tapes resembled what the site should have looked like around the time of Arthur Montgomery's disappearance.

"Can I look at these here?" Shane asked once they found the three tapes.

"Sure. Any idea what you're looking for?"

"Absolutely none."

"Good luck."

Rewinding each tape to the beginning, Shane prepared to watch over thirty-six hours of film. Each tape could record for twelve hours.

By fast-forwarding, Shane could still see what was recorded and not have to watch every minute of recording. It took two hours to go through the first tape. The most noteworthy occurrences recorded included a car full of young women smoking pot and a bat which had gotten itself tangled in a bale of fencing. After an hour or so, it managed to free itself.

Reluctantly, Shane began the next tape and fast-forwarded his way through it as well. The screen remained absolutely inactive until mid-morning. A digital readout in the upper left hand corner of the screen indicated that it was eight-twenty-two in the morning. Shane almost didn't notice the movement on the screen at first. It was just rising dust, but then he saw that it became thicker and quickly dissipated. As if a car had pulled up just off-screen. Watching the tape at normal speed, Shane waited to see if anything else was caught on tape.

There it was.

A flash of movement on the left side of the screen. Was that an arm? Shane decided to watch for awhile longer before he rewound the tape.

Then again, an arm and part of someone's upper body flashed onto the screen. The arm was waving up and down.

Another minute passed and without warning, what looked like a man being pushed onto the ground made its way onto the screen. It was a man. He was scrambling on the ground. His hand picked up a pipe and he stood up. It looked like he was yelling.

The man on the screen was Arthur Montgomery.

There was no doubt about it. Shane couldn't believe it. He rewound the tape and watched the doctor falling to the ground again. Then he was gone off the screen once more. Half-an-hour later the tape ended.

Shane left the second tape at the spot where the doctor appeared on screen and began watching the third tape. Much like the first tape, nothing of interest was recorded on it.

"Find anything?" Harry Gable walked into the trailer as the third tape was rewinding.

"Possibly," Shane said trying to conceal his excitement. "Could I borrow this tape?" Shane asked holding up the second tape.

"Sure. Keep it if you want, we've got enough of the bloody things."

"Thanks, Harry."

Shane jogged back to his car, sighing in relief when he saw that it hadn't accidentally been run over by one of the huge lumbering vehicles which dominated the site. After a day and a half of investigating the origins of the Meadowvale Clinic and talking to practically everybody involved he couldn't wait to show the tape he'd found to Haskins.

Chapter 59

▼

The instance at which Carl Sanford first became aware that he was being watched happened Saturday evening, innocently enough while he was sitting at home reading one of his many unread psychiatry periodicals in the comfort of his den.

Against numerous admonishments, his fourteen year old son, Terrence, a tall, lanky, athletic, upstart of a youth, interrupted him during his "quiet hour" he enjoyed after dinner.

Ambling into the dimly-lit den, Terrence said hesitantly, "Uh, Dad? I just thought you should know there's a big, dark car outside with two guys in it checking out our house."

"How many times have I told you not to come in here after dinner?" Carl fumed, angry at the impetuousness of youth and the grief his ulcer was giving him. Despite swallowing a stomach-full of Pepto each day and the acid inhibitor his doctor had him on, his condition seemed to be deteriorating due to the constant and never-ending barrage of aggravations he had to put up with, both at home and at work. "Why would anyone be watching our house? They're probably looking for houses for sale or waiting to pick up one of the neighbors."

"They've been there for three hours, ever since you got back from work. They look like Feds or something."

That's it, Carl thought at the time, TV time was being seriously limited from here on in at the Sanford household. Was everyone in this world paranoid except for him? Maybe there was something in the water other than fluoride.

"Terrence, I doubt that they're *Feds*, as you so eloquently put it, and even if they were, what on earth would they be doing watching our house? Now, shoo, I've got to catch up on some reading." Terrence skulked out of the room and picked up his game of three on three in the driveway. He ignored the car and its occupants.

Inside, Carl grew increasingly agitated. The thought of being watched, in conjunction with the steady and unnerving noise of his son's basketball game outside were enough to drive him to distraction.

"Honey, you look tired," his wife Melissa, came into the room and wrapped her small arms around her husband's neck tenderly, "Why don't you come up to bed with me? Hmmm?" she suggested. Carl turned to his wife of nineteen years and saw concern in her face. Why was everyone so concerned about him? Couldn't they just mind their own business. He wanted to tell her to get lost.

Instead, he said, "Not now dear, I want to finish this article I started, and then I have some paperwork to do." Melissa Sanford took the hint and left the den without saying a word. Like Carl, Melissa disregarded Terrence's claims that their home was being watched by government agents.

For the eighth night in a row, Melissa Sanford went to bed before her husband and knew that she would be asleep long before he retired.

Proving his wife right, although he didn't know it, Carl climbed the steps to the master bedroom two hours later.

Brushing his teeth and examining his facial wounds, Carl ruminated over how little he had accomplished that day. Lost in his own depressing thoughts, he wouldn't have looked out the small bathroom window if a movement outside in the street hadn't caught his eye.

The interior light of a car flashed on and off ever so briefly. Just long enough for Carl to catch sight of it out of his peripheral vision. His son was right. There was a car parked outside the front of their house.

Carl quickly turned off the light in the bathroom, closed the door so the light from the hallway wouldn't cast his silhouette, and peered through the vertical blinds down onto the street below.

From what he could tell, the car looked like a late model sedan. There were two people sitting in the front of the vehicle. Just like his son had told him. Both sat motionless. Carl couldn't see their faces or tell whether they were looking his way.

The lights of the car came on and cut a brilliant swath of light down the darkened street. Carl could hear the ignition start. Slowly, almost reluctantly, the car pulled away. John Haskins had told his agents to be as obvious and menacing as possible. The mock surveillance had begun.

Early the next morning, Carl pushed the thought of the mysterious car from his mind and went about preparing his breakfast while at the same time, mentally planning the rest of his day. It wasn't until he was stopped at a set of lights downtown that he gave the previous night's occurrence any thought or credence.

Stopped three cars back, the same car, or at least what appeared to be the same car, a dark, late model sedan, appeared to be following him. Carl closed his eyes and shook his head to ensure he wasn't imagining things, seeing things that weren't really there. Another glance in his rearview confirmed that the car was indeed there. Apparently following him.

Carl turned right once the lights turned green, a departure from his usual route. Normally he went straight. Taking a few more random turns, Carl drove on, hoping to prove to himself that no one was following him. He drove through a crowded parking lot and continued on his way to work. All the while, he kept his eye on the mirror. It looked like he had lost his tail. Or, more likely, he thought to himself amused, there was no one there in the first place. The scenario reminded him of the classic television series, *The Streets of San Francisco*. All it lacked was a high speed chase down Nob Hill and a young Michael Douglas burning rubber hot in pursuit.

By the time he arrived at the Clinic, Carl was in better spirits, and actually looking forward to diving into a mass of work he had put off for the past two weeks. Since the Clinic opened, he seldom had a moment to himself, what with his new patients and the incessant and impossible demands Flemming heaped upon him. This was the third Sunday in a row that he sacrificed to his career. No rest for the wicked, he supposed.

Only a few other cars were parked in the lot. Although some were later models, few of them were dark, and not one of them was a sedan. Smiling at his heedless worrying, Carl almost failed to notice the dark, late model sedan, creeping along the roadway, just outside the grounds' outer perimeter, on the other side of the tall, wrought iron gates. His initial reaction was to go up to his office and put it out of his mind, but then he decided to put an end to whatever was going on.

Angrily, and without thinking about what he was doing, Carl put down his armload of papers and began jogging towards the car. As he approached, the car sped off. Carl was unable to read the license plate or get a good look at the people inside. Again, there were two of them.

For the rest of the day Carl continued spying the late model sedan. It wasn't as brazen as it had been initially, but it continued to be a constant presence. One which threatened to push Carl over the edge. When he approached Grant Foley about it, his colleague's response was one of impatience. Now, Carl Sanford won-

picions about Emily Jenkins, the patient of Carl Sanford who had killed herself five years ago, and the iatrogenesis they believed had been going on at the psychiatric hospital and was continued at the Meadowvale Clinic. Ed also revealed his suspicions about insurance fraud. Agent Haskins once in awhile inserted a question where it seemed pertinent, but otherwise wrote everything they said down in his notepad.

"So you think Emily Jenkins, Lisa Parsons, and Jim Wells were experiments?"

Rachel answered the question. "We think Emily Jenkins was the very first patient they seriously worked on. None of Sanford's files preceded hers. I don't know about Jim Wells and Lisa Parsons though."

"I want to ask you a few more questions later," John finally said when he had taken a dozen or so pages of notes, "but I've got to keep track of what's going on down here as well. Can you two stick around for awhile?" John asked Ed and Rachel.

"Sure," they replied in unison.

Back in Rachel's office, Ed asked "So what are you going to do now that the upper echelon of the Clinic has been wiped out?"

"I don't know. Maybe go into private practice. I might even stay here. The Clinic can still help people and a lot of good work is still being done here. Maybe it's my chance to move up the ladder. What about you? I saw you talking with your boss. Did you get your job back?"

Ed shrugged. "No, I didn't."

"You're kidding me?"

"Nope, remember that guy I told you about, Bernard? He's taken my place. I'm going to be promoted if Hal has anything to say about it." A huge smile spread across Ed's face.

Rachel leapt off the corner of her desk and gave Ed a big hug. "Ed, that's great. I'm so happy for you."

"Well, I never doubted for a second that things would work out," he put his pencil in his mouth and held it like a cigar. Rachel gave him a playful punch to the shoulder.

Chapter 72

▼

Two hours later, Agent Haskins re-joined Rachel and Ed in Rachel's office.

"So how goes the battle?" Ed mused.

"It's going great. The body we found was Montgomery's, perfectly preserved. And we found a bloodstained jacket beside it with a monogrammed handkerchief tucked in the breast pocket. The initials were W.F. Can you believe it?"

"I hope the bastard fries," Rachel said. Just the thought of what Flemming had been doing to Amanda and the other patients sickened her.

"I think we've got enough on him to make sure he doesn't see another patient ever again," John said. "Also, almost everything you told me and suspected has proven correct. Doctor Sanford hasn't stopped talking for over two hours. We can't shut him up. Flemming is answering most of our questions. The orderly Kevin Cheung and Grant Foley have both taken the fifth, and we have one more person in custody now. It seems one of the other orderlies, Dean Campbell was also involved somehow. We're not sure how yet, but Sanford insists he and Kevin Cheung were responsible for 'acquiring' Jim Wells along with several other patients-to-be."

"What about Emily Jenkins, Lisa Parsons, and Jim Wells?" Rachel asked.

"Sanford admits that the Jenkins woman was his first serious attempt at iatrogenesis. He claims he didn't know what the effects would be. I don't think that will gain any sympathy from the DA though. Lisa Parsons was also part of their experiments but she had been a heavy drug user beforehand and didn't respond properly to their so called treatment."

"And Jim?" Rachel asked.

dered to whom he could turn. Flemming would undoubtedly have the same reaction Foley had. He could not tell his wife, because she would want to know why her husband was being watched. No, there was no one he could tell.

Did someone think that he knew what happened to Arthur Montgomery? Was that why the FBI Agent had talked to him Saturday morning even though Montgomery had disappeared six months ago? The fact was he knew very little. He knew that Flemming and Montgomery had gotten into a row over the project. Montgomery apparently had ethical concerns regarding the whole thing. He also knew that Montgomery never showed up for work the same morning. What he didn't know was exactly what had happened to him, and how Flemming was involved with his disappearance.

He was sure Flemming was responsible for the disappearance, as Flemming himself made perfectly clear in his veiled threats. Carl recalled a distant conversation he had shared with Grant Foley the week before. After leaving Flemming's office, Foley had told him; *"Remember what happened to Arthur Montgomery,"* referring to the fact that Montgomery had opposed the project. Something which he himself wished he had done from the beginning. How could he forget. The man vanished off the face of the earth. Now it seemed like he was back to get his revenge, much like the infamous Montezuma. The accumulated stress of the past week resulted in even more severe gastro-intestinal pains however. Something which even his little pink panacea couldn't aid.

The next day, Monday, Carl Sanford ate lunch by himself in the Clinic's secluded courtyard. He chose a narrow metal bench painted a dark forest green underneath a group of young saplings. Eating his sandwich slowly, he peered through the overhanging canopy of foliage almost expecting to see a silent black helicopter hovering above. The courtyard's beauty did little to soothe Carl's tattered nerves.

For the time being, no one was watching him as he ate in the courtyard and no silent, black helicopters loomed overhead.

For the time being.

Chapter 60

"Thanks for meeting me so soon," Rachel said to Ed when they met at the Chinese Restaurant. Mrs. Liu came by and took their order. Water for Rachel, Dr. Pepper for Ed.

"It's not like I was busy doing anything else," Ed replied. "So what's up?"

"I think I figured out what they've been doing to their patients."

"Doctor Sanford and whatshisname?"

"Doctor Flemming. Yes. I can't believe I didn't think of it earlier."

"Think of what?"

"Iatrogenesis."

"Iaccocawhat?"

"Iatrogenesis." Rachel repeated.

"Layman in the room. What the heck is iatrogenesis?"

"When a physician or psychiatrist incurs within a patient a particular disease or disorder."

"Kind of like when you go to the hospital to get a few stitches but end up getting a cold as well?"

"No, that's nosocomial. Iatrogenesis is caused by a doctor. And I think that's what they're doing with patients at the Meadowvale Clinic right now. They're intentionally creating multiple personalities in their patients."

"How can they do that?" Ed asked confused.

"Let me give you an example. Do you remember the first day we met? We sat in the courtyard?"

"Yes."

"Now do you remember what was in the courtyard?"

"Sure," Ed listed the types of plants he recalled, the trees, the benches, the pond and the footbridge.

"Do you remember the two other people in the courtyard at the time?"

"The clinic staff?"

"No, they were patients."

"I thought they worked there?"

"No, they were patients."

"Okay."

"Do you remember them arguing?"

"Not really."

"They were yelling at each other."

Ed's face was a mask of concentration. "I think I remember them talking loudly. What's your point?"

"My point is that the two people in the courtyard *were* clinic staff and *not* patients and they were *not* arguing. In fact they didn't say a word the entire time we were there. However, I've already got you doubting your memory. With only a small suggestion, you're willing to believe that the two people in the courtyard were patients and that they were arguing.

"Now imagine I was your doctor and you placed all your confidence in me. Memory is very malleable. With enough time and drugs, and who knows what else, I could have you remembering whatever I wanted you to. That's what I think the doctors at the Clinic are doing to their patients, only worse."

"Worse?"

"I think they're suggesting to their patients that they were physically and sexually abused as children and that they have developed multiple personalities as a coping mechanism."

"Those are pretty lethal suggestions."

"Exactly."

"And you think they were doing the same at the San Francisco Psychiatric Hospital?"

"Yes."

"How do you know all this?"

Rachel explained the anomalies she discovered in Jim Wells' EEG readings and how they resembled those of someone faking dissociative identity disorder. That, coupled with the facts that Flemming had claimed Jim had DID and that she found no symptoms of the disorder, had led her to believe that Jim was not genuinely suffering from DID but thought he was.

"And how do they do this to the patients?"

"Through hypnosis and possibly drugs. That must have been what Amanda meant when she said Doctor Sanford was talking about others. He wasn't talking about other patients, he was talking about other personalities. He wanted to drag them out and meet them." Rachel remembered when Amanda repeated Dr. Sanford's words, *"He's talking about there being others. He's saying that he'll take care of us. That he only wants to talk to us and meet the others."*

"That would explain her memories," Ed said; his mind was racing at the implications.

"It may also explain the two separate numbers on Doctor Sanford's patient records. The first number probably indicated the number of personalities the patient had to begin with while the second number represented how many personalities were going to be placed iatrogenically."

"But what about Jim Wells? I thought you said he didn't have DID?"

"He didn't."

"But the other patients did? Including Amanda?"

"Yes, and I know what you're trying to say. I think Jim Wells was an experiment."

"What kind of experiment?"

"An attempt to iatrogenetically create within, a normal person, multiple personalities."

"Is that possible?"

"I think so. Deliberately inducing alters has been used as a means of treating DID patients before. It's not uncommon. There's no doubt that alters can be created iatrogenetically. A number of years ago, a Canadian psychologist, Doctor Nicolas Spanos and his colleagues conducted an experiment where they demonstrated that personalities could be developed in regular people not suffering from DID."

"So it can be done?"

"Apparently so. If the conditions were right and you had someone who knew what they were doing. They have everything they need at Meadowvale and Doctor Sanford is an excellent hypnotist."

"What about Flemming?"

"He's an expert when it comes to DID. Wait a minute!" Rachel snapped her fingers and practically leaped out of her seat. A few of the other customers in the restaurant gave her baleful glares.

"What?" Ed asked.

"I now know why Doctor Flemming's method of treating people with DID is so effective."

"Why's that?"

"Because he's the one who's given them the disorder in the first place. It must be easy to remove alters you yourself induced. As horrifying as the concept is, it's also brilliant."

"Brilliant, horrifying, and confusing," Ed said. He stared across the table at Rachel, his Dr. Pepper untouched.

"How do you mean?"

"Let's assume the doctors at the Clinic are playing God with their patients. What I don't understand is why?"

"Why they're doing it?"

"Yes. Why go to all the trouble? That's the sixty-four thousand dollar question."

"The Meadowvale Clinic was built largely because of Doctor Flemming's 'breakthrough' in treating these people. The Clinic not only offers the doctors intellectual autonomy, but earns them more respect than they could get anywhere else. You wouldn't believe how much the scientific community reveres respect and prestige. Flemming has written over a dozen papers on his method of treatment alone."

Ed recalled his first conversation with Rachel when he first went to the Meadowvale Clinic, *"We have a saying in our world 'Publish or Perish.' If you don't get published you may as well kiss your career good-bye."*

"So his revolutionary method of treatment is all a scam."

"It would appear so."

"This is bigger than sexually abusing patients."

"Much bigger."

"If Jim Wells didn't have DID but was given it, and let's say he didn't kill himself, he would be treated like a normal DID patient, right?"

"I guess so. What are you getting at?"

"Only the fact that the Clinic would be charging his insurance carrier for bogus treatment."

"But Jim didn't have an insurance carrier, he was a pro bono patient."

"Maybe he was an experiment like you said. Patient zero, the subject, a human guinea pig. Once they proved to themselves that they could give Jim DID, what would stop them from doing it to others?"

"Absolutely nothing," Rachel exclaimed understanding what Ed was implying.

"If they were treating patients who didn't actually have to be treated, and could take as long as they want, do you realize how much they could milk from the insurance carriers?"

"Thousands, I would imagine."

"Hold on to your hat. As part of my work on the Meadowvale portfolio, I had to figure out how much treatment costs for all the different types of dissociative disorders. If my calculations are right, and I have every reason to believe they are, do you know how much it costs to treat a patient with DID for one month at your Clinic? Take a wild guess."

"Close to ten thousand dollars?" Rachel guessed, though she thought her guess might be much too high.

"Try thirty thousand dollars."

If Rachel Miller was less of a lady, her jaw would have dropped. "Thirty thousand dollars?" she asked in disbelief.

"You heard me. If a patient with DID receives two years of treatment, it can cost that person's insurance carrier upwards of three million dollars. Of course the patient doesn't care how much it costs, hell, why should they, insurance is paying for it, right?" Ed was livid. "I can't wait to get my hands on Doctor Sanford and Doctor Flemming. Their days of insurance fraud are over."

"We have to put a stop to all of this. They can't be allowed to continue."

"I'm way ahead of you."

"What are you going to do?"

"I'm going to collect everything I have on Meadowvale, or had rather, and show it to Hal, my boss. I'm going to tell him what's going on over there." Ed stopped talking and paused. Anxiety plagued his face

"Good God!" he finally exclaimed as the reality of the situation they were discussing so casually finally dawned upon him. It was like a crushing weight bearing down on his shoulders. Now he knew what Atlas felt like. "What they're doing is insane. What would that do to a person's mind?"

"I think what happened to Jim Wells is answer enough," Rachel answered with little intonation in her voice.

"Do you think that's what happened to Emily Jenkins as well?"

"It seems more than likely. I would be hard pressed to think of it as a coincidence."

"What about the other patients then? Do you think they might have another Jim Wells over there?'

"It wouldn't surprise me and if all we've said so far is true, Amanda's life is certainly in danger," Rachel got up out of her seat so quickly that she upset her chair.

"Where are you going?" Ed called out after her.

"I've got to go to the Clinic and see if I can get Amanda out of there."

"Can't you do that afterwards?"

"It may be too late. Besides, if Sanford and Flemming find out that we know what they're up to, they might do something to her to make sure she doesn't talk. It makes me wonder what really happened to Lisa Parsons."

"How long do you think you'll be?"

"Give me an hour. I'll meet you back here."

"Call me on my mobile if you're going to be late. I'm going to see my ex-boss and let him know what's going on. Good luck."

"You too."

Chapter 61

▼

"What's a good looking woman like you doing in a place like this?" Desmond Galen asked the dead woman who lay before him.

Galen adjusted the height of the microphone hanging suspended over his next patient and looked curiously at the woman who lay prone on the dissecting table. Cause of death was not immediately apparent. Standing at six foot two, with wavy dark hair and dead blue eyes with flecks of gray, Galen could have more easily passed for a real estate agent or stock broker than a pathologist. Presently, he tingled with anticipation. After twenty-three years as a pathologist, he always looked forward to a challenge. Most people who came his way died in such boring and predictable fashions. It was the odd case where the cause of death eluded him that truly excited him.

The preliminary exam had already been carried out on the patient, as Galen liked to refer to the people who required his services, where the body was weighed and measured. The plastic bags that had been wrapped around her head and hands to preserve evidence had been removed. The victim, aged between eighteen and thirty-two, was in good health, good physical condition, and exhibited no outward signs of mutilation or struggle. She had been found in her present condition by two hikers early in the morning just outside the city. The body had been dumped unceremoniously in the forest, naked and without any clue as to the young woman's identification.

Desmond Galen switched on the microphone and began his examination. A thin sheen of sweat collected on his forehead despite the air-conditioned atmosphere of the 'operating room'. The first thing he did was look for was any bodily fluids which may have leaked out before or after death took place. He checked all the body's orifices and kept an eye open for blood, urine, fecal matter, and cerebrospinal fluid. He then swabbed the mouth, nose, and anal and vaginal cavities. He noted no damage to the perineum, which often indicated rape. He spoke calmly and clearly for the microphone as he described his findings. So far nothing out of the ordinary but also no obvious signs of what had brought this woman's life to such a premature end.

A careful examination of the body's surface revealed nothing of interest. No scars, tattoos, or interesting birth marks. Galen collected samples of facial and pubic hair, dirt from behind the woman's fingernails, and placed them on a counter alongside the swabs he had taken earlier.

Next came the dissection of the body. The skin parted easily under the sharp edge of the stainless steel scalpel and the muscle tissue underneath obliged just as willingly. Galen then cut the sternum with a Stryker saw and pried open the ribcage emitting a sickening crunch. If they last this long, most people who have never witnessed an autopsy, usually pass out at this stage.

The body's inner marvels revealed, Galen confirmed the presence of all of the major organs and noted no damage. Before removing the organs and scrutinizing them in turn, he had to collect the woman's body fluids. Galen paused to shrug his shoulders and roll his neck in an effort to ward off a cramp in his neck which he often developed when he worked. The room itself was empty as the other pathologists all had lunch at this time.

Once he had bottled ample samples of blood, urine, and cerebrospinal fluid, Galen set to work on the stomach. Along with the intestinal contents, liver, and vitreous humour, the jelly-like fluid behind the lens of the eye, the stomach contents were crucial in any post-mortem examination. Time of death can be closely estimated given the digestion or partial digestion of its contents, and in cases of suspected poisonings, the stomach must be examined carefully.

After carefully maneuvering the stomach over a large stainless steel tray, Galen cut it open with a pair of scissors and dumped its contents into the tray for inspection. He placed the tray on the counter next to him and rummaged through the stomach's contents curious as to what his patient had eaten last. From all appearances, it looked like Jane Doe had last eaten a submarine sandwich with the works. Galen turned back to the cadaver intending to begin the removal of the intestinal contents when something caught his eye. Something was caught alongside the inner wall of the stomach. Something plastic.

"What do we have here?" Desmond Galen muttered aloud. Using the scissors, he pried the foreign object out of the stomach and held it up under the light for examination. His dead blue eyes suddenly came to life.

"Well I'll be damned, if that isn't the strangest thing I've ever seen."

Chapter 62

▼

"Smile, Doctor Montgomery, you're on Candid Camera," with the push of a button, John Haskins froze the larger than life image of Arthur Montgomery's twisted facial features on the large screen TV.

Shane Pavletic, Susan Baxter and John, stood in a small, darkened room on the thirteenth floor of the building which housed the San Francisco FBI staring silently at the missing doctor. After six months of pursuit, seeing the face of their quarry brought them all a quiet satisfaction.

"That picture was taken on the morning of Montgomery's disappearance according to the contractor who built Meadowvale," Shane explained. He took the remote control from John and brought the tape to the spot where a cloud of dust could be seen rising and falling.

"Correct me if I'm wrong, but it looked like a car or truck just drove by off-screen," John said.

"That's what I thought as well. Unfortunately, that's all there is on the tape, but at least we know where he was that morning."

"Excellent work, Shane. Why don't you tell Shane what you found, Susan?"

Susan opened a folder she was holding and withdrew several sheets of paper. She sat down on the corner of a large desk and scanned their contents.

"Like both of you, I have an inherent distrust for Walter Flemming," she began. "I was originally supposed to take another look at all of the doctors who work at Meadowvale, but I decided to focus on Flemming. As we've already scoured their personal lives for the slightest misdemeanor, I decided to look more closely at their work. All the doctors at Meadowvale and Montgomery himself, were highly specialized within the field of psychiatry. Their expertise ranges from hypnosis to drug therapy. Aside from their involvement with Meadowvale and their high levels of expertise, the only other thing they have in common is their phenomenal rate of success when it comes to the treatment of their patients, patients with Multiple Personality Disorder in particular. I've talked to numerous psychiatrists, some who admire the Meadowvale doctors and others who openly criticize them. What I've discovered is that the Meadowvale doctors seem to treat their patients much quicker than their counterparts and at a much higher success rate."

"So what does that tell us?" Shane asked, wondering where Susan's observations were leading.

"That tells us that the doctors at the Meadowvale Clinic are either very good at what they do, or something not quite on the level is going on."

"What do the people you've talked to think?"

"After interviewing over twenty psychiatrists from all over California, I wouldn't place my bets on the quality of work being done at Meadowvale," Susan answered cryptically.

"Spell it out for me," Shane said.

"Several of the psychiatrists I've talked to have tried to duplicate the Meadowvale methods for treating patients with dissociative disorders with little to no success. In fact, some subjects were better off without the treatment. I've been told that the theory behind the treatment methods is sound but the amount of time involved is unrealistic. None of those psychiatrists who attempted to duplicate the treatment could do so within the timeframe set out by the Meadowvale experiments."

"So if they're not treating the patients like they say they are, then they're fudging their results," Shane concluded simply.

"It's more complicated than that," Susan retorted.

"How so?"

"Most of the studies conducted by Flemming and his colleagues prior to their move to Meadowvale were controlled by other psychiatrists who will firmly attest to the condition of the subjects both before and after the treatment."

"You mean the patients were in fact cured?"

"Not in all cases but those who weren't cured, showed remarkable improvements in their condition and behavior, all with little to no signs of recidivism."

"So what are we looking at here?" Shane asked more perplexed than ever.

"A mysterious method of treating mentally ill patients which has a remarkable success rate yet doesn't seem to work when anyone else attempts to duplicate it."

"And you think something isn't quite right and…"

"…and Arthur Montgomery found out about it…"
"…and didn't like what was going on, so…"
"…so he was disposed of," Haskins finished their thought. "I think it's time we had a chat with Spracken."

Chapter 63

Rachel's poor VW Rabbit was trembling by the time she peeled into the Meadowvale parking lot. The car hadn't been driven so fast in its entire existence. Once its ignition was killed, the engine emitted a series of disturbing clicking and pinging noises as it cooled. Rachel wasn't around to hear them. She had already dashed inside the Clinic.

The building's interior was exactly as she remembered it yet it somehow seemed foreign to her. Daniella was alone behind the reception desk amidst ringing phones and piles of paper. Muzak flowed gently out of carefully hidden speakers. It was like she had stepped into another dimension where everything was the same but she was changed. Rachel headed for the elevators.

She pressed the button for the sixth floor. She wanted to pick up the copy she made of Amanda's file with the two numbers written on it and Jim Wells' EEG readings and his CT scan results. She would need proof to back up her claims. She still wasn't entirely sure whom to contact. Should she call one of her old profs in hopes that they would at least comprehend the ramifications of what she was postulating? Should she call the police and risk having to spend hours trying to explain to them what was going on? Wait! What about that FBI guy, Agent Haskins? Perhaps he could help. Rachel would look for his card as soon as she got to her office.

God, this elevator is taking forever, Rachel thought. That was when she noticed it had stopped at the third floor. The elevator doors slowly slid open. Rachel was terrified that either Flemming or Sanford would step in. Much to her relief, Grant Foley stepped into the elevator with her. A white lab coat hung on his wiry frame and he carried a thick metal binder which he used to scratch his ribs with.

He smiled. "Going up?"

"Doctor Foley, am I glad to see you. I need to talk with you right away." Rachel hadn't even thought of telling Foley what she knew. Now that he was here though, Rachel couldn't understand why she hadn't thought of him earlier. He would help her put a stop to the atrocities being carried out within these walls. He would know what to do, who to contact. Most importantly of all, he would understand what she was talking about.

"Can't it wait, Rachel? I'm kind of busy right now."

"No, it can't!" Rachel punched the large red Emergency Stop button on the panel of buttons next to the door. The elevator jerked to a halt.

"Rachel? What is this about? Start the elevator back up. I have work to do," Foley said impatiently.

"Grant, I have to tell you something…" Rachel began.

"Really, Rachel, this isn't the way to get my attention."

"Would you shut up and listen!?" Rachel screamed at the top of her lungs. Within the confines of the small enclosure, the sound was deafening. Grant Foley didn't make a sound.

"Thank you. I apologize for yelling but I have to tell you something that I found out about Doctor Flemming and Doctor Sanford."

Foley's eyebrows shot up. "Oh?" was all he could manage to say.

"I've learned that they are iatrogenically inducing alters into patients here at the Clinic. They did the same thing at the Psychiatric Hospital. I have proof."

"Rachel, those are accusations of the gravest nature. Professional misconduct, violation of the doctor-patient relationship, and a slew of other misdemeanors. I must insist you show me this proof."

"I have it in my office. I'll show you right now." Rachel said, grateful that Foley would at least hear her out. She allowed the elevator to resume its course. Once in her office, she locked the door and let Foley look at the copy of Amanda's file and Jim Wells' EEG readouts and CT scan results. She told him all about her suspicions regarding the deaths of Jim Wells and five years previously, Emily Jenkins. She also told him about Carl Sanford's files and how they disappeared. She finished off by telling him how she had Amanda Rutherford hypnotized and that she had broken through an implanted mental block which was designed to prevent her or anyone else from discovering what was being done to her.

"Who else knows about this, Rachel?" Foley finally asked once she was done recounting everything she had learned.

For reasons she couldn't explain later, she decided not to tell him about Ed's involvement. She wasn't sure if she was trying to protect him or herself.

"Nobody. Just me."

"Good." Foley furrowed his brow, his eyebrows knitted tightly and he looked like he was squinting. Rachel knew he was deep in thought.

"I think we had better get out of here and talk about this more."

"I was going to get Amanda. She's one of the patients they've been victimizing. I think her life may be in danger."

"Good idea. Grab everything you have which can be used as evidence and meet me at the elevator. I have to lock up my office and get my keys."

Rachel hastily scooped up the copied file, the EEG readouts, the CT films, and a few pages of notes she had made over the past week. They were filled mostly with questions and suspicions.

As she glanced through her notes, she came across the card Agent Haskins from the FBI had given her. She dialed the number but was informed Agent Haskins was in a meeting. She left a message on his voice mail saying she urgently needed to speak with him and left Ed's mobile phone number with him.

Foley was already waiting at the elevator for her when she came out of her office.

"Got everything?" he asked as they stepped into the elevator.

"Everything."

"Excellent." He pushed the button and the elevator doors slid quietly shut and the car began to descend.

Rachel got out on the third floor and grabbed Amanda. She needed little cajoling to get her out of her room.

"Have you talked to the authorities yet Rachel?" Foley asked when she and Amanda stepped into the elevator.

"No, not yet," she said, not mentioning the message she had just left for Agent Haskins. "I wanted to talk to someone who would understand what I was trying to say first. If I went to the police they would think I was nuttier than a double-nut fruitcake."

"Well, it's a good thing that you came and talked to me first."

Rachel sighed as she watched the floor numbers flash downwards. She felt like a heavy burden had been lifted from her. Finally she understood what was going on and someone actually believed her. She couldn't wait to get out of the Clinic. Amanda was holding her hand. The bright red LED readout flashed 1 and Rachel prepared to step out of the elevator. Instead, the doors did not open and the elevator continued its downward descent. It stopped in the basement.

"You pushed the wrong button." Rachel told Foley.
"No, actually I didn't," Foley said coldly.

Chapter 64

All three mobile phones rang at once. Agents Haskins, Pavletic, and Baxter looked at each other curiously. They each answered their respective phones and chose a corner of the room to talk privately in.

"Agent Haskins speaking," John said as he leaned against the wall.

"Hi, Honey, it's just me," John's wife said, "Sorry to call you at work, but I just wanted to remind you that my parents are coming in tonight so don't be surprised when you get home."

"I won't, thanks for callling, love you."

"I love you too." John disconnected. Shane and Susan were still talking on their phones so he used the time to check his messages. There was only one. It was from Doctor Miller at the Meadowvale Clinic. He wrote down the number she left and tried calling but it was busy.

"Hello?" Shane spoke into his mobile. He opened the blinds to the room and sat on the windowsill looking out at the skyline.

"Agent Pavletic?"

"Yes?"

"Hi, it's Harry Gable from Gable and Sons Construction. We met this morning at the site. You were looking at some videotapes."

"Hi, Mister Gable, yes I remember. What can I do for you?"

"After you left, I was talking to my sons about what you were looking for, I hope that's okay?" a hint of worry crept into his voice.

"Of course, nothing wrong with that."

"Good, anyway, my son Hank asked me if you had found anything regarding that doctor's disappearance. I told him that you took one of the tapes you were looking at and he asked me which date."

"And?" Shane prodded.

"So I told him and he goes and says 'Oh, that was the same day that Doctor Flemming was here.'"

"Did you say Doctor Flemming? As in Walter Flemming?" Shane asked.

"Yeah. Hank says that Flemming was out there that morning looking around. It was sometime between eight and nine o'clock, before any of the workers arrived but my son came onto the site just as Flemming was leaving. At first he didn't recognize him."

"Is your son positive it was Flemming that he saw that morning?"

"Oh, no doubt about it. We talked with him lots about how the construction was going. I thought he was going to ask help build the place, he was so anxious to get it done."

"Thank you for calling me, Mister Gable, I have to let you go, but I'll be in touch shortly."

"Agent Baxter," Susan answered.

"Hi Sooz, it's Trish," a woman's voice gushed into the phone. Trish was Susan's roommate and also an FBI agent who worked in Missing Persons.

"Hi, Trish, can I call you back, I'm kind of busy with the Meadowvale case."

"That's why I'm calling. You'll never believe what we found today."

"A missing person?" Susan asked impatiently.

"Yes, but it's what was found inside her that was so interesting."

"Inside her?"

"Inside her. Two hikers found a Jane Doe in the woods early this morning and called SFPD. She was wearing her best birthday suit with no ID."

"How did she die?"

"Chemical cocktail, they're still trying to sort out the ingredients."

"So you don't know who she is?"

"Actually we do," Trish answered cryptically, "Halfway through the autopsy, a Doctor Desmond Galen was inspecting Jane Doe's last meal when he found something rather peculiar in her stomach."

"Spare me the suspense, what was it?"

"An identification bracelet."

"A what?"

"An identification bracelet. One of those plastic bracelets you get at the hospital."

"What does this have to do with my case?"

"The bracelet was from the Meadowvale Clinic and belonged to a woman named Lisa Parsons."

Chapter 65

▼

The elevator doors swished open and revealed the basement hallway. The bare cinder-block corridor was dimly lit and oppressive. A cold draft of air made its way into the elevator. Rachel shuddered, not because of the draft, but because standing in the middle of the hallway was Walter Flemming.

"Hello, Rachel," Flemming said coolly with restraint. "I was wondering how long it would take for you to catch on." Foley grabbed Rachel by the arm and began pulling her roughly out of the elevator. Once he was standing in the hallway, Rachel pressed the control panel for the elevator. She had no idea which button she hit or which floor it would take her to. At the moment, she didn't care. Foley turned around at the sound of the doors closing and was greeted by a swift kick to the groin. His hand released Rachel's arm as he crumpled into a heap on the floor, grabbing himself and writhing around in pain.

"No!" Flemming yelled as he realized what was happening. He made a mad dash for the closing doors but was a micrometer too late. The door closed safely and Rachel felt the elevator ascending. She took a big breath and tried to collect her thoughts. She was trembling. So was Amanda. The doors slid open on the second floor. She stepped out quickly, still shaken, but was all of a sudden pushed violently back in. Her head hit the back wall of the elevator car and her body slumped to the ground. The lights in the elevator seemed to be receding. The last thing she saw before slipping into unconsciousness was the blurry silhouette of Carl Sanford.

Chapter 66

"Assistant Director Spracken isn't seeing anyone this afternoon, Agent Haskins," Roger Chambers informed Haskins and his agents in a pompous tone. Chambers served as Spracken's secretary and primary screener. Nobody entered the Assistant Director's office without going through him first.

"Tell her it's urgent that we see her," Haskins said cooly.

"I said, she is not seeing anyone this afternoon," Chambers repeated snidely.

"I heard you the first time, Roger. But if you don't let me in to see Assistant Director Spracken by the count of three, Agents Pavletic and Baxter are going to seriously ruin your day," Haskins glanced at his agents who stood at attention behind him. Both smiled wickedly at Chambers.

"I can't let you…"

"One," Haskins interrupted him.

"Wait, you can't…"

"Two."

"What are you going to…"

"Three. Agent Baxter, Agent Pavletic. Please detain Mister Chambers while I have a word with Assistant Director Spracken."

Shane and Susan advanced rapidly from either side of the desk and knocked Roger out of his chair and pinned him to the floor behind his desk. Haskins ignored Chambers' pathetic pleas, knocked on Spracken's office door and let himself in.

Assistant Director Julie Spracken looked up in annoyance from her desk but smiled upon seeing Haskins enter the room.

"I see I need a more assertive secretary," Spracken said witnessing the scene outside her office.

"I apologize for the interruption, but it is rather urgent."

"Please have a seat."

"May Agents Pavletic and Baxter join us?"

"If you think it necessary. Is this about Doctor Montgomery?"

Haskins waited until Shane and Susan had entered the office and made themselves comfortable before answering, "Doctor Montgomery and more."

Haskins then told Spracken everything he and his agents had discovered in the past twenty-four hours. The videotape Shane had discovered with footage of Arthur Montgomery and Hank Gable's claim that he saw Walter Flemming on the construction site the same morning. The suspicious methods of treatment used on dissociative patients by the doctors at the Clinic. The discovery of Lisa Parson's body and the bracelet she chewed off and swallowed before she was killed.

Haskins admitted that they still did not know exactly what was going on at Meadowvale but they believed it was something much bigger than the disappearance of Arthur Montgomery.

Spracken remained silent, pondering over all of the information she had just received trying to make sense of it all.

"We do have enough to bring Flemming in for questioning," Shane said mistaking Spracken's silence for an invitation to continue.

"Have you tried calling Doctor Miller?" Spracken asked finally.

"The last time I tried it was busy, let me try again." Haskins punched in Ed's phone number. His heart did a sommersault when he heard it ringing.

Chapter 67

"Well, where is she?" Hal Rosenberg asked Ed outside the Chinese restaurant.

Ed's teeth bore down on his HB pencil. He looked around anxiously. She should have been here by now, or she should have at least called. An hour and a half had passed since they left the restaurant. Rachel wouldn't be thirty minutes late without good reason.

"I don't know. I think I'd better try calling her."

Ed withdrew his mobile and quickly punched in Rachel's office number. Her cheery voice came on after two rings informing Ed that she wasn't in at the moment. Ed hung up in disgust.

"She's not at her office," he said.

"Do you think she already went to the police?" Hal asked.

"No, she wanted to go together. She must be in trouble. I'm going to go to the Clinic and see if I can find her."

"What should I do?" Hal asked.

"Do you have your cell phone on you?"

Hal patted his breast pocket. "Always."

"If you don't hear from me within half an hour, call the police and tell them…I don't know, tell them something. Make something up, just make sure they get there."

"Ed, before you go…" Hal said.

"Yeah?"

"I'm sorry about what happened."

"No worries, just make sure to give me a raise when I get back. Wish me luck."

"Good luck."

Ed bolted across the street where he had double parked his truck and tore out of the parking lot. Halfway to the Clinic, his mobile rang, electronically beeping *Video Killed the Radio Star*, interrupting his thoughts. He sighed in relief.

"Rachel, I was getting worried," he said into the phone.

"This isn't Rachel, I'd like to speak to Dr. Miller please," John Haskins said from the other end.

"Who's this?" Ed asked.

"This is Agent John Haskins with the FBI. Who is this?"

"This is Ed Morgan, a friend of Dr. Miller's. Where is she?"

"I don't know, I just got a desperate call from her asking me to call her back as soon as possible. What's going on?"

"What has Rachel told you so far?"

"Not much. What can you tell me?"

Ed turned off his stereo and told Agent Haskins everything he and Rachel had just discussed.

"I'll meet you at the Clinic," Haskins said when he was finished, "don't do anything. We'll be right there."

Ed thanked Agent Haskins and increased his speed. He turned on his stereo and turned up the volume using *Duran Duran* to keep his mind off worse case scenarios.

Chapter 68

Rachel's car was in the parking lot when Ed arrived at the Clinic. The guard at the gate recognized his truck and tried to flag him down but Ed ignored him. He hoped the old coot hadn't called anyone inside the Clinic to warn them of his arrival.

Nobody tried to stop him as he got into the elevators. He still had his visitor's pass with him. On the sixth floor, the door to Rachel's office was locked. Ed kicked the wall in frustration. Where would she be? She said she was going to pick up proof of what she knew and then get Amanda. Ed ran for the elevators. Which floor were the long term patients on again? Ed recalled Rachel explaining who occupied each floor, *"The third floor is dedicated to the housing of long-term patients. Those patients who stay with us for an indefinite period of time."* Amanda would be on the third floor.

The elevator doors opened on the third floor and Ed was greeted by a nurse he didn't recognize. His name tag identified him as Lester.

"I'm looking for Rachel Miller!" Ed shouted to him.

"And you are?"

"Dr. Pepper!" Ed yelled as he stalked out of the elevator towards the nurse.

"Sir, you can't come on this floor!" Lester yelled back.

"I need to find Rachel Miller, she was supposed to pick up a patient, Amanda Rutherford." Ed was yelling now too.

Kevin Cheung entered the reception area and quickly assessed the situation. Both he and Lester moved around the desk they were standing behind.

"Neither Doctor Miller nor the patient you mentioned are here right now. I'm going to have to ask you to leave, Mister Morgan." Kevin Cheung told Ed. It was against Clinic policy to reveal information of any kind about patients but Kevin hoped that by telling Ed that Rachel and Amanda weren't on the third floor, he could get him to the elevator and out of the building. Let the police deal with him.

"I'm not leaving until I find Rachel." Ed pushed Kevin aside. Kevin bounced back and with Lester's help, they were able to force Ed back into the elevator. Ed struggled against the two nurses and tried to knee Lester but only managed to slide his knee off the other man's hip. Kevin threw a punch to Ed's kidney and then one in the gut bringing him down to his knees. Pushing him over, Kevin sat on Ed's back and twisted his arm behind his back.

"I'll call Doctor Flemming," Lester grabbed the phone and dialed an internal number. Ed couldn't hear him because Kevin's hand was pressed against one ear and his other ear was pressed firmly to the ground.

"Take him downstairs, Kev," Lester called out.

The hand squishing his ear was removed temporarily as Kevin pushed one of the elevator's buttons. Ed felt the car going down.

"One wrong move and I'll break your arm and pull it out of its socket. Understand?" Kevin spat into Ed's ear. His arm was jerked upward to punctuate the question. A river of pain flowed through his arm. He could feel the man's hot breath on his neck.

"I got it," Ed replied. He was pulled roughly to his feet when the car stopped. The elevator indicator revealed that they were in the basement. Ed was haltingly led through the same corridor that Rachel was dragged through moments before by Sanford.

He was thrust into a mid-sized room, his arm still pinned in an unnatural angle behind his back. The room resembled the rest of the Clinic in its decor and sterile environment.

Situated in the middle of the room was Rachel.

Chapter 69

Rachel was strapped down by four-point leather restraints in what looked like a mockery of a dentist's chair. Dentists were no great fun, but as far as Ed remembered, they never had to tie down their patients. Walter Flemming was standing to the side of her. Carl Sanford was in the room as well. There was no sign of Amanda. A look of relief swept across Rachel's face when she saw that it was Ed entering the room. It was quickly replaced by a flash of anger when she saw that Kevin Cheung was holding him.

Ed's face was masked in pain. "Hey, Rachel. Have you met my new friend?"

Rachel smiled despite the situation.

"Ah, Edwin, nice of you to join us," Flemming said.

"Nice of you to invite me." Kevin gave Ed's arm a twist. Ed grunted in agony.

"Yes, sorry there could be no engraved invitations, but speaking of in-grave. You don't leave me with a lot of choice."

"Well you could just let me go and I promise I won't tell anyone what you and your pals are doing to people's minds."

"I wish I could but unfortunately you have put me into what is known as the kidnapper's dilemma. As much as I may want to let you go, there is nothing stopping you from going to the authorities," Flemming replied.

Ed flinched as Kevin gave his arm another twist, "Would you please stop doing that? You're really becoming a pain in the…Aghhh!"

"Really Edwin, you mustn't antagonize Mister Cheung."

"Thanks for the tip." Ed looked at Rachel once more, she seemed out of it, groggy.

"Where's Amanda?" Ed shot at Flemming.

"Doctor Foley is taking care of Miss Rutherford," Flemming replied calmly.

"Foley's in on your little scam as well?" Ed asked surprised.

"That's none of your concern. What you should be worrying about is who's going to miss you and will they ever find your corpse."

Ed glared at Flemming. Synapses were firing like mad in his head and Ed acted on pure reflex, he knew it was a long shot, but he had to try.

"Is that what you told Arthur Montgomery too?" he asked in a vain attempt at delaying the inevitable.

Kevin Cheung's grip loosened for a split second and Flemming's face went slack. He regained his composure quickly enough but Ed knew he had hit a nerve.

"Yeah, that's right," he continued "Rachel and I found out what you did to Arthur Montgomery. The police and the FBI are on their way right now."

"He's bluffing." Kevin Cheung said over Ed's shoulder.

"Perhaps. But he'll never entertain anyone again with those bluffs, now will he? I have to take care of Doctor Miller, Mister Cheung. Would you be so kind as to introduce Edwin to Miss Parsons?"

"Certainly." Kevin answered with a sneer and started moving out of the room.

"Wait!" Ed shouted. "What are you going to do to Rachel?"

"Something we psychiatrists call iatrogenesis."

"You can't do that!" Ed yelled.

Flemming beamed. "Of course I can. It's quite simple really. Doctor Sanford and I are specialists at it. All I have to do is inject her with this," Flemming held up a large needle, it looked like something out of the middle ages, "and Doctor Sanford does the rest."

"What's that?"

"A chemical cocktail. Just a little Sodium Amytal and a few other mind-altering treats."

Truth serum, Ed thought. "They'll know that Rachel would never develop DID."

"On the contrary, Edwin. Not only will she develop DID, but she'll also develop amnesia. She won't remember anything. Your girlfriend will be a mental vegetable by the time we're through with her. Everyone at the Clinic has noticed her acting strange lately, some may even describe it as paranoia."

"That's because she found out what you were doing to patients."

"True, but no one else knows that. Besides, there's a history of DID in her family. Precedent has been set."

Ed's face revealed his puzzlement.

"Oh? You weren't aware of Rachel's dysfunctional family. Well, let me enlighten you. It seems Rachel's sister, one Theresa Miller, developed DID at a very young age and it killed her at the ripe old age of twenty-three. She was certifiable."

"Bullshit!"

"Such vulgarity doesn't become you, Edwin."

"You're a liar, a murderer, and a bastard!"

"'It is the providence of knowledge to speak and it is the privilege of wisdom to listen.' A doctor and a poet said that. Perhaps you should heed his advice," Flemming spat.

"Perhaps you should kiss my...Aughh!" Kevin Cheung cranked Ed's arm skyward. At the same time, Ed jumped and twisted himself in midair towards Kevin. It was the opportunity he had been waiting for. He tore his arm loose from Kevin's painful grip and swung it in an arc directly into Kevin's face.

Cartilage crunched.

Kevin's nose gushed blood onto the bright white floor and his hands shot up to his face. Ed grabbed him by the head and brought his knee up into his chest. Kevin went sailing backwards into the wall. He was down but not out. Ed rushed over to him and kicked him in the midsection.

In between kicks, Ed yelled "I told you, not to, do that, again!" Ed turned around to deal with Flemming and was knocked backwards by the old doctor. He was stronger than Ed would have thought, or liked. He stumbled on Kevin Cheung's body and fell to the ground. Kevin sprang up and seized the advantage. He was on top of Ed within seconds.

"What are you? The freakin' Energizer Bunny?" Ed cried. Kevin punched him in the face.

"No more games," Flemming said. His voice was icy cold. "Get him out of here and make sure no one *ever* finds the body!"

Kevin heaved Ed's limp body off the floor and began dragging him to the door. His nose was still dripping copious amounts of blood. Ed watched helplessly as he was pulled further and further away from Rachel. She looked at him with pleading eyes. There was nothing Ed could do.

Just as his feet were dragged past the door, he felt Kevin's grip on his shirt weaken and then fall away entirely. Ed wondered why he had stopped. He looked up behind him and saw Kevin standing perfectly still.

He was looking into the barrel of a very large handgun.

Chapter 70

"Don't even breathe funny," John Haskins said as he prodded Kevin back into the room. Ed stood up with difficulty. He looked past Agent Haskins and saw four more FBI agents clustered in the hallway.

"Thank God, you showed up," Ed said, pulling himself up off the floor, as Haskins handcuffed Kevin.

"Where's Flemming?" Haskins asked.

"He's right here...what the hell?" Flemming was no longer in the room. A door beside the two-way mirror was slightly open.

"Shit." Ed ran through the door and found Flemming trying to escape through a narrow basement window. It looked like he was stuck. His legs wriggled frantically as they searched for leverage. Ed was about to pull the doctor back in when he saw the large needle Flemming was going to stick into Rachel lying on its side on the floor.

"You got him," John exclaimed when Ed brought Flemming back into the room where Rachel was being unstrapped.

"I think now might be a good time to question him," Ed said with a mischievous grin. Flemming was massaging his posterior. Rachel, though still groggy and sore, managed to laugh.

"Good work, son." Agent Haskins handcuffed Flemming and handed the doctor and Kevin over to two of his agents. Shane Pavletic squeezed in through the door as the other agents left.

"John? I think you'd better come with me. I think we found Doctor Montgomery."

Chapter 71

▼

The Meadowvale Clinic's large open foyer was bustling with activity. An EMS team was on hand; they tried to convince Rachel to lie down but she refused. FBI agents and SFPD officers were everywhere. Over ten vehicles with flashing blue and crimson lights were parked just outside the front entrance. Grant Foley, Carl Sanford, Walter Flemming and Kevin Cheung were each sitting in the back of their very own cruiser wearing their new chrome accessories.

The entire Clinic staff was congregated in little groups in the lobby as well. They looked on with the intensity of the most dedicated rubberneckers waiting to be questioned in turn by the SFPD and the FBI. It would be a long time before any of them went home.

Hal Rosenberg stood near the front doors and beckoned Ed over when he saw him emerging from the elevator with a group of FBI agents. Ed and Hal spoke for a few minutes while Rachel tried to convince the EMS team that she was all right.

"Ed, once again I want to tell you how deeply, deeply sorry I am for ever doubting you."

"It's no big deal, Hal, really." Ed said modestly.

"It is a big deal son. I didn't believe you when you tried to tell your side of the story this weekend. Hell, I hardly listened to you. I can never forgive myself for that. I hope you can forgive me though. When you come to work tomorrow both Steinbeck and Wainfleet want to talk to you."

"With me? Why?"

"Do you realize how much money you've saved our company? A bloody fortune. Christ, five more days and it would have been our malpractice insurance that those doctors out there fall back on," Hal waved his arm towards the cruisers outside. "If you and Doctor Miller hadn't persisted, especially you after you had no earthly reason to, and unearthed this Byzantine plot of theirs, Steinbeck and Wainfleet would have faced dozens of suits. Maybe even hundreds. I feel sorry for the San Francisco Psychiatric Hospital's insurance carrier. They're going to have a hell of a lot of claims on their hands. I'll see you tomorrow morning in Mister Steinbeck's office. I believe he might have a promotion in mind if I have my say." Hal winked and slapped Ed on the shoulder.

Once Ed was through talking with Hal, Agent Haskins called Ed and Rachel over to his side. He was standing near the entrance to the Arthur Montgomery auditorium. Shane Pavletic led them into the auditorium. A group of five FBI agents, including Susan Baxter, were crouched over an odd looking high-tech contraption at the far end of the auditorium, right next to the right wall. The machine they were huddled around looked like a black box attached to a bicycle wheel, it was fitted with a screen. *PulseEKKO* was printed across its side.

Shane, Haskins, Ed, and Rachel approached the group. The operator of the machine looked up and smiled. He was a slight man with buckteeth, little hair and a round head that bobbed up and down as he spoke. He wore the same type of jacket as the other agents, with FBI emblazoned across the back in big bold yellow letters but didn't look like an FBI agent himself. In reality, he wasn't. He was a geologist who was often called in by the FBI when his expertise was required.

"Agent Haskins, long time no see," Eugene Gibson exclaimed.

"Eugene, thanks for coming out on such short notice." John turned to Ed and Rachel, "Eugene is a geologist from Stanford. He helps us from time to time when we need his expertise and the use of his GPR, Ground Penetrating Radar." John glanced at Eugene, who was studying the small digital screen on the machine. He leaned over and whispered to Ed and Rachel, "Around the office we refer to him and his machine as Echo and the Bunnyman."

"I heard that," Eugene looked in mock indignation. His head bobbed some more.

Rachel, Ed and John all laughed.

"So what do you have for us, Eugene?" John leaned over the machine trying to see what was on the screen.

"It looks homosapien to me," Eugene replied. "Have a look." He moved over so that John, Ed and Rachel could see the screen clearly. A fuzzy image of what looked like the upper body of a human could be seen on the screen. The machine wasn't large enough to reveal an image of the entire body at once.

"Let's dig it up to be sure, but I think we've found our doctor." John stood up and patted Shane Pavletic on the back. "Excellent work Shane, drinks are on me tonight. You too, Susan." Susan Baxter smiled.

"How did you know to look for Doctor Montgomery here in the auditorium?" Rachel asked as she, Ed, and John left the auditorium.

"One of my agents Shane found a surveillance tape which recorded Montgomery here at the Clinic when it was first being built. It looked like he was fighting with someone on the site. That alone didn't help us much, but we got a call a few hours later from a guy named Hank Gable, one of Harry Gable's, as in Gable & Sons Builders, sons. Hank told us that he remembered seeing Doctor Flemming at the site the same morning Montgomery disappeared. He also said that there was some graffiti in the foundation which could only have been put there that afternoon. Surveillance tapes didn't catch anyone else at the site that morning though. Bringing in Eugene and his GPR was a longshot, but it looked like it paid off. We think Flemming and Montgomery got into an argument here at the site and Flemming killed him to keep him quiet. We can't link Flemming to the murder yet but hopefully something will come up."

Ed told Agent Haskins about his conversation with Flemming less than an hour ago and how spooked Flemming had become when Ed mentioned Montgomery's name.

"Unfortunately, that still doesn't prove anything."

"So how did you know what was going on here?" Rachel asked, still groggy from the Valium she had been given and confused as to how the FBI had come charging in like the cavalry.

"I got your message and called the number you left and Ed filled me in. That and we discovered a few things on our own," John told them about the tapes from the construction site and the discovery of the identification bracelet inside Lisa Parsons' stomach.

"It sounds like you know more than we do," Ed said.

"We will soon. With Flemming drugged up on Amytal Sodium and Doctor Sanford begging to confess, I imagine we'll be brought up to speed soon. Sanford is so scared he'd probably confess to the Lindbergh kidnapping. Before I start questioning any of them though, could you two fill me in on what you uncovered."

For the next half hour, Rachel and Ed went over everything they had discovered in detail with Agent Haskins; the discrepant vanishing files, Amanda's purposely repressed memories, the death of Jim Wells and his EEG readings, and what Flemming had revealed to them downstairs. They then explained their sus-

John referred to his notepad. "Sanford says Jim was Flemming's idea and that as far as he knows, the man never had any mental illness at all. They tried inducing alters into him but obviously failed. They already have another subject that they started experimenting on. A woman named Sandra Hillock. She's been here for a few days."

"What's her condition?" Rachel asked concerned.

"She's physically fine, but mentally we don't know yet. She's very confused and can't tell us anything. She's being brought to San Francisco Psyc. right now. You were right about the insurance fraud though Ed. That was part of their plan all along. They were going to rip-off their patients' insurance carriers for everything they could. We found some files in Flemming's office which outlined the entire scam. If they hadn't been caught, they would have made millions and it all would have been taken in through the Clinic. They may never have been caught. I have to admit, I'm still having a hard time coming to grips with what those doctors were doing to their poor patients."

"Are there any other patients here at the Clinic who were part of their project?" Ed asked.

"Unfortunately, yes. I've got Doctor Sanford making up a list right now. Apparently they were going to be transferred, according to Sanford, meaning they were to be disposed of permanently. Sanford said they had finished with them and had no more use of them. It seems you two uncovered the doctors' plans just in time. You saved a lot of lives. Hopefully, we'll learn everything we can over the next few days. Then it's going to be a matter of treating those patients for the treatment they've been receiving."

"At least the worst is over," Ed said quietly.

"Let's hope so. Hey, can I borrow your phone for a second, Doctor Miller?" John asked.

"Sure. What's the number?"

John rhymed off a local pizzeria phone number. "My agents and I are going to be here all night going through the Clinic's records and questioning the rest of the staff. We need some food to keep us going."

Rachel put the phone on speaker mode so that John could just talk to the machine.

The phone was picked up at the other end. "Davinci's Pizza."

"Yes, hello. This is Agent John Haskins with the FBI, I'd like to order a dozen large pizzas with a variety of toppings. Mix them. It's your call. And say forty cans of soda. Again, mix them up."

"Is this for pick-up or delivery?"

"Delivery, please."

"Where to?"

"The Meadowvale Clinic."

"Are you talking about the new mental hospital?'

"Yes," John couldn't be bothered to educate the man on the other end of the line.

"Did you say you were an FBI agent, sir?"

"Yes, Special Agent John Haskins. There's about a dozen of us here. There are a few police officers here as well."

"Where are all the doctors if you don't mind my asking?"

"Most of them are locked in our cars, one of them is here with me."

"You're calling from the mental hospital?"

"Yes."

"And you say you're an FBI agent and there are more FBI agents and cops there, and most of the doctors are locked up in cars?"

"That's right. They're going to jail. Listen, how long will it take for those pizzas to get here?"

"Why don't you try someplace else." The phone on the other end was hung up.

John stared at the phone. "He hung up on me," he said in shock.

Ed and Rachel burst out laughing.

"I can't believe he hung up on me."

"Can you blame him?" Rachel asked still laughing. Ed was doubled over.

"Hey Rachel, I know a nice little Chinese Restaurant we can go to, if you're hungry?" Ed asked once he stopped laughing.

"I'd like that." Rachel said and held out her arm. Ed slipped his arm through hers and walked her out of the office. As they waited for the elevator to take them out of the Clinic, Ed withdrew his pencil from his pocket. As he stepped into the elevator, he snapped it in half and threw the halves in a garbage can. Rachel took his free hand in hers and smiled.

"Don't you need that?" she asked.

"Not anymore."

As the elevator descended and Rachel pushed the day's events out of her mind she gave Ed's hand a squeeze. He squeezed back. Rachel didn't think her dreams would bother her for a long, long time.

978-0-595-37529-5
0-595-37529-4

Printed in the United Kingdom
by Lightning Source UK Ltd.
117317UKS00001B/200